VICKSBURG

☆ ☆ ☆

THE CIVIL WAR BATTLE SERIES
by James Reasoner

Manassas

Shiloh

Antietam

Chancellorsville

Vicksburg

Gettysburg

Chickamauga

Shenandoah

Savannah

Appomattox

☆ ☆ ☆

VICKSBURG

James Reasoner

CUMBERLAND HOUSE
NASHVILLE, TENNESSEE

Published by
CUMBERLAND HOUSE PUBLISHING, INC.
431 Harding Industrial Drive
Nashville, Tennessee 37211
www.cumberlandhouse.com

Cover design by Bob Bubkis, Nashville, Tennessee.

Library of Congress Cataloging-in-Publication Data.

Reasoner, James.
    Vicksburg / James Reasoner.
        p.   cm. — (The Civil War battle series ; 5)
    ISBN 1-58182-163-8 (hardcover : alk. paper)
    ISBN 1-58182-372-X (paperback : alk. paper)
    1. United States—History—Civil War, 1861–1865—Fiction. 2. Vicksburg (Miss.)—History—Siege, 1863—Fiction. I. Title.

PS3568.E2685 V53 2001
813'.54—dc21   2001017263

Printed in Canada

1 2 3 4 5 6 7 8 9 10—08 07 06 05 04

For Skeeter, Nicky, and Zach

VICKSBURG

Chapter One

A SCREAM RIPPED THROUGH the quiet stillness of the night, and Cory Brannon cracked his head against the bottom of the wagon as he sat up abruptly. Wincing from the pain, he closed his hand around the butt of his pistol and rolled out from under the wagon. He looked around for the source of the scream.

Nearby, Cory's massive friend Pie Jones had scrambled from underneath one of the other wagons. The vehicles were parked in thick shadows under some trees alongside the road, but even in the darkness someone as big as Pie was hard to miss. He had an Enfield rifle in his hands, one of the weapons brought to Texas from England to assist the Confederacy in its struggle against the Northern invaders.

"What the hell was that?" Pie hissed toward Cory. "A catamount?"

"It sounded more like Lucille," Cory replied as he got to his feet and started toward the wagon where Lucille Farrell and Rachel Hannah were supposed to be sleeping.

Cory loved Lucille, the woman he intended to make his wife as soon as they returned to Vicksburg. But the wagon train was still on the road between Marshall, Texas, and Monroe, Louisiana, and they had already survived one attack by renegades who were after the supplies and guns in the wagons. There was no telling when trouble might crop up again.

Col. Charles Thompson, the leader of the wagon train and the man responsible for setting up this vital lifeline between Vicksburg and Texas, came around one of the other wagons carrying a torch. Allen Carter, the head teamster and Thompson's second-in-command, followed behind him. The wooden peg that had replaced Carter's right leg below the knee sank into the soft dirt as he limped along hurriedly. Carter had one of the British Enfields in his hands, too.

11

"That cry came from the ladies' wagon, I believe," Thompson said as he and Carter joined Cory and Pie. The four men approached the wagon in question, tense in their anticipation of possible trouble.

A canvas flap had been drawn across the opening behind the driver's seat, closing off the covered bed of the vehicle to give the young women some privacy. Now, as Cory and the others approached, the flap was pushed back and a woman with fiery red hair stuck her head through the opening. "It's all right," Rachel Hannah called to the men. "Lucille just had a nightmare, that's all."

Cory stopped and let out his breath, unaware until this moment that he had been holding it. "Can I see her?" he asked.

"I don't know . . . ," Rachel began.

Then Cory heard sobbing coming from inside the wagon, and he started toward the vehicle again, determination etched on his normally friendly face. Rachel obviously knew that she wasn't going to stop him from reaching the woman he loved, so she climbed out of the wagon, pulled her cotton wrapper more tightly around her, and jumped down lithely from the driver's seat, forestalling Pie's attempt to hurry forward and help her. Rachel was tall and quite attractive, even with her red hair tousled from sleep.

Cory went past her, grabbed the wheel closest to the seat, and clambered up. He pushed through the canvas flap and announced himself, "Lucille? I'm here, Lucille. Are you all right?"

Lucille Farrell was sitting upright in the narrow sleeping area that had been arranged between stacks of crated supplies. Enough light came into the back of the wagon from the torch Colonel Thompson held outside for Cory to see the tear-streaks on her cheeks as she looked up at him. Her long, thick, honey-blonde hair was disarrayed from the tossing around she had been doing in her sleep.

"Oh, Cory," she said in a wretched voice. "He came back again."

"No, he didn't," Cory said firmly as he knelt beside her and slipped an arm around her shoulders. "It was just a dream, Lucille. That renegade wasn't here. He can't hurt you."

She turned her head and buried her face against his shoulder. "Why won't he leave me alone?" she sobbed. "Doesn't he understand that I had to kill him?"

He just held her and made soft, soothing noises. There was nothing he could say. Lucille had killed one of the renegades when they attacked the wagon train a couple of days earlier. She had probably saved her own life and Cory's life in the process. But she had to come to terms with the fact that she had pulled the trigger of the Kerr revolver and put a bullet in the middle of a man's chest. Lucille had witnessed more than her share of violence in her life, but never before had she killed a man.

The renegade had richly deserved killing, thought Cory. The gang would have slaughtered everyone on the wagon train in order to get their hands on the supplies it was carrying.

Flour, sugar, guns, and ammunition. Those things were more precious than gold and gems now, in October 1862, and the city of Vicksburg, Mississippi, where the supplies were headed, was a prize most coveted by the hated Yankees.

Ever since New Orleans had fallen to the Federals earlier in the year, the Yankees had set their sights on Vicksburg. Already Union forces were in control of the upper and lower ends of the mighty Mississippi River, and if the Northerners could take Vicksburg, they would close an iron fist around the entirety of the river. That would split the Confederacy in half, cutting off the flow of supplies from the west, and more important, it would open the river to Northern commerce. Midwestern farmers, accustomed to shipping their crops down the river to New Orleans and on to the rest of the world from there, had lost their market when the Confederate batteries at Vicksburg closed the Mississippi. The war was already quite unpopular in some sections of the North, and it would only become more so as long as it interfered with commerce. The political pressure on Abraham

Lincoln to reach a peaceful settlement with the Confederacy would only intensify. So Vicksburg had to fall for the Yankee invasion to succeed.

Cory and those with him on this wagon train were equally determined that it would not.

The supply line from Texas had been the idea of Colonel Thompson of the Mississippi Home Guard; he was also Lucille's uncle. During the early days of the war, the Vicksburg, Shreveport, and Texas Railroad had been completed as far as Monroe, and from that Louisiana town to Marshall, the largest city in eastern Texas, was only a distance of 120 miles. The colonel, with help from Cory and Pie, had led the first wagon train from Monroe to Marshall and returned with wagons full of supplies that were then taken to Vicksburg on the railroad.

While bound for Monroe the first time on horseback, before the trains had started running, the three men had rescued Rachel from involuntary servitude at a tavern owned by a brutal man named Grat. Rachel had been close-mouthed about her past and how she had come to be a virtual prisoner of the tavern owner, but evidently she was the well-bred daughter of a wealthy planter, Rutherford Hannah, who had owned a plantation called Cottonwood Point, near Baton Rouge. That information had come out when she took a room at a boarding house in Monroe owned by an acquaintance of the Hannah family.

Lucille had come to Monroe on the railroad with her Aunt Mildred, the colonel's wife, for a visit before the first wagon train left for Texas. Cory had met and fallen in love with Lucille the previous winter when he was taken under the wing of her late father, Capt. Ezekiel Farrell, owner and operator of the steamboat *Missouri Zephyr*.

The *Zephyr* had been destroyed during the battle in which the Yankees had taken Fort Henry, and Captain Farrell had fallen at the battle of Fort Donelson, dying in Cory's arms. Cory had promised the captain that he would find Lucille and take care of her, and that vow had led him to a conquered Nashville, where she had gone to stay with her aunt and uncle. Lucille had vanished, though, along with Colonel and Mrs. Thompson, and Cory's search for them had taken him to the battle of Shiloh and ultimately to Vicksburg, where he had been reunited finally with Lucille. Being drawn into the colonel's plans for the wagon train had postponed Cory's plans to marry Lucille, so he had been glad to see her when she made her visit to Monroe.

He hadn't been prepared, though, for her insistence that she and Rachel accompany them on the journey to Texas.

Until this trip, there hadn't been any trouble. But the wagons had never carried anything quite as valuable as those British rifles and pistols until now, either.

As Cory held Lucille and tried to calm her, he wondered if Jason Gill had had anything to do with the attack on the wagon train. Gill was an ardent abolitionist and Yankee agent provocateur who had crossed paths with Cory several times in the past. Gill had made a specialty of stirring up trouble for the Confederacy, and Cory had spotted him in Monroe several months earlier. The abolitionist had disappeared, but Cory thought he might still be in the area, on the lookout for anything he could do to hurt the Southern cause, such as looting the wagon train of its vital cargo. Gill could have recruited those renegades and deserters for the raid . . .

Or the men could have simply been thieves, Cory told himself. Jason Gill didn't have to be responsible for everything bad that happened in the world.

But a lot certainly had happened, both good and bad, since Cory had first laid eyes on Gill in New Madrid, Missouri, the previous winter.

Lucille had stopped shuddering and crying, and as Cory held her, he felt her deep, regular breathing. She had slipped back into sleep. He hoped her slumber wouldn't be disturbed by nightmares this time.

Moving slowly and carefully, he lowered her to the pallet where she slept. She stirred a little but didn't awaken, and he was thankful for that. He stood up, muscles unkinking from the strained position in which he had been sitting. The arm that had been around Lucille was numb, too. He massaged feeling back into it as he quietly climbed out of the wagon and dropped to the ground beside the vehicle.

Colonel Thompson, Pie, Rachel, and Allen Carter were standing several yards away, talking in low voices. Rachel turned and asked, "How is she?"

"Asleep again," he said. "She dreamed that the man she killed came back for her."

Rachel shivered. "The poor thing."

"Lucille is a strong young woman," said Thompson. "She'll get over this."

Pie scratched his beard and said, "Shoot, if'n I was Miss Lucille, I wouldn't worry none 'bout ventilatin' that sumb—I mean, that fella. If she hadn't stopped him, he'd've likely stuck that knife in poor ol' Cory here."

Cory nodded. "Yes, but she probably never hurt anybody else in her life until she was forced to kill that man. That's something that takes some getting used to."

Even after Shiloh, killing still bothered Cory. Not as much as it once had; he could do whatever was necessary to protect himself and those he loved.

But he hoped he never got to the point where he didn't blink at the idea of dealing out death.

The colonel slipped his watch from the pocket of his trousers and flipped it open. "Almost two o'clock," he said. "Allen, your watch is nearly over. Go on to sleep. I'll take the guard duty."

"You're sure, Colonel?" asked Carter.

"Of course."

Carter nodded his thanks and limped toward the wagon under which his son, Fred, was sleeping. Fred was Cory's age, in his early twenties, but his mind was more like that of a six-year-old. Despite that, he could handle a team of mules and drive a wagon quite well, and his friendly smile made everyone else on the wagon train glad to have him around.

Pie stretched then offered. "Reckon I better get some more shuteye, too. But let me walk you back to your wagon first, Miss Rachel."

"That won't be necessary, Pie," she told him with a smile. "It's only a few feet from here."

"Yeah, well, you never know when somethin' might happen."

Still smiling, Rachel shook her head and held out her hand toward the big man. Pie took it, closing his sausagelike fingers tenderly around her slender ones, and they walked toward the wagon where Lucille was sleeping.

That left Cory to crawl back under his wagon and curl up in his blankets. The autumn days in Louisiana were hot and muggy, but it was beginning to get colder at night now, a harbinger of winter. Cory lay down and tugged the blankets around him, pillowing his head on his folded coat.

He was a long time getting back to sleep, though. Memories of the terror he had seen in Lucille's eyes haunted him until he finally dozed off.

❧

THE WAGONEERS were awake early the next morning, and the wagons were rolling by sun-up, as usual. Rachel had taken over the handling of one of the wagons after its driver had been killed during the raid a few days earlier. Lucille was the only member of the party who wasn't driving a wagon. She sat perched on the high seat beside Rachel.

She had seemed normal enough at breakfast, pitching in to help with the cooking and then the cleaning up after the meal. Except for some faint circles under her eyes, no one could have known that she'd had a bad night.

Cory knew, though, and his efforts to talk to her about it had been rebuffed.

"Thank you for helping me last night, Cory," she had told him when he asked her how she was doing, but then she'd added, "I really don't want to talk about it, though."

"But, Lucille—"

"I'm all right, Cory, really," she'd insisted.

He had no choice but to go along with her wishes.

As the wagons rolled east along the road that would take them to Monroe, Cory cast an eye toward the sky. Thick gray clouds had moved in during the night, and a chilly breeze—the first one he had felt in Louisiana—was blowing. He hoped that a storm wasn't moving in. It wouldn't take much rain to muddy the road and slow the wagons to a crawl. He had hoped they would reach Monroe this afternoon, but if they got a downpour . . .

That was exactly what happened. Before noon, the skies opened up, and rain fell in buckets.

Cory pulled on a slicker and tugged down the brim of his hat, but that didn't keep him from getting saturated. Rivulets of water sneaked insistently under the slicker and dripped from the brim of his hat. The mules plodded grimly on as he slapped the reins against their backs and called out to them. At times the rain was so hard he could barely see the rumps of the animals as they pulled the wagon.

He hoped Lucille had retreated into the wagon she was riding, but he doubted if that was the case. Since Rachel had to be outside on the driver's seat, Lucille was probably right there beside her, stubbornly huddled in a slicker.

The pace slowed. At midday, Colonel Thompson called a short halt for lunch. Cooking fires were impossible in this weather, so the group had to make do with jerked meat and hardtack. This was like being back with the army, Cory thought miserably as he sat in the mud underneath the wagon and gnawed at a square of the tough, barely palatable hardtack.

Well, not exactly like being in the army, he realized as Lucille came over and crawled in beside him. Even damp, she was a whole lot prettier than any soldier he had ever served with.

"Do you think we'll reach Monroe today?" she asked.

Cory shook his head. "I don't know. We might have, if not for this blasted rain."

Lucille sighed and said, "I hope we do. I'd love to sink down into a tub of hot water right about now."

Cory swallowed hard, but it wasn't from the food he was eating. In his mind's eye, he saw Lucille sitting in a bathtub, a vision of pink skin and frothy soap bubbles and tendrils of steam wisping up from the heated water . . .

A clap of thunder brought him back to wet, forlorn reality. "I reckon we'll get there when we get there," he said, sounding more harsh than he intended to.

"I know. I'm just ready to be home, that's all." She was sitting close enough to him so that he could feel the tiny shudder that went through her. "I don't think I want to go on any more of these trips."

That was the best news Cory had heard in quite a while. Once they got back to Vicksburg, they would get married and then Lucille would stay where it was safe while he and the others continued to bring in supplies from Texas.

But would Vicksburg really be safe? he suddenly asked himself.

As long as the Yankees were on the rampage, was any place in the South truly safe?

Cory couldn't answer that question, so he was glad when the wagon train got under way again a few minutes later. As long as he was working and had an immediate goal in mind, he didn't have to think too much about the future.

The rain let up in the middle of the afternoon and finally stopped, but the damage had been done. The road was slick in some places and so muddy in others that the wagons continually threatened to bog down. The teams had to be kept moving constantly, except on the occasional stretches that were packed harder. Then the wagons were stopped and the drivers jumped down to scrape mud off the wheels.

The sky remained overcast, bringing on an early dusk. The colonel lit a lantern and hung it from his brake lever. The other drivers did the same. Cory had been over this route often enough so that he knew they were only a couple of hours out of Monroe—under normal conditions. On these bad roads, the rest of the journey might take twice that long. Clearly, though, the colonel intended to push on as long as possible in hopes of reaching the town tonight.

Men, women, and beasts were all thoroughly exhausted when the wagon train finally rolled into Monroe long after dark. Lights still shone in a few windows, but many of the buildings were dark. Anybody with any sense was already sound asleep, Cory thought as he wearily brought his wagon to a halt in line with the others in front of the railroad depot.

He clambered down from the seat and stretched, easing muscles sore from the long day's work. He, Pie, and the colonel would stay at the depot, in a small bunk room that the VS&T provided for railroad employees. Lucille and Rachel had rooms at Miss Fay's boarding house, and Cory wanted to see Lucille safely back there before he turned in himself.

Colonel Thompson assembled the group briefly and thanked everyone. "You've done yeoman service, as usual, men. And ladies." He inclined his head toward Lucille and Rachel. "I'm proud of all of you, and I'm certain the Confederacy is, too."

Allen Carter replied, "We're just glad for the opportunity to help, Colonel." He put his arm around Fred's shoulders. "Come on, son, let's go home." The two of them lived in a small cabin on the edge of the settlement, within easy walking distance.

Thompson shook hands with the drivers who were local men. The two soldiers who had been sent from Vicksburg stayed at the depot as well. One of them suggested, "Reckon we'd better stand guard over them wagons tonight, Colonel?"

"Yes, of course," replied Thompson. "I want two men on watch at all times. I hate to ask that of anyone after this grueling trip, but if anything happened to those supplies now . . ."

He didn't have to finish the sentence. No one wanted to lose the guns and supplies after the danger and hard work they had endured to get them here.

It was quickly decided that the two soldiers would stand the first watch, but it would be a short one, only until midnight. Then Cory and Pie would take over, followed by Colonel Thompson and one of the troopers. They matched to see who would get only a short nap before coming back to finish out the night's guard duty.

Cory linked arms with Lucille. "I'm sure you're exhausted," he said. "Let's get you to Miss Fay's."

"I did less work than anyone else," Lucille said. "Perhaps I should volunteer to stand guard with Uncle Charles, so that poor Private Keegan can get some more sleep."

"I'm sure he'll be all right," Cory said quickly as he and Pie began walking down the street with the two young women. After everything that had happened, he didn't think it would be a good idea to put a rifle in Lucille's hand and tell her to shoot anybody who tried to steal the supplies.

It had rained in Monroe, too, and the streets were muddy. The four of them carefully avoided the puddles they could see, but the night was so dark it was hard to miss all of them. A small lantern was burning on the porch of the boarding house, and as they drew closer to it, Cory was grateful for the glow that it cast, feeble though it was.

They had just reached the steps that led up to the porch of the house when the front door opened and a man stepped out. A light was burning behind him, throwing his bulky body into silhouette, but his rough-hewn features were visible in the yellow glare of the porch lantern. Rachel stopped in her tracks and cried out in horror as she looked up and saw him standing there, a self-satisfied smirk on his face.

"There you are, woman," Grat said. "They told me down at the depot you might be back tonight. Come along, now. It's time to go home."

Chapter Two

PIE MOVED QUICKLY IN front of Rachel, thrusting out a tree-like arm to shield her. Grat made no move to come down the steps and seize her, however. He just stood there wearing that ugly grin.

Cory felt Lucille stiffen beside him. She had never seen Grat before, but she had heard about him from Cory and no doubt from Rachel as well. "Is that—" she began.

"It is," Cory said.

"Mister, I don't know what in blazes you think you're doin' here," rumbled Pie, "but you better just skedaddle back where you come from."

"I'm not going anywhere without that redheaded hellion," Grat said. He folded his arms stubbornly and nodded toward Rachel. "Look at her. She knows she has to go with me."

Cory glanced at Rachel and saw a mixture of fear, anger, and resignation on her face. The emotions warred briefly, and anger abruptly won, at least temporarily. "No!" she spat. "I won't go with you. I won't go anywhere with you, Grat!"

"Yes, you will," Grat said calmly. "The boys've been missin' you back at the tavern, Rachel. They say there's nobody who can warm a bed like you."

"You son of a bitch!" Pie's hands clenched into fists, and he started to rush up the steps to the porch.

Grat stepped back quickly, his right hand dipping under his coat and coming out with a revolver. He leveled the gun at Pie and thumbed back the hammer.

Cory lunged after Pie, grabbing the big man's arm and hauling him to a stop halfway up the steps. "Wait!" he said. "Damn it, Pie, hold on. He's liable to shoot you."

"A bullet or two ain't gonna stop me from gettin' my hands 'round his neck," Pie said.

"Pie, no," Rachel said shakily. "He . . . he'll kill you."

"And I'd be within my rights to do it, too," said Grat, his smug smile reappearing. "A man's got a right to defend his property from them that'd steal it."

"Property!" thundered Pie. "What the hell are you talkin' about?"

"Her," Grat said, pointing with his free hand at Rachel.

"Hell, she ain't property. She ain't even your wife. She told us you never did marry up with her proper-like."

"Of course not. A white man can't marry a darkie."

Cory's eyes widened, and Lucille gasped in shock. They looked at Rachel, who stood there, hands trembling slightly as she held them at her side, a deathly pallor on her face. Slowly, Pie turned around to look at her, too.

"Slave?" he said, his voice barely above a whisper.

Grat's voice lashed out mockingly. "Tell your friends the truth, gal. Tell 'em about how I bought you from Rutherford Hannah's widow 'cause she didn't want you around remindin' her how her precious husband fathered a bastard brat from some darkie maid."

For a long moment, Rachel didn't say anything. Then, so quietly that the others had trouble hearing her, she said, "She was an octaroon. My mother was an octaroon."

"Don't matter. One drop of darkie blood's enough," Grat sneered. "She was a slave and that makes you a slave, and I bought you all legal-like from Miz Hannah. So you are my property, gal, and I'm takin' you back to the tavern with me."

Cory's brain was spinning at these unexpected revelations, but he knew he had to think of a way to protect Rachel from Grat. He and Pie and Colonel Thompson had jeopardized their mission for the Confederacy to rescue her, and ever since she had been a staunch friend to them. Slave or not, they couldn't let her fall back into Grat's brutal hands.

"Prove it," he heard himself saying. "You have to be able to prove it."

Grat nodded. "Sure, I can do that." Without lowering his pistol, he reached inside his coat with his other hand and brought out a folded paper. "Got the bill of sale from Miz Hannah's overseer right here. It's got the gal's name on it, and he wrote out her description, too, right down to the mole on the inside of her thigh. I reckon you boys have both seen that mole, as handy as she is at spreadin' her legs."

Cory still had a hand on Pie's arm. He felt his friend tremble with barely suppressed rage.

"I can kill him," Pie growled. "It don't matter how many times he shoots me, I can still get my hands on him and kill him."

"Take another step and I'll blow your brains out," Grat threatened.

Cory's right hand drifted toward the butt of the Colt holstered on his hip. "You can't down us both, mister," he said. "If you shoot Pie, it'll be the last thing you ever do, because I'll put a bullet through your head. And if you go for me instead, he'll get hold of you and tear you apart."

Grat hesitated, and the barrel of his gun began to waver a bit.

From the bottom of the steps, Rachel suddenly shouted, "Stop it! Stop it, all of you! I don't want any of you to die because of me. I'm not worth it!" Her hands came up and covered her face as she began to sob.

Lucille went to her and put an arm around her to try to comfort her. Looking up at the tense tableau on the steps of the boarding house, Lucille said, "Let me go get Uncle Charles, Cory. He can straighten out this mess, I'm sure."

"Ain't nothin' to straighten out," Grat insisted before Cory could say anything. "That gal is a runaway slave, and she belongs to me. I'm takin' her home."

"You'll have to kill me first," Pie breathed.

The barrel of Grat's pistol started to come up again, and Cory steeled himself for action. He wondered if he could draw and fire his Colt before Grat got off a shot. He didn't think it was very likely . . .

"Here now!" a stern voice sounded. "What's going on here?"

Cory recognized Colonel Thompson's voice. He glanced over his shoulder and saw the colonel striding down the road toward the boarding house. At his side were Luther Bradley, the stationmaster, and another man Cory didn't know.

"It'll be all right now," Lucille told Rachel. "You'll see."

Thompson came to a stop and balefully regarded Grat. "I had hoped never to set eyes on you again, sir," he said. "What are you doing here, and why are you pointing that gun at my young friends?"

"You'd best stay out of this, old man," snapped Grat. "It ain't none o' your business, either, just like it's none o' theirs."

Lucille spoke up. "That horrible man is claiming that Rachel is a runaway slave, Uncle Charles. He says he's come to take her back."

The stranger who had come up the road with Thompson was in late middle age with white hair under his hat and sweeping white mustaches. With an air of authority he turned to the tavern keeper. "Runaway, is it? You got any proof of that, mister?"

Grat brandished the paper he had taken out of his coat earlier. "Right here," he said. "A legal bill of sale for that slave."

The stranger looked curiously at Rachel. "Don't appear to me that she's a darkie."

"She's got darkie blood. Her ma was an octaroon. But what business is it of yours, anyway?" Grat demanded harshly.

The stranger pushed back the lapel of his black frock coat so that the badge pinned to his vest was visible. "I'm the sheriff o' this here parish, mister, and you'd better keep a civil tongue in your head."

"Sorry," Grat muttered. "Didn't know you was the law." His attitude brightened. "But since you're here, Sheriff, maybe you can tell these folks that I'm within my rights. I bought and paid for this gal. She's mine."

The sheriff thrust out his hand as he started up the steps. "Lemme see that paper."

Pie said desperately, "Sheriff, can't you see he's lyin'? You can't let him have Rachel. You just can't!"

The sheriff took the paper from Grat and began to read it by the light of the lantern hung beside the door. "Just hold your horses, boy," he said to Pie. "We'll get to the bottom o' this."

With the dangerous situation momentarily eased, Cory was able to tug Pie back down to the bottom of the steps. He left the big man with Lucille, and the two tried futilely to console Rachel. Cory turned to join Colonel Thompson and Luther Bradley. "I'm glad you showed up when you did, Colonel," he said quietly. "I'm afraid in another minute or two there would have been gunplay."

"Even from down the street I could tell that something was wrong," Thompson said. "I found Mr. Bradley and Sheriff Wiggins in the depot and spoke to them. Mr. Bradley told me that someone had been there earlier asking questions about Miss Hannah. From his description I knew it must be Grat."

"I'm mighty sorry I told that gent anything about her," Bradley said ruefully. "It never occurred to me that he might mean to cause trouble for y'all."

"You couldn't have known," Thompson said.

Bradley leaned closer to Cory and asked, "Is that redheaded girl really a darkie?"

Cory just shrugged. Rachel hadn't denied Grat's charge. If she really was a runaway slave, it would explain a lot of things.

Sheriff Wiggins cleared his throat and rattled the piece of paper he had taken from Grat. "Well, now," he said, "this here looks like a legal bill of sale, right enough. It's dated and witnessed, and there ain't no denyin' this young woman matches the description writ down on it."

"That's what I told you," said Grat. Now that he appeared confident of getting his own way without having to fight for it, he lowered the hammer on his pistol and tucked it away under his coat. "The gal's mine. Ain't that right, Sheriff?"

Wiggins shrugged, then said sharply, "You there! Girl!"

Rachel looked at him, her tear-streaked face set in stony lines.

"You got anything to say for yourself?" asked Wiggins. "Do you deny that you're the slave called Rachel?"

"Rachel is my name," she said tautly. "My father gave it to me. His name was Rutherford Hannah."

"It don't make no never-mind who your daddy was if your mama was a slave," the sheriff said impatiently. "Now, is that true or ain't it?"

Rachel's jaw trembled a little. "It's true," she finally said.

Wiggins refolded the paper and handed it back to Grat. "Then what'n hell are we arguin' about? You belong to this gentleman here, and I reckon you got to do whatever he says."

"No!" roared Pie, and he would have swarmed up the steps again if Cory hadn't grabbed one arm and Colonel Thompson the other. Even with both of them hanging on, they could barely hold him back.

"I thought you had better sense than to run off," Grat said to Rachel. "You ought to've knowed that sooner or later I'd find you and take you back. As soon as somebody told me they'd seen you over here in Monroe, I came right on to get you." He crooked a finger. "Let's go."

At the bottom of the steps, Rachel didn't budge.

"Come on, damn it!" Grat said. "You got to do what I tell you. The sheriff said so."

Pie looked around in a miserable, mute appeal. His eyes went from Cory to Thompson, from Lucille to Bradley to the sheriff. Then he looked at Rachel, but she dropped her gaze and wouldn't look at him. Slowly, she raised her foot to the first step. As if she were climbing the steps of a gallows, she went up to the porch where Grat was waiting.

Cory's pulse hammered in his head. He saw eager faces peeking through gaps around the curtains over the windows in the front of the house and knew that Miss Fay and the other boarders were watching Rachel's humiliation. Bitterness welled up in his throat.

"Come along, Private Jones," Thompson said quietly but firmly to Pie. "There's nothing we can do here."

"But—"

"As much as we may dislike it, that man has the law on his side," said Thompson. "It's a private matter. We can't interfere."

Cory wanted to interfere. He wanted to pull his gun and put a bullet in the middle of Grat's ugly, gloating face. He didn't care if Rachel was a slave. He didn't care about property rights. Rachel was his friend, and he wanted to help her.

But he knew he couldn't, not with the sheriff right there. He'd just get himself locked up, and then he couldn't take care of Lucille or help the cause. Besides that, if there was gunplay, Lucille might be hurt. Cory couldn't risk that.

So he stood there, knowing that a part of him would be forever ashamed of his inaction, and watched like the others until Rachel reached the top of the steps and went to stand beside Grat. Her head was still down.

Wiggins made shooing motions with his hands. "You folks better go on about your business," he said. "This is all over."

"I won't go in there," Lucille said in a low, angry voice. "I won't stay under the same roof as that man."

Luther Bradley offered, "You can come home with me, Miss Farrell. My wife and I will be glad to put you up for the night. You can have the room our daughter had 'fore she got married and moved out."

Lucille managed a faint smile as she nodded. "Thank you, Mr. Bradley. I appreciate it very much." She glanced back at the boarding house as she turned away. "I'll never set foot in there with those harpies again."

So Lucille had spotted Miss Fay and the others at the windows, too, thought Cory. He shared her anger at them.

Grat jerked a thumb at Rachel. "Get on inside," he snapped. "I ain't lettin' you out of my sight again."

They disappeared into the boarding house as Cory and Colonel Thompson succeeded in turning Pie away from the place. Getting him started down the street toward the depot was easier than Cory expected it would be. Pie shambled along, bearlike, and after a few steps his back began to heave.

He was crying, Cory realized, a quiet, wretched sobbing unlike anything he ever would have expected to come from his massive friend.

⌇

THE TROUBLE had made Cory forget about how tired he was. When they reached the station, he and Colonel Thompson steered Pie inside, past the parked wagons and the two soldiers who were standing guard. All three of them sat down on one of the hard benches in the waiting room.

Still agitated, Pie ran his fingers through his beard and his hair, making him look more like some sort of wild man than ever. "You should'a let me kill him," he said without looking at Cory. "You should'a let me kill him."

"Then you would have been a murderer and a fugitive from justice," Thompson said crisply.

"Would've been worth it to save Rachel from that bastard."

"Pie," Cory said tentatively, "she's a slave."

Pie's head snapped around, his expression furious. "I don't care about that!" he said. "You think I give a damn?"

Slowly, Cory shook his head. "No. I didn't think so. I reckon I don't, either."

"Gentlemen, I'm quite fond of Miss Hannah, as well," said Thompson, "but the law is the law. We cannot go against it."

Pie used the back of his hand to paw at his eyes for a moment, then stood up and began to pace back and forth. The depot's waiting room was dimly lit by a single lantern, and its glow threw huge, shifting shadows on the walls as Pie moved back and forth in front of it.

"She told me about how Grat made her go with fellas at the tavern," Pie said. "Well, not really told me, I reckon, but she'd start to say things and then stop all of a sudden, and I knew what she meant. She was mighty ashamed of the things she's done. I told her she didn't need to blame herself, that it wasn't her fault. But just hearin' what little she did tell me . . . it made me want to tear that fella apart with my bare hands."

"We'd all like to do that," the colonel said. "Unfortunately, he has the sheriff on his side."

Pie swung around. "There's got to be a place where there ain't no sheriffs. Where folks just care about what's right and wrong, not what some piece of paper says."

Thompson shook his head and said, "I'm afraid laws are the price we pay for a civilized society."

"You call it civilized when a man like Grat can torment a gal like Rachel, and the law says it's all right?"

Cory clasped his hands between his knees and leaned forward. He was frowning darkly as he wrestled with questions he couldn't answer. "Listen," he said, "aren't we fighting a war because of the whole idea of slavery?"

"We're fighting a war because the North tried to dictate—unconstitutionally, I might add—what the South should be allowed to do," Thompson replied crisply. "And when we would not go along with their bullying, they launched an armed invasion of our homeland. I can't speak for everyone in the Confederacy, of course, but that is why I'm fighting."

"Then you don't believe in slavery, Colonel?"

Thompson took his pipe out of his coat pocket and stuck it in his mouth. His teeth clamped down on the stem. "Whether I believe in it or not, our laws permit it. Our laws. The question is, do we have the right to make our own laws, or does that right reside in Washington? I believe in states' rights."

"My family never had any slaves," said Cory. "I don't reckon my father believed in holding down any other man when he wouldn't be held down himself."

"I never owned any slaves, either. You don't need them to run a bank."

"But we knew folks who did. Some of them were pretty bad
. . ." Cory thought about Duncan Ebersole, owner of the plantation called Mountain Laurel. Ebersole was known throughout
Culpeper County for the harshness of his overseers. "But some
of them weren't. They treated their slaves decently. But slaves
were still slaves."

Thompson took the pipe from his mouth and pointed the
stem at Cory. "I believe that if the Union had just left us alone,
all the slaves would have been freed within the next ten or
twenty years." The colonel shook his head. "Now, if there's any
sort of settlement, or if we actually win the war, I fear the problem will continue to fester for much, much longer."

Suddenly, Pie stepped over to the bench and slammed a fist
down on it. The blow was so hard Cory felt the bench jump
underneath him.

"Damn it!" Pie thundered. "You two are sittin' here talkin'
while Rachel's down yonder with that snake!"

"But what can we do, Pie?" Cory asked miserably. "You
heard the sheriff—"

"The sheriff can go to hell! I'm goin' to get Rachel."

As Pie swung toward the doorway, Luther Bradley appeared
there. The stationmaster had taken Lucille to his house to get
her settled in for the night with his wife. He said, "I thought I'd
find you gents still up." He put out a hand to stop Pie. "Better
hold on there, young fella. When it comes to the law, Dan Wiggins means what he says. If you try to take that girl back, he'll
come after you with a shotgun, and he won't hesitate to use it."

"I don't care," Pie said. "I got to help Rachel."

Solemnly, Bradley shook his head. "There's not a thing you
can do, son."

For a moment, Cory thought Pie was going to bull his way
past Bradley and head for the boarding house anyway. Then,
instead, Pie slammed his fist against the wall of the waiting
room. Cory was a little surprised that the planks didn't crack
under the impact.

"It ain't right," Pie said. "It just ain't right."

Bradley patted him on the shoulder. "I know, son, but it's—"

"Don't tell me it's the law. I'm sick o' hearin' that."

Colonel Thompson stood up and came over to him. "Perhaps you ought to get some sleep, son" he suggested. "I've often found that regardless of how bleak things may look in the middle of the night, they take on a distinctly better appearance in the morning."

Pie didn't look like he believed that for a second, but after a few moments he slowly nodded his shaggy head and turned toward the door of the bunk room.

Cory came to his feet. An idea was tickling around in the back of his brain, and he didn't know if he ought to share it with Pie or not. Then he thought about the way Pie had sobbed as they were walking down here, and he knew he had no choice.

"Colonel, I think Pie and I ought to check the mules before we turn in," he said. "You can go on, though."

Thompson's eyes narrowed in suspicion. "What are you up to, Mr. Brannon?"

"Nothing," Cory said. "I just want to make sure the mules get rubbed down all right."

"What you want is to go back down there and cause a commotion at that boarding house."

"No sir," Cory insisted. "I don't intend to set foot in that boarding house."

"You give me your word of honor on that?"

"Word of honor," said Cory.

Pie knuckled his eyes. "I ain't sleepy," he said. "Maybe it'd make me feel better to move around a mite."

The colonel still didn't look convinced. "I don't mean any insult—" he began.

"Then don't insult us by not believing us," Cory said. "We're just going to the corral by the wagon yard."

"All right. But I want you back here in less than a half-hour."

Cory nodded. "Yes sir."

Bradley yawned and looked at his watch. "Damn, it's nearly midnight. I got to get some shuteye." He smiled at Thompson. "Don't worry, Colonel. I'll walk with these boys down to the corral. It's sort of on my way home, anyway."

"Very well. Good night, gentlemen."

"Good night, Colonel," Cory said. Pie didn't say anything.

The night air was chilly as the three men walked the couple of hundred yards to the wagon yard, where the mule teams had been taken earlier. Bradley grunted a good night and left them there. As soon as the stationmaster was out of earshot, Pie closed his hands around one of the bars of the corral and leaned on it. Inside the enclosure, the mules appeared to be settled down peacefully for the night.

"I don't care what you told the colonel," said Pie. "You dragged me off down here for a reason, Cory. What is it?"

"I was thinking about what you said earlier," Cory replied. "About how there had to be a place somewhere that the law didn't matter, only what was right and wrong. I think I may know of a place like that."

One of Pie's hands left the corral pole and closed on Cory's arm. "Where?"

"We've been there." Cory took a deep breath. "Texas."

Chapter Three

F OR A LONG MOMENT, Pie stared at Cory. Then the big man
said, "They got law in Texas. It's part of the Confederacy,
ain't it?"

Cory nodded. "Yeah, but you've heard the people in Marshall talk about how uncivilized parts of the state are. Why, out
west there are still wild Indians."

The clouds overhead were starting to break up, shredded by
the chilly north wind. The gaps let moonlight come through,
and in that faint illumination, Cory saw Pie suddenly smile.

"Uncivilized don't sound so bad to me right now. I reckon I
wouldn't even mind the Injuns if it meant Rachel'd be safe from
Grat." The big man hesitated for a second, then went on, "But
if we took off for the tall and uncut like that, it'd mean I might
never see you again, Cory."

Cory felt a pang of loss just talking about it. But he just put a
smile on his face and nodded. "I know. But Rachel's worth it,
isn't she? I know if it was Lucille, I'd risk anything for her."

Pie dragged his fingers through his beard. "Yeah. Rachel's
worth it, all right. But how're we gonna get her away from Grat?"

"That is a problem," Cory admitted. "I gave the colonel my
word we wouldn't go to the boarding house, at least tonight."

Pie shook his head. "We can't wait. Grat'll probably leave for
the tavern first thing in the mornin'."

Cory agreed. He thought for a minute, then said, "We either
have to break our word . . . or find someone who didn't promise
the colonel anything."

"Who around here would help us?"

"Lucille would," Cory answered without hesitation. "I'll bet
Allen Carter would, too."

"I hate gettin' them mixed up in my trouble . . ."

39

"We're your friends, Pie," said Cory. "Your trouble is our trouble, too."

Pie nodded appreciatively. "I'm much obliged. Can't tell you how much."

"We don't have Rachel yet," Cory reminded him. "What we need is some sort of distraction that'll get Grat out of the house. Then Lucille can sneak in and bring Rachel out. We'll have a couple of horses saddled and ready. If you ride the rest of the night, you'll be a long way toward Texas by morning."

"We'll have to take some supplies," said Pie, getting into the spirit of the plan they were forming. "I'm a good shot and there's plenty of game, so I reckon we can live off the land if we have to, 'specially once we get to Texas. Where'll we go when we get there, though?"

Cory remembered the soldier who had befriended him at Fort Donelson. "There's a river called the Brazos," he said. "A fella once told me that the land along it is some of the best in the world, and it's wide open for settlement. It's far enough out on the frontier that you ought to be safe there. The two of you could build a cabin and have a farm."

Pie got a faraway look in his eyes. "Sounds mighty nice. Somewhere along the way we could find a parson to marry us, so once we got there we could raise a whole passel of young'uns." He heaved a deep breath. "Yes sir, mighty nice."

"Come on," Cory said. "Let's go get Lucille."

They both knew where the stationmaster lived, and they even knew which room had belonged to the Bradleys' daughter. That was where Lucille would be. Moving silently in the darkness, the two young men approached the house.

"Has Mr. Bradley got a dog?" Cory whispered.

Pie shook his head. "Don't know. I hope not."

Luck was with them. No canine sentry came bounding out to bark at them as they carefully and quietly slipped up to the house. Cory went to the window of the room where Lucille was sleeping and softly tapped.

There was no response, so he tapped again, a little louder this time. He had visions of Luther Bradley throwing open the window and sticking out a shotgun, but that didn't happen. Instead, after a moment, the curtains were pushed back and a dim white shape appeared on the other side of the glass. It leaned closer to the window, and Cory was able to make out Lucille's puzzled features.

When she saw that her nocturnal visitors were Cory and Pie, she opened the window and leaned out, pulling the wrapper she wore more tightly around her. "Cory!" she said in a whisper. "What are you doing here? Have you lost your mind?"

"Nope," he told her with a grin.

"But . . . but you can't be here. It's improper!"

He grew more serious as he said, "I know that, and I'm sorry, Lucille. But we're here on an important matter. We need you to help us rescue Rachel from Grat."

"Well, why on earth didn't you say so?" Lucille flashed a smile at them. "Wait just a minute and let me get dressed."

She didn't lower the window, just closed the curtains as she retreated into the room. Cory and Pie turned their backs to the house and waited until they heard Lucille at the window again. As they turned around, she was climbing out of the house. Cory took her arm to steady her as she dropped lightly to the ground.

Lucille was dressed as she often had on the *Missouri Zephyr*, in boy's clothing—a linsey woolsey shirt, brown whipcord trousers, and boots. Instead of tucking her hair up under a cap, it was loose around her shoulders. Cory thought she looked as beautiful in the moonlight as he had ever seen her.

"I know, this garb is scandalous," she said, "but considering what we're up to, I wanted to be able to move quickly."

"Good idea," Cory told her.

"What are we going to do?" Lucille asked as they moved away from the Bradley house.

"We have to come up with something that'll get Grat out of Miss Fay's," said Cory. "Then we figured you could go in the back and get Rachel. Pie and I will be waiting outside with a couple of saddled horses."

"We're goin' to Texas," Pie said proudly.

"Texas?" repeated Lucille. "My goodness. Isn't that rather . . . drastic?"

"We got to go somewhere that Grat'll never find us. I figure we'll be safe if we can get on out to the frontier."

"Safe from Grat, perhaps. But what about Indians and wild animals and . . . and . . . well, I've heard what an untamed wilderness western Texas is!"

Pie grinned confidently. "Then I reckon Rachel and me'll help tame it a mite."

"You're sure this is what you want to do?"

Pie nodded. "I'm sure."

"But you haven't asked Rachel yet."

"Well . . . no, 'course not. She's shut up in that house with that Grat fella."

"What if she doesn't want to go?"

Cory said, "Of course she'll want to go. She'll do anything to get away from Grat."

"You're sure of that?" asked Lucille.

Cory felt doubts creeping into his head. He was certain that Rachel didn't want to be with Grat, but would she be willing to go on the run, to abandon everything she had known and set off for the frontier? He felt like that was the case, but he had to admit that he couldn't know for sure.

Pie had no doubts. "She'll go," he declared, and that was good enough for Cory. Of all of them, Pie knew Rachel the best. They had spent a lot of time talking these past few months.

"All right, then," said Lucille. "How are you going to get Grat out of the boarding house?"

Pie scratched his head. "We ain't quite figured that'un out yet. Have we, Cory?"

"No," Cory was forced to admit. "I thought about yelling that the house was on fire, but if we did that, Grat would just bring Rachel out with him. We have to separate the two of them somehow, some way."

"We thought we'd get Mr. Carter to help us," said Pie. "Maybe he can come up with somethin'."

"It has to be something that would appeal to Grat," mused Lucille. "The problem is, we don't know him that well. You only spent part of one night at his tavern, right?"

Cory nodded. "And while we were there he just stayed behind the bar and served drinks and glared at us."

"Did he drink himself?"

Cory thought back to that night, months earlier, when he had stopped at the tavern with Pie and the colonel. He nodded. "I saw him down several mugs of beer, and some shots of whiskey, too. It didn't seem to make him drunk, though."

"So we know he likes to drink. What else?"

"He's a greedy sumbitch—I mean son of a gun," said Pie. "Seemed like he was more upset about the money Rachel cost him by runnin' off than anything else."

Lucille nodded. "All right, he likes money and he likes to drink. What about cards? Does he play poker?"

Cory shrugged. "I don't know. I didn't see a game going on while we were there. It's certainly possible, though."

They reached the little cabin where Allen and Fred Carter lived. The place was dark, and Cory hated to disturb them after the long day they'd all had bringing the wagon train into Monroe. Clearly, though, he and Pie and Lucille needed help coming up with a scheme that would get Grat away from Rachel.

Cory knocked on the door. A moment later, he heard a thumping sound that he recognized as Allen Carter's wooden peg hitting the planks of the floor. "Who's there?" Carter called.

"Cory Brannon," he responded. "And Pie and Miss Farrell."

The door opened, and Carter stared out at them in confusion. He had a pistol in his hand, but it was held with the barrel down alongside his leg.

"What is it?" he asked. "Is there trouble with the wagons?"

"No sir," Cory said. "But we need your help."

"He's got Rachel," Pie broke in. "That fella Grat who was holdin' her prisoner at his tavern."

Carter stepped out of the cabin and quietly pulled the door closed behind him. "Fred's asleep, and I don't want to disturb him," he said. "Now, what's this about something happening to Miss Hannah?"

"You've heard us talk about Grat," said Cory.

Carter nodded. "The tavern keeper. Sounds like a bad fella."

"He's plenty bad. He beat Rachel and . . . ," Cory glanced at Lucille, not wanting to be too indelicate in her presence.

"And forced her to prostitute herself," Lucille said bluntly, making Cory's eyes widen slightly. "He heard that she was here in Monroe and came to get her."

"What about the law?" asked Carter. "Somebody should have fetched the sheriff. Grat can't hold her against her will."

"Well . . . the law says he can," Cory explained. "Rachel's mother down on that plantation . . . she was a slave."

Carter stiffened and said harshly, "What?"

"The law says Rachel's a slave, too," said Pie, "'cause she's got her mama's blood in her. But it ain't right, Mr. Carter. It just ain't right."

"Was she freed?" asked Carter. "Given her manumission papers?"

"No sir," Pie admitted grudgingly. "The lady who owns the plantation sold her to Grat."

Carter took a deep breath. "I don't hold with helping slaves run away from their masters."

"I don't care what the law says," Pie shot back. "Rachel ain't no slave."

"What is it you want from me?"

Cory said, "We thought maybe you'd help us get Rachel away from Grat so that she and Pie can go to Texas."

"Run away, you mean." Carter shook his head. "I won't do it. I like Miss Hannah, never would have thought she was a slave, but I lost this leg at Manassas fighting for our rights to do as we please down here in the South. I'll not go skulking around in the night like some . . . some damned abolitionist!"

Pie made a noise deep in his throat, and Cory moved smoothly between him and Carter. "This is different," Cory said. "You know Rachel. You know how much she helped out with the wagons."

Carter shrugged. "I'm sorry to hear about her trouble, but the law is still the law."

"I'm gettin' damned tired o' hearin' that," rumbled Pie.

Carter used his free hand to rub his eyes for a moment, then said, "I'll do this much. I can't help you, but I won't say anything about what you've told me tonight. If you manage to get her away from Grat and the sheriff asks me about it, I'll tell him I haven't seen you since we parted ways at the depot earlier and that I don't know a blasted thing about it. That's all I can do."

Cory saw that Carter wasn't going to be swayed. Grudgingly, he nodded. "All right, if that's the best you can do."

"Be grateful I don't go warn the sheriff what you're up to," snapped Carter. He went inside.

Disappointed, Cory, Lucille, and Pie turned away from the cabin and started walking back toward the other end of town. They had gone only a couple of hundred yards when they heard the rapid patter of footsteps behind them.

Cory turned around quickly, his hand moving to the Colt on his hip. A slender figure loomed up out of the shadows, and a familiar voice said, "It's just me."

"Fred?" Cory exclaimed.

Lucille said, "Fred, what are you doing here? You shouldn't be wandering around in the dark."

"I came after you," Fred Carter said. "I heard you talking to my pa. I want to help you."

Cory knew that Allen Carter wouldn't have let his son leave the cabin in the middle of the night. "What did you do, sneak out the window?"

Fred laughed delightedly. "I did," he said. "I pretended to be asleep. And then Pa went back to bed. And I climbed out the window just like you said, Cory." His voice became somewhat solemn. "I want to help Miss Rachel. I heard you tell Pa she was in trouble."

Fred couldn't possibly understand the depth of the trouble Rachel was in, but Cory was touched by the young man's concern for her. He put a hand on Fred's shoulder and said, "Thanks, Fred, but I don't know of anything you can do to help."

"But I want to!"

"And we're much obliged," Pie told him. "There just ain't nothin' you can do. You best run along home now."

"Wait a minute," said Lucille. "Maybe Fred *can* help us."

Cory frowned at her. He'd felt bad enough about bringing her into this and possibly putting her in danger. But at least Lucille fully comprehended what they were doing. Fred didn't.

"Lucille, I don't know if this is a good idea—" he began.

"You haven't even heard my idea," she broke in.

Cory supposed that was true. The night was slipping away, and he hadn't had any sleep in what seemed like ages. "Go ahead. It can't hurt to listen," he said, none too gallantly.

Lucille put her hand on Fred's arm. "Fred, do you know what it means to pretend?"

He grinned. "Sure. Sometimes I pretend I'm a bird, and I flap my arms and go flying all around town."

"That's right. Do you think you could pretend that you're lost and afraid of the dark?"

"But I'm not lost." Fred turned and pointed. "My house is right back yonder. And I haven't been afraid of the dark for a long time. A year, at least."

"That's why I said you'd have to pretend," Lucille explained patiently.

"Oh. Yeah, I understand now."

"Good." Lucille pointed up the street toward Miss Fay's. "You know where the boarding house is?"

"Yep. Pa did some odd jobs for Miss Fay after he came back from the war with his leg shot off."

Cory grimaced but didn't say anything.

"All right. I want you to go down there and knock on Miss Fay's door. Knock hard, so everybody in the house can hear you. Do you like to yell?"

Another grin. "Oh, yeah."

"Well, you can yell all you want, as loud as you want," Lucille told him. "Cry and pretend that you're lost and you're really scared. Make the biggest racket you can."

"That'll wake everybody up," Fred said worriedly.

Lucille nodded. "That's what we want. When the people come out, tell them you need somebody to take you home."

"How do you know Miss Fay will ask Grat to do that?" Cory wanted to know.

"I don't," admitted Lucille. "But I've been around Miss Fay enough to know that she's not going to go traipsing off to the other side of Monroe in the dark. Most of the boarders are old, and they won't want to go, either."

Cory grunted. "Seems like a pretty shaky plan to me."

Lucille turned and planted her fists against her whipcord-clad hips. "Do you have a better one, Coriolanus Brannon?"

That brought a laugh from Fred. "Cor . . . io . . . lan . . . us," he said, dragging out the name. "That's funny."

Cory bit back the snappish remark he almost made and took a deep breath. "All right, I don't have a better plan," he admitted. He looked at Pie. "What about you?"

Pie's massive shoulders rose and fell. "I got no plan at all, 'cept to get out o' here with Rachel."

"I guess we can give it a try. At the very least, maybe the commotion Fred raises will bring Grat downstairs. We'll have to move fast, though."

Lucille nodded. "I can do that. I know my way around the house really well. I can get in the back door and up the back stairs before anybody knows I'm around."

"How will you know which room Rachel's in?"

"There was only one vacant room," said Lucille. "Miss Fay keeps it for people who are only going to be in town for a short time, rather than for her regular boarders."

The plan actually might work, Cory thought. "All right," he said, "let's give it a try. Pie and I will go down to the corral and get the horses ready. You and Fred go on to the boarding house, but don't start until I give you the signal."

"Come on, Fred," Lucille said, taking the young man's hand. He went with her, smiling happily.

"You reckon this is gonna work?" asked Pie as he and Cory hurried toward the corral next to the wagon yard.

"I don't know," Cory admitted honestly. "But like Lucille said, I don't have a better idea."

⁓

FIFTEEN MINUTES later they were ready. Leading two of the horses on which they had first ridden to Monroe several months earlier, Cory and Pie moved stealthily through the darkness. As they neared the boarding house, Cory handed the reins of one the animals to Pie, then he slipped forward until he heard Lucille whisper his name from the thick shadows underneath a tree.

He put out his hand and touched her, unable to see her. She took his hand and squeezed. "We're ready," she whispered.

"Fred's with you?"

"Right here, Coriolanus," said Fred, his voice a little louder than Cory liked.

He made a shushing noise, then leaned closer to Fred and whispered, "Can you count to ten?"

"Sure can. Want to hear me? One, two—"

"Wait, wait," Cory said. "Lucille and I are going around to the back of the house. As soon as we're gone, you count to ten and then go up on Miss Fay's porch and start carrying on like Lucille told you, all right?"

"Sure. Count to ten, then go up on the porch and start carrying on." Fred hesitated, then said, "I'm not really lost, or scared of the dark, you know."

"We know," Lucille assured him. "We know how smart and brave you are, so we know you can do this."

"Yes ma'am."

"We're going now," Cory told him. "Start counting, Fred."

Holding tightly to Lucille's hand, Cory hurried around the boarding house, giving it a wide berth so they wouldn't be heard. Pie was supposed to be in place already behind the house.

He was. Cory spotted the big man and the two horses in the shadows next to a shed that Miss Fay used as a smokehouse. As they came up next to the shed, Cory could smell the hams hanging inside it.

Before any of them could say anything, they heard shouting from the front of the house and thumping sounds as Fred pounded on the door. Fred certainly was raising a ruckus, just as they had told him. From back here, the house was still dark, but Cory imagined lamps and lanterns being lit as the inhabitants were roused from their sleep and went to find out what all the commotion was.

A few moments later, they heard a hubbub of voices from the front porch. Lucille whispered, "I'd better go."

Cory caught her arm before she could start toward the rear door of the house. "What if Grat's still in the room with Rachel?" he asked anxiously. That thought had just occurred to him.

"I'll say I went downstairs and then got mixed up and came back to the wrong room. Grat doesn't know me. He might not even recognize me." Lucille tugged her arm free. "Cory, I've got to go."

He didn't stop her this time, though every bit of him wanted to go with her. He would only slow her down, he told himself. He didn't know the layout of the boarding house like she did.

Cory and Pie waited tensely as Lucille opened the rear door and disappeared inside the house. The sound of Fred's wailing still came from the front porch. He was carrying on in grand fashion. Surely Grat would be curious enough to go downstairs to see what was going on, Cory told himself.

Fred's cries died away, but Lucille had not yet appeared. It seemed to Cory as if she had been inside for an hour. He muttered, "I don't care what I told the colonel, I'm going in there."

"Hold on," Pie said, touching his arm. The big man's voice was breathless and eager as he went on, "Look there!"

The rear door opened again, and two figures slid out, moving as rapidly and silently as ghosts. Like phantoms they crossed the back yard to the shed, and as they reached the shadows, the taller of the figures threw herself forward into Pie's arms.

"Oh, Pie!" Rachel said in a half-sob. "I knew you'd come for me. I just knew it!"

"You'll be all right now," he told her as he patted her back and stroked her hair. "Ain't nothin' ever gonna hurt you again."

"Where are we going?" Rachel asked as she leaned back slightly in Pie's embrace.

"Texas," he told her. "As far west as we can go, so far that Grat'll never find us, even if he comes lookin' for us."

Rachel nodded. "Yes. I know him. He's a coward. He won't come out on the frontier where it might be dangerous."

Cory was getting impatient. Pie and Rachel needed to mount up and get out of here.

"There's just one more thing 'fore we leave," Pie said. He swallowed hard and went on, "Rachel, soon as we get the chance . . . will you marry me?"

For a moment, she didn't say anything, just looked into his eyes as if she could not believe what she had just heard. Then, with a slight catch in her voice, she said, "Oh, yes, Pie. I'll marry you—if you'll have me as your wife."

"I never wanted anything more," he told her. His mouth came down on hers.

Cory waited as long as he could, then cleared his throat and stepped forward to put one hand on Pie's shoulder, one hand on

Rachel's. "This is very nice, very romantic," he said. "But you two need to get out of here before Grat comes back."

Pie broke the kiss and nodded. "Cory's right. Let's go."

Holding Rachel's hand, he turned toward the horses. She would have to ride astride, since they didn't have side saddles, but she didn't care. She hiked up her skirt and mounted quickly, with Pie's hand on her arm to steady her. Then he swung up into the saddle of the other horse.

"Cory, Lucille," he said, "I can't even start to thank you."

"You don't need to," said Lucille. "Just live a good life out there in Texas. Be happy together."

"We will be," Rachel said. "I know that."

Cory reached up and shook hands with Pie. "Tell the colonel how sorry I am 'bout everything," Pie said.

"Don't worry. I'm pretty sure he'll understand."

"Good luck, Cory. Watch out for the Yankees."

Cory grinned. "The Yankees better watch out for me."

Lucille took Rachel's hand and squeezed it hard for a second, then let go and stepped back. Cory moved alongside her and put his arm around her. Both of them waved as Pie and Rachel turned the horses around and put them into a fast trot that carried the two of them away into the night. It was dark enough so that they vanished quickly.

"Do you think they'll be all right?" Lucille asked, a tiny quaver in her voice.

"They'll be all right," Cory said. "They've got each other. For now, that's all they need."

Chapter Four

CORY HAD BARELY GOTTEN back to the depot and rolled up in his blankets in the bunkroom when the trouble started. On his way in, he had spoken to the two soldiers on guard at the wagons and asked them not to say anything to the colonel about when he arrived. They had agreed reluctantly, guessing that Cory had been off trying to help Pie in some way. They were fond of the big man, too.

Colonel Thompson was sleeping soundly; quiet snores emanated from his bunk. Exhaustion from the long day had claimed him.

Despite the tension he still felt, Cory probably would have dozed off, too, had it not been for the shouting that suddenly came from outside.

Thompson snorted and rolled over. "What—what—" he said as he sat up. "What in blazes is going on out there?"

Cory knew. He recognized Grat's voice as the tavern keeper yelled curses and demanded to see the colonel. Obviously, the two sentries had stopped him.

Cory sat up on his bunk, mumbling and rubbing his face as if he, too, had just been awakened from a sound sleep. His gun belt was coiled on the floor next to his bunk. He bent over and snagged the Colt, saying to the colonel, "Must be somebody after the wagons!"

"Good Lord, you're right!" exclaimed Thompson as he snatched up his revolver and bolted from the bunk. Cory was right behind him, following the colonel as he naturally would if trouble cropped up.

In stocking feet, they rushed through the dimly lit lobby and out through the front doors of the depot. In the light that came from inside the building, Cory saw Grat standing there in the street, nightshirt hastily tucked into a pair of pants. The tavern owner carried the same pistol he had brandished earlier to threaten them at the boarding house and glared at the two guards. As Cory and Thompson emerged from the depot, he turned toward them and shouted, "Damn it, where's that gal?" He started to lift the pistol.

Cory thought this might be his opportunity to end Grat's threat, but Colonel Thompson stepped forward into the line of fire. "Get hold of yourself, man!" snapped Thompson. "Put that gun down!"

Faced with four armed men as he was, some sense finally penetrated Grat's fury. He let his gun hand drop back to his side, but his face was still contorted with rage as he said, "I've sent for the sheriff. I want that slave of mine back!"

"If you've lost Miss Hannah again, that's no concern of ours," Thompson said. "She's certainly not here."

"Damn it, you're probably hidin' her—"

"Are you calling me a liar, sir?" Thompson cut in coldly.

Grat pointed at Cory. "He done it, him and that big one. They stole Rachel from me again!"

"Don't be insane. Mr. Brannon and Private Jones have been asleep in the station—" Thompson stopped as he glanced over his shoulder and saw Cory standing there alone. Clearly, he hadn't noticed until now that Pie was nowhere to be seen. "Where is Private Jones?"

Cory looked around, trying to appear confused. "I don't know, Colonel." That wasn't exactly a lie, he thought. At this moment, he didn't know precisely where Pie was, only that he and Rachel were somewhere west of Monroe, heading for Texas as fast as their horses would carry them.

Thompson turned to the sentries. "Have you seen Private Jones leave the railroad station tonight?"

"No sir," one of the men answered without hesitation. "We haven't seen hide nor hair of him since we started standin' guard. Ain't that right, Trout?"

The other guard nodded. "Yep."

"I guess he could have . . . slipped out while I was asleep."
If he had actually been asleep tonight, Cory added to himself.
He didn't have to fake a jaw-cracking yawn. "I was really tired.
Still am."

"I told you!" crowed Grat. "Maybe this little son of a bitch
didn't have anything to do with it, but the big one sure did!"

Cory felt anger well up inside him. "I don't take kindly to
being called names, Grat." He stepped forward.

Thompson moved between them again. "We'll get to the
bottom of this," he said. "Exactly what happened, Mr. Grat?
When did you notice that Miss Hannah was gone?"

"Shortly after that half-wit raised such a ruckus at the boarding house."

Thompson shook his head and said, "I don't understand.
What are you talking about?"

Grat took a deep breath and controlled his anger with a visible effort. "Some addle-brained kid turned up on the porch of
the boarding house. He'd wandered away from home and was
carryin' on about bein' lost and afraid of the dark. Somebody
had to take him home, and none of those old codgers who live
there were willing to do it. The old bat who runs the place asked
me to."

So Lucille had been absolutely right about how her plan
would work out, thought Cory. She would be glad to hear that.

"I wasn't just about to let that gal run off again, so I went
upstairs and locked her in the room before I left," Grat went on.

"Perhaps Miss Hannah climbed out the window," suggested
the colonel.

Grat shook his head. "It's painted shut. Nobody had bothered it."

Cory wondered how close Lucille had come to running into
Grat while she was sneaking into the house. She hadn't said anything about it, but maybe she hadn't mentioned it because she
wouldn't want him to know how dangerous her actions had
been. He wondered, too, how she had gotten the door unlocked.

Thompson looked at Cory again. "Mr. Brannon, you gave me your word of honor that you would not go back to the boarding house tonight."

"I never set foot in the place," Cory said honestly, putting plenty of indignation in his voice. "Neither did Pie, at least while I was with him."

"But Private Jones is gone now."

Cory just shrugged.

A slender figure carrying a lantern trudged up to the depot. Sheriff Dan Wiggins looked quite angry about being rousted out of bed. "What's goin' on here?" he demanded. When he spotted Grat, he added, "Not you again!"

"I demand justice!" Grat spat out angrily. "I got a slave that's run away again!"

"If she's run away, then you ain't got her," Wiggins said dryly. "What happened?"

Quickly, Grat told the story again, and at the mention of Fred's part in it, the sheriff glanced sharply at Cory and Thompson. "Half-wit boy, eh?" he grunted when the tavern keeper was finished. "Sounds like the Carter boy. You know anything about this, Colonel?"

"Not a blessed thing," Thompson replied fervently. "The first I knew of it was when Mr. Grat started making so much noise out here it sounded like Ulysses S. Grant himself was riding in!"

"Lord, spare us that," said the sheriff. "Where's that big fella who was with you?"

Thompson hesitated then said, "Private Jones appears to be missing, too."

Wiggins grunted again. "Well, there you go. Him and the darkie gal run off together. Hate to think a white man'd do such a thing, but some folks take leave o' their senses now and then."

"That's all you can say about it, that they ran off together?" raged Grat. "Ain't you goin' after them? That bastard Jones is a slave stealer!"

"It's the middle of the night," snapped Wiggins. "I ain't goin' nowhere but back to bed. This ain't no emergency."

"You've got to get a posse together—"

"In the mornin', I'll ride out and see if I can find any tracks, so's I can figure out which way they was goin'. Then I'll send word to the authorities to be on the lookout for 'em. That's about all I can do, Grat."

Grat fumed. Cory heard his teeth grinding together in frustration. "I'll go after them myself!" he threatened.

"You do that. Me, I'm goin' back to bed." Wiggins gave them all a sour look and turned to walk off down the street, going back the way he had come.

Grat glowered at Cory and the colonel. "You ain't gettin' away with this," he said. "I know you had somethin' to do with it. I'll even the score with you later. And when I find that darkie, I'm taking a blacksnake whip to her! I'll flay the hide off her back! She won't never run away again!"

There was a faint tremble of emotion in Thompson's voice as he said, "I can't stop you from dealing however you wish with your legal holdings, sir, but I can tell you this: I'm here on an official mission for the Confederate States of America, and Private Jones is still under my command. If you interfere with my men, or my mission, in any way . . . I'll have you hanged, sir. I'll have you hanged from the nearest tree."

Grat stared at him, flabbergasted. Finally, the tavern keeper was able to say, "But . . . but you can't—"

"I assure you, I can and I will," said Thompson. "Now get away from these wagons. They're government property."

Grat backed up but didn't turn away. He pointed a shaking finger at Thompson and said, "You ain't heard the last of this!"

"I devoutly hope that I have."

Finally, Grat turned and stalked off, muttering curses. The colonel stood, his back ramrod-stiff, and watched him go.

"Well, what do you know?" Cory said into the silence that followed Grat's departure. "I never would have thought that Pie—"

"Oh, shut up!" Thompson snapped in exasperation as he turned toward the depot entrance. "I'm not going to ask you any more questions, Mr. Brannon, because I don't want to listen to any more lies."

Cory wanted to protest that he hadn't told any lies—well, not really—but he decided it would be best not to push the colonel right now. Thompson had his suspicions, but that wouldn't stop him from standing up for the men under his command. Later on, when some time had passed and the whole situation had cooled down, maybe then Cory would tell the colonel the truth.

Or maybe not.

CORY MANAGED to get a couple of hours of sleep before Colonel Thompson woke him to take his turn on guard duty. The colonel stood watch with him, and they both pulled a double shift, guarding the wagons and their cargo until dawn. It was a long, uncomfortable time for Cory. He knew that the colonel knew he'd had something to do with the disappearances of Rachel and Pie, but he couldn't yet tell him what he had done or that he had involved Lucille in the matter.

Finally, so exhausted he was practically stumbling, Cory headed to the Bradleys' house to see Lucille. She was already up, helping Mrs. Bradley make breakfast. The stationmaster's wife invited him to join them. He accepted gratefully.

A cup of coffee, several thick slices of ham, and a stack of flapjacks renewed Cory's strength and made him feel almost human again. Sitting across the table, Bradley commented, "That fella Jones was a good man. Reckon we'll miss him around here."

"Yes sir."

When Cory left, heading back to the depot, Lucille went with him. When there was no one within earshot, she asked, "What happened after you brought me back here last night?"

Quickly, Cory described the scene Grat had made at the train station, concluding by saying, "Your uncle's convinced I had something to do with it, but he doesn't suspect you."

"I'll tell him the truth—"

"No!" Cory said. "Better to just let things lie. Grat can't prove anything against any of us, and neither can the colonel. And the sheriff's not interested in causing trouble for us or going after Pie and Rachel."

"I wonder if we'll ever see them again," Lucille said wistfully but hopefully.

"Maybe. I was thinking about going to Texas someday, after the war is over."

Lucille looked over at him. "Oh, you were, were you?"

This was an opportunity to ask her to marry him, Cory realized, so that they could go to Texas together. But he felt a sudden, unanticipated surge of nervousness and changed the subject. "You didn't tell me that you almost ran into Grat in the boarding house."

"How do you know that?" asked Lucille, clearly surprised.

"He said he went back upstairs to lock Rachel into her room before he took Fred home. That would have been about the same time you were going up to her room from the back."

"I heard him coming and hid in the rear stairwell until he was gone," she said with a nervous look in her eye. "I'm just glad he didn't come along a few seconds later. Then he would have found me unlocking the door with my key."

"Is that how you got her out? I was going to ask you about that, too."

She laughed softly and a little mischievously. "All the locks are the same in Miss Fay's house. That's why most of the boarders never lock their doors. All of them have keys that will open any door in the place."

Cory shook his head. Luck had been on their side, all right.

But maybe it was about to desert them, he thought as he heard angry voices and looked up ahead to the depot. The crates of supplies and munitions from the wagons were being unloaded and carried onto the platform so that they could be put on the train from Vicksburg that would be rolling in later this morning. Colonel Thompson and Allen Carter were supervising the work, and Fred Carter was standing by and watching. But Grat was there, too, haranguing the young man.

"Damn it, who put you up to that trick?" demanded Grat. His face was mottled with anger, and he had shoved it so close to Fred's face that spittle was spraying the young man's cheeks. "Answer me, you damned half-wit!"

Cory breathed, "Oh, no!" and broke into a run toward the depot. Fred looked scared and upset, as if he were about to cry. If he broke down under Grat's yelling and told what had really happened the night before . . .

Allen Carter was coming toward Fred and Grat, too, hurrying from the other end of the platform. His peg thumped heavily against the planks as he rushed to his son's defense as fast as he could. Before Cory could reach them, Carter came up to Grat, grabbed the tavern keeper's shoulder, and jerked him around.

"What the hell do you think you're doing, yelling at my boy like that?" Carter asked as he pushed his face into Grat's just as Grat had been doing to Fred.

Grat sneered back at him. "So you're the half-wit's pa? You should keep a better eye on the dumb little bastard!"

Cory stopped in his tracks, astounded by Grat's callous gall. If there was a dumb bastard here, he thought, it was Grat.

Sure enough, the heavy muscles in Allen Carter's shoulders suddenly bunched, and his right fist came up in a punch that was almost too fast for the eye to follow. The blow sledged into Grat's jaw and knocked him backward into Fred. Fred skittered out of the way so that Grat went off the end of the platform and landed hard in the dirt.

Carter thumped to the edge of the platform, fists clenched, and shouted down at Grat, "Get back up here, mister! I ain't done whippin' you yet!"

Grat growled a curse and started to reach under his coat. He hadn't noticed Cory standing a few feet away. Cory palmed out his Colt, thumbed back the hammer, and said, "Go ahead, Grat. Pull a gun on an unarmed man. Everybody here will tell the sheriff that I killed you to save Allen's life."

He wasn't quite sure where the bravado came from, but it succeeded. Grat slowly withdrew his empty hand from underneath his coat.

Colonel Thompson stalked to the end of the platform. "By God, now what is it? I should have known that I wouldn't be fortunate enough to be done with you, Grat."

The tavern keeper pointed at Fred. "That's him," he accused. "That's the boy who lured me away from the boarding house last night so you could steal my slave!"

"I never stole a slave in my life," Thompson said coldly.

"Well, *he* did," Grat said, jerking his head toward Cory. "Him and that big darkie-lover!"

Still breathing hard with anger, Carter turned toward the colonel and asked, "What's this all about?"

"Miss Hannah disappeared last night, as did Private Jones. Mr. Grat here seems to think the two events are connected."

"He does, does he?" Carter's gaze flicked toward Cory for a second. Carter kept his word, though, and made no mention of Cory and Pie's visit to his cabin the night before. "What's that got to do with my boy?"

"He's the one who was carryin' on at the boarding house," said Grat, who pushed himself to his feet and started brushing off some of the dust that clung to his clothes. "They used him to distract me so they could steal the gal!"

Carter turned toward Fred, and once again Cory waited anxiously. If Fred denied being at the boarding house, he would quickly be caught in the lie, because Miss Fay and everyone else there had seen him and recognized him.

"What about it, Fred?" Carter asked quietly. "Were you at the boarding house last night?"

Fred licked his lips nervously then bobbed his head up and down. "Yes, Pa. I didn't mean to go down there, though."

"Then why did you?"

"I . . . I couldn't sleep last night. I thought I'd get up and go for a walk. I . . . I got turned around, I guess. I didn't know where I was." Tears started to roll down Fred's cheeks, and his shoulders shook. "I was scared! It was dark, and I couldn't find my way home!"

"Nobody sent you down there?"

"N-no sir."

Cory breathed again as relief flooded through him, then felt an immediate flash of guilt and shame. Because of him and his friends, Fred had just told a lie to his father. Cory didn't know if Fred had ever lied to Carter before. He hated to think that he might be partially to blame for the first lie the young man had ever told.

Maybe that was the lesser of two evils, as the old saying went. He hoped so.

Carter regarded his son intently for a moment, then said quietly, "If you couldn't sleep, you should have woken me up."

"I . . . I knew how tired you were, Pa. That's why I slipped back in, as quiet as a mouse."

"We'll talk more about this later," Carter said. He turned back toward Grat, and his voice was sharper. "All right, mister, you heard for yourself that my boy didn't have anything to do with your slave being missing."

"He's lying," snapped Grat. "I still say he was put up to it. He lies pretty good for a half-wit, but you're the one who's addle-pated if you believe him."

Carter glanced over at Cory. "Put your gun up."

Cory hadn't realized he still was holding the Colt alongside his leg. He lowered the hammer and slipped the revolver back into its holster.

"Allen," the colonel said warningly, "I think you should go back to supervising the unloading of the wagons."

"With all due respect, Colonel, no sir." Carter started down the steps at the end of the platform. "This fella's said too much, and he's got to answer for it."

"Stay away from me," said Grat. "I don't want to fight a damn cripple."

"Then you should have watched that mouth of yours," Carter said as he reached the bottom of the steps. He balanced on his single leg and the stout wooden peg and began rolling up the sleeves of his shirt.

Grat took a step back, still sneering, his eyes darting around. "Forget it. You got too many friends around to help you once I start to get the best of you."

Carter looked around, his gaze taking in Cory, Thompson, and the other members of the supply-line operation. "I'd take it as a personal favor if nobody was to interfere," he said mildly.

Thompson hesitated, then said, "I think this is a mistake, Allen, but if that's the way you want it, I won't order you not to do this."

"Wouldn't do any good if you did, Colonel. I ain't in the army no more."

Grat took another step back. "Wait just a minute!" he said anxiously. "He said that if I give any of his men any trouble, he'd have me hanged."

"I'll rescind my statement . . . temporarily," said Thompson.

"How about it?" Carter said, staring at Grat. "You're hell on wheels when it comes to bullying a kid who's not right in the head. How are you when it comes to cripples?"

The words lashed at Grat. Breathing heavily, he stood in silence for a moment then said again, "I ain't goin' to fight you."

"All right." Carter started to turn away. "Crawl back in your hole, then, like the maggot you are."

Grat's face contorted. He suddenly clasped his hands, clubbing them together, and swung his arms up. Cory called, "Allen, look out!" but it was too late. Grat's fists came down in a smashing blow on the back of Carter's neck.

The treacherous attack sent Carter falling hard against the end of the platform. Cory heard Lucille gasp behind him, and Fred leaped forward anxiously and cried out, "Pa!"

Thompson exclaimed, "By God, sir, I'll thrash you myself!"

"No!" Carter put his hands against the platform and pushed himself up. "Fred, stay back." He shook his head, then turned and took a step toward Grat. "My turn now."

Knowing that the fight could not be avoided, Grat lunged forward, trying to use his superior speed and agility to get in another blow before Carter could strike. Carter blocked the punch with his left forearm, though, and sunk his right fist into Grat's midsection. Grat started to double over, and Carter hit him in the face with a left.

Grat staggered but didn't go down. Instead, he caught his balance and flung himself toward Carter in a flying tackle that the handicapped man could not avoid. Both men went down as Grat wrapped his arms around Carter's waist.

Lucille gripped Cory's arm tightly as Grat, who was on top, began to pound blows into Carter's body. Cory wanted to help his friend, but Carter had asked that no one interfere. Up on the platform, Colonel Thompson had an arm around Fred's shoulders, holding him back as well.

Carter grunted under the onslaught of punches but finally managed to get his hands up. He caught hold of the lapels of Grat's coat and tossed the tavern keeper off him. Both men rolled over in the dust and struggled to stand up. With the advantage of two good legs, Grat made it upright first. He launched a kick at Carter's head.

Carter jerked aside and grabbed Grat's boot. With a heave, he threw Grat down again. This time as the two men grappled, it was Carter who wound up on top, and he drove a right and then a left into Grat's face. Grat's head bounced hard off the ground under the force of the blows.

Carter continued the assault, his fists rising and falling, rising and falling, until Grat's face was crimson from the blood that poured from his nose and the cuts that the one-legged veteran's punches had opened above his eyes. Grat had stopped fighting back and seemed to be only half-conscious now.

Colonel Thompson hurried down off the platform and snapped, "Cory, give me a hand!" Cory knew what the colonel meant. They stepped up behind Carter and bent down to grab him under each arm. They hauled him off Grat before he could beat the tavern keeper to death.

Carter jerked against their grip, but only for a second. Then he slumped and let them pull him away. Grat lay there on his back, his face a mask of red, his chest rising and falling rapidly as he struggled to draw in breath through his pulped nose.

"What's all this?" drawled the sheriff from behind Cory, Thompson, and Carter.

The colonel turned, letting go of Carter. "There you are, Sheriff." He leveled a finger at Grat. "I want that man locked up. He attacked my associate, Mr. Carter."

"Is that so?" asked Wiggins. "Looks like he come out on the short end of the stick."

"That doesn't matter. Grat provoked the fight. Mr. Carter was merely defending himself."

"That ain't the way it was," Carter said, his chin coming up defiantly. "I threw the first punch."

"Only because Grat was bullying your son," Thompson insisted. "And then you had turned away when Grat struck you from behind."

Wiggins said, "Hit you from the back, did he? And went after poor ol' Fred before that? I reckon that's disturbin' the peace if I ever heard tell of it." The sheriff looked around and got nods of agreement from Bradley and everyone else who had witnessed the altercation. No matter what, no one was going to say a good word for a man who attacked someone who had lost a leg in the service of the Confederacy.

"Gimme the loan of a couple o' your soldier boys," Wiggins went on, "and have 'em drag Grat down to the jail. I'll keep him locked up overnight, then send him on his way in the mornin'. Maybe you and your folks ought to pay a visit to Vicksburg, Colonel. Time you get back, things ought to've settled down."

"Perhaps you're right, Sheriff." Thompson turned to Carter. "Allen, how would you and Fred like to see Vicksburg?"

"Can we go, Pa?" Fred asked eagerly. "I never been to a big town like that."

Carter was rubbing his bruised knuckles. "I guess that would be all right," he said.

"Seems like a good idea to me," said Wiggins. As two men lifted Grat to his feet and began to half-carry him down the street, the sheriff glanced back at the little group standing beside the platform. "Oh, by the way, I ain't forgettin' 'bout that runaway slave gal and that big fella from your bunch who's missin'. I'll get on their trail . . . one o' these days."

Cory knew the sheriff was telling them he wasn't going to pursue Pie and Rachel. That was good news. By the time Grat healed enough from the beating he had received at Carter's hands, Pie and Rachel would be long gone, across the border in Texas. Grat would never find them.

Once Grat and the sheriff were gone, the colonel said, "Well, we had best return to our task of unloading the wagons. The train will be here shortly."

As if it had been waiting for his pronouncement, the shrill, wailing sound of a locomotive whistle came floating over the air from a distance. It reminded Cory a little of Pie's mouth harp, and he remembered the evening they had sat on the porch of the colonel's house in Vicksburg while Pie played "Dixie."

Now the big man was gone, and Cory never had learned to play as well as he had hoped.

Someday, he thought, touching his shirt pocket where he carried his own mouth harp.

Someday in Texas.

Chapter Five

FRED CARTER STOOD ON the platform at the front of the train's single passenger car and leaned far out, tightly gripping the railing around the platform so that he wouldn't fall. "Look at that!" he cried happily. "I never seen such!"

Standing beside Fred, his father nodded. "Vicksburg's a mighty big town," Allen Carter agreed. "My company came through here when I joined the army."

The city was visible, perched on the bluff high above the Mississippi, as the train rolled toward the Vicksburg, Shreveport, and Texas depot on the west side of the great river. Cory leaned a hip against the railing on the other side of the platform and smiled as he saw how impressed Fred was. Fred had never seen a town larger than Monroe. Vicksburg, spread out on the bluff with the massive courthouse dominating the landscape, had to be a spectacular sight to Fred's eyes.

The train had left Monroe that morning after being loaded with the supplies and munitions from the wagon train. The crates of Enfield rifles and Kerr revolvers, along with plenty of ammunition, rode securely in one of the boxcars, watched over by a couple of guards.

Lucille came out of the car and joined Cory on the platform. She wore a neat blue traveling suit and hat and didn't look in the least as if she was just back from a grueling overland journey to Texas. She looked fresh and beautiful, in fact, at least to Cory's eyes.

True to her word, Lucille had not gone back to the boarding house. Her things had been gathered up from her room and brought to the Bradley house by the stationmaster's wife.

"It'll be so good to see Aunt Mildred again," Lucille said now as she stood on the platform next to Cory, swaying slightly with the motion of the train as it slowed. "She never said much

71

in her letters about my going back and forth to Texas with you, but I'm pretty sure she thought I was mad!"

"She'll be glad to see you, too," said Cory. "She'll be even happier when she hears you're not going back."

Lucille frowned slightly. "You're not going to do anything foolish, are you, Cory?"

"What do you mean by that?"

"I mean, you're not going to decide that you're not going back to the wagon train just because of me, are you?"

Cory had been considering that possibility during the train ride. Losing both him and Pie as teamsters would be a problem for Colonel Thompson, but only a minor one. Now that the supply-line operation was rolling along smoothly and successfully, there were plenty of soldiers who could take their places on the wagons.

"I don't know," he began slowly. "I was thinking about staying here in Vicksburg for a while . . ."

"Because of me?"

"Because the colonel doesn't really need me anymore."

"So you'd run out on him?"

Exasperated, Cory said, "It's not the same as running out on him. I went with him to help set up the supply line, but it's operating fine now and can go on without me. I never intended to stay away from you—"

"And you didn't," Lucille pointed out.

"Only because you came with me to Texas. Blast it, Lucille, I've got to consider that promise I made to your father."

"The promise to take care of me, you mean?" Lucille shot back at him. "Did you ever stop to consider, Cory Brannon, that I can take care of myself?"

Cory glanced over at Allen and Fred Carter. Both of them were smiling, and he had the feeling they were laughing to themselves as they listened to the conversation that was threatening to turn into an argument. Cory was grateful when the train jolted to a stop and steam poured from the escape valves. He hoped the distraction would be enough to let him get away with not answering Lucille's question.

As if to help him out even more, the colonel emerged from the car, stepping onto the platform and saying fervently, "It's good to be back."

"Yes sir, it is," Cory agreed.

"We can't stay long, of course," Thompson went on. "A few days at most. Then we'll have to return to Monroe and start the next trip to Texas."

"Cory's not going," Lucille said quickly, before Cory could even give her a warning look.

The colonel's eyebrows lifted in surprise. "Really, Mr. Brannon? This is the first I've heard of such a decision."

"That's because I haven't actually made a decision yet," Cory said, giving Lucille an exasperated glance.

"Cory and Lucille have been fightin'," Fred put in.

Trying not to grin, his father took Fred's arm and turned the young man toward the depot platform. "This is none of our business," Carter told Fred. "It's a family matter."

"We're a family," Fred protested.

"We sure are, but not this one. Come on. We'll see if we can find some fellas to help us unload those supplies."

They got off the train and started toward the doors leading into the station. Behind them, Colonel Thompson clasped his hands behind his back and solemnly regarded Cory and Lucille. "Now," he said, "what's all this about?"

"Cory's disloyal to the Confederacy," declared Lucille.

"I am not!" Cory glared at her for a second then turned back to Thompson. "Listen, Colonel, I was just thinking that maybe this time when you go back to Monroe, I wouldn't go with you. You don't really need me now. Everything's going so well."

"Thanks in part to the assistance that you and Private Jones have furnished the project," Thompson pointed out. "Now Private Jones is gone, and it appears that you soon will be leaving it as well." He sighed. "I remember Zeke's telling me that you were a wanderer by nature, Cory. I suppose that impulse has struck you again."

"No, that's not it at all," Cory said in frustration. "I want to stay here."

I want to settle down, to marry Lucille, to stay in one place for a while.

Those were the words in Cory's mind and on the tip of his tongue, but he didn't speak them because a voice called, "Colonel Thompson!"

The three people on the platform turned to see an officer with a rather bushy goatee emerging from the station and striding toward them. Cory recognized the markings on the man's uniform as those of a general, and a second later that was confirmed by Colonel Thompson, who stepped down from the train, came to attention, and saluted. "General Pemberton. What can I do for you, sir?"

"I received word by telegraph from Monroe that you were on your way back. I thought perhaps you could give me a report on the state of our supply line from Texas."

"Of course, sir. You didn't have to come down here yourself. You could have sent an aide—"

"Vicksburg is important, Colonel. Important to the Confederacy and important to me." Pemberton's face was grim. "After failing to stop the Yankees from taking New Orleans, I'll be damned if I'm going to let them waltz in and take over Vicksburg, too."

"Of course not, sir," Thompson said quickly.

"I have a carriage waiting. We'll go to my headquarters for our conversation."

There was nothing Thompson could do but agree. He glanced over his shoulder as he was leaving, though, as if to tell Cory and Lucille that their discussion was not over.

"I won't have you neglecting your duty on account of me," Lucille announced before Cory even had a chance to gather his thoughts again.

"We can talk about this later," he said as he took her arm. "Right now, we ought to get you home. You were anxious to see your aunt, remember?"

"You're trying to distract me from the matter at hand, Cory Brannon—" Lucille stopped short and took a deep breath. "But you're right. I do want to see Aunt Mildred. I suppose we can continue this argument another time."

"I'm not arguing," Cory said as he helped her down to the station platform. He linked arms with her and led her into the building. "I just want to do what's best."

"And how do you know what's best?"

That was a good question, thought Cory. And as he let his memory play back over all the decisions he had made in his life, he realized it was one that he had often answered incorrectly.

"Come on," he muttered. "Let's see if we can find a buggy."

Just as Cory had said, Lucille was glad to see her aunt, and the feeling was returned. Mildred Thompson, a petite, red-haired, attractive woman in middle age, threw her arms around Lucille and hugged her tightly. "You dear girl!" she exclaimed. "It's so good to have you back home. Let me look at you." She moved back and put her hands on Lucille's shoulders. "My, you're as beautiful as ever. All that gallivanting back and forth doesn't seem to have hurt you a bit!"

"I'll echo those sentiments, Mrs. Thompson," said the guest Cory and Lucille found sitting in the parlor of the Thompson home, sipping tea when they arrived. "Miss Farrell is the very picture of loveliness."

Cory frowned as the words came from Lt. Jack O'Reilly's mouth. He wasn't happy to see O'Reilly. He was even less so as he heard the young lieutenant of artillery flatter Lucille.

O'Reilly was one of the first people Cory and Pie had met when they came to Vicksburg. The commander of one of the artillery batteries overlooking the Mississippi, O'Reilly had been none too polite when they'd inquired about Col. Charles Thompson. In fact, he'd been downright rude, and when Pie had tried to volunteer to join the army and become a gunner, O'Reilly had refused him, offering him only a job as an ammunition hauler.

Later, when Cory had discovered that O'Reilly was also acquainted with Lucille and her aunt and uncle and was a frequent dinner guest at their home, he had tried to make himself like the lieutenant, but that had proven to be impossible. O'Reilly was smooth enough to have ingratiated himself with both Lucille and Mildred, and according to the colonel he was a decent if unimaginative officer, but as far as Cory was concerned O'Reilly was a smug, arrogant son of a bitch.

He couldn't very well spout words like that in Mrs. Thompson's parlor, however, so he extended his hand and forced himself to be pleasant to this unexpected visitor. "Good to see you again, Lieutenant."

"Yes," O'Reilly replied curtly. His handshake was a cold, brief touch. "Back from your latest jaunt, eh?"

Cory would hardly call bringing a wagon train of supplies from Texas a "jaunt," especially when this time the trip had included an attack by renegades. But he didn't want to mention anything about that in front of Mrs. Thompson, so he merely nodded and said, "Yes, that's right."

O'Reilly cocked an eyebrow. "I suppose some people don't mind traipsing off while others remain to protect the city."

Cory's jaw tightened. Surely Lucille and Mrs. Thompson could see that O'Reilly was insulting the colonel as well as him. But if they did, they gave no sign of it. Mrs. Thompson hugged Lucille again and said, "Sit down and tell us all about your trip."

Lucille's eyes flicked toward Cory for a second, and he had a pretty good idea what she was thinking. She was remembering the attack on the wagon train and the man she'd been forced to kill. That was hardly proper conversation for a parlor, either.

"Oh, it was just a trip," Lucille said as she settled onto the settee and patted the cushion beside her, indicating to Cory that he should sit with her. She went on, "Lots of heat and dust starting out, and then rain and mud."

"I fear it will be a wet winter," said O'Reilly as he sat down in an armchair and picked up his cup of tea from the small table beside him.

"Where is Charles?" Mrs. Thompson asked. "He did come back with you, didn't he?"

"General Pemberton met us at the depot," said Cory, casting a glance at O'Reilly, who allowed a flicker of jealousy to show in his eyes. The general in command of Vicksburg's defenses didn't seek out the counsel of a lowly artillery lieutenant. "They went to the general's headquarters."

"Well, I'm sure he'll be here as soon as he can. But where's Private Jones? I have an apple cobbler baking in the oven."

Cory leaned forward slightly and clasped his hands together between his knees. "Pie . . . ," he began. "Well, Pie's not with us anymore." It hurt to say that.

Mrs. Thompson gasped and put a hand to her mouth. "Oh, no! You mean he . . . he passed away?"

"Oh, no!" Cory and Lucille said together, hastily. Cory went on, "He's fine, as far as I know. But he, uh, resigned his place in the home guard and left Monroe when we got back there. I'm not sure where he is now."

"He did? I'll swan. I never thought he would do such a thing." Mrs. Thompson shook her head sadly.

"I'm sure he did what he thought was best," said Lucille.

"Hmmph!" O'Reilly put in. "Sounds like a deserter to me. He'll be lucky if he's not shot. But then, I knew as soon as I saw that big lummox that he wasn't very smart."

Cory saw both Lucille and her aunt frown, and he knew a moment of glee when he realized that Lieutenant O'Reilly had finally overplayed his hand. O'Reilly's easy charm wasn't going to get him out of this one.

"I think Private Jones is a fine young man," Mrs. Thompson said crisply. "I always enjoyed having him here in my house."

"He was always a good friend to me," Lucille said.

"Oh, I'm not saying he was a bad fellow." O'Reilly tried hard to recover. "I'm sure he had many fine qualities. He just, um, never would have made a regular soldier."

Pie had been a hell of a soldier as far as Cory was concerned, and he knew the colonel agreed with him. Or at least, Thompson had felt that way until Pie had disappeared with Rachel.

It was all water under the bridge now, Cory told himself. He changed the subject by asking Mrs. Thompson, "How have things been here in Vicksburg?"

O'Reilly took it upon himself to answer before his hostess could say anything. "The blasted Yankees continue to sneak up the river to shell us. But they've done little damage to our defenses, and they certainly haven't affected the morale of the city or its defenders."

"That's right," Mrs. Thompson agreed. "The lieutenant and the others manning the gun batteries have done a gallant job of holding off the Yankees."

"We make them pay every time they show their ugly faces on the Mississippi," O'Reilly asserted proudly.

That was all well and good, thought Cory, but he didn't like the idea that Federal gunboats were still lobbing shells into the city. The bombardment might have been fairly ineffective so far, but there was no guarantee it would stay that way. In light of this continuing danger to Vicksburg, he was more determined than ever not to leave Lucille here alone. He would remain at her side whether she liked it or not.

"That's enough talk about the war," Mrs. Thompson said. "Lieutenant, you will stay for supper tonight, won't you?"

O'Reilly drained the rest of the tea from his cup and then said, "I'm truly sorry, ma'am, but I won't be able to accept your invitation, though it does me great honor that you would extend it. I have to be on duty this evening."

That was just fine, thought Cory. He would rather not have O'Reilly's presence casting a further pall on his first night back in Vicksburg.

"But I'll be free tomorrow night," O'Reilly added.

"Then you must come," Mrs. Thompson said with a smile. "You're always welcome at our table, Lieutenant."

"Thank you, ma'am."

Cory tried to hide the disappointment he felt. His jaw tightened again when O'Reilly shot a glance of triumph at him. O'Reilly had made it clear in the past that he was interested in Lucille. All the more reason for him to go ahead and ask Lucille to marry him as soon as possible, Cory told himself. Once their engagement was official, O'Reilly would have no choice but to take himself out of the picture.

O'Reilly left the house a few minutes later, kissing the hands of both Mrs. Thompson and Lucille as he did so. Cory clenched his teeth in frustration as he watched the sickening display. The women didn't seem to mind, though. Evidently they had forgotten O'Reilly's unfavorable comments about Pie.

When the three of them were alone again, Mildred Thompson said briskly, "Now, tell me what else happened during this trip, Lucille."

"But . . . but I told you, Aunt Mildred—"

"Not all of it," her aunt said tenderly. "I saw the look in your eyes and sensed the hesitation in your voice, dear. Something happened that you don't want to talk about."

Cory tried to step in and protect Lucille. "Maybe it would be better—"

"I'm the closest thing this poor girl has to a mother, Cory. It's not good to hold everything inside. I want to help, but I have to know what happened."

Suddenly, tears welled from Lucille's eyes and rolled down her cheeks. "I . . . I killed a man," she choked out.

"Dear Lord," breathed Mrs. Thompson. She took hold of both of Lucille's hands. "What happened?"

"The wagon train was attacked," Cory said flatly. He wanted to spare Lucille from having to tell the story, now that he could see Mrs. Thompson was determined to have it. "A bunch of deserters and thieves were after the supplies we were carrying." He didn't mention his theory that Jason Gill might have had something to do with the raid. "One of the men climbed into the wagon where Lucille and I were. He had a knife, and my gun was empty. Lucille saved our lives by shooting him."

Mrs. Thompson put her arms around her niece. "What a dreadful thing to have to do!" she exclaimed. "But you had no choice. You were so brave, my dear."

"Even if there was no choice, a man is still dead because of me," Lucille said. She wasn't sobbing, but tears continued to trickle down her face.

Bluntly, Cory said, "That man is dead because he decided to desert from the army and become a thief and a renegade. He brought his fate on himself, Lucille."

"Cory is right, child. When a man decides to do evil, he has no one but himself to blame if he comes to a bad end."

Lucille wiped her eyes. "Thank you," she said quietly. "Thank you both. I know you're right, but still . . ."

Still, it was hard to live with yourself after you'd killed a man, thought Cory. He knew that from experience.

Unfortunately, it got easier as more men died. That was one of the lessons of war, and this conflict that had set North against South was a brutally effective teacher.

꙳

THE FIRST few days after Cory and the others returned to Vicksburg passed surprisingly pleasantly. No Federal gunboats shelled the city, and an illusion of normalcy stole over the citizens. After the strain of everything that had happened since summer, it was easy to fall into the trap of believing that now everything was going to be all right, even though deep down most people knew that probably was not the case. The Yankees would be back. Gaining control of the Mississippi River was too important to them for Vicksburg to be left alone.

But despite what he suspected the future would bring, Cory enjoyed the lull. Even the presence of Jack O'Reilly at dinner a couple of times couldn't completely spoil his mood. Cory was spending time with Lucille, and for now, that was all that really mattered to him.

She returned to her previous practice of baking treats for the soldiers who manned the guns overlooking the river, but now Cory went with her when she delivered them, so O'Reilly couldn't flirt so blatantly with her. Whenever they spoke, though, O'Reilly usually managed to work in a subtle jibe about the fact that Cory was no longer contributing to the defense of Vicksburg except as, in O'Reilly's words, "the guardian of the apricot tarts."

With an effort, Cory controlled his temper at those moments, but it made him uneasy when he pondered the situation and realized that in a way, O'Reilly was right. That restless feeling grew worse when Colonel Thompson departed for Monroe to begin another wagon train journey to Texas.

"Good luck, my boy," the colonel said as he stood on the platform of the Vicksburg, Shreveport, and Texas depot and shook Cory's hand. "In my absence, I know I can count on you to look after the ladies."

"Yes sir," Cory affirmed, but the words threatened to stick in his throat.

Lucille hugged the colonel. "You be careful, Uncle Charles, you hear?" she said huskily.

He patted her on the back as he returned the embrace. "Of course. Don't you worry about me."

Thompson turned to his wife, and they embraced and kissed. Like Lucille, Mildred Thompson was trying hard not to cry. Neither of the women succeeded. Tears trickled down their cheeks as they said their good-byes.

Cory moved back a couple of steps, not wanting to intrude on a family farewell. Of course, once he and Lucille were married, he would be part of the family. The right moment to ask her, however, had not presented itself, but he was sure that it soon would.

Allen Carter and Fred came along the platform. Fred hurried up to Cory and said, "You're coming back with us, aren't you, Cory?"

Shaking his head, Cory said, "I'm afraid not, Fred. Remember I told you I was staying here in Vicksburg with Lucille?"

"I want you to come back. You're my friend."

Cory felt a pang of regret. With Fred, everything was boiled down to its essence. Fred liked Cory, so he wanted him to come back with them. It was as simple as that.

Carter put a hand on his son's shoulder. "Don't pester Cory about this, Fred. He's made up his mind."

"But Pie left, and now Cory's not going to be with us, either. It's not fair."

"Life usually isn't," said Carter, and Cory couldn't blame him for the faint tinge of bitterness that crept into his voice. Thus far, life had certainly dealt Allen Carter a bad hand in many ways. He had lost a leg in battle, and he would always have to worry about Fred and who was going to take care of him, especially after Carter was gone.

But at least the two of them were together now, Cory told himself. Hard times were easier to face when you weren't alone.

The train had steam up, and the locomotive's whistle blew. Allen Carter and Fred hurried aboard. Colonel Thompson hugged his wife again then turned toward the train. He went briskly up the steps of the passenger car and paused at the top to look back. He lifted a hand in farewell as the train began to move away.

Cory joined the others in waving. They stood there on the station platform until the train had disappeared from sight, heading westbound toward Monroe.

He slipped an arm around Lucille's shoulders, which were shaking slightly as she cried soundlessly. After a moment, she said, "Will we ever see him again?"

"Sure we will," said Cory. "The colonel can take care of himself. I know that for a fact."

"But it's dangerous out there," Mrs. Thompson said, "and growing more so all the time. And I know Charles. Sometimes he's too fearless for his own good."

"The colonel will be fine," Cory insisted.

But if Jason Gill had had anything to do with the attack on the wagon train, chances were there would be more trouble. Gill wasn't the type to slink away after a single defeat. He would try again and again, bolstered by self-righteousness and arrogance.

Cory kept those thoughts to himself as he went on, "We'd better get back to the ferry landing."

Mrs. Thompson dabbed at her eyes with a lace handkerchief. "You're right, of course. Charles wouldn't be happy if he knew how we were carrying on."

Cory walked with them down to the river. They had left the buggy at the landing on the other side. In a short time, they would be home.

But as they started across the Mississippi on the ferry, Cory found himself looking back, looking toward the west. He felt the old familiar tug, the siren's song that summoned him, whispering in his ear that he needed to be moving, to be seeing new places and doing new things.

He took one of Lucille's hands in both of his and held on tightly. She looked at him and smiled, but he could tell that she didn't understand.

Neither did he. He had everything he wanted in life right here. He had reached the end of the restless journey that had brought him so far from his home in Virginia. Why would he ever need anything else?

But still his head turned, and he listened for the unheard whistle of the faraway train.

Chapter Six

CORY HURRIED DOWN THE street, looking from time to time at the piece of paper in his hand. Mildred Thompson had written a shopping list on it—molasses, flour, bacon, a few other items—and the name and address of a market. He was relatively familiar with Vicksburg by this time and had no trouble finding the place.

He just wasn't prepared for what he found when he finally got there.

A line of people, mostly women but some men and children, too, stretched out the door of the establishment and into the street. Cory stopped and frowned as he looked at the crowd. He wondered if the market was always this busy. Mildred and Lucille usually handled the shopping. They hadn't come today because Mildred was feeling poorly and Lucille wanted to stay home and take care of her aunt. So Cory had volunteered, thinking it would be a simple enough errand. When he was younger, he had sometimes taken the wagon into Culpeper to pick up supplies at Michael Davis's emporium.

To the best of his recollection, there had never been crowds like this in Culpeper. Cory gave a little shake of his head and walked toward the market. He would just have to stand in line and wait his turn, he supposed.

It was early November, and the air was cool and damp. Thick clouds gathered overhead, and through the gaps between them a deep blue sky was visible. If the overcast thickened more, it might rain later, thought Cory, and he hoped if there were showers they would hold off until he got back to the Thompson house.

He was thinking about that and not paying any attention to the person standing in line in front of him, but a sudden sharp poke in the chest made him grunt in surprise. He looked down and saw a wizened, elderly woman who was a head shorter than he. She wore a patched, faded dress and a sunbonnet. "What're you doin' here?" she demanded.

"Uh, I'm waiting to buy some supplies," answered Cory. He held up the scrap of paper with Mrs. Thompson's list written on it. "See?"

The old woman brushed aside the list. "That ain't what I meant a'tall. You're young, and you 'pear to be reason'bly healthy. How come you ain't in the army?"

Cory didn't like the question. "I've never actually signed up—"

"Pshaw. I can see that. You think I'm blind?"

"No, ma'am—"

"How come you ain't off fightin' Yankees?"

Cory was slightly irritated. "I have fought the Yankees," he protested. "At Fort Henry and Fort Donelson and Shiloh." That statement usually shut up anyone who questioned his loyalty to the Confederacy.

The old woman's head bobbed up and down. "Heard tell o' them places. But you ain't there fightin' now."

Cory didn't see any reason why he should have to explain himself to this annoying woman, but he said, "I've been helping bring in supplies from Texas. That's why I haven't enlisted."

"Oh." The woman nodded. "I got three sons an' seven grand-sons in the army. Reckon I oughta say I did have. They's all dead now."

Cory's eyes widened at the matter-of-fact tone in which the old woman announced such a horrible thing. "I . . . I'm sorry," he managed to say.

"It's a powerful burden, all right. I just thank the Lord my husband didn't live to see the day." Tears glistened in the woman's eyes but didn't spill from them. "Whenever I see a young feller like you, it gets me to thinkin' o' my boys. That's all. I didn't mean no offense."

"No ma'am."

The woman turned back toward the market. The line was moving a little. "Mebbe we'll get some victuals 'fore night," she muttered hopefully.

Cory took a deep breath. He was ashamed of himself now for getting annoyed at the old woman. At the same time, the questions she had asked made him uneasy. He had fought on the side of the Confederacy, had fought well. Why hadn't he ever made it official by enlisting in the army?

There was Lucille to consider, of course, and his vow to her father. But other men had made vows and then joined the army anyway. Maybe there were times when the greater good had to override personal considerations. How was a man to know what was really right . . . ?

A man's voice from behind him brought him out of his reverie. "Cory?" it asked. "Cory Brannon, is that you?"

Cory turned and saw a well-dressed man standing there. The newcomer was about forty years of age with sleek dark hair under a cream-colored planter's hat. His handsome face was a little florid, showing signs of the excessive life he had led. He wore a brown cutaway coat and tight trousers of the same shade. Black boots came up high on his calves. His shirt front was white as snow and covered with lace, and his cravat was held in place by a pin with a glittering gem on it. An expensive cigar smoldered between the fingers of his left hand.

"Mr. Kincaid?" Cory exclaimed in surprise.

"Palmer," the dapper man said heartily. His large free hand clapped Cory on the shoulder. "We're old friends, lad. No need to call me mister."

Friends? Not really, thought Cory, although he was grateful to Palmer Kincaid for the help he had provided when the *Missouri Zephyr* slipped out of Cairo, Illinois, under the very noses of the Yankee gunboats. But Cory had never expected to see Kincaid again, and that was perfectly all right with him.

Palmer Kincaid owned the Staghorn Saloon, one of the more popular establishments in Cairo's tenderloin district, or at least

he had the last time Cory had seen him. Union soldiers patronized the place, and Kincaid had seen no problem with taking
Yankee money. At the same time, he was friends with Capt.
Ezekiel Farrell and other Southern sympathizers. The Staghorn
had served as a meeting place for Farrell and other men who
would never bow to the yoke of Northern oppression, and when
Farrell had needed help to escape Cairo, Kincaid had provided
it—albeit a little grudgingly.

Now he was in Vicksburg, a city that was still a Confederate
stronghold. Obviously, thought Cory, things had changed.

"What are you doing here?" he asked, knowing that the
question might sound a little impertinent but not really caring.
Lucille regarded Palmer Kincaid as an uncle, but Kincaid hardly
felt toward her as he would toward a niece. Back in Cairo, Cory
had seen the desire in the gambler's eyes whenever he looked
at Lucille.

"I decided a change of scenery would be a good idea," said
Kincaid. He took a puff on the cigar. "I sold the Staghorn and
came south."

"I'll bet the Yankees didn't like that much."

Kincaid chuckled. "There are ways of getting around the
Yankees. A clever man can always find ways around the obstacles life places in his path."

And Palmer Kincaid was nothing if not clever. He had
proved that by being able to lead his double life in Cairo for as
long as he had.

"How's Mr. Jimmerson?" asked Cory. The first time he had
met Kincaid had been during a meeting at the Staghorn in
which Captain Farrell had conferred with Avery Jimmerson,
who owned a local cotton mill.

Kincaid grimaced slightly and shook his head. "Poor Avery
is in prison, I'm afraid. The Yankees discovered that he was
dealing with the enemy. At that, though, he was lucky. Certain
officers were of the opinion that he should be hanged instead of
imprisoned. Fortunately for Avery, cooler heads prevailed."

Cory found himself wondering if Kincaid had sold out the cotton trader. Kincaid would do almost anything if the price was right. On the other hand, Jimmerson's arrest might have been what prompted Kincaid to flee Cairo and head south. Jimmerson had frequented the Staghorn, after all, and so had other men who were carrying on illicit trade with the Confederacy.

Casually, Kincaid waved his hand in a dismissive gesture. "We can't do anything for Avery, and life goes on, I suppose. How did you come to be in Vicksburg? Are Zeke Farrell and his lovely daughter here as well?"

"Captain Farrell is dead," Cory said soberly. "He was killed at Fort Donelson."

Kincaid's eyes narrowed. "Oh. I didn't know. Well, I'm mighty sorry to hear that. Zeke was a good man." The gambler sounded sincere. "What about Lucille? Is she all right? Is she here in Vicksburg?"

"She's fine. She's living here with her aunt and uncle." And we're engaged to be married, Cory wanted to add. That way Kincaid would know right away that Lucille was spoken for.

But Cory knew he couldn't do that until he had asked Lucille to be his wife. If Kincaid said something to her about an engagement, she would be furious at Cory's presumptuousness.

"Well, I'm glad to hear that, at least," Kincaid went on. "I'll have to call on her and tender my condolences on the death of her father. I'm sure you can give me the address. You were quite fond of Lucille, if I remember correctly."

"Yes," said Cory. "Quite fond."

Kincaid glared at him for a moment, and his attitude turned toward impatience. Finally Cory realized that he was waiting for the address. Reluctantly, he gave the gambler directions to the Thompson house.

After thanking Cory, almost as an afterthought, Kincaid asked, "And what are you doing these days?"

"I've been helping Colonel Thompson, Lucille's uncle, set up a supply line over to eastern Texas."

Kincaid cocked an eyebrow. "Really? That's interesting. I suppose with traffic so severely curtailed on the river, the flow of supplies into the city has diminished considerably."

"That's right. We bring goods from Texas on a wagon train, then load them onto a regular train in Monroe, Louisiana." Cory wasn't giving away any secrets. Most of Vicksburg's citizenry knew how the railroad was being used to bring in supplies from the west.

"And you helped arrange this?"

"That's right." Cory couldn't help but feel proud. He'd been nothing more than a pilot's cub on the riverboat the last time Kincaid saw him, and only a few months removed from a desperate, starving, half-frozen existence as a wharf rat in New Madrid, Missouri. Now he was a vital part of the operation that was bringing much-needed food and munitions into Vicksburg.

Or at least he had been, before he'd decided not to go back to Monroe with the colonel.

"My, my," muttered Kincaid. "You have come up in the world, haven't you, Cory? Are you on some 'special mission' for the Confederacy at the moment?"

Cory glanced down at the piece of paper in his hand and then at the line into the market. He was still bringing up the rear. "No, I'm, ah, doing the marketing for Lucille's aunt."

A smile tugged at the corners of Kincaid's mouth. "Oh," he said. "Well, I'm sure that's important, too." He put the cigar between his lips and continued around it, "Tell Lucille that I'll be by to call on her and her aunt, will you?"

"Of course."

"I'll try to come along this evening." Kincaid gave Cory a curt nod. "So long."

Cory returned the nod but didn't say anything. Kincaid strolled on down the street, heading toward the edge of the bluffs, home to most of the city's less reputable taverns and gambling halls. He might have had to leave Cairo in a hurry, one jump ahead of trouble, but one thing you could say about

Palmer Kincaid, thought Cory: The man knew how to land on his feet. He could find a poker game in any of the waterfront dives and make a living that way. With his skill, Kincaid might well wind up owning the place in a few days.

But Cory still didn't like him and didn't trust him. How much of that was motivated by jealousy, Cory didn't know. Captain Farrell had been friends with Kincaid, and Farrell had been a good judge of character.

After all, the captain had taken a stinking wharf rat and made something out of him, hadn't he?

CORY HAD never realized what a depressing experience shopping could be. When he finally made it into the market, the apron-wearing man behind the counter informed him, "No more molasses," before Cory could even speak. "You can have a dab of sorghum. We got a little left."

"What about flour?" asked Cory. "I need a pound."

The storekeeper just snorted contemptuously. "Half a pound, no more. Better make it last, too."

Cory wanted to argue, but there were people waiting behind him and he knew they were just as anxious to buy supplies as he was. He nodded grudgingly. "I suppose a side of bacon is out of the question?"

"Can give you a few slices," the storekeeper replied in a surly tone, "but it'll cost you."

Indeed it had, Cory thought as he left the market a few minutes later with a much smaller paper-wrapped package under his arm than he had expected to be returning with. And less money in his pocket than he had expected, too. The few supplies he had been able to buy had taken all of the Confederate scrip Mrs. Thompson had given him, plus a few coins of his own.

He wore a frown on his face as he walked back toward the house. If things were already this bad when supplies were still coming into Vicksburg, what would it be like if the Yankees were ever successful in cutting off the city entirely? If nothing else, this morning had made it abundantly clear to him just how important it was to keep the supply line to Texas open.

When he reached the house and gave the provisions to Mrs. Thompson, who was up and about and feeling better, she sighed. "Poor Mr. Krause tries, but he simply can't get enough merchandise for his market," she said.

Cory didn't feel that sympathetic toward the storekeeper. "He was pretty rude."

"Imagine how he feels, having to turn away customers who have been coming to him for years. We've only been here a few months, but some of the people who shop at his market have been going there for a long time."

Cory shrugged. "I suppose so."

Mrs. Thompson hefted the package in her hand and said, "Well, we'll simply have to make do. This is certainly better than nothing. Thank you, Cory."

He nodded and then went in search of Lucille, finding her in the parlor, sitting near the fireplace and mending a pair of trousers. Cory thought at first the garment belonged to the colonel, but then he realized with surprise that the trousers were his. There was something so domestic about the scene that it sent a pang of emotion through him. He swallowed hard as Lucille looked up at him with a smile.

"How was your trip to the market?" she asked.

"All right. Your aunt's condition has improved."

"Yes, she was able to rest for a while, and that made her feel stronger."

Cory had considered not telling Lucille about his encounter with Palmer Kincaid, but he didn't want the gambler simply showing up on the doorstep with no warning. He said, "You won't guess who I spoke to while I was waiting at the market."

"I have no idea. Who?"

"Palmer Kincaid."

Lucille lowered the mending to her lap and looked up at him with a surprised smile on her face, almost gleeful. "Uncle Palmer?" she exclaimed. "Really? My goodness, what's he doing in Vicksburg?"

"He sold his place in Cairo and came south. I got the impression he was in some sort of trouble with the Yankees."

"I don't doubt it. Father always said that despite appearances, Uncle Palmer was a staunch supporter of the South."

Cory's instincts told him that Kincaid was a staunch supporter of whatever put the most money in his pocket, but he kept that thought to himself. Lucille would probably be offended if he commented on Kincaid's mercenary nature.

"He said he was sorry to hear about your father," Cory went on. "And he said he would come by to call on you."

"I should hope so," said Lucille. "I'll certainly be glad to see him, as I'm sure you were, Cory."

Cory just shrugged and didn't say anything. He went over and sat down in an armchair then toyed with one of the doilies on its arms for a moment before saying, "Thank you for mending those trousers, Lucille."

She had the needle and thread moving again. The tip of her tongue was stuck in one corner of her mouth as she concentrated. She tied off a stitch, then said, "I'm afraid I'm not much of a seamstress. There was never much opportunity to practice while I was on the *Zephyr*. If you need to know how to avoid a snag in the river, though, I can do that."

Cory knew that was true. Lucille could have made an excellent riverboat pilot—if women were allowed to do such things.

"Well, I appreciate what you're doing," he said. "I'm no good at all with a needle and thread."

"It's just . . . something I wanted to do."

Now was the time, Cory told himself. He would never have a better opportunity to ask her to marry him.

He leaned forward a little in the chair. "Lucille, I . . . There's something I want to ask you . . ."

She was working on another small rip in the trousers. "What is it, Cory?" she asked without looking up.

He wished he could see her eyes. He knew that if he could look into her eyes as he spoke, he could read the truth of her response there.

"Lucille . . ."

"I'm listening . . ." She was starting to sound a bit impatient now, but she still didn't raise her eyes from her mending.

There was nothing he could do except plunge ahead, Cory told himself. He said, "Lucille, I was wondering if—"

Mildred Thompson appeared in the doorway of the parlor and said, "Lucille, I need someone to draw a bucket of water."

Cory shot to his feet. "I'll do that, Mrs. Thompson," he said. He held out a hand toward Lucille. "You just stay where you are. I'll be right back. Don't move."

He rushed out of the parlor, turning toward the rear of the house and heading for the water pump. As he did so, he heard Mrs. Thompson observe, "My, that young man certainly is anxious to help."

He was anxious to get back to the parlor and finish asking Lucille to marry him, that's what he was anxious about, he thought as he snatched up the bucket by the back door and stepped outside. The pump handle was close to the door. He worked it quickly, filling the bucket from the spigot.

When he came back into the kitchen, he saw to his dismay that Lucille had left the parlor and followed her aunt into the room. The private moment he had hoped for was gone.

"I'll take that," Lucille said as she held out her hands for the bucket. Cory gave it to her, and she continued, "You were about to ask me something . . . ?"

"I was?" he said. "I don't recall now what it was."

"Oh?" Lucille sounded disappointed. "Well, maybe it will come back to you."

"Maybe," Cory agreed. He turned toward the doorway, feeling his mood growing more bleak with every step he took.

Abruptly, he stopped. For months now, ever since he had come to Vicksburg and found Lucille again, he had been postponing the one thing that he had meant to do as soon as he saw her again. Through all the grim days at Fort Donelson and the hell that had been Shiloh, he had clung to the hope that he would be with Lucille again and ask her to be his wife. That dream had sustained him through everything he had been forced to endure. Why, when they were reunited at last, had he failed to grasp the dream?

He couldn't answer that question—but he could make certain that it wouldn't continue to plague him. Quickly, so that he wouldn't have time to ponder on what he was about to do, he swung around and said, "Actually, I do want to ask you something, Lucille. I want to ask you to marry me."

The handle of the bucket slipped from Lucille's fingers, and it crashed to the floor, turning over and spilling the water. "Oh!" she cried, stepping back from the spreading puddle.

Cory sprang forward. "I'm sorry," he said. "I'll get something to mop up that mess—"

Lucille's hand shot out and closed on his arm. "What did you say?" she demanded huskily as she stared at him with an intense gaze that felt as if she were looking right through him.

The power he saw in her eyes shook him. He forgot completely that they were not alone, that Mildred Thompson was standing across the kitchen by the stove, looking a little surprised but very pleased.

"I asked you to marry me," Cory said almost too quietly. "I want you to be my wife, Lucille. I want us to be together for the rest of our lives."

"You want me to . . . marry you?" Tears welled from the corners of her eyes.

"Well . . . only if you want to," said Cory.

"Oh . . . oh, yes."

Then she was in his arms, and both of them were standing in the puddle of water, and neither of them cared. Their mouths met, and the warmth and sweetness that Cory tasted there was dizzying. He let the sensations wash over him, glorying, reveling in the smell and taste and feel of the woman he loved. His heart was pounding harder, he realized, than it had in the heat of battle.

Lucille drew her mouth an inch away from his and murmured, "Of course I'll marry you." Then she kissed him again.

Cory had no idea how much time had passed before he became aware that Mrs. Thompson was saying something. "Charles will be so happy," she said. "He's always thought you were a fine young man, Cory."

Cory and Lucille turned toward her, and Cory's arm went around Lucille's shoulders in a natural embrace. "I'm sorry," he said. "I know I should have asked the colonel's permission first before I even approached Lucille—"

"Nonsense," Mrs. Thompson said briskly. "If you're worried about Charles's approval, you don't have to. I know he'll be pleased. In fact, while he was here he mentioned to me that you would probably ask for Lucille's hand in marriage soon."

"He did?" Cory was surprised. "How did he know?"

Mrs. Thompson came closer, put one hand on Cory's shoulder and the other on Lucille's. "Don't be silly. Everyone knows how you two feel about each other. You're perfectly matched."

"Lucille's perfect," Cory said with a rueful grin. "I don't reckon many people would describe me that way."

"I would," Lucille said softly, looking up at him.

Beaming with joy, Mrs. Thompson went on, "Now, there's the matter of deciding when the wedding will be."

"Soon," Cory and Lucille said at the same time, then looked at each other. Lucille blushed, and as Cory watched her, he felt his own face growing quite warm. Still, it was good to know that she'd had some of the sort of passionate thoughts that he'd had.

"Of course," agreed Mrs. Thompson. "In times of war, it's best not to wait too long for anything that's important. And I can't think of anything that's more important than a wedding." Suddenly, she frowned. "But we'll have to wait for Charles. I'll send word to Monroe, but I'm sure he's already set off for Texas."

Cory suppressed a groan of dismay. He hadn't even considered the colonel's whereabouts. Mrs. Thompson was right; it would be five or six weeks before Colonel Thompson could get back to Vicksburg. And since Lucille's aunt and uncle were the only relatives she had left, he couldn't very well expect her to have her wedding without both of them in attendance.

"It's all right," he said. "We'll wait for the colonel."

Lucille looked up at him worriedly. "Are you sure?"

Cory gave a little laugh that he hoped didn't sound too forced. "Of course. It wouldn't be a proper wedding without your uncle here. He'll have to give away the bride."

"That's right, dear," said Mrs. Thompson. "I wish your father could be here, but I'm sure Charles will be honored to walk you down the aisle."

Lucille moved closer to Cory and rested her head against his shoulder. "I think my father *is* here," she said in a half-whisper. "I can feel him here with us, and I think he's happy."

"I think so, too," Cory said, his voice choked with emotion. Captain Farrell had given him his life back—and more. The captain had given him the woman he loved, the woman with whom he would spend the rest of that life.

And as he drew Lucille and her aunt into an embrace, he whispered, "Thank you, Cap'n."

He liked to think that somewhere the captain heard.

Chapter Seven

CORY HAD NO IDEA so many different things went into getting married. He spent the rest of the day with his head in a whirl as he listened to Lucille and her aunt discussing all the details of the wedding.

There was the matter of the church, of course. Lucille and the Thompsons were Methodists, which meant that Cory's Baptist mother would regard them as only one step up the ladder from heathens. But it wasn't his mother who was marrying into the family, Cory reminded himself, and he didn't care what denomination Lucille followed. He had no objection at all to their getting married in the First Methodist Church in downtown Vicksburg.

Providing that Yankee mortars hadn't leveled the building before the wedding could take place.

That grim thought intruded into Cory's head, but he forced it away. He wasn't going to allow the war to ruin his happiness on this day.

"I was thinking about a Christmas wedding," Lucille suggested as she and her aunt sat at the kitchen table and sipped tea. "Uncle Charles will certainly be back by then."

Mrs. Thompson clasped her hands together. "That's a wonderful idea, dear. Not Christmas Day itself, but perhaps Christmas Eve."

Lucille nodded and added, "That's exactly what I was thinking, Aunt Mildred."

Cory wasn't sure how appropriate it would be for one's wedding night to take place on Christmas Eve, but if that was what Lucille wanted. . . . Anyway, weddings and such were more for the bride and her family than they were for the groom.

That thought made him realize that none of his family would be able to attend the ceremony. Virginia was much too far away for any of the Brannons to make the trip, especially when much of the area between there and Vicksburg was occupied by Federal forces. And Will and Mac were in the army, so of course they couldn't leave.

He had missed his brother Titus's wedding to Polly Ebersole, Cory told himself, and though he regretted that, there was nothing he could do about it. This was the same thing. Though the bonds of family could never be broken, his life was here now with Lucille, not in Virginia.

The only thing really settled by evening was that if it could be arranged with the church, the wedding would take place on Christmas Eve. Lucille and Mrs. Thompson had moved on to discussing the dress Lucille would wear. Cory didn't think they even noticed when he got up and went into the parlor. He built up the fire against the damp chill that tried to steal in from the waning day outside.

A knock on the front door drew Cory's attention. With a frown, he remembered that Palmer Kincaid had said something about stopping by this evening.

The frown turned into a smile as Cory recalled his earlier impulse to tell Kincaid that he and Lucille were engaged. At the time, it hadn't been true, but now it was, and Cory knew he could count on Lucille in her happiness telling Kincaid all about it. The gambler would see that he had no chance of winning Lucille's affections for himself, so with any luck, he would simply offer his congratulations and then bow out of the picture as gracefully as a gentleman should.

When he went to answer the door, however, he found a Confederate lieutenant standing there, not Palmer Kincaid.

"Cory Brannon?" the lieutenant asked.

Taken aback with the surprise, Cory answered, "Yes. What can I do for you?"

"I have a message for you from General Pemberton, sir." The lieutenant held out a folded piece of paper sealed with wax. "The general instructed me to wait for your reply."

What the devil? . . . Cory hesitated, then took the paper from the young officer. "I don't know why General Pemberton would be writing to me," he muttered.

"Then I suggest you read the message, sir," the lieutenant suggested without a hint of sarcasm.

Cory shrugged and broke the seal. He unfolded the paper and quickly scanned the lines written on it. The message was a request for Cory to present himself at the general's headquarters at nine o'clock the next morning.

"The general further instructed me to say, sir, that although he cannot command you to accept the invitation contained in his missive, it concerns a matter of utmost urgency to the Confederacy and to Vicksburg."

Cory's head was spinning. He was baffled by this unexpected affair. But he couldn't refuse a request from the commanding officer of Vicksburg's defenses, so he nodded. "Please tell the general that I'll be there."

"Thank you, sir." The lieutenant came to attention and started to salute, then stopped and settled for a curt nod instead, since he was dealing with a civilian and not a fellow soldier. He turned and went back to the street, walking briskly away. As Cory watched him disappear into the gathering shadows, he noticed that it had started to rain lightly.

Still staring at the piece of paper in his hand, Cory slowly closed the door and turned back toward the parlor. As he did so, Lucille and Mrs. Thompson came out of the kitchen. "Who was that at the door?" asked Mrs. Thompson.

"An officer with a message from General Pemberton," Cory said. He held up the paper so that they could see the official seal on it.

"What in the world? Doesn't the general know that Charles has gone back to Texas?"

Cory shook his head. "The message isn't for the colonel. It's for me."

"For you?" exclaimed Lucille. "What does he want?"

"He wants to see me at headquarters tomorrow morning."

"Why?"

Again, all Cory could do was helplessly shake his head. "I have no idea."

But even as he spoke, a shiver went through him. Whatever General Pemberton wanted, the chances were it wouldn't be anything good.

∽

CORY KNEW little about Gen. John C. Pemberton, only that the man had been in charge of the Confederate defenses at New Orleans—defenses that had failed to prevent Yankee Adm. David Farragut from capturing the Crescent City. Pemberton had been placed in full command at Vicksburg only a few days before Cory's most recent arrival in the city, superseding Gen. Martin Luther Smith, who had helped with the plans for establishing the supply line from Texas.

One of the newspapers in the Thompson household contained a story about Pemberton's taking command, and in it Cory read: "In General Pemberton we have a man worthy of trust and confidence. Free from ostentation, an indefatigable and untiring worker, he has traversed the whole department and overlooked all our works of defense. Where work is needed, he has done it at once. His whole mind is absorbed in the great business before him."

That sounded promising, but Cory was less impressed by what Mrs. Thompson had to tell him about the general.

"He's a Yankee, you know," Mrs. Thompson said at the breakfast table the next morning after Pemberton's message had been delivered to Cory. "From Philadelphia."

"How did he come to fight for the Confederacy?" asked Cory.

"He married a Virginia girl. A Thompson, in fact, one of Charles's distant relatives. Martha, I believe her name is. Charles served with General Pemberton during the Mexican War. He was wounded and decorated for gallantry. General Pemberton, that is. Charles was decorated, too."

Lucille said, "I don't like this. You're not in the army, Cory. General Pemberton shouldn't be able to order you around."

"He didn't give me an order," Cory pointed out. "He simply asked me to see him."

"A request from a general is the same thing as an order."

Cory shrugged. "You may be right. But I don't suppose it'll hurt anything to go see what he wants."

When breakfast was over, Cory slipped into a dark brown corduroy coat and brushed off his hat before he settled it on his head. Lucille came with him into the foyer and lifted herself on her toes to kiss him before he left. Cory's arms went around her, and he didn't want to let go. Finally, though, he knew he had to if he was going to arrive at Pemberton's headquarters on time.

The rain of the night before had stopped, but so recently that the streets were still wet. Cory was grateful for the showers; they had helped keep Palmer Kincaid wherever he was, instead of visiting the Thompson house. Lucille had been so excited over the engagement that she seemed to have forgotten entirely about Kincaid's presence in the city.

Cory had to pass through several levels of sentries and aides before he reached General Pemberton's office in the downtown Vicksburg building that had been commandeered as military headquarters. The last man he saw before Pemberton himself was a lieutenant colonel, who ushered him into the general's office. "Mr. Brannon, General," the colonel announced.

Pemberton, who was sitting behind a desk littered with papers, came to his feet. Cory had seen him before, so he recognized the erect military bearing, the dark brown hair and beard, and the spotless, faultlessly creased uniform. Pemberton greeted him crisply, "Thank you for coming, Mr. Brannon." He gestured toward a chair in front of the desk. "Please have a seat."

Cory felt as if he should have saluted, but he suppressed the impulse. He took off his hat instead and sat down.

Pemberton got right to the point. "I have need of a man to carry out a particular mission for me, Mr. Brannon, and Colonel Thompson suggested that you might be an appropriate choice."

"Me, sir?" Cory asked. "But I'm not in the army."

"I realize that. Therefore I cannot order you to accept this assignment. I know from speaking to Colonel Thompson that you have served the Confederacy on several occasions in the past, and it is my hope that you will consent to do so again."

"If there's anything I can do . . . ," Cory began, but in the back of his brain a small voice was crying out for him to refuse. Whatever it was that Pemberton wanted, he ought to say no. After all, he was soon to be a married man. His wife would be his first responsibility.

"As you may be aware, General Grant recently has been placed in command of the Federal Department of the Tennessee," Pemberton went on, not giving Cory a chance to say anything else. "We have . . . agents, if you will . . . who keep us informed of such things."

Spies, that was what he meant, thought Cory. Word of Grant's promotion had come from Confederate spies behind the Yankee lines.

"I believe you have faced Grant before, Mr. Brannon, at Forts Henry and Donelson and at Shiloh."

"Well . . . I was there for those battles. But I was just a . . . a common rifleman, and not an officially enlisted one at that. I wouldn't really say that I've gone up against General Grant, sir."

"You are familiar with his tactics, however. He is not a man to sit back and wait."

Cory thought about the battles in which he had participated during the past year and shook his head. "No sir, I don't suppose he is."

"Therefore, it is safe to assume that Grant, knowing the importance that his president and commander-in-chief places on the capture of Vicksburg, will move on the city posthaste."

"I, uh, wouldn't be surprised, sir."

A large map of the region hung on the wall behind the general's desk. Pemberton rested a fingertip on a line that ran from western Tennessee down into central Mississippi. "This is the Mississippi Central Railroad. Over here—" He moved his finger to another, roughly parallel line to the east. "The Mobile and Ohio. The word from our agents is that General Grant plans to advance to the south along one of these rail lines and thereby position his army to launch an assault upon Vicksburg from the east. He must be prevented from doing so."

Cory nodded, remembering the two-pronged attack on Fort Donelson and how successful it had been.

"General Braxton Bragg commands our forces in Tennessee," continued Pemberton. "Do you, by chance, know him, Mr. Brannon?"

"Ah, no sir, I'm afraid not." Pemberton still had an inflated idea of his importance, thought Cory. What in blazes had Colonel Thompson told the general about him, anyway?

Pemberton nodded. "I thought you might; he was at Shiloh. But no matter. Bragg is a good man, but sometimes a bit reluctant to act. I have sent him telegraphic messages apprising him of what I believe General Grant's plans will be and suggesting that his aid will be needed to thwart them, but from the tone of his replies I do not believe that General Bragg places sufficient weight on the threat." Pemberton stepped back over to the desk and picked up a sealed envelope. "That is why I want you to deliver this letter to him, Mr. Brannon."

Cory's eyes widened in surprise. "You want me to take a letter all the way to Tennessee to another general?" he asked, too shocked to worry about whether he was following military protocol or not.

"That is correct," Pemberton said with a solemn nod.

"But . . . but why me? Why not just send it with one of your army couriers?"

Pemberton sighed. "Because I am appealing to Bragg not as a fellow officer but as one gentleman to another." His voice dropped as he went on between clenched teeth, his words now somewhat measured. "It . . . pains me . . . to have to beg for help, Mr. Brannon, especially when it should be forthcoming without having to take such desperate measures."

Cory was beginning to understand the situation. Pemberton's pride had been wounded deeply by the loss of New Orleans to the Yankees, and now he was faced with a similar situation here in Vicksburg. Yet, evidently this General Bragg was dragging his feet about providing the help Pemberton needed to hold the city.

"Then this is . . . an unofficial communication with General Bragg, sir?"

"Decidedly so, Mr. Brannon."

Cory took a breath. What Pemberton was asking him to do wasn't exactly spying; he would just be carrying a letter, after all. But it was beyond the pale of normal military procedure.

Cory caught himself. He was thinking as if he were on the verge of accepting the assignment when what he had to do was refuse, in no uncertain terms and as quickly as possible.

"I'm getting married on Christmas Eve," were the words that came out of his mouth instead.

Pemberton's eyebrows rose. "Indeed? Well, then, congratulations are in order, Mr. Brannon. You should be back from Tennessee by then, secure in the knowledge that you have helped protect the city so that you and your bride can begin your lives together without the Yankees on your doorstep."

Cory swallowed an impulse to laugh. Pemberton was a skillful manipulator of words and situations, no doubt about that.

"I walked here most of the way from Tennessee, you know," Cory said. "It took me most of the summer."

"You'll have the best horse we can find for you. If you like, I'll detail an officer to travel with you, so that you won't have to make the journey alone. He can't be made privy to the details of the message you'll be carrying, of course, since that would defeat the purpose of employing a civilian courier."

Whatever was in his letter to Bragg, Pemberton didn't want it to ever become part of the official military record, Cory mused. Which meant that Pemberton was taking a chance by putting it in the hands of a civilian, a messenger over whom Pemberton had no real control. The general was that desperate to get the aid he needed to stop the Yankees from capturing Vicksburg.

After a moment of silence, Pemberton lifted a hand and rested it over his eyes. "I've assumed too much," he said as his shoulders sagged. "From what Colonel Thompson told me, I thought you would be the man to carry out this mission, Mr. Brannon. I apologize for wasting your time."

When Thompson and Pemberton had spoken, the colonel had had no way of knowing that Cory would soon be engaged to Lucille. Cory reminded himself of that fact. He also thought about what he and Lucille, along with everyone else in Vicksburg, would be facing if U. S. Grant—"Unconditional Surrender" Grant, he had been dubbed after the fall of Fort Henry—were to show up with a Yankee army just outside town. The prospects were not good.

"All I'd have to do is deliver the letter to General Bragg?" he asked to be sure.

Pemberton looked up quickly. "That is correct."

"Then I could return here?"

"Of course. As a civilian, you would be free to go wherever you wished—as long as you didn't run into too many Yankees on the way."

There was that to consider, Cory reminded himself. The trip could be dangerous.

And yet, if it would help save Vicksburg . . .

And if he could be back in time to marry Lucille on Christmas Eve . . .

"I'll do it," he said abruptly. "I'd be honored to deliver the letter to General Bragg, sir."

Pemberton stood there and folded his arms across his chest. Only a slight increase in his breathing indicated what he was really feeling. He gave Cory a curt nod. "Thank you, Mr. Brannon, on behalf of the Confederacy." He picked up the sealed envelope from the desk and handed it to Cory, who slipped it into a pocket inside his coat. Pemberton was business-like again as he went on. "Would you wish to have an officer travel with you?"

"That would probably be a good idea."

Pemberton summoned the colonel in the outer office and said, "Have Lieutenant Ryder report here immediately."

A few minutes later, the young lieutenant who had delivered Pemberton's summons to Cory the previous evening came into the office, snapped to attention, and saluted. "Lieutenant Ryder reporting as ordered, sir."

Pemberton returned the salute then said, "At ease, Lieutenant. I believe you're acquainted with Mr. Brannon."

Ryder's eyes flicked over to Cory for a second. "We met yesterday afternoon, sir, at the home of Colonel Thompson of the Mississippi Home Guard."

"Indeed. Lieutenant, Mr. Brannon is going to Tennessee. I want you to go with him."

Ryder stiffened. "Sir?"

"You heard me, Lieutenant."

"Yes sir."

The lieutenant was even more confused than he had been at first, Cory thought. And since Pemberton's message to Bragg had to be kept a secret, Ryder wouldn't even get the luxury of an explanation.

"You will assist Mr. Brannon to reach Tennessee safely, where the two of you will locate General Bragg. Mr. Brannon knows what to do then."

Ryder glanced at him again, and Cory nodded.

"Yes sir," said the lieutenant, accepting the orders without question. "And after that, sir?"

"You will return to your duties here, Lieutenant."

"When will we leave, sir?"

Pemberton looked at Cory then said, "As soon as possible."

"Yes sir."

Pemberton extended his hand across the desk toward the lieutenant. "Godspeed, son."

Ryder hesitated, then shook hands with the general. Cory got to his feet and clasped the general's hand, too.

"Draw the best horses you can find from our stables," Pemberton instructed them. "I'll leave those decisions to you. Requisition the necessary supplies for the both of you as well. And good luck."

"Thank you, sir," Cory said. The lieutenant saluted again then turned sharply and marched out of the office, accompanied at a more leisurely pace by Cory.

Ryder waited until they were outside to look at Cory, then he demanded in amazement, "Who the hell are you, anyway?"

Cory stuck out a hand and said, "Cory Brannon, from Culpeper County, Virginia, but lately of Vicksburg, Monroe, Louisiana, and Texas."

Baffled, the lieutenant shook hands with him. "Hamilton Ryder," he introduced himself. "My friends call me Ham."

"I had a friend named Pie," said Cory.

That just confused Ryder even more. Like many of the young officers in the Confederate army, he was about Cory's age. A few inches shorter than Cory, he was slender and wiry, with a shock of dark brown hair. He took off his hat now and ran his fingers through his hair in confusion.

"I'm not supposed to understand any of this, am I?"

Cory shook his head. "Not really. I can't tell you why we're going to Tennessee, only that you're supposed to help me get there without the Yankees shooting or capturing us."

Ryder lifted a hand and shook a finger at Cory. "You're a spy," he accused.

"If I was, could I tell you?"

The lieutenant sighed in exasperation. "All right. Let's get over to the stables and pick out some horses."

As they walked along the street, Cory felt a deep sense of unease that threatened to turn into pure panic. What had he done? What had he been thinking? Out of a burst of ill-advised loyalty to the Confederacy—and, he had to admit, the same sort of restlessness and longing for adventure that had always plagued him—he had agreed to undertake a covert mission that would take him away from Vicksburg and the woman he loved just at the time when he needed most to be with her. Lucille would be furious when she found out they were going to be separated during the weeks leading up to their wedding.

Or would she? Cory asked himself. Surely she would be disappointed, but Lucille had always understood the concept of duty. Cory might not be a soldier, but he was a citizen of the South just as she was. Sometimes, other considerations had to come before personal ones.

Besides, he thought, he would be back by Christmas Eve. There was plenty of time to ride to Tennessee and back. All the time in the world, in fact . . .

Chapter Eight

ACTING ON AN IMPULSE, Cory invited Hamilton Ryder to the Thompson house with him for lunch. He realized that another person would put a strain on the provisions he had been able to buy, but he thought that if the lieutenant were there, Lucille might be able to understand a little better how important the mission was that Cory had accepted. And after spending more than a year in the army, Ryder seemed quite gratified by the possibility of a home-cooked meal.

The lieutenant was from Tennessee, Cory learned as they talked while selecting their mounts for the journey. Ryder had been born and raised in a small town south of Nashville called La Vergne. Cory had never heard of it, but Ryder spoke fondly of the place, naturally enough.

"My father is the editor of the local newspaper," said Ryder, "so there was always a great deal of talk around the dinner table about politics. We knew the war was coming long before it did."

That was true of most people, thought Cory, but he didn't say anything. The lieutenant was still puzzled by this assignment and somewhat resentful of the secrecy involved, but he seemed to make an effort to be friendly, and Cory didn't want to spoil that.

"My mother passed away so long ago I barely remember her," continued Ryder, "so it was just my father and my brothers and myself."

"How many brothers?" Cory asked.

"Three. All of them older than me."

"I have four brothers. I'm next to the youngest. Our sister is the baby of the family, though," Cory said with a grin, remembering Cordelia.

"After Fort Sumter, my brothers all enlisted in the army, so I did, too. My father was opposed to it, but since I'm of age, there was nothing he could do."

118 • *James Reasoner*

Cory thought about Ryder's father, a widower with all four sons in the army and facing death at the hands of the enemy. He couldn't blame the man for wishing that at least one of his boys had stayed home. It was all too possible that the elder Ryder could find himself alone in the world by the time the war ended. Men were dying all over.

They saddled the horses they'd selected and led the animals toward the Thompson house. Vicksburg was chilly but peaceful. Cory didn't miss the sound of the mortars on the Yankee gunboats at all. Sooner or later, though, they would be back. He was certain of that.

As they walked, Cory told Ryder a little about his family and touched briefly on the events of the past year. Like nearly everyone else, the lieutenant was impressed by the fact that Cory had been at Shiloh.

"I was in New Orleans at the time, serving with General Pemberton," Ryder said, "but we heard a great deal about what went on during that battle. Grant was lucky he was able to turn the tide on the second day."

Cory didn't think anyone had been particularly lucky at Shiloh, especially the men who had fallen in the bloodbath of the Hornet's Nest and the savage fighting around the old log church. He knew that before Shiloh, most people in the South had still clung to the hope that the war would be short, a hope born in the heady triumph of Manassas. But Shiloh had opened their eyes to the fact that the war would most likely be long and hard and brutal, and nothing that had happened in the six months since then had changed their minds.

"I was just glad that I survived, and that I didn't wind up in a Yankee prison camp," he said. "I thought that was where I was headed after Donelson fell, but they paroled us instead."

Ryder looked sideways at him. "You've done a lot considering that you're not even in the army."

Cory shrugged and shook his head. "I've just been in the wrong places at the wrong times, I reckon."

And this current dilemma he was in was a prime example of that, he thought.

When they reached the house, Cory was surprised to see a fancy black buggy parked in front of the picket fence. A fine-looking bay horse was hitched to the vehicle. Obviously, Lucille and Mrs. Thompson were entertaining a visitor, but Cory had no idea who it could be.

He should have known, he told himself a few moments later as he stepped into the parlor and found Palmer Kincaid making himself at home on the settee next to Lucille.

The gambler looked up and greeted Cory with a smile. "There you are!" he said. "Lucille was just telling me the wonderful news." He stood up and extended his hand. "Congratulations! I must say I envy you, Cory. You're getting one of the loveliest women in the world as your bride."

"I know," Cory said as they shook hands. He glanced toward the settee and saw that Lucille was blushing with pleasure at the compliment.

"Uncle Palmer and I have been catching up," she said.

Kincaid let go of Cory's hand and turned to Lucille, his expression becoming solemn. "And of course I offered the dear girl my condolences on the tragic passing of her father." He shook his head. "Tragic."

Mrs. Thompson came into the parlor from the hallway. "I thought I heard someone come in," she said. "My goodness, Cory, who's this?"

Cory swept a hand toward the young officer who had accompanied him from Pemberton's headquarters. "Everyone, this is Lt. Hamilton Ryder. Lieutenant Ryder, allow me to present my fiancée, Miss Lucille Farrell . . . her aunt, Mrs. Mildred Thompson . . . and Mr. Palmer Kincaid—late of Cairo, Illinois."

Ryder stepped forward with his hat under his arm and took the hand that Lucille offered him. "I'm honored, Miss Farrell." Turning to Mrs. Thompson, he repeated the sentiment, then shook hands with Kincaid and added, "Illinois, eh? A Yankee?"

Cory was well aware that what Ryder had just said bordered on an insult. Kincaid merely smiled faintly, however, and replied, "Hardly. I was born in Natchez. My line of work took me up north."

"And that is . . . ?"

"Businessman. I owned an establishment in Cairo known as the Staghorn."

"A saloon and gambling den, you mean?" Ryder asked coolly and with a hint of censure.

Cory was starting to like the lieutenant, who evidently had taken the same instinctive dislike to Palmer Kincaid that Cory himself felt.

Kincaid seemed determined not to take offense. He smiled and shrugged. "Call it whatever you like. What's important is that I've sold it and come home to the South, where I belong."

"Welcome home, then," said Ryder.

Lucille and Mrs. Thompson were both aware of the subtle dueling that was going on, and they didn't much care for it, thought Cory. However, their innate hospitality prevented them from saying anything negative to a guest.

Ryder turned toward the women, clasped his hands behind his back, and smiled. "Mr. Brannon has invited me to be your guest for lunch, ladies, but I'll certainly not take it amiss if you'd prefer to disinvite me, since he was perhaps a bit hasty in his actions." Ryder shot a glance toward Cory.

"Absolutely not," Mrs. Thompson said without hesitation. "You're more than welcome, Lieutenant. My, my, with Mr. Kincaid as our guest as well, our table will be full again for the first time in ages! That's a sight that will do my heart good, I'm telling you."

So they had invited Kincaid already, Cory thought. Well, he supposed he could put up with the gambler's presence—for Lucille's sake.

He would have preferred, though, that Kincaid not be around when it came time to tell Lucille that before the afternoon was over, he would be on his way to Tennessee with Lieutenant Ryder. The sooner he got there and delivered the letter to General Bragg, the sooner he would be back, he told himself.

Mrs. Thompson said, "If you young people will excuse me, I'll see to what needs doing in the kitchen."

Lucille rose quickly. "I'll help you, Aunt Mildred."

"Oh, no, that's not necessary—"

"I insist." Lucille went past Cory with a swish of skirts, a swirl of perfume, and a quick smile meant for him alone. Just being that close to her made his heart pound.

With the departure of the women, that left Cory, Ryder, and Kincaid alone in the parlor. Kincaid lowered himself to the settee and slid a cigar from a vest pocket. He didn't offer one to Cory or the lieutenant, just struck a sulfur match on his thumbnail and lit the tightly rolled tobacco cylinder.

Cory gestured toward an armchair and said to Ryder, "Have a seat." He lowered himself into one of the other chairs.

Ryder said, "So you've only recently arrived in Vicksburg, Mr. Kincaid?"

"Quite recently. I arrived only the day before yesterday."

"Is that your buggy outside?" asked Cory.

Kincaid smiled. "Yes, it is. Nice, isn't it?"

"Did you come from Cairo in it?"

"No, no," Kincaid replied with a shake of his head. "I traveled by train and horseback most of the way. Even a bit by shank's mare. No, until yesterday evening, the buggy belonged to a man named Cochran."

"Red Mike Cochran?" asked Ryder, sounding surprised.

Kincaid drew deeply on the cigar then leisurely expelled a cloud of smoke. "I believe someone called him that. We were sitting across the table from each other in a game of chance."

Cory remembered where he had heard of Red Mike's Saloon. It was one of the most notorious, and most lucrative, establishments of its sort in Vicksburg. Obviously, Ryder was aware of its unsavory reputation, too.

"I do not believe I have ever heard of Mr. Cochran's losing a poker game," Ryder commented.

"He lost this one," said Kincaid. "He was convinced his pair of ladies and his pair of tens were going to beat me, but he hadn't reckoned on the trio of sixes in my hand."

"So you won the buggy from him?" asked Cory.

"The buggy . . . and his place."

Cory's eyes widened. "You won Red Mike's?"

Kincaid puffed on the cigar again. "Do you think I should change the name or leave it as it is? Kincaid's has more class, but everyone knows Red Mike's."

Cory leaned back in the armchair and cocked his right ankle on his left knee. "It didn't take you long, did it?"

"To establish myself in Vicksburg, you mean?" Kincaid shook his head. "I don't believe in wasting time."

Ryder asked, "May I ask how Mr. Cochran took it when you beat him?"

Kincaid's reply was curt. "Badly."

"Is he still alive?"

"Of course! I'm not a barbarian, Lieutenant. I simply had him escorted out of the place by some of my new employees." Kincaid shrugged. "I haven't seen him since."

Cory frowned. He wasn't happy that Kincaid had won Cochran's saloon. That meant the gambler would be around town for a while. If Kincaid hadn't been so successful, he might have moved on. Now he would be in Vicksburg where he could come calling on Lucille and Mrs. Thompson any time he wanted while Cory was gone on General Pemberton's mission. Kincaid knew that Cory and Lucille were engaged, but if his sights were set on Lucille, would such a thing really matter to a man like him? Maybe it wasn't too late to back out . . .

But it was, Cory realized. He'd given the general his word. He had to take that letter to General Bragg.

But at least he could postpone until after lunch the moment when he would have to break the news to Lucille.

As Cory had figured it would be, the fare at the table in the dining room was rather sparse. A few biscuits, a bowl of greens with a small chunk of fatback in it, and buttermilk that had been chilled on the back steps. The way Kincaid exclaimed over it, though, it might as well have been a feast.

When the meal was finished, Kincaid got to his feet and said, "I really hate to run, ladies, but I have a business that demands my attention. Thank you so much for your hospitality."

"Why, you're as welcome as you can be, Mr. Kincaid," said Mildred Thompson. "I know you were a good friend to my brother Ezekiel, which means that you'll always be welcome in this house."

"You're as gracious as you are beautiful, madam," Kincaid said as he took her hand for a moment. Then he turned to Lucille and held out his arms. She came into them, gleefully hugging him tightly.

"I'm glad you came to Vicksburg, Uncle Palmer," she said.

Kincaid patted her lightly on the back as he returned the embrace. "And I'm glad to be here, child. If there's ever anything I can do for you, please just let me know."

Cory's jaw tightened and his forehead creased in a frown as he watched Kincaid hugging Lucille. The gambler seemed to be enjoying the embrace way too much, he thought. Kincaid held her long enough.

Cory was about to say something when Kincaid finally released Lucille and stepped back. He gave Cory and Ryder a brisk nod and turned toward the hallway.

"I'll see you out," Cory said quickly. He followed Kincaid into the foyer of the house, making sure that the gambler didn't turn back. Kincaid took his hat and a silver-headed stick from the table just inside the door, then paused before going out to give Cory a sardonic smile.

"I'll be seeing you, Mr. Brannon," he said.

"Sure," Cory said easily. Kincaid would find out soon enough that he was leaving town for a while.

The door closed behind Kincaid. Cory looked at it for a second, then took a deep breath.

"You don't like him, do you?" asked Hamilton Ryder in a quiet voice, startling Cory. He hadn't heard the young officer come up beside him.

Before answering, Cory shot a glance toward the rear of the house. He could hear the two women bustling around in the kitchen, out of earshot as long as he kept his voice low.

"No, I don't like him at all," he said. "Is it that obvious?"

Ryder shrugged. "You hide it fairly well most of the time . . . except when he touches Miss Farrell."

"She thinks of him as a kindly old uncle," Cory said between gritted teeth, "but he doesn't feel that way about her at all."

"I know. But don't you think Miss Farrell is intelligent enough to see that, too?"

"Intelligence has nothing to do with it," said Cory. "She's known him since she was a child. She trusts him. It would never occur to her to think anything bad about him."

"It's a shame, then, that you have to leave Vicksburg."

Eyes narrowing, Cory looked at him. "Just now, I thought about not going."

Ryder shrugged again. "It's your choice. I don't even know what it's about, remember?"

Cory didn't know how to answer that, but he didn't really blame the lieutenant for being somewhat resentful. After all, Ryder would be putting his life on the line, too, by accompanying Cory into Tennessee.

Before they could continue the conversation, Lucille and Mrs. Thompson emerged from the kitchen. "I'll see about those supplies," Ryder said quickly to Cory, then picked up his hat and turned toward the women. "Thank you, ladies. This has been the most pleasant hour I've spent in a long, long time."

"Please come back to visit us as often as you like, Lieutenant," Mrs. Thompson said.

Ryder said his farewells and left, and Cory knew he couldn't postpone what he had to do any longer. He said, "Lucille, could I talk to you in the parlor?"

She looked a little surprised. "Why, I suppose so."

"I'll leave you young people alone," said Mrs. Thompson, taking her cue that Cory wanted some privacy. She went upstairs to her bedroom.

Cory took Lucille's hand and led her into the parlor. She was looking at him rather apprehensively as he sat them both down on the settee. "Cory," she said, "something is wrong. I can tell." Her eyes suddenly widened. "Oh, my God! You've decided that you don't want to get married after all."

"No! Not at all." He took both of her hands in his. "I love you, Lucille, and I want more than ever to make you my wife. That's exactly what I'm going to do on Christmas Eve."

She relaxed a little and squeezed his hands. "Well, what is it, then? As long as we're going to be together, whatever you have to tell me can't be all that bad."

"It's just that . . . for part of the time between now and then . . . we can't be together."

Her worried frown came back. "Why not?"

There was no choice now but to plunge ahead, Cory told himself. "Because I have to go to Tennessee. General Pemberton has asked me to see a man there, but my mission is a secret."

Lucille gasped. "The general wants you to be a spy?"

Quickly Cory shook his head. "No, not a spy. Just a . . . a courier, I guess you could say. I've been asked to deliver a letter to another general."

"But . . . but why can't he send it with a regular soldier? Why does it have to be you who takes it?"

"Your uncle told him I'd be a good man for the job, I suppose." Cory laughed wryly. "That's what I get for making the colonel feel confident in me."

Lucille pulled her hands away. Her eyes blazed at him as she said, half crying, "No! It's not fair! We're engaged. We shouldn't have to be apart."

Cory couldn't tell if she was angry at him or Pemberton or both of them. "I tried to refuse—" That was stretching the truth a little, but at least he had thought about turning down the general's assignment. "—but it's important for the Confederacy—"

"Damn the Confederacy!"

The words were no sooner out than Lucille's hand lifted to her mouth in horror that she had spoken them. "I didn't mean that," she rushed on. "It's just that . . . our lives are important, too, Cory. You . . . you just asked me to marry you, for goodness' sake! There's so much to do . . ."

"You and Mrs. Thompson can arrange everything. I know the wedding will be perfect. We have to wait until Christmas Eve anyway. That's six weeks away. I should be back from Tennessee in a month or less."

"But it could be a dangerous trip, especially for someone who's alone."

"I won't be alone," Cory said.

Understanding dawned in Lucille's eyes. "Oh. So that's why you brought Lieutenant Ryder with you. He's part of this, too."

"He's going with me."

"When . . . ," Lucille took a deep breath. "When will you be leaving me?"

"Later this afternoon," Cory replied miserably.

Lucille flinched almost as if she had been struck. "Today?" she whispered.

Cory nodded. He wanted to take her into his arms, but he hesitated, unsure of how she would react. She was still a little angry at him, he thought.

She took the decision out of his hands by putting her arms around him and leaning against him. "I can't tell you not to go," she said, "but I can warn you that you had better be careful and come back to me in one piece."

"I intend to do that," Cory said, relieved that she wasn't going to pitch a tantrum.

Although why he should have been worried that she would, he didn't know. During times of trouble, Lucille had always been cool-headed and competent, every inch her father's daughter. He remembered how, following a bombardment by Yankee gunboats, she had calmly set about tearing strips off her petticoats and bandaging the wounds of the soldiers manning one of the Confederate batteries.

"Right now you should make the best of the time you have left and kiss me," she suggested.

Cory nodded. It was a good suggestion. He brought his mouth to hers, felt the heat and tasted the sweetness as she opened her lips. The kiss sent his emotions tumbling out of control. How could he leave her, even for a few weeks? How could any mission for the Confederacy be more important than what he held right here in his arms?

There were no answers, other than the fact that he had given his word.

So he held her tightly and wished this moment would never end, knowing all the while that it had to.

⟲

LT. HAMILTON RYDER returned in the middle of the afternoon, leading his saddle horse as well as a pack mule with a pair of saddlebags slung over its back. Cory was watching for him and came out of the house to meet him. The gun belt with the holstered Colt was strapped around his waist, and he had a small pouch of provisions that Mrs. Thompson had insisted he take with him. It held some biscuits, a few slices of bacon, and a couple of apples.

"That way I'll know that you'll have at least one good meal while you're on the road," Mildred Thompson had said when she gave the small bundle to him. Tears had glittered in her eyes. Breaking the news of his leaving to her had not been easy, although it wasn't the ordeal that telling Lucille had been.

"Ready to go?" Ryder greeted him.

"I've said my good-byes, if that's what you mean."

"A soldier often doesn't have that luxury," Ryder pointed out. "He just goes where he's told to go and does what he's told to do."

Cory nodded. "I know. And you probably think less of me because I'm a civilian and I'm complaining."

"Soldiers complain, too," Ryder said with a grin. "They probably spend more time doing that than anything else. And as for being a civilian . . . well, I wasn't conscripted. Enlisting was my own choice. So I can't hold it against you that you haven't, especially considering the fact that you've fought for the Confederacy anyway." He put out a hand. "I meant no offense."

Cory returned the grin and shook Ryder's hand. "All right. I suppose since we're going to be together for a while, we might as well be friends."

"That's right."

Cory's horse was tied in front of the house. He was reaching for the reins when the front door banged open and Lucille called desperately, "Cory!"

He turned toward her in surprise as she ran down the walk, holding up her skirts so she wouldn't trip on them in her haste. She jerked open the gate in the picket fence and practically threw herself into his arms, staggering him slightly. He had no choice except to return the embrace. Her mouth found his and clung to it with an unbridled hunger.

When she finally took her lips away, his heart was pounding unmercifully and he couldn't seem to catch his breath.

"I love you, Cory Brannon," she said fiercely. "Don't you ever forget it!"

"I . . . I won't," he managed to say. "I love you, too, Lucille."

She kissed him again then pulled back. "Go," she said. "Go on. Now."

He jerked his head in a nod, knowing she was right. He tugged the reins loose from the fence and swung up in the saddle, and beside him, Ham Ryder did the same. Cory turned the horse and heeled it into motion. He didn't trust himself to look back as he began to ride down the street. The lieutenant fell in alongside him, leading the pack mule.

After a few moments, Ryder chuckled. "Well, I'm not as worried as I was about this mission."

Cory swallowed hard, still fighting the impulse to turn around and gaze back at Lucille, even though he knew that would only make things harder on both of them. "Why's that?" he asked.

"Because if there was ever a man with a good reason for getting back safe and sound, it's you. I figure some of that's bound to rub off on me as well."

Cory looked over at him, laughed, and shook his head ruefully. "We'll get back," he said, never doubting it for a moment.

By Christmas Eve . . .

Chapter Nine

GENERAL BRAGG HAD BEEN busy.

Earlier in the summer, he and Gen. Edmund Kirby Smith had rendezvoused at Chattanooga and determined to launch an invasion of Kentucky. Since the beginning of the year, the Federals had moved strongly into Kentucky and Tennessee and now controlled most of both states, threatening to move farther south. Confederate morale was low. To stem the tide of defeat and regain some of the ground that had been lost to the Yankees, Bragg and Smith knew they had to be aggressive.

Smith struck first, leading an army of ten thousand men on a rapid march that brought them to the Union-occupied town of Richmond, Kentucky. Confederate cavalry under the command of Col. John Scott were the first ones to engage the enemy, near the hamlet of Rogersville, a short distance south of Richmond. An afternoon-long cavalry skirmish on August 29 ended with nightfall and found both armies moving up to confront each other in the morning.

Gen. Patrick E. Cleburne's division was in the forefront of the Southern forces. At dawn on August 30, Cleburne's division advanced, accompanied by two batteries of artillery. The gunners got in the first action, fighting a long-range duel with Union batteries as the infantry on both sides attempted to maneuver into favorable positions. Expecting reinforcements from Gen. Thomas J. Churchill's division, Cleburne committed his men to the attack. Cleburne himself was wounded by a ball that ripped through the left side of his face, which forced him to relinquish command to Gen. Preston Smith. The Yankees put up a staunch defense, and the Confederate thrust into Kentucky seemed to be in danger of collapsing before it even got started properly.

The timely arrival of Kirby Smith, along with Churchill's division, changed all that, tipping the odds in the Southerners' favor. The Yankees began to fall back, rallying several times in new defensive lines but unable to hold them against the storm of Rebel rifle fire and artillery bombardment. Overrunning the Federal positions, the Confederates managed to capture almost the entire garrison that had been stationed at Richmond. The first engagement, though in doubt for a while, was now a decisive success.

Meanwhile, Bragg, with an army three times the size of the one Smith led, began his part of the invasion by driving into the western part of the state, some one hundred miles west of Smith's line of attack. On September 13, his forces neared the town of Munfordville, on the Green River. The stream at this point was spanned by a Louisville and Nashville Railroad trestle, and since the L&N was an important part of the Yankee supply line, Bragg decided to destroy the bridge, which was defended by a small force of Union troops in a nearby fort.

The job of starting the ball rolling went to John Scott's cavalry, which had found itself in the same situation in General Smith's advance on Richmond. After the Confederate capture of that city, Scott and his men had been detached from Smith's forces and transferred to Bragg's. Scott and Gen. James Chalmers's brigade moved against the Yankees in a show of force. However, despite being outnumbered, the Union commander, Col. John T. Wilder, refused to surrender. Scott and Chalmers attacked, but they were beaten back.

With a far superior force at his command, Bragg did the reasonable thing and placed Munfordville under siege. The standoff did not last long. A struggle for command inside the Yankee fort between Wilder and Col. Cyrus Dunham was resolved finally with Wilder giving the orders. On September 16, under a flag of truce, Wilder conferred with Confederate Gen. Simon Buckner, who convinced him that it was indeed hopeless to hold out. The Federal garrison at Munfordville surrendered the next morning, September 17. With this obstacle removed from his path, Bragg and his army moved on to the settlement of Bardstown.

By early October both Bragg and Smith were ensconced comfortably in Kentucky, holding firmly to the ground they had gained. Since the Confederates were now in position to threaten Louisville, the Union-held capital of Kentucky, as well as the Ohio River, a vital transportation artery for the Yankees, the Northerners had no choice but to respond. Gen. Don Carlos Buell, who earlier in the year had triumphantly captured Nashville without a shot being fired, moved northward with his army into Kentucky to confront Bragg and Smith.

It was bad weather for battling. The region was gripped by the worst drought in years and unseasonable heat. The search for water prompted the Federals to march toward the town of Perryville, south of Frankfort and Lexington, where a small creek known as Doctor's Fork was rumored to have water.

The Confederates were already at Doctor's Fork, guarding the skimpy water supply. With the Yankees moving in on them, conflict was inevitable, and on the morning of October 8, 1862, Union forces under the command of Brig. Gen. Philip H. Sheridan launched an attack on the Confederate right. By midday Federal units under Gens. Alexander McCook, Thomas Crittenden, and Charles Gilbert had become involved, opposed by the forces of Buckner, Cleburne (who had recovered from the sound suffered at Richmond), Gen. Leonidas Polk, and Gen. William Hardee. The Confederates were reinforced at the ends of their line by Gens. James Cheatham and Bushrod Johnson as well as by cavalry under Gen. Joseph Wheeler. The battle stretched in a long, slightly arching front over several miles of what had once been green and beautiful Kentucky landscape, which was now brown due to the drought.

Bragg himself was in the town of Perryville, some two miles east of the battle. Unusual atmospheric conditions prevented him from hearing the roar of cannon and the rattle of musketry until late in the afternoon. When he finally received word of the action and rode forward, he found that the troops on both sides had battled to a near standstill. The only Confederate advance had come at the northern end of the battle, where McCook's forces had been pushed back a considerable distance. Darkness brought the fighting to a halt, and at first Bragg was determined to continue the defense of the Confederate position when the sun rose again the next morning.

By that time, however, he had reconsidered, having received reports that he was outnumbered by Buell's army. Bragg issued orders for the Confederates to withdraw, and they began pulling back south, toward Tennessee. Buell pursued, but only tentatively, allowing the Southern forces to complete their retreat. Bragg's soldiers pulled back all the way through eastern Tennessee, finally coming to a stop and setting up headquarters at the settlement of Tullahoma, a good distance southeast of the state capital, Nashville.

Buell's lackadaisical pursuit of Bragg immediately landed him in hot water with his superiors. He was subsequently replaced by Gen. William S. Rosecrans, who brought the Union army back to Nashville.

So, as winter approached, the invasion of Kentucky had come to nothing, and Bragg and his men prepared to hunker down and wait for spring before resuming operations. Things were happening elsewhere in the region, however, and telegraphic messages from Gen. John C. Pemberton, in command at Vicksburg, soon began to catch up to Bragg. Pemberton, fearing that Union General Grant was about to move on the city, appealed for whatever aid Bragg could give him. With the bitter taste of defeat still in his mouth, Bragg was not inclined to respond too rapidly to Pemberton's plea.

He had other problems on his plate, too, such as what to do with a certain brigadier general of cavalry who had been summoned to Tullahoma from western Tennessee. Although Bragg admired this general's instinctive grasp of strategy, the man had no formal military training, indeed little education of any sort. He had risen through the ranks after enlisting as a private when the war began, and while his successes in a series of cavalry raids had won him fame of a sort, Bragg simply did not believe he was suited to command a large force, so he had to find something else for the man to do.

The brigadier's name was Nathan Bedford Forrest.

RIDING ACROSS Mississippi and Tennessee was certainly quicker and easier than walking, Cory discovered, but spending long days on horseback had a few disadvantages, such as sore muscles and a rump that took a pounding from the saddle. He had become a fairly good rider during the first trip he and Pie and Colonel Thompson had made to Monroe, Louisiana, but that hadn't prepared him for the rigors of the journey he was now making with Lt. Hamilton Ryder.

Ryder wasn't a cavalryman, either, and for the first week he complained long and hard every night in camp. After a while, Cory learned not to pay any attention. He concentrated instead on studying the map Ryder had brought. Cory took a stub of pencil and traced in a likely route for them to follow. He didn't know exactly where General Bragg's headquarters were situated, only that they were southeast of Nashville.

He wasn't sure where the Yankees were. That meant he and Ryder had to be careful not to ride into the middle of an enemy force. The delays caused by that caution chafed at Cory, who wanted more than anything else to find Bragg, deliver Pemberton's letter, and then get back to Vicksburg—and Lucille—as rapidly as possible.

They followed the railroad to Jackson then angled northeast, cutting through the corner of Alabama and into the lower eastern part of Tennessee. Two weeks had passed since they had left Vicksburg, and both young men were finally becoming accustomed to long days in the saddle.

As they rode, they talked about their homes and their families, until Cory thought that he knew Ham Ryder pretty well.

For his part, he explained about his father's passion for Shake-speare—a passion that had extended to naming his oldest son for the Bard of Avon himself and the rest of his children for characters in the plays. He talked as well about the Brannon farm in Virginia's Piedmont region, near Culpeper. As he spoke, Cory heard a wistful longing in his voice. He had never been able to control his wanderlust, but at the same time, it would be good to pay a visit to the farm someday and see his family again.

Inevitably, the conversation turned to what Cory and Ryder planned to do when the war was over—assuming, of course that they survived.

"I thought I might go to New York," Ryder said. "Or maybe Chicago or San Francisco."

"Why?" asked Cory.

"To work, of course. I'm going to be a journalist. I'd take over the newspaper when my father gives it up, only my older brother Seth already has his eye on that. So I'll be a reporter instead. For *Harper's Weekly*, perhaps."

"That's a lofty goal, I suppose. I could understand if you wanted to go to those places just so that you could see them for yourself. I've felt like that a lot of times."

"Surely you have goals of your own," Ryder said. "Other than to marry Miss Farrell, I mean."

Cory smiled. "That's the most important one. As long as I can do that, I don't really care about anything else."

"Of course you do! There must be something you want to accomplish with your life."

"Well . . . ," Cory didn't have to think too long about it. "When I was younger I always wanted to go to Texas. I've been there now, but only to the eastern part. I have a good friend somewhere farther west. He was heading for a river called the Brazos. I'd like to visit him and see that country for myself. I've been told there's plenty of good land there for the settling."

Ryder laughed. "I haven't known you for long, Cory, but somehow I just can't see you as a farmer, even in Texas. If you'd wanted to do that, you could have just stayed in Virginia with the rest of your family."

"Maybe I could do something besides farm. There are other ways to make a living."

"By then you'll have a wife and half a dozen children. You'll have to do whatever you can to get by."

"The wife and children don't sound bad," Cory said with a grin. "We'll make it just fine."

Ryder sighed. "I envy you, Mr. Brannon. You're a man who knows what you want out of life."

That was true, thought Cory. And the main thing he wanted was to be married to Lucille.

The weather was cold but dry. Cory and Ham pushed deeper into Tennessee, and when they stopped for the night, they did so at a small farmhouse. The man who stepped out of the house to greet them did so with a shotgun tucked under his arm. He wore a black patch over his left eye, and that side of his face was covered with thick red scar tissue. Clearly, he had been in a bad fire, and Cory suspected it had come about as a result of battle. The farmer wore threadbare gray uniform trousers and a woolen shirt.

The man relaxed a little at the sight of Ryder's uniform. "Thought you boys might be Yankees come to call," he said. "Glad to see I was wrong. Step down off those horses."

"Good evening, sir," Ham said. "We were wondering if we might impose on your hospitality."

"You from Tennessee?" asked the farmer. "Sound like it."

"La Vergne," Ryder replied with a grin as he and Cory dismounted. "Up close to Nashville."

"I know where it is. Damn Yankees all over the place up there now. Sorry to be the one to tell you, son." The man's voice was thickened slightly by his injuries. He had to speak out of the right side of his mouth.

"That's all right, sir, I knew." Ryder stepped forward and extended his hand. "Lt. Hamilton Ryder. This is Cory Brannon."

The farmer shook hands with Ham and glanced at Cory. "You ain't a soldier?"

"He's on a special assignment," Ryder said before Cory could reply.

The man seemed impressed. "Well, I'm pleased to meet you, son." He shook hands with Cory. "Name's Jeremiah Mingus."

"How do you do, Mr. Mingus."

A laugh came from the farmer. He gestured at his face. "Not so good since last spring. Got this at Shiloh."

Cory nodded and said, "I was there."

Mingus clapped him on the shoulder. "All the more reason for you boys to come in and have some dinner with me. Ain't gonna be much, you understand, but y'all are welcome to share what there is. Welcome to bed down in my barn tonight, too. Liable to be pretty chilly."

Mingus had a pot of thin stew simmering over the low flames in the fireplace. He dished it up along with some hardtack that wasn't too bad when it was allowed to soak for a while in the stew. There were a few chunks of meat floating in the stew; Cory wasn't sure what sort of animal they came from, but he didn't ask.

"We're looking for General Bragg," Ryder said when they had finished the meal and pushed their chairs back from the rough-hewn table. Night had fallen, and the farm house's single room was lit only by the fire and a single candle on the table.

"I hear he's bivouacked up at Tullahoma," said Mingus. "Came runnin' back there after he let hisself get licked by the Yankees up in Kentucky."

Ryder leaned forward and frowned. "Our army has been up in Kentucky?"

"You ain't heard about it? Our boys did right smart for a spell, but then they run into the Yanks at a place called Perryville."

"We lost the battle there?" asked Cory.

Mingus shrugged. "Heard tell it was pretty much a stand-off, but that didn't stop Bragg from tuckin' his tail 'twixt his legs and runnin' back down here to Tennessee."

Cory saw Ryder's mouth tighten in disapproval. The lieutenant didn't like to hear anyone talking like that about one of his superior officers. Yet, as a former soldier who still bore the marks of his service and always would, Jeremiah Mingus had earned the right to complain.

"I'm sure General Bragg did what he thought best," Ham said.

"Maybe so, but if Forrest had been there, we wouldn't've turned tail, I'll bet you."

"Bedford Forrest?" The question came from Cory.

"That's right," Mingus said with a nod. "He's been rangin' all over the state, burnin' bridges and tearin' up railroad tracks and gen'rally makin' life purely miserable for those blue bellies. Leastways, he was until Bragg called him in to headquarters. You must'a heard of Forrest, son."

"I know him," said Cory. "I met him at Fort Donelson, before it fell."

"Well, then, you know what sort o' fightin' fool he is. No sir, if Forrest had been in charge, we'd still be up yonder in Kentucky, confoundin' those Yankees."

Cory suspected the farmer was right. More than once, he had heard Forrest espouse his simple but effective theory of warfare: "War means fightin', and fightin' means killin'." A force under the command of Bedford Forrest was nearly always on the attack, retreating only when absolutely necessary.

It would be good to see Forrest again, thought Cory, if the general was still at headquarters when he and Ryder got there. The main thing, though, was just to reach Bragg and deliver Pemberton's letter. Cory asked, "How far is it to Tullahoma?"

"Thirty-five, forty miles, maybe. I ain't so good with distances. You might could make it tomorrow if you push your horses pretty hard."

The mounts had already been pushed hard, but maybe they could dredge up the strength and stamina for one more day's ride. Cory's heart beat a little faster when he considered the possibility that in less than forty-eight hours, he might well be on his way back to Vicksburg.

And Lucille.

THE CONFEDERATE headquarters camp at Tullahoma was smaller than Cory had expected. He and Ryder entered it not long before nightfall on the day after their overnight sojourn with Jeremiah Mingus. Braxton Bragg's headquarters were in a commandeered house on the edge of the settlement. The sentries on duty there didn't mind admitting Lieutenant Ryder, especially after he told them that he had come all the way from Vicksburg on an urgent mission and had to see the general, but they balked at allowing Cory inside.

"He's a civilian," one of the troopers said. "What if he's a spy o' some sort, come here to assassinate General Bragg?"

Cory sighed in frustration. "I'm not a spy," he said. "How many times do I have to explain that?"

"Then what're you doin' here?" the soldier wanted to know.

"I have—" Cory had started to say that he had a message for the general from the commanding general at Vicksburg, but then he recalled Pemberton's insistence that everything about this mission remain a secret. "I have to see him," Cory concluded, knowing even as he spoke that his limp statement wasn't going to do any good. The hardheaded sentry wasn't to be swayed.

The soldier suddenly snapped to attention as a footstep sounded behind Cory and Ryder. Cory's companion glanced back at whoever had come up behind them then abruptly stiffened, too, just as the guard had done. Worriedly, Cory turned his head to look, and as he did so, a gauntleted hand came down on his shoulder.

"As I live and breathe," said Brig. Gen. Nathan Bedford Forrest, "I'll be damned if it's not Cory Brannon."

Ryder and the sentry both gave the general crisp salutes, which Forrest returned rather casually. He had changed very little since Cory had seen him last, a few weeks after the battle at Shiloh. The lean, almost hawkish face, the high forehead, the longish dark hair and neatly trimmed beard, and most of all the keen and intelligent eyes . . . all those things were the same. The insignia on his hat and uniform were different, however. Forrest had been a colonel the last time Cory had seen him, and now he was a general.

Cory didn't salute, but he turned around and came to a pose that closely resembled attention. "General, sir," he said. "It's good to see you again."

Forrest took his hand and pumped it enthusiastically. "What in the world are you still doing here? Did you ever find that gal of yours?"

"Yes sir, I did. She's in Vicksburg."

Forrest's eyebrows arched. "Then I'm doubly surprised to find you here."

No more so than he himself was, thought Cory. "I'm looking for General Bragg, sir," he said.

Forrest grunted. "Then you've come to the right place. Come along with me."

"Sir, this man is a civilian," the sentry said tentatively.

Forrest regarded the soldier with a stony stare. "So? He's well known to me. I'll vouch for him."

The sentry moved aside, quailing a little under the intensity of Forrest's gaze. "Of course, sir," he muttered as he cast his own eyes toward the ground.

Forrest inclined his head toward Ryder and said to Cory, "This young fellow a friend of yours?"

"Lt. Hamilton Ryder, sir," Ryder said briskly. "At your service, sir."

"Yes, he's with me," said Cory.

Forrest crooked a finger as he started into the house. "Then you come along, too, Lieutenant."

They walked through a small foyer, and Forrest muttered under his breath, "Damned rigmarole. I suppose it's necessary, though, if there's to be any sort of military discipline." He paused at the entrance to what had been a parlor before the house had been commandeered. "The general and I don't see eye to eye on most things," Forrest added, quietly enough so that he wouldn't be overheard. "If your business here is with him, perhaps it wouldn't be a good idea after all for you to be seen with me."

Cory had come too far to turn back now. All he needed was a moment to turn over the letter to General Bragg, and then the whole matter was out of his hands.

"That's all right, General. I'll take my chances."

Forrest grinned quickly. "That's always been my policy, too. Come along."

They entered the parlor and found that several desks had been moved into the room. On the far side, near the fireplace, was a table, and at the table sat a man with deep-set eyes, a prominent nose, and a dark, gray-shot beard. Cory knew immediately that he was Braxton Bragg.

The subordinate officers working at the desks stood up and saluted as Forrest came into the room. Forrest sketched a return salute that was more of a wave than anything else, then took his gauntlets off and strode across the room toward Bragg.

Bragg was a full general while Forrest was only a brigadier, so the cavalryman came to attention and gave Bragg a proper salute. Behind him, Ryder did the same, while Cory stood to one side, trying to look properly respectful even if he didn't have to follow military protocol.

"Good evening, General Forrest," Bragg said when he had returned the salute. "What can I do for you?"

"I came to speak to you concerning the weapons that have been supplied to the men of my brigade, General—or rather the weapons that haven't been supplied."

Bragg's expression began to tighten.

"But," Forrest went on, "I'll defer for the moment to my young friend here, who apparently has a pressing need to see you. This is Mr. Cory Brannon, a former comrade in arms, and his companion, Lieutenant Ryder."

Bragg's dark, hooded eyes cut over toward Cory. "Comrade in arms, eh? You're not in uniform now."

"Nor was he when he fought at Fort Donelson or Shiloh," put in Forrest smoothly. "But that didn't stop him from serving with distinction. Fact is, when I charged those Yankees at Fallen Timbers, if Cory hadn't lent a hand I might not have gotten out of there alive."

Cory found himself a little embarrassed at the praise. He was glad that Bragg got right down to business by asking, "Well, what is it, son?"

"I have a message for you, sir." Cory reached under his coat and stepped forward. He took out the envelope and held it toward Bragg.

The general made no move to take the envelope. In fact, he looked at it as if Cory were offering him a dead rat. "Who's it from?" he asked.

"I really can't say, sir. All I know is that it's important."

"Blast it!" Bragg leaned forward and snatched the envelope out of Cory's fingers. "I don't like this sort of skulkery." He tore open the seal, slid out Pemberton's letter, and unfolded it. His eyes quickly scanned the writing. He gave a surprised grunt.

"With the general's permission . . . that's all I was supposed to do . . ." Cory began to edge away from the table. His mission was completed now.

"Stand right there!" snapped Bragg. He stuffed the letter back in the envelope and tossed it aside. "I'll have to think about this. In the meantime, I don't want you to leave this camp, Mr. Brannon."

Cory felt his heart sinking. He'd wanted to spend the night here then start back to Vicksburg first thing in the morning. It was almost December now, and he had a wedding to attend.

Bragg looked quizzically at Ryder. "And what's your part in all this, Lieutenant?"

"Only to see that Mr. Brannon reached you safely, General."

"I see. Well, you've both carried out your orders—for now. But keep yourselves available, understand?"

"Yes sir," said Ryder. Cory just nodded, trying not to look too disappointed.

"Dismissed," Bragg said curtly to the two young men. Then, to Forrest, he went on, "Pull up a chair, General, and we'll talk about those weapons."

Ryder caught Cory's eye and angled his head toward the door. They went out, walking through the foyer and onto the front porch.

When they were back on the road where they had left their horses, Cory said miserably, "What do we do now? I never dreamed we'd have to stay here."

Ryder shrugged. "Orders are orders. In the absence of any to the contrary from a superior officer, I have to do what General Bragg tells me to do. But you don't."

"You heard him. He said for me not to leave the camp."

"It's true that martial law has been declared all across the Confederacy and civilians do have to submit to military authority. But I don't think anybody would stop you if you were to just ride away."

Cory thought about it, thought long and hard. Then he shook his head. "Maybe the general won't take too long making up his mind to do . . . whatever it is he's going to do. There might be some message he wants me to carry back to Vicksburg. I can wait a while, I suppose." He smiled. "Besides, I wouldn't mind getting to talk to General Forrest again. Catch up on old times, I suppose you could say."

Ryder looked at him for a moment, then grunted and shook his head. "You are the damnedest sort of civilian I've ever met, Mr. Brannon," he declared. "You wind up in the middle of battles, you're at the beck and call of generals, and you act like you're old friends with one of the most famous cavalry officers in the entire Confederacy. How do you manage to do all that?"

"Luck?" Cory suggested with a grin.

But he didn't say if that luck was good or bad. In truth, he really didn't know.

Chapter Ten

Chapter 160

GENERAL BRAGG HADN'T TOLD Cory and Lieutenant Ryder where to wait or what to do while they were waiting, only not to leave the camp. They led their horses to a stable that had been taken over by the army and turned the mounts over to hostlers who would see to graining and watering the animals. Then the two young men strolled down the street to an officers' mess tent, following the smell of coffee.

The food wasn't too appetizing—hardtack, fatback, and greens—and the coffee was mostly roasted grain that tasted burned, but it had been a long day for Cory and Ham and they ate hungrily. The mess sergeant hadn't wanted to feed Cory at first, until Ryder had explained that Cory was there on the express orders of General Bragg himself.

As they were finishing the meal, General Forrest came into the tent. Cory spotted him right away. Forrest carried himself with an air of command that just naturally made all eyes turn toward him. He glanced around the tent until he found Cory and his companion, then strode toward them.

"Figured I'd find you boys in here," he said as he came up to the table where they were sitting. "Young men typically have prodigious appetites. I know I always did. Never got enough to eat. 'Course, that could've had something to do with the fact that my family was mighty poor." Forrest grinned. "Come on along with me, both of you."

Cory and Ryder got to their feet. "Where are we going, sir?" asked Cory.

"I'm quartered in a house not far from here. Since you've already eaten, I won't offer you supper. But we might find a cup of better coffee or tea to warm a cold night."

Ryder gave Cory a worried glance, and Cory knew the lieutenant was concerned about the propriety of socializing with a general. Cory tried to look confident that everything would be all right. He wasn't sure if he brought it off or not.

The small house where Forrest was living was nearby and took only a few minutes for the three of them to reach. The chilly day had turned into a cold night. A gusty wind whipped the silk-lined cloak that Forrest wore.

The house was warm, though, and an elderly woman met them just inside the door to take their hats and coats. Forrest smiled at her and said, "Thank you, Mrs. Carson." To Cory and Ryder, he added, "This is Mrs. Carson's house, which she has graciously opened to us."

Cory could tell that the woman was proud to have such a famous officer quartered at her house. Holding the hats and coats, she said, "I'll just put these away, and then I'll bring you and your guests some tea, General."

"That would be fine, Mrs. Carson, just fine."

"Will the young gentlemen be dining with us?"

"No, ma'am," Cory said quickly. "The lieutenant and I have already eaten." Supplies might not be as sparse here as they were getting to be in Vicksburg, but he was sure the old woman didn't have an abundance of food in the house.

"All right . . . but what about a piece of pie afterward? It's already baked."

Cory and Ryder both grinned. They couldn't help it. Ryder said, "Thank you, ma'am. I don't know about my friend here, but I'd enjoy that very much."

"Absolutely," Cory said.

"Come along into the parlor, gentlemen," said Forrest. He led the way into the cozy little room as Mrs. Carson bustled off. The general waved Cory and Ryder into chairs, then sat down himself on a divan near the fireplace. "Lieutenant," he said sternly to Ryder, "what is said in this room remains in the room, do you understand?"

"Yes sir," Ryder replied, but he was clearly puzzled by Forrest's meaning, as was Cory.

The next moment, they both understood, as Forrest continued in a quiet voice, "I hope your business with General Bragg isn't too important, Mr. Brannon, because the man is a fool. An absolute ass."

Ryder's eyes widened in shock to hear a field-grade officer speak so bluntly about another field-grade officer. Cory was less surprised, having known Forrest before. He was well aware of the cavalryman's tendency to speak his mind.

Cory leaned forward in his chair. Since his fate, to a certain extent, was tied up in what Bragg might decide to do, he wanted to know as much as he could about the man. "Why do you say that, General?"

Forrest snorted in disgust. "He can't make up his mind."

Cory didn't like the sound of that. Fast, decisive action by Bragg was what would get him back to Vicksburg sooner rather than later.

"I was with him in Kentucky during the early stages of the invasion," Forrest continued. "My men were performing quite admirably at Munfordville, accomplishing every task given to them—which mainly had to do with killin' Yankees, of course. But then he sent me back down here. He said I was to recruit more men and train 'em. I did that, while Bragg was muddling around up yonder and then finally running for home. And when he got back, he relieved me again." Forrest shook his head. "He even tried to send me a new chief of artillery when I've got a perfectly good officer doing that job. I wouldn't stand for it, of course. Lieutenant Morton stayed on, although not in command of anything."

"So what are you doing now, sir?" asked Cory.

"Waiting for Bragg to make up his blessed mind. And begging him for more rifles for my men. Hell, I'd almost settle for new flints for the rifles they already have. Some of 'em are useless for anything except bustin' Yankee heads open."

Forrest stretched out his long legs and crossed them at the ankles. He was more relaxed now, more informal, the way Cory had often seen him at Fort Donelson. Strictly speaking, Forrest wasn't much of a military man—but he was one hell of a soldier, in Cory's opinion.

Ryder looked confused. He didn't know what to make of this conversation.

Mrs. Carson came in with a teapot and cups on a silver tray. She served the tea then announced, "Dinner will be ready shortly, General."

"Thank you, madam." Forrest gave her another smile, but when Mrs. Carson had left the room, his expression grew serious again. He turned to Cory and said, "What is your business with Bragg? You don't have to answer that, mind. I'd just like to give you a hand if I can."

Cory hesitated, remembering what he had been told by General Pemberton about the need for absolute secrecy. However, there was no one in the Confederate army Cory trusted more than Bedford Forrest. He said, "It stays in this room?"

Forrest nodded.

Cory looked over at Ryder. "You won't repeat any of this?"

"I've already had to pretend I wasn't hearing several things tonight," Ryder confirmed with a disapproving glance at Forrest that made the general chuckle. "I suppose I can pretend a little while longer."

"All right." Cory turned his attention back to Forrest. "The letter I gave General Bragg was a personal plea for help from General Pemberton in Vicksburg. General Pemberton has been sending wires to Bragg asking for assistance, but Bragg keeps ignoring them."

"Of course he does," said Forrest. "He's too busy dithering around and making life difficult for officers who actually want to accomplish something."

Cory didn't have to ask who Forrest had in mind with that comment. He went on, "General Pemberton didn't want to appear to be begging for help, so he sent a letter through unofficial channels—"

"With you."

"That's right. That way there won't be any record of it."

Forrest shook his head. "Foolish vanity on General Pemberton's part. And foolish intransigence on Bragg's. What is the situation in Vicksburg?"

Cory had been away from the city for more than two weeks, so he didn't know for certain what was going on there now. He quickly explained, though, about the growing shortages of supplies and how they had tried to deal with the problem by setting up the supply line from Texas.

Forrest immediately viewed the situation from a cavalryman's perspective. "One brigade of Yankee cavalry could put a stop to that in a hurry, just by tearing up some tracks and burning a few bridges." He laughed. "I've some small experience in such matters."

Cory clasped his hands together between his knees. "If Grant launches an overland advance from the north while at the same time the Yankee gunboats increase their bombardment of the city, Vicksburg will be in a bad position. And that's what the reports indicate is about to happen." It might even be happening already, he thought. He had no way of knowing.

"There's an old saying about being between a rock and a hard place," mused Forrest. "That's where Vicksburg's going to find itself."

Lieutenant Ryder spoke up. "Begging the general's pardon, but if Grant conducts an operation like that, then his supply lines will be stretched out."

"Indeed they will," Forrest said with an approving nod.

"And if someone were to disrupt Grant's supply lines, then he couldn't carry out an invasion."

"Are you in the cavalry, son?"

"No sir. I'm one of General Pemberton's adjutants."

"Well, you think like a cavalryman, so you may be wasting your talents." Forrest grimaced briefly. "My apologies if I spoke too harshly of the general earlier. I don't really know the man."

"No offense taken, sir." Ryder paused, then added, "When you're in trouble, I don't really see anything wrong with yelling for help as loud as you can."

That practical attitude surprised Cory a little. Maybe Ryder wasn't as by-the-book as he seemed.

"My headquarters are at Columbia right now," Forrest said. "That's over west of here. I want to get back there tomorrow, after I've spoken to Bragg again about those rifles, and have a look at my maps and talk to my scouts. I think there are some things we can do to put a bur under Grant's saddle."

Cory felt his spirits lift. If Vicksburg was in trouble, there was no better man to get the city out of it than Bedford Forrest.

"In the meantime . . . are you sure you don't want something else to eat besides that pie?"

Cory thought of Pie Jones, long gone to Texas. He would have felt better if Pie was with him right now—but that was impossible. Cory looked at Ryder, who shrugged.

"I suppose we could eat a little, if there's plenty," Cory said.

Forrest grinned. "Growing lads. Their appetites never disappoint." He rose to his feet. "Come along. I'll tell Mrs. Carson to set two more places in the dining room."

THERE WAS a spare room in Mrs. Carson's house, and that was where Cory and Ryder spent the night. That came as no surprise to Cory, who had expected Forrest to offer the hospitality of his temporary quarters.

The next morning, Forrest went to speak with Bragg one more time while Cory and Ham took a look around the camp. They were checking on their horses when Forrest found them.

"Saddle up, boys," Forrest said cheerfully. "You're coming to Columbia with me."

Cory's jaw dropped. "But . . . but I can't!" he protested. "I have to get back to Vicksburg."

"Not just yet," said Forrest. "I want to keep you with me for a while, and General Bragg agrees."

"Why?" Ryder asked coolly.

"Why did the general agree? Or why do I want you boys in my command?"

"Both."

"You're a couple of bones that the general has decided to toss to me," explained Forrest, "since he's not going to give me the guns or flints or firing caps that I've asked for. And I want you with me because I'm convinced we're going to receive orders to perform a few raids in Grant's rear, just as the three of us speculated last night."

Cory shook his head. "I'm not in the cavalry. I'm not even in the army."

"You're mighty good at killin' Yankees, though. And as for you, Lieutenant Ryder, I recall your mentioning last night while we were talking that you had aspirations to be a newspaper reporter someday."

Ryder looked as confused as Cory felt. What did Ryder's journalistic ambitions have to do with anything?

"That's right, sir."

"Good. I need an aide-de-camp with the ability to write good reports for me. Clear, well-written reports, I should say. I wouldn't expect a man to stray from the truth just to make me and my command look better."

Cory wasn't sure of that. He knew what a proud man Forrest was. He was sure the general wanted the official reports to reflect him in as favorable a light as possible.

"But I'm attached to General Pemberton's command, sir," Ryder pointed out.

Forrest shook his head. "Not any longer. General Bragg will put through a transfer order for you, making you part of my brigade. The Old Brigade, we call it, though it's not so old at all. I just started to raise it a few weeks ago."

"But I have to get back to Vicksburg," Cory said stubbornly.

"You're on the books as a civilian scout," Forrest told him. "And since you've been paid in advance, you have no choice but to serve out your obligation."

"Paid?" repeated Cory incredulously. "I haven't been paid anything, general!"

Forrest reached in his pocket, took out a coin, grabbed Cory's hand, and slapped the coin into his palm. "There," he said. "You're now a civilian employee of the Army of the Confederate States of America."

Cory wanted to argue that this wasn't fair, that he couldn't possibly go on any sort of cavalry raid with Forrest. He had a fiancée waiting for him back in Vicksburg and a wedding in less than a month.

At the same time, he felt somewhat honored that Forrest thought so highly of him as to practically force him to come along. Forrest wouldn't have done that if he didn't believe that Cory would be a valuable addition to his brigade.

"How long will it take?" he asked.

Forrest shrugged. "No tellin'. We won't really know until we get to western Tennessee. And I ain't leaving Columbia until I've tried again to get more rifles out of Bragg."

"I'd have time, then, to write a letter to Lucille."

"You'll have time to write her half a dozen letters, more'n likely before we move."

Cory was aware that Ryder was looking at him strangely. He didn't return the lieutenant's puzzled gaze. Instead he nodded to Forrest. "I'll go with you, but I have to get back to Vicksburg by Christmas Eve."

"I can't make any such promise, Mr. Brannon," Forrest said sternly.

"I'm just telling you," said Cory. "When the time comes, I'm leaving, pay or no pay, no matter how I'm being carried on the muster books."

"You'd desert just to get back to that gal?" Forrest frowned.

Cory ignored the dark look and said, "Yes sir, I sure would."

Suddenly, Forrest threw back his head and laughed. "Damn, it must really be love! Come on, you two, saddle up those horses. We've got to be ridin'."

COLUMBIA WAS about fifty miles northwest of Tullahoma, which put it almost due south of Nashville. Only a small detail of cavalry had come to Bragg's headquarters with Forrest, so the group—now including Cory and Lieutenant Ryder—was able to set a fast pace back to their camp. Still, Forrest didn't push them so hard that they covered the ground in one day. They spent one night on the road, camping on the edge of a burned field. Cory wondered if the fire that had scorched the field had been the result of natural causes, or if it had been started by an exploding artillery shell.

The cavalrymen built several fires over which they boiled coffee and warmed food. Cory and Ryder found themselves seated next to one of the small blazes on a fallen log, holding their hands out toward the flames to ease the chills that had set in during a day of riding.

"Why did you let him do it?" Ryder asked abruptly, his voice quiet so that only Cory could hear it.

"Do what?"

"Browbeat you into coming along with him. He had no right to do it, and with Miss Farrell waiting for you in Vicksburg."

"You have friends in Vicksburg, surely."

Ryder gave a short, humorless laugh and added a wink. "None like Miss Farrell."

Cory inclined his head in acknowledgment of the other's point, then said, "It's hard to say no to General Forrest. It was difficult enough when he was a colonel, and it certainly hasn't gotten any easier."

For a moment, Ryder didn't say anything, then, "And it'll be exciting, won't it?"

Cory looked sharply at him. "What do you mean by that?"

"Just that you have a hard time saying no to anything that sounds the least bit adventurous, don't you? That's why you get into these things. Luck has nothing to do with it. Another man might take the more sensible course, but not Cory Brannon."

Cory felt a flush of anger welling up inside him. "What the hell are you talking about?" he demanded. "You don't have any right to talk to me like that, Ham! You've only known me for a couple of weeks."

Ryder shrugged. "Maybe so, but I know what I see."

"Well, you see it wrong," Cory said with a frown. "I'm just trying to do the best I can for the Confederacy, that's all."

"A noble goal," said Ryder dryly. "And if you can smell powder smoke and hear the roar of battle in the process, all the better for you."

"You're crazy," Cory muttered. "I just want to get this over with and get back to Lucille." He turned on the log so that he was no longer looking at Ryder, ending the conversation.

The lieutenant didn't press the issue, but later that night, as Cory was rolled up in his blankets and trying to get to sleep, Ryder's words came back to him. And deep down, like it or not, Cory had to admit to himself that his insightful friend might be on to something.

Back during the summer, when Colonel Thompson had proposed setting up the supply line to Texas and asked for Cory's help, Cory had pondered the quickness with which he had accepted. It was easy enough to rationalize his decisions; he'd had plenty of practice ever since he had ridden away from the Brannon farm in search of . . . something. He hadn't known then what it was, and he still didn't. He had thought that he'd found what he was looking for in Lucille, and in many ways, that was true. She filled a hole inside him, completed him in a way that no one else had ever been able to do.

Yet when Forrest had told him he was coming along on the cavalry raid, Cory had put up only a token resistance before agreeing. Was he really so hungry for adventure that he would answer any call so long as it carried with it the potential for action?

He had left Lucille twice, first to go to Texas with the colonel and then to carry out the mission for General Pemberton. Now he was prolonging his absence even more. Perhaps it wasn't too late to talk to Forrest and get out of this.

But what harm would it do to at least visit the general's camp at Columbia? If he knew what Forrest was planning, he could take a potentially valuable report back to Pemberton.

That thought eased Cory's mind enough for him to fall asleep finally. He didn't dwell on the possibility that such a report to Pemberton might be yet another rationalization . . .

FORREST'S COLUMBIA camp came as something of a surprise to Cory. It numbered some thirty-five hundred men covering a large open field. Most of the brigade had no tents, but the ones who didn't had fashioned rough lean-tos out of branches. Smoke rose from dozens of cooking fires as the general and his companions rode in late the following afternoon.

"We have three regiments here," Forrest explained to Cory and Ryder. "You'll need to know this, Lieutenant, since you'll be expected to keep up with them."

"Yes sir," Ham acknowledged.

Forrest pointed to an area of the camp. "That's the Fourth Tennessee Cavalry under Col. James W. Starnes. Over there, the Eighth Tennessee under Col. George Dibrell; my brother Jeffrey serves with them. And there, the Ninth Tennessee, Col. J. B. Biffle's lads. We also have the men left from Colonel Russell's Fourth Alabama Cavalry and a fine battery of seven guns under Captain Freeman, my chief of artillery—no matter what Generals Bragg or Wheeler may say about replacing him."

Several officers emerged from one of the tents to greet Forrest as the general brought his mount to a halt and swung down from the saddle. Cory and Ham did likewise, while behind them the other members of the party scattered to their respective regiments to care for their horses and get something to drink.

Forrest introduced the two newcomers to the members of his staff: Maj. John P. Strange, the brigade adjutant; Lt. Charles Anderson, Strange's assistant; Maj. C. S. Severson, the quartermaster; Capt. Gilbert Rambaut, the chief commissary officer; the chief surgeon, Maj. J. B. Cowan; and a young man still in his teens, Lt. William M. Forrest, introduced by his proud father as one of his aides. "Lieutenant Ryder will be working with you, Willie," the general told the boy. "The two of you will be responsible for all staff reports."

"Yes sir, General," Willie said with a nod. Cory thought the boy might resent having someone else brought in to take over some of his responsibilities, but the smile of welcome and the handshake Willie gave Ryder were unmistakably genuine.

"Mr. Brannon here will be functioning as a civilian scout," Forrest went on. "Some of you may remember him from Fort Donelson and Shiloh."

Cory hadn't met any of Forrest's staff at those places, but the officers greeted him pleasantly anyway.

"Any luck with General Bragg, sir?" asked Major Strange.

"None to speak of," Forrest replied curtly. "We may have to take things into our own hands, gentlemen. The enemy possesses firearms, after all."

Cory had to think for a second to understand what Forrest meant, then he realized the general was talking about foraging for rifles and flints and firing caps. Forrest and his men had been functioning largely as irregulars ever since their daring escape from Fort Donelson, so they were experts at living off the land and taking what they needed from their enemies. They would continue to do so if that was the only option available to them.

"Come along inside," Forrest said to the small group of officers, including Cory and Ryder among them. "I want to take a look at the maps."

A lamp was lit inside the tent, casting its light over several maps spread out on a folding table. Forrest called Cory up beside him and pointed out their location, putting it in relation to Bragg's headquarters at Tullahoma and the Federal forces that were now massed in Nashville under Rosecrans.

"There's Murfreesboro," Forrest said with a grin as he pointed to another dot on the map. "We whipped the Yankees pretty good there a while back. Chased them nearly all the way to Nashville, in fact. That was a good fight. They didn't expect as many of us to show up where we did." He looked across the table at Cory. "You know the secret to winning any battle, don't you, Mr. Brannon?"

"What's that, sir?"

"Get wherever you're goin' fustest with the mostest," said Forrest with a grin, drawling out the words in an exaggerated accent. "That'll win most battles."

"Yes sir," Cory agreed.

Forrest leaned forward over the maps. "Now, let's see if we can figure out what we're going to have to do to make life miserable for Grant . . ."

Chapter Eleven

LIEUTENANT RYDER FIT RIGHT in as a member of General Forrest's staff, but Cory wasn't so fortunate. As the days passed and the Old Brigade remained encamped at Columbia, Cory's impatience grew. He wanted to be back with Lucille, and it was beginning to look as if Forrest was never going to do anything other than squabble with General Bragg about supplies. A furious Forrest had found out that Bragg had sent a letter to one of his superiors in the War Department in Richmond boasting of an excess of munitions, but still Bragg refused Forrest's request for more rifles and flints and firing caps for the weapons he did have. The telegraph messages he received from Bragg often sent Forrest into fits of anger.

Gen. Nathan Bedford Forrest in the grip of rage was a sight to behold, but also one to avoid if at all possible. When angered, Forrest's face flushed redly and his eyes bulged and widened until it seemed they were about to pop out of his head. He ground his teeth together and his lips drew back in a snarl of savage fury. His men knew to step lightly around him when he was in such a mood, because sometimes his anger blinded him to the point that he might strike out at someone without even knowing who they were.

Such displays were something of an aberration, however. Most of the time Forrest was friendly, even courtly, every bit the Southern gentleman. He dressed well, in clean uniforms that were enlivened by brightly colored sashes and cloaks. As a mark of his rank, a saber hung at his side in a gleaming brass scabbard, even though he had little or no idea how to properly use such a weapon. He could hack blindly back and forth with it, but that was about all. He was much more dangerous with the pair of Colt revolvers that were holstered at his hips.

The weather was less than pleasant. A raw, cold wind blew most of the time, and at night the temperature plunged below freezing. Seeing as it was now December, that was not at all unusual or unexpected, but it made for harsh conditions. The flimsy wooden lean-tos that sheltered most of the Old Brigade, including Cory and Ryder, did little to block the wind, although they did stop the dry, powdery sleet that fell from time to time.

Cory was sitting in his lean-to one afternoon, huddled next to a tiny fire, when the sound of boots crunching on the frozen ground made him look up. He saw Ryder coming toward him. The lieutenant's hat was pulled down tightly, and his shoulders were hunched against the cold.

"The general wants to see you," Ryder said as he came up to the lean-to.

Cory's muscles had stiffened from the chill. He winced as he got to his feet and straightened. He hated cold weather worse than anything and had ever since he had nearly frozen to death in New Madrid the previous winter.

"What does he want?" Cory asked as he started walking toward Forrest's tent with Ryder.

"I don't know," Ham replied with a shrug. "He didn't tell me. But I know he just got another wire from General Bragg."

Cory felt his spirits rise. Maybe they were on the verge of actually doing something. The nearly two weeks of inactivity had been hell on his nerves. If he'd left Tullahoma for Vicksburg, he would be almost back there by now, he told himself. Almost back with Lucille.

It was warmer inside Forrest's tent, of course. Cory was grateful for the warmth as he stepped through the entrance flap behind Ryder. He found Forrest standing at the table, which was surrounded by the other members of the general's staff.

"Come in, Cory," Forrest greeted him. "We've been waiting for you."

"Sorry, sir. I came as soon as Lieutenant Ryder told me you wanted to see me."

Forrest waved off the apology as Cory took his place by the table. "No harm done." He looked around at the group. "Now that we're all here, I want you to know that I have received orders from General Bragg. We are to break camp immediately and proceed with all due speed to western Tennessee, where our mission will be to operate in the rear of the Federal invasion force that General Grant is leading south toward Vicksburg."

There was nothing in Forrest's statement that Cory hadn't already known or guessed, but still, hearing it put into words quickened his pulse a little. General Bragg had made the right decision—but he should have made it a couple of weeks earlier, thought Cory.

"What about our request for more weapons and firing caps?" asked Major Severson, the quartermaster.

Forrest's expression, eager a second earlier, now turned bleak. "General Bragg has refused it. We are to proceed with the means at hand, with a view toward bettering our situation ourselves, should the opportunity arise."

One of the officers muttered a bitter curse; Cory wasn't sure which one. But it could have been any of them, because they all felt the same way. Their mission might well prove to be the salvation of Vicksburg, but all the same, Bragg's orders bordered on throwing them to the wolves.

Cory looked down at the map. "How are we going to get across the Tennessee River?" he asked. He didn't know if it was his place to speak up or not, but the question worried him.

"That will be a problem," admitted Forrest. "The river is quite wide, and our scouts report that there are chunks of ice floating in it that would pose a danger to any sort of boat or raft. Also, the Yankee gunboats are still patrolling the area. But get across we must, because we can't strike at the Yankees otherwise. And I intend to hit them, gentlemen. I intend to hit them very hard."

Forrest didn't know any other way to proceed, thought Cory. The general was always on the attack.

"That's all for now," Forrest went on after a moment. "Begin preparations to break camp and get the men moving." The staff officers nodded and turned to leave the tent. Forrest added, "Remain behind a bit, Mr. Brannon. I need to speak with you."

Cory tensed. If Forrest wanted to speak with him alone, it couldn't be about anything very good. But Cory nodded anyway. "Of course, sir."

Ryder hesitated before going out, but Cory gave him a nod, indicating that it would be all right, whatever Forrest had in mind. Ryder left the tent with the other officers. The general hooked a three-legged stool with the toe of his boot and drew it toward him.

"Get another stool and sit down." Forrest grinned and said, "Now you're finally going to earn your pay as a civilian scout." There wasn't a hint of irony in the general's voice.

"What is it you want me to do, sir?"

The grin fell away from Forrest's mouth. With a grimace, he said, "Something has to be done about those flints and firing caps, Mr. Brannon. I've given up on getting any more rifles out of Bragg, but without the flints and the caps, many of the weapons we already have are useless! That's why you have to go to Memphis."

Cory's eyes widened. If Forrest had said that he was sending him to the moon, Cory couldn't have been more shocked. "Memphis?" he repeated weakly.

Forrest nodded. "That's where the Yankees have their head-quarters for all of western Tennessee. There's a supply depot there with plenty of flints and firing caps."

"My God!" Cory couldn't stop the exclamation from escaping his mouth. "You want me to go to Memphis and steal them from the Yankees?"

"The . . . requisitioning of certain supplies is already arranged. All you'll have to do is pick up the shipment and bring it back to us. We'll rendezvous at the Tennessee River. It'll take us about a week to get there from here and probably a day or two to get across. So you'll have to move fast. Once we're on the other side of the river, we'll be in enemy territory, and we'll need those flints and caps by then."

Cory's head was spinning. Forrest was entrusting him with a job on which the success of the entire mission might well hinge. "You want me to go alone?" he asked hollowly.

"You can take Lieutenant Ryder with you, I suppose. I know you lads are friends. But he'll have to wear civilian clothes. Can't very well waltz into Memphis wearing a Confederate uniform, now can he?"

"He won't like being a spy," Cory said.

"He's a good soldier. He'll follow orders."

Cory nodded. He supposed Forrest was right. The general was right, too, about the importance of moving quickly.

"I'll do it," he said. "But when Ham and I get back to the Tennessee and meet you there with the flints and caps, I'm going home to Vicksburg while I can still get there. If Grant isn't stopped, the city may be surrounded."

Forrest regarded him narrowly for a moment, then nodded. "Fair enough. If you're successful with this mission to Memphis, you'll have done your share to ensure our triumph, and Grant *will* be stopped."

Cory drew a deep breath. "I'll find Lieutenant Ryder and tell him."

"This won't be easy, you know," said Forrest. "You'll have to move fast through country that's crawling with Yankees. I'll tell you who to contact when you get to Memphis, but the Yankees will be on the lookout for spies. Getting back may be even harder than getting there."

"I know," Cory said as he put his hands on his knees and pushed himself to his feet. "But I have a reason for getting there and back as fast as I can."

"The lovely Miss Farrell," Forrest said with a grin.

"I intend to marry her as planned on Christmas Eve in Vicksburg," Cory said.

Then he went to find Ryder and tell the lieutenant that he'd just been volunteered for duty behind enemy lines.

～

JUST AS Cory expected, Ham Ryder wasn't pleased.

"I won't go without my uniform," he insisted.

"Then you won't go, period," Cory said. He rubbed his hands together for warmth. "I'll do the job myself." He started to turn away and leave Ryder beside the rope corral where he had found him.

Ryder reached out and put a hand on his shoulder. "Wait a minute," he said. "You really mean to ride all the way to Memphis, steal a bunch of percussion caps, and get back to the river by the time Forrest and the rest get there?"

"Someone has to. And I won't actually be stealing the caps. Someone else is going to be doing that, some agent we already have in Memphis, I assume. I'm just going to pick them up and bring them to the general."

Ryder shook his head. "It's insane. It can't possibly be done."

"If it's not, Grant will march on Vicksburg and likely capture the city. If there's anything I can do to stop that, I'm going to."

Ryder hesitated. "It still sounds crazy to me . . ."

"But you're going with me anyway, aren't you?" said Cory as a grin broke out on his face.

"All right, I suppose I am," Ryder said with an exasperated sigh. "Someone's got to look after you." He glanced down at his clothing. "I don't like giving up the uniform, though."

"You can put it back on when we rendezvous with Forrest at the river. Right now you need to find some civilian clothes while I get our horses ready."

"One more thing. You brought it up yourself—how are we going to get across the river?"

"There's an old saying," mused Cory, "about crossing a bridge before you get to it . . ."

"But there *isn't* a bridge! That's the problem."

"I didn't say it applied exactly."

With another sigh and a shake of his head, Ryder went to look for some clothes.

$$\backsim$$

WHEN THEY rode away from the camp at Columbia less than half an hour later, Ryder was wearing his boots, brown corduroy trousers, a gray woolen shirt, and a thick jacket of darker gray wool. His hat had been replaced by a cap that was a little too big, so that it came down over his ears. He complained about it as he and Cory rode west.

Cory was more worried about Ryder's boots. They were clearly military issue . . . but a lot of civilians in the South wore military castoffs these days. On the other hand, no soldier in his right mind would have gotten rid of a pair of serviceable boots, not with the shortages of decent footwear in the army.

They would just have to trust to luck, Cory decided. With the legs of the trousers worn on the outside of the boots, maybe they weren't too obvious.

General Forrest had insisted on giving Cory a second pistol, so now he wore a brace of Colts under the tails of his coat. Ryder carried a pistol as well, but neither of them had a rifle or carbine. If they ran into trouble, they would have to rely more on speed and cunning to get them out of it, rather than armament.

Their route led them west under a leaden gray sky. Rather than carrying a map with them, which might have been considered proof that they were spies if they were captured by the Yankees, Cory and Ryder had studied the maps in Forrest's tent until they had the roads memorized. Their first objective was to reach the settlement of Clifton, on the Tennessee River, which was also where Forrest intended to cross the stream with his cavalry.

More men would be sent out in front of the main body to prepare for the river crossing, but Cory and Ryder were moving much more quickly even than that work party. They spent one night on the trail, then reached Clifton around the middle of the next day. Skirting the town itself, they rode up to the river and reined in. Cory tried not to feel too discouraged as he gazed out over the wide gray stream. Ice was rimed along its edges, and large chunks of ice floated in the river itself.

"Well, what do we do now?" asked Ryder, sounding as grim as Cory felt.

"There must be a way across," Cory said, hoping for some sort of inspiration. He didn't want his mission to be a failure before it even got started properly. If he failed, Forrest's raid undoubtedly would fail, too, and Vicksburg would be in greater danger than ever before.

Suddenly, movement on the river caught Cory's eye. He lifted himself in the stirrups to peer out over the water. He saw an old man with a long white beard poling a small flatboat toward them from the other side of the river.

Ryder had seen the old man, too. "Charon come to ferry the dead across the Styx," muttered the lieutenant.

"I don't care about the Styx, I just want to get across the Tennessee," said Cory.

They watched while the old man made his slow way across the river and finally poled the flatboat up to the eastern bank. "Howdy!" the old-timer called. "You boys need a ride?"

"We surely do," Cory said. "Can you take us across?"

The white beard bobbed up and down as the old man nodded. "Yep. But it'll cost you."

Forrest had given Cory some money for just such necessities. "How much?"

The old man tugged at his beard, thought it over, and then said, "Five dollars."

"I have Confederate scrip—"

"No sir," the old man cut in. "Got to be Yankee money."

"I have that, too," Cory said. Forrest had a supply of cash that had come from Yankee paymasters, gathered in the raids of the past few months. Cory reached into his pocket, brought out a handful of coins, and selected a U.S. five-dollar gold piece, an 1861 liberty head half-eagle. He tossed the coin to the old man, who caught it easily and then bit it to test its authenticity. The old-timer regarded the marks his teeth had left on the coin, then nodded.

"Come aboard," he invited. "Hold on tight to them horses, though. Can't have 'em movin' around much or they'll tip us over and dump us all in the river. It's so cold we'd freeze to death in a hurry."

Cory and Ryder dismounted to lead their mounts onto the flatboat. The animals balked at stepping out onto the boat, but after a few minutes Cory and Ryder succeeded in getting them aboard. The old man used the long pole to push away from the bank and send the boat out into the current.

The Tennessee's flow carried the flatboat downstream, so the crossing wasn't made in a straight line. They landed on the far side about a quarter of a mile downstream from where they had started. That was all right with Cory and Ryder. They were just glad to be off the flimsy craft and back on solid ground.

"What's your name, old-timer?" Cory asked curiously when he and Ryder had disembarked.

"Call me Charlie," replied the old man.

"Charon," Ryder said under his breath.

"No, I said Charlie. Can't you hear right, boy?"

Cory grinned and said, "Thanks, Charlie."

The old man tugged on his beard again. "You know, for another dollar, I could plumb forget all about seein' you boys. Anybody was to ask me did I ferry anybody across today, I could say no."

Cory took out another coin and tossed it to him. "We appreciate that, Charlie."

The old man took off his battered hat and waved at them as they rode away. When they were out of earshot, Ryder said, "I don't much like the idea of bribing civilians."

"Better that than having him tell a Yankee patrol that a couple of men crossed the river today."

"How do you know he won't take your money and tell the Yankees anyway?"

"I don't," Cory admitted. "But you can't go through life without trusting some people and hoping for the best."

"And here I thought you were a cynic."

"Just a fella trying to get where he's going," said Cory.

〜

THEIR ROUTE took them about thirty miles north of Pittsburg Landing. It was in the woods south of that settlement that the tiny log church known as Shiloh was situated. Being that close to the scene of the battle of only eight months ago brought back bad memories for Cory, and his sleep that night was restless. He and Ryder had kept moving until long after dark, finally stopping when both they and their horses were too exhausted to continue. They made a cold camp in some woods, gnawed on hardtack and jerky, and rolled in their blankets to spend a frigid night in the open.

Between the cold and the nightmares that plagued his slumber, Cory was more than ready to wake up and get moving again before dawn the next morning. They angled southwest, circling around the little town of Purdy, and headed for the Memphis and Charleston Railroad, which they could follow all the way west to Memphis.

Everything about the next two days blended together in Cory's mind. He and Ryder pushed their mounts as hard as they could, paralleling the railroad but staying out of sight of it for the most part, avoiding roads and riding across open country so they would be less likely to encounter Union patrols. Whenever they spotted riders in the distance, they took to the woods and hid until it was safe to proceed. Speed was vital, but so was stealth. If they were captured, their mission would be ruined.

They skirted Grand Junction, Lafayette, and Colliersville to the north. On the evening of December 13, 1862, they approached Memphis. The occasional stretches of woods had given way to flat farmland where there was no place to hide. They had to trust to darkness to hide them as they made their way into the city. A light rain began to fall as they reached the outskirts, and even though Cory didn't like being wet, he was grateful for the rain. It would help keep the Yankees indoors somewhere they could be warm and dry.

Forrest had instructed him to find a tavern called the Oxbow and ask for a man named Russell. Cory didn't know if that was a last name or a first name, but he supposed it didn't matter. As he and Ryder walked their horses along a street that was growing muddy, he watched for someone he could ask about the Oxbow.

Pedestrians were few and far between tonight, and the first two that Cory stopped had no idea what he was talking about. Then he hailed a passing wagon, and the teamster gave him directions. The Oxbow, as it turned out, was only three blocks along this same street. He and Ryder would have found it for themselves soon enough, thought Cory.

He saw only a few Union soldiers on the street, and they paid no attention to him and Ryder as they hurried on about their business, whatever that might have been. A few minutes later, the two reached the Oxbow and dismounted. A shed next to the building housed several horses, so they led their mounts in there and tied them out of the rain, which was growing harder. They dashed through the downpour back to the door of the tavern and went inside, stopping to shake water off their hats just beyond the door.

"Shut that damned door!" a voice bellowed. "I don't need any more drafts in here!"

That was true enough. The Oxbow was in a ramshackle frame building. Wind whipped through gaps around the planks of the walls, and rain dripped through the roof in a couple of places into buckets that had been set out to catch the drips. A fire roared in a large black cast-iron stove in a corner of the room, giving off enough heat to make the air stifling close to it, but not enough to reach all the rest of the room. The bar ran along the rear wall, and a few rickety tables sat around the room. The Oxbow had about a dozen patrons at the moment, no more.

Cory and Ryder closed the door and went to the bar. A small man with a heavily wrinkled face and iron-gray hair stood behind it, wearing a filthy apron that marked him as the tavern keeper. He was the one who had shouted at Cory and Ryder when they came in.

"What do you want?" he asked in a surly voice.

"Beer," said Cory, and Ryder nodded in agreement. The bartender drew two tin cups of beer from a keg and set them on the bar, then scooped up the coin Cory had dropped there. Cory lifted his cup and took a sip of the brew, found it thin and watery and bitter. He tried not to grimace as he lowered the cup and asked, "Is Russell around tonight?"

"That no-good drunken layabout!" exploded the bartender. "Of course he's here. Where else would such a worthless tramp be?" The man pointed across the room toward a table near the stove. "There he is, soakin' up heat like a no-good cat. Lazy as a no-good cat, too."

Cory and Ryder turned and saw a man sitting at the table, his head down, pillowed on his arms. Cory glanced at Ryder and angled his head in that direction. They picked up their cups and walked across the room.

Cory could hear the snores coming from Russell before they got there. They pulled back a couple of rough-hewn chairs and sat down. As they did so, Ryder put a hand on Russell's shoulder and shook him. "Hey! Wake up!"

Russell stirred and sleepily lifted his head, rapidly blinking bleary eyes as he looked at the two strangers. His hair was pure white, and his face was gaunt and haggard. He looked considerably older than he really was, Cory decided.

"Your name Russell?" Cory asked.

"Tha—" The white-haired man belched. "That's right. Who're you?"

This man was a hopeless drunk, Cory thought grimly. Why in the world had whoever was in charge of the Confederate espionage network chosen him to serve as an agent? He would probably betray all sorts of secrets for the price of a shot of whiskey.

Cory leaned closer to Russell, grimacing as he smelled the man's breath. With the rain pounding on the roof and water plopping steadily into the buckets, there was enough noise so that no one in the room could overhear as Cory hissed, "Forrest sent us."

"Who?" asked Russell, peering owlishly at Cory.

Cory didn't want to raise his voice any more. He moved still closer to Russell and repeated, "Forrest."

Russell shook his head. "Never heard of 'im." He put his hands on the table and awkwardly pushed back his chair. "I got to be goin'."

"Wait!" Ryder said. "We have to talk to you."

"Don't know you, don't wanna know you," Russell practically snarled. "Go 'way. Leave a feller alone." He turned toward the doorway and stumbled a little as he began making his way out of the tavern. None of the other customers paid any attention to his departure.

Cory and Ryder looked at each other helplessly. "What do we do now?" asked Ryder.

"We have to go after him," Cory said. "We have to make him understand."

The door was just swinging shut behind Russell. Cory and Ryder stood up and hurried after him, hoping that the man hadn't had time to give them the slip. They went out into the rain and looked both directions along the street. Cory bit back a curse as he realized that he couldn't see Russell anywhere.

"Go that way," he said to Ryder, waving to the right. "I'll check the other direction." He broke into a trot that carried him past the shed where the horses were.

A shadowy shape darted out from the shed as Cory passed it, and an arm like an iron band suddenly looped around his throat and jerked him almost off his feet as he was dragged back under the roof of the shed. The choking grip was so tight that he couldn't make a sound.

Something hard and round pressed up against the side of his head, and a voice whispered, "Talk fast, son, and you'd better say the right things or I'll blow your brains all over the street."

Chapter Twelve

THE RIGHT THINGS? Cory couldn't say *anything*, couldn't make any sound except a choking gurgle.

But then the arm across his throat eased its grip, and his captor pressed the gun barrel harder against his head. "Talk, damn you!"

"Let him go!"

The shouted words came from the street. Cory's eyes darted in that direction, and he saw Ham Ryder standing there, pistol drawn and leveled. "Let him go or I'll shoot!" the young lieutenant continued.

Cory hoped that Ryder wasn't too nervous. Ryder's pistol was pointing at him as much as it was at the man who had grabbed him. The gunman knew that, too, because he laughed and said, "Go ahead and shoot, sonny. You'll just kill your friend here."

Cory recognized the voice now. All traces of drunkenness were gone, but it definitely belonged to the man known as Russell. And since it was impossible for anyone to have sobered up that quickly, the only explanation was that Russell hadn't been drunk to start with. He'd only been acting when they tried to talk to him inside the tavern.

In a hoarse whisper, Cory grated out, "Put the gun down, Ham."

"But—" Ryder began.

"It's all right," Cory went on. "Russell's not going to shoot me, are you, Russell?"

"I damned sure will unless you convince me I shouldn't."

"You wouldn't want to kill one of the men General Forrest sent to get those flints and firing caps," Cory said.

He felt Russell relax slightly, but the gun barrel stayed where it was, pressed against his head. "What's the name of Forrest's brother?" asked Russell.

184 • *James Reasoner*

"The one who's a major in the Eighth Tennessee, under Colonel Dibrell? His name is Jeffrey."

Russell grunted, and the gun finally went away from Cory's head. Cory heaved a sigh of relief as Russell let go of him. He lifted a hand and rubbed his neck as he turned around.

"A man can't be too careful," said Russell. "Memphis is full of Yankees, and they're all on the lookout for spies."

Ryder came closer. He was still holding his pistol. "Are you the man we're looking for?"

"Of course I am," snapped Russell. "Who else could I be?"

"A Yankee spy, maybe?"

"Don't be a damned fool."

"You wanted bona fides from us," said Ryder. "Perhaps you should return the favor."

"I don't carry identification papers!"

"No, but if you know the name of General Forrest's brother, perhaps you know the name of his son, too."

Cory wished he had thought of that. He had been prepared to take whatever Russell said at face value.

"Oh, all right," Russell said. "The general's son is named William, but he's called Willie. He serves as one of his father's aides-de-camp."

Ryder nodded and slipped the weapon back into its holster under his coat. "I suppose you're really who you claim to be."

"Thanks," Russell said wryly. "Now, can we get out of here? With all these horses, it stinks to high heaven in this shed!"

Cory couldn't argue with that. "Where are we going?"

"I have a room not far from here. Come on."

Cory was still a little worried that this might be some sort of trick, so he kept a hand on the butt of one of his pistols as he and Ryder followed Russell through the rain-drenched streets. All of them were soaked by the time they reached a dingy rooming house. Russell led them up a rear flight of stairs into a dark hallway. He opened a door and then scraped a lucifer into life. The inconstant glow from the sulfur match revealed a tiny room furnished only with an iron bedstead with a thin mattress on it and a porcelain chamber pot on the floor.

"Welcome to my humble abode," Russell said with a chuckle as he ushered Cory and Ryder into the room. The sodden clothing of all three men dripped onto the floor. Before the match burned down, Russell used it to light a candle stuck to the windowsill.

The room's single window had no shade or curtain, but it was filthy enough that no one could possibly see through it, Cory noted. That griminess, however, might have been deliberate on Russell's part.

"Keep your voices down," Russell warned them. "These walls are mighty thin. Now, you said you've come for the caps."

"And flints," Cory said.

Russell shook his head. "I've got fifty thousand firing caps, that's all. No flints. Couldn't get any. Forrest'll have to make do with what he has."

"That's what General Bragg told him," Ryder said.

Russell grinned. "I guess Bragg was countin' on Forrest being good at scavenging. Forrest got word to me weeks ago that he was going to need caps."

"Then you *are* a Confederate agent?" asked Cory.

"I'm a fella who knows how to lay his hands on things," replied Russell, still grinning. "And how to get well paid for them. However, in the case of a noble cause like the Confederacy, I don't mind putting off my payment for a while."

Cory was glad to hear that. Forrest hadn't given him enough money to *buy* the firing caps.

"All right," Cory said. "Give them to us, and we'll be on our way. We have to get back as quickly as we can."

Russell shook his head. "Can't do that."

Ryder stiffened and put his hand on the butt of his pistol. "I thought you said you'd postpone the payment."

"Ease off, boy. I meant the caps aren't here. I'll have to take you to 'em."

186 • James Reasoner

Cory felt a surge of impatience. "Then why did you waste our time by bringing us here? Why didn't you take us straight to wherever they are?"

"I had to make sure you fellas were on the up and up. I ain't quick to trust a man. That can get you killed in my line of work."

"But you trust us now?" asked Ryder.

Russell shrugged. "I reckon."

"Then let's go."

"Sure, sure." Russell bent over and blew out the candle.

They made their way out of the boarding house. The rain had slacked off to a steady mist. Russell led the way through the streets of Memphis. Cory tried to keep track of the twists and turns of their route, but soon he was hopelessly lost. He wished they had gotten their horses from the Oxbow and brought the animals with them. They'd have to rely on Russell to lead them back to the shed. And that worried Cory, because he still didn't fully trust the man. From the worried look on Ryder's face, neither did the lieutenant.

Russell took them along a tree-lined street into a neighborhood of large houses. The people who lived here had to be wealthy, thought Cory. When they came to a gate in a tall, black wrought-iron fence, Russell opened it and stepped through onto a flagstone pathway that led across a vast yard dotted with shrubbery. There were flower beds along the path that would probably be a riot of beautiful colors in the spring, but now, in the dead of winter, they were just beds of mud.

Warm yellow lamplight glowed from the windows of the house as they approached it. Cory could make out tall white pillars along the front. This was more than a house, he thought, it was a mansion.

Why would the firing caps be here? he wondered.

Russell led the way to a side door and knocked. It was opened a moment later by a large black man in butler's finery. The man seemed to be expecting them. He stepped back and silently ushered them inside.

Cory heard music and laughter coming from another part of the house. He frowned. Was there a party going on? A ball of some sort?

"Thank you, Leander," Russell said to the butler. "Is she upstairs?"

The black man nodded solemnly without saying anything.

Russell seemed to know where he was going. He motioned for Cory and Ryder to follow him along a hallway. Opening a door, he went into a small room that was dominated by a huge mahogany wardrobe. There was also a dressing table with a razor and a pan of water on it. Tendrils of steam curled up from the water basin.

"If you gentlemen will excuse me for a moment, I'll try not to be long."

Something was different about Russell's voice. It was smoother now, more cultured, not the coarse growl it had been earlier in the evening. Cory and Ryder glanced at each other in surprise as Russell began stripping off his dirty clothing.

The next ten minutes wrought a miracle of transformation. Russell washed and shaved and opened the doors of the mahogany wardrobe to select a white silk shirt with frills on the breast, tight trousers of brown fawnskin, and a darker brown cut-away coat. He drew on clean socks and then slid his feet into expensive slippers. After shrugging into the coat, he took a dark gray silk cravat from a hook and tied it expertly, then held it in place with a diamond stickpin. The man who turned to face them looked totally different from the drunk they had found slumped over a table in the tavern. Russell smiled and said, "All right. Now we can go see Miss Arabella."

Cory wasn't sure what was going on, but he and Ryder had placed themselves in Russell's hands, so there was nothing to do but follow where he led. That was upstairs, along a curving stair-case that overlooked a large room crowded with people. Cory saw dozens of Union officers drinking and dancing and talking with an assortment of beautiful young women of all shapes, sizes, and colors. The only thing the women had in common was their scanty attire.

Cory felt himself beginning to blush. Russell had brought them to a bawdy house!

And a very successful one, judging by the crowd. Ryder leaned closer to Cory and warily whispered, "There are Yankees down there!"

Russell heard him and waved a hand negligently. "Don't worry about them," he assured Ryder. "Those gentlemen are too busy to pay any attention to us, and even if they did, they'd just think you were two more pigeons about to be clipped in my game. You see, I play a hand or two of poker in my spare time, whenever I'm not busy running this place for Miss Arabella."

So in addition to being a Southern agent and a thief, Russell was also a gambler and a whoremaster, thought Cory. A fine man to entrust with the fate of Vicksburg.

On the other hand, if Russell could deliver what they needed, that was all that really mattered.

The three of them took the stairs all the way to the third floor of the mansion, then Russell led them down a corridor to a pair of double doors. He knocked twice, then once again. It must have been a signal, because a woman's voice called, "Come in, Simon."

Russell opened one of the doors and stepped inside. Cory and Ryder followed and found themselves in a luxuriously appointed bedchamber. The bed itself, a huge four-poster with pink lace curtains hung around it, dominated one side of the room. A large rolltop desk was on the other side of the room, and at the desk sat the woman who had spoken to them. She wore a gauzy green wrapper that went well with her fair skin and dark red hair. She was writing something in a ledger that lay open on the desk. When she put the quill aside and turned toward her visitors, Cory saw that she was perhaps thirty years old. She had green eyes a shade darker than her gown and a small mole on her right cheek near her mouth. The gown was very low-cut, so that the swells of her breasts were revealed. Cory thought he glimpsed the edge of a dark brown nipple.

Then he realized he was staring and tore his eyes away from the woman's cleavage. He saw that she was smiling at him in amusement, and that just deepened his embarrassment. He felt as if his face were on fire, he was blushing so hard.

"Are these the men you've been waiting for, Simon?" the woman asked.

"That's right. Bedford Forrest sent them."

"Good. Having all those percussion caps in the hiding place you selected for them made me a bit nervous at times." The woman's voice was slow and smoky and made Cory clench his hands into fists.

Russell chuckled and went over to the bed. He knelt beside it and reached under the ruffle that hung around it. A second later he pulled out a pair of canvas pouches attached together with a thick leather strap. He straightened and brought the pouches over to Ryder.

"Here you are. Fifty thousand firing caps from the Federal armory. There are 100 tins in each pouch, 250 caps in each tin."

Ryder took the pouches. "A horse will be able to carry these with no trouble."

"That was the idea," Russell said with a nod. "They're well packed and wrapped in oilskin to protect them from moisture. You shouldn't have any problem with them."

"Thank you," Cory said. "You don't know what you've done. If we can get these to General Forrest—"

"Then he can kill more Yankees," the woman cut in. "Kill more Yankees and send the rest of the bastards packing."

"From the look of things downstairs, you seem to like the Yankees," Ryder observed. Cory stiffened. The lieutenant had no business making remarks like that to people who were trying to help the Confederacy.

The redhead didn't seem offended. In fact, she gave a throaty laugh. "I don't mind taking their money," she said. "I take a lot of it. So does Simon here, with his card games. The war will be over someday, and when it is we intend to still be right here, doing business as usual."

"In the meantime, if we can aid the cause, however slightly . . . ," added Russell.

Cory caught hold of Ryder's sleeve. "Come on. We have to find our way back to the horses."

"No need for that," said Russell. "I had them brought here. You'll find them out back in the stable. They've been fed and watered and rubbed down."

"Perhaps you'd like to spend the night and leave in the morning," suggested Arabella. "I'm sure we could find a couple of the girls who aren't too busy to keep you company."

Cory swallowed hard and thought about Lucille. He kept her image in his mind as he said, "Uh, no, but thank you, ma'am. We had better be riding."

Ryder nodded curtly in agreement. Cory was embarrassed by their surroundings, but Ryder seemed morally outraged.

"Well, gentlemen," Arabella said. "Good luck to you."

"Thank you, ma'am," Cory said.

Russell opened the door. The huge black butler was waiting just outside. "Leander will take you to your horses," Russell said. He put out his hand. "Good luck."

Cory shook his hand. Ryder did, too, after a second's hesitation. They stepped into the hall and the door closed behind them with a soft click. Cory took a breath and told himself not to think about what might transpire in there later tonight.

Leander led them downstairs and out the back of the house to the stable. Their horses were waiting as Russell had said. Cory and Ryder swung up into the saddles, and Ryder arranged the pouches so that they hung on either side of his horse with the strap over the animal's back.

"Thank you, Leander," Cory called to the butler. Leander just inclined his head gravely. Cory wondered if the slave could even talk.

He and Ryder rode off into the mist, their horses' hoofbeats muffled by the heavy air. After a few minutes, Cory said, "You were rude back there."

"I don't care," said Ryder. "I don't like that sort of people. I don't like having to accept help from them."

"I'd make a deal with the devil himself if it meant saving Lucille and helping the Confederacy."

Ryder glanced back over his shoulder. "Let's hope that's not exactly what we've done."

FINDING THEIR way out of Memphis was difficult, but eventually they found the railroad station and followed the tracks out of town to the east. No one else seemed to be abroad on this dark, cold, wet night, and that was just fine with Cory.

He could have been in where it was warm and dry, he reminded himself, sprawled on a silken comforter laid atop a downy mattress, his every need attended to by one of Miss Arabella's young, willing, perfumed lovelies. The thought made him sigh.

Then he felt a twinge of guilt. He was engaged to be married; he had no business even thinking such things. The prettiest, sweetest, smartest woman he had ever known was waiting for him back in Vicksburg. None of the girls at Miss Arabella's could even begin to compare with Lucille.

But a night's sleep in a soft, warm, dry bed . . . *that* would have been nice.

The horses were trotting along beside the railroad right-of-way. Cory and Ryder didn't have to be as circumspect about their travel now that it was the middle of the night. Ryder said, "Do you think we'd better push on all night?"

"That might be asking too much of the horses," Cory said. "But we'll keep going as long as we can. We'll stop after a while for a short rest."

"Fine." Ryder's voice was still curt and angry.

"What is it?" Cory asked. "Why were you so upset back there? Haven't you ever been in a whorehouse before?"

"As a matter of fact . . . I hadn't until tonight. But I suppose you have."

"Well . . ."

"Never mind. I was just raised to believe that such things were wrong. My parents didn't hold with gambling or drinking or . . . or any of those other things."

Cory couldn't stop himself from laughing. When Ryder stiffened as if he'd been insulted, Cory said quickly, "I'm not laughing at you, Ham, really. I was just thinking about my mother. She's the most hardshell Baptist you'd ever want to meet. All my life she tried so hard to raise me right, to keep me on the straight and narrow, and what happened? As soon as I got old enough I went a-roaming and got into all sorts of things she'd probably think were positively scandalous." Cory chuckled. "Well, at least she's still got my brothers and my sister to be proud of. Except for maybe Titus."

"What's wrong with him?"

"Nothing's *wrong* with him. He just has a wild streak in him. He takes a drink now and then, and he likes to fight. Come to think of it, Mama got mad at my brother Will for a while, too."

"He was the sheriff, before the war?"

"That's right. Will could fight, too, and he could handle a gun better than anybody I've ever seen. My mother didn't like that." Cory shrugged. "But she forgave him, I reckon. At least, I hope so, anyway."

They rode on in silence for a while, then stopped to rest the horses. The rain had stopped completely, but the bare branches of the trees were still dripping. Cory gnawed some jerky while Ryder chewed on a piece of hardtack. They didn't sit down for fear of dozing off. When they judged that the horses had rested enough, they mounted up again and rode on. The sky in the east was gray with false dawn.

When the real thing arrived a couple of hours later, it brought with it a sky that was still overcast but with some breaks in the clouds where blue shone through. Cory and Ryder moved away from the railroad, keeping it in sight but not so close that anyone on a passing train would be likely to spot them.

At midmorning they rested again, this time forcing their way deep into a grove of trees. Cory slept for a couple of hours while Ryder stood watch, then they switched places. Cory was still tired and his eyes felt gritty, but after he woke Ryder, they saddled up and rode on. Cory tried to count the days since they'd left Forrest's headquarters at Columbia. By his reckoning, it was December 15. Forrest ought to be reaching the Tennessee River today or the next, Cory thought.

That meant he and Ryder couldn't let up, couldn't afford to relax. They had to get to Forrest's camp with the firing caps as soon as possible.

Twice during the afternoon they had to seek shelter in the brush when they spotted Union cavalry in the distance. Each time, they were able to avoid being seen by the Yankees and pushed on when the patrols were gone. The clouds thickened in the late afternoon, and the cold rain started to fall again before dusk. Cory didn't mind too much, although he was very tired of being wet and chilled to the bone. The bad weather functioned as added concealment, however, and for that Cory was grateful.

Once again, the two young men rode most of the night, stopping just barely long enough for their horses to rest. The animals were still tired, and so were Cory and Ryder. Cory caught himself swaying in the saddle, on the verge of dozing off, more than once.

It was still raining the next afternoon, December 16. Cory had taken the lead, moving out about ten yards in front of Ryder. His head kept nodding forward from exhaustion, and although he fought it, his eyelids finally drooped closed without his even being aware of it. He was sound asleep but instinctively hanging on to the reins.

He didn't know they had come to a creek until his horse started down the bank. The sudden change in angle threw Cory forward in the saddle and made him jerk his head up and exclaim in surprise. His eyes opened and saw the creek in front of him. The little stream was flowing fast from all the rain the past few days, but it was narrow and didn't appear to be too deep. Fording it wouldn't be a problem.

The problem was that on the far side of the creek, about thirty yards away, were more than a dozen mounted Yankees sitting under some trees while they waited for the downpour to ease up.

The rain wasn't so hard that Cory couldn't see the blue-clad cavalrymen, which meant they could see him, too. One of them let out a yell and pointed as Cory reined in sharply. Several more of the Yankee soldiers swung their horses toward Cory. One of them shouted something. Cory couldn't make out the words, but he knew it was a command to halt. The Yankee patrol would have orders to stop and search any civilians.

Even the most cursory search would turn up the tins of percussion caps. Cory started to jerk his mount around, calling to his companion, "Ham, get out of here!"

He caught a glimpse of Ryder, whose horse had just reached the top of the creek bank. Ham was as startled by the sight of the Yankees as Cory. He hauled on the reins, desperately trying to turn his horse, and Cory started up the bank toward him.

Cory's horse struggled to climb the bank. The rain had made it muddy and slippery. He heard a booming sound from across the creek, but it wasn't thunder. Mud spurted into the air a few feet to his right where a bullet plowed into the bank.

Several more shots rang out from the Yankees. Flight was enough to convince them that the two strangers were the enemy. Cory leaned forward over the neck of his horse, making himself as small a target as possible. He jammed his heels into the animal's flanks, urging as much speed as he could from the exhausted horse.

So far he hadn't been hit, Cory realized. The rain and the poor light made for bad shooting. Given a little luck, he and Ryder could escape from the Yankees, he told himself. After what seemed like an eternity, his horse finally reached the top of the creek bank and surged over it. On flat land again, the horse could stretch its legs and really run.

But not for long, and not for very far. The animal was too worn out for that.

As Cory put his horse into a gallop, he spotted Ryder ahead of him, leaning forward in the saddle just as Cory had done. Cory followed Ryder's lead, swerving around trees, crashing through underbrush, leaping his horse over fallen logs. It was a mad, breakneck ride, and all the while Cory was aware that the Yankees could be right behind them. He didn't hear any more shooting, but that might have been because the thudding hoof-beats and the pounding of blood inside his head drowned out any other sounds.

Slowly, Cory began to catch up with Ryder. They were riding side by side as they broke out of a stand of trees into a large open field. There was no cover out here, Cory realized, so all he and Ryder could do was get across it as fast as possible. "Come on!" he shouted.

As they started across the field, Cory glanced over and saw that Ryder was still hunched over the neck of his horse. He realized suddenly that something was wrong. He yelled to him, but Ryder didn't look up.

Cory threw a quick look over his shoulder. They were halfway across the dangerously open area, and he expected to see the Yankee patrol emerging from the trees behind them. The field was empty, though. Maybe they had given the Yankees the slip, Cory dared to hope. The horses raced on toward another stand of trees on the far side of the field.

When they reached the thick growth, Cory veered his horse closer to Ryder's and reached over to grab the reins. They slid loosely from Ryder's hands. Cory pulled both horses to a stop.

He glanced again at the other side of the field as he leaped to the ground. Still no Yankee cavalry in sight.

Ryder let out a groan and started to fall. Cory caught him, staggering under the sudden weight. He caught his balance before both of them fell in the mud, then carefully lowered Ryder to the ground. Their clothes were soaked from the rain, but the back of Ryder's coat felt sticky, too.

Cory sobbed as the realization of what had happened hit him. One of those Yankee bullets that had whipped harmlessly past him had struck Ryder in the back. Somehow, Ryder had managed to stay in the saddle and lead the way to safety during the wild pursuit. Now, though, the last of his reserves of strength had deserted him.

Keeping one eye on the field, Cory knelt beside his wounded friend. He rolled Ryder onto his side. A look at the shirt under Ryder's coat showed Cory a large dark stain. The bullet had ripped all the way through Ryder's body, leaving him bloody front and back, despite the rain.

Cory slipped an arm under Ryder's head to support him. Ryder's eyes flickered open, and his hand closed over Cory's arm. "The . . . caps," he said. "Get . . . the caps."

"Don't worry about the caps, damn it," said Cory. "You're wounded, Ham. We've got to get you patched up."

Ryder licked his lips, then shook his head. "All . . . torn up . . . inside . . . Too bad to . . . do anything about it." His fingers tightened on Cory's arm. "Get the caps . . . to Forrest."

Cory felt tears rolling down his cheeks. Unlike the rain, they were hot and burned like fire. "We'll both take the caps to Forrest," he said in a choked voice.

"No! No . . . Go on, . . . Cory . . . now." Ryder took a deep, shuddering breath and winced at the pain it caused him inside. "Take . . . both horses . . . switch off . . . faster . . . that way. Get to Forrest . . ."

"I can't just leave you here!"

"Can't do . . . anything else."

Cory looked at the field again. Still no sign of the Yankees, but it could be that the patrol was searching the area. They might find him yet unless he put more distance between him and them.

Ryder was right. Logically, Cory knew that. But they had become friends over the past few weeks, and he couldn't bear the thought of just leaving Ryder here to die, or to be found by the Yankees.

"Ham, I . . . I don't want to leave you . . ."

"You're . . . wasting precious time." Ryder sighed. "Wish you were . . . a soldier . . . then I could . . . order you . . . to get out . . . of here . . ."

His eyelids closed. Another shudder went through his body, and Cory felt the life going out with it. Fighting back more sobs, he whispered, "Yes sir, Lieutenant Ryder."

Gently, he lowered Ham Ryder's head and then stood up. The lieutenant was lying underneath a tree, his face calm and smooth now that the pain was over. Cory took off his hat and passed a hand over his own face, then drew in a deep breath and squared his shoulders. He moved to Ryder's horse and unslung the pouches containing the firing caps. A moment later, he had arranged the pouches over the back of his own mount. He swung into the saddle and caught up the reins of Ryder's horse. Switching mounts from time to time was a good idea; it would let him travel even faster. And speed was what he needed now.

He looked back once, when he was twenty yards away, but the rain and the fading light made the shape lying under the tree indistinct. Cory swallowed hard and rode on, and eventually the rain washed the tears from his face.

Chapter Thirteen

BEDFORD FORREST, LEADING A force of twenty-one hundred men, left Columbia, Tennessee, on December 10, 1862, bound for the western part of the state where he intended to raise hell with the Union supply lines stretching down into northern Mississippi. Two smaller parties had been sent on well ahead of the main body of Forrest's troops. Nothing had been entered in the record book about the first group, which was unofficial and known only to Forrest. The second group, however, was charged with finding some way to get hundreds of men and horses across the Tennessee River in the shortest possible time.

It took five days for Forrest and his men to reach the Tennessee near the town of Clifton, where the river was approximately three-quarters of a mile wide. When they got there on December 15, they found that the advance party had been busy. The Confederate horsemen had found enough lumber to hammer together two small flatboats, and they had commandeered another one from an old, white-bearded man who lived on the riverbank.

No more than two dozen men and horses could be crowded onto the boats at a time, so getting more than two thousand troops across the river was going to be a lengthy process, Forrest realized. He issued orders setting up a picket line along the riverbank for more than a mile north and south of the point where the crossing would be made. If any Yankee gunboats came steaming along, the general wanted to have as much warning as possible of their pending arrival.

A light, cold rain was falling, but it grew heavier as the first men and horses were loaded onto the boats. The advance party had cut down quite a few saplings and trimmed and peeled them to make poles. Some of the cavalrymen temporarily became boatmen, poling the craft upstream for a distance of nearly half a mile, staying close to the eastern shore where the current was weaker. From there the men pushed the boats farther into the river, letting the flow take them and float them across and downstream so that they landed on the western side at a point almost opposite from where they had left the eastern bank. Then the tedious process was repeated to return for the next load.

The rain was an icy, driving downpour that made life miserable for man and animal alike. But Forrest knew that it also served a very valuable purpose. The Yankees would be less likely to be patrolling the river in such weather, and even if they were, the visibility was so bad that observers on a Union gunboat in the middle of the Tennessee wouldn't be able to see much on the banks.

The slow ferrying of men and horses continued the rest of the day on the fifteenth, on through the night, and then the day and night of the sixteenth as well. By the gray, still overcast but no longer rainy morning of December 17, everyone was across the river, even the battery of seven guns. The previous day, Forrest had scouted along the stream and found where a small creek flowed into the Tennessee. On his order, the two flatboats his men had built were towed a short distance up this creek and sunk. They could be hauled out of the water and repaired later to carry the men back across the river—assuming they survived the raid to return this way.

The white-haired man whose boat had been commandeered was allowed to go his way. He did so, but not before muttering several complaints about what the cavalry mounts had done to his vessel.

With the dangerous crossing completed, Forrest moved his force some eight miles deeper into western Tennessee, well away from the river and any Yankees who ventured along it. They made camp and built some small fires, a most welcome relief after several cold and wet days. Despite the brigade's relative newness—many of them were little more than raw recruits who had undergone only a few weeks of cavalry training—morale was high in the camp.

Morale wasn't enough by itself, though, Forrest knew. Many of his men had only enough firing caps for a dozen shots, and others had none at all. If they encountered the enemy now, they wouldn't stand a chance.

So he waited, and hoped that Cory Brannon and Lieutenant Ryder, his unofficial emissaries to Memphis, had been successful in their mission.

IF HE looked half as bad as he felt, then he must look like hell, thought Cory as he rode into Forrest's camp. Gaunt, hollow-eyed, his face covered with a week's worth of beard stubble, he clutched the horse's sides tightly with his knees to keep from falling off. The horse wasn't in much better shape, and neither was the animal Cory was leading.

The pickets had challenged him, then, recognizing him from the time he had spent in the camp at Columbia, passed him on. Major Severson, the quartermaster, saw him and came up to him as Cory reined in. "My God, Brannon," the major said. "What happened to you?"

Cory started to dismount and half-fell out of the saddle, catching himself on the horse's mane. As he straightened, he mumbled, "Got to see . . . the general." He took the pouches off the horse and swayed as he draped them over his left arm.

Severson took his other arm to steady him. "Come along. I'll take you to General Forrest's tent."

As Cory stumbled along, he asked, "What day is it?"

"The seventeenth."

"When did you . . . get here?"

"We established this camp this morning, after we finished crossing the river," Severson told him.

Cory nodded in weary satisfaction. He hadn't slept since the encounter with the Yankees that had cost Ham Ryder his life. He had pushed on regardless of how tired he became, changing from one horse to the other so that he could keep going. He wasn't sure if he had eaten anything or not—the past twenty-four hours were a little blurry in his memory—but if he had, it had been while he was in the saddle.

Mostly he had spent the time cursing himself. It was his fault Ryder was dead, he told himself over and over. If he had been alert, he would have reined in before he reached that creek. He never would have gone riding down the bank in plain sight like that, so that the Yankees would have had to be blind not to see him. His carelessness had cost Ryder dearly. Ryder would never become a newspaperman now, would never see those places he had dreamed of visiting and writing about.

All my fault, Cory thought now, but he was dry-eyed as he castigated himself. He had cried himself out the day before.

The major pushed aside the entrance flap of a tent and ushered Cory inside. Bedford Forrest looked up from a camp stool at a folding table and uttered the same exclamation that Cory's appearance had prompted from the quartermaster.

"My God!" Forrest came quickly to his feet. A long stride put him in front of Cory. "Are you all right, Mr. Brannon?"

Cory used both hands to lift the canvas pouches containing two hundred tins of percussion caps. "The . . . caps you needed . . . General," he got out. "Sorry . . . no flints. Couldn't get them."

Gingerly, Forrest took the pouches from Cory and looked down at them with a fierce grin. "Now we can fight!" he said. He raised his eyes again to Cory's haggard face, and his voice was much more gentle as he went on, "And you can go back to Vicksburg, Mr. Brannon. You've done your duty."

Cory shook his head. "Not yet," he said. "There's still Yankees . . . that need killin'—"

With that, his eyes rolled back, and a black curtain dropped over his consciousness. He thought he felt his knees buckling but couldn't stop them. He fell but was out cold by the time he hit the muddy ground at the feet of Forrest.

MOVING AS many men as quickly as Forrest had did not go unnoticed. Union spies were aware that the cavalry force had left Columbia, and when they passed the word, there was no doubt in the minds of the Federal commanders about where Forrest was going, at least in a general sense.

General Rosecrans in Nashville immediately wired General Grant in Oxford, Mississippi, that Forrest was on the move. Rosecrans suggested that Union officers along the rail lines be especially watchful for trouble. A few days later, Rosecrans's warning was reinforced by word from Gen. Jeremiah C. Sullivan, in command at Jackson, Tennessee, that Forrest had crossed successfully the Tennessee River.

Grant suspected what Forrest was up to. The Yankee commander had figured out already that it was going to take a combined assault to take Vicksburg, and a viable supply line was mandatory if the overland part of the operation was going to have any chance of succeeding. Accordingly, he had set up two such lines, one along the Mobile and Ohio Railroad from Jackson, Tennessee, to Corinth, Mississippi, the other following the Mississippi Central Railroad from Jackson to Grand Junction, just above the border between Tennessee and Mississippi. Grant's own forces had moved down the Mississippi Central all the way to Oxford. He established his headquarters there, with his supply depot being set up some thirty miles back up the rail line at Holly Springs.

But if Forrest was able to disrupt rail traffic, the flow of supplies to Grant's army would come to a halt. Without supplies, Grant would not be able to march on Vicksburg from the northeast, as he intended to do while Admiral Farragut's gunboats pounded the city from the Mississippi River. Knowing that

Forrest had to be stopped, Grant issued orders sending more men back to Jackson, the vital junction point where the railroads came together.

Jackson had to be defended successfully—or more than likely, all of Grant's plans would come to nothing.

THE FIRST thing Cory became aware of was the smell of coffee. The aroma reminded him of early mornings in the farmhouse back in Virginia. He slowly realized that he was smelling real coffee, not the mixture of grains that passed for coffee in most army camps. His stomach cramped painfully, bringing him more fully awake. His eyelids began to flutter.

"I thought that might wake you up," a voice said from somewhere close by.

Cory forced his eyes all the way open and saw that he was lying on a cot inside a tent. Sitting next to the cot on a stool was Bedford Forrest. The general had a tin cup in his hand. Spirals of steam wafted up from the cup.

"If you can sit up, I'll give this to you," said Forrest. "I don't want you spilling it, though. Coffee's more precious than gold around here. The only things more valuable are powder and shot and firing caps—of which, we now have plenty, thanks to you, Cory."

Cory pushed himself into a sitting position. A wave of dizziness and nausea swept over him but subsided. He reached for the coffee that Forrest held out toward him, but he pulled his hand back when he saw how badly it was shaking.

"Wait," he said hoarsely. His lips were painfully chapped and cracked from the cold weather, and his voice sounded to his ears like a rusty hinge.

"Take your time," Forrest told him. "There's no hurry."

Cory sat on the cot for several minutes, then finally reached for the coffee again. This time his hand was steady enough to take the cup and raise it to his lips. He sipped the hot, strong brew and closed his eyes in appreciation of it. Forrest handed him a biscuit—not a piece of hardtack, but a real, honest-to-God *biscuit*, and Cory bit into it eagerly. He had never tasted anything as good in his life, he thought.

Strength seeped back into his body. He ate the biscuit and drank all the coffee, and he was still ravenous. But at least his hunger and thirst had been eased somewhat, and as he looked around, he found that his head was clear enough for him to recognize the inside of General Forrest's tent.

That meant that he'd been lying in the general's cot.

For a second Cory was afraid that they'd laid him on the cot after he passed out, muddy boots and all. To his relief, he saw that his boots and his outer garments had been removed.

Forrest leaned forward, clasped his hands together between his knees, and smiled. "Damned fine work, Cory," he said. "We couldn't push on into Yankee territory without those caps you brought us. It would have been suicide."

"But you would have done it anyway, General, since those were your orders."

Forrest shrugged. "I don't like losing men, not without making the Yankees pay for every damned one of them. But you made the decision easier."

"That's about all I did right," Cory said bitterly.

"You're talking about Lieutenant Ryder?" Forrest raised his eyebrows. "I was told that you came into camp alone, leading a second horse. I assume the lieutenant was lost during the course of your mission?"

"I got him killed," Cory said. "It was my own stupid fault."

"Tell me about it," suggested Forrest.

Cory did so, explaining how his weariness had allowed him to let down his guard and blunder headlong into the Yankee patrol at the unnamed creek. "I was the closest one to them when they started shooting," he said. "The bullets should have hit me, not Ham."

"Bullets have a mind of their own sometimes. There's no way of knowin' why they miss one man and hit another."

Cory shook his head. "It's still my fault. I can't blame it on fate or luck or anything like that. If I'd been more alert, I might have spotted the Yankees in time for us to hide from them. They never would have seen us if I hadn't ridden right into their laps."

"I won't argue with you, and while I regret Lieutenant Ryder's death, what's done is done. You successfully completed the task that was given to you, and you deserve congratulations for that." Forrest paused, then added, "You deserve to go back to that young lady of yours. I'm sure Miss Farrell is anxious to see you again."

The mention of Lucille made Cory think about what day it was. "How long was I unconscious?" he asked.

"A few hours. This is the night of the seventeenth." Forrest grinned. "You have time enough to make it back to Vicksburg for that Christmas Eve wedding of yours."

Without thinking about what he was doing, Cory shook his head. "I'm not going back to Vicksburg," he said, just as he had that afternoon when he delivered the percussion caps to Forrest. "Not yet. I want to ride with you, General. I owe that to Ham."

Forrest regarded him severely. "And what about what you owe to Miss Farrell?"

Cory took a deep breath. "Lucille will understand. Ham gave his life to help make your operation a success, General. I have to see it through for him."

"You mean you want vengeance. You want to kill some of the Yankees who killed your friend."

Forrest's voice was harsh as he spoke the blunt words. Cory couldn't honestly disagree with him, either. Anger and the need for vengeance burned inside him. He might not shed any more tears for Ham Ryder, but the grief was still there. The grief . . . and the guilt.

Cory looked down at the ground. "Just let me ride with you, General," he said quietly. "I think I've earned that much."

"Indeed you have. Very well, then. Your employment as a civilian scout attached to his unit will continue." Forrest got to his feet and looked down at Cory. "But you'll have to explain everything to Miss Farrell when you get back. I'll fight Yankees all day, every day, but I'll be damned if I'm going to face up to a bride who's been left waiting at the altar."

THE CONFEDERATE cavalry broke camp before dawn the next morning. The night before, Cory had gotten dressed and drawn more rations, then pitched his bedroll in a tent with some of the junior officers. Still tired from his ordeal, he had slept soundly despite the cold and the muddy ground. The notes of the morning bugle call seemed to come only seconds after he had closed his eyes. The sky was still dark gray with night as Cory stumbled out of the tent with the rest of its occupants.

Forrest wasn't trying to be quiet or stealthy about anything. In fact, he made sure that plenty of drumming and bugling went on as the men moved out. By spreading out his men, he made it look as if his forces were much larger than they actually were. Cory figured that out as the group began to ride toward the northwest.

He was up front with Forrest and several of the other officers. Only the outriders were ahead of them. "We're bound for Lexington," Forrest announced. "From there we can advance due west toward Jackson."

The Yankees had to know they were coming, thought Cory. It was only a matter of time until they ran into some resistance. Sure enough, just as dawn was breaking, one of the outriders came galloping back to the column of cavalry.

"Yankees up ahead, General!" the trooper called as he hauled his mount to a halt. No sooner were the words out of his mouth than the sound of guns popping came floating through the cold morning air.

Forrest's mouth curved in a grin of anticipation. "It's about time!" he said. He turned in the saddle and bellowed, "Prepare to charge!"

There was no hesitation in Bedford Forrest, thought Cory. The general was ready to attack, any time of the day or night, no matter what the situation.

Cory drew one of his Colts. He was ready to fight, too. More than ready.

Forrest shouted the command that sent more than two thousand horsemen surging forward at a gallop. Cory looked keenly ahead, his eyes searching for a flash of blue that would mark the position of the Yankees. Instead, a couple of minutes later as the leading horses splashed through a shallow creek, Confederate outriders came racing up to report that the Yankees were falling back toward Lexington. The Federal troops had put up only a brief skirmish, then lit out.

Forrest paused only long enough to order a pursuit. He twisted in his saddle and called to one of the officers, "Captain Gurley, take your company around to the north and hit the Yankees from the flank if they decide to make a stand!" Then with a shouted cry of anticipation this wizard of the saddle once more put the spurs to his mount.

Cory stayed with Forrest as the group split. The men commanded by Captain Gurley, he recalled, were Alabamans, some of the remnants of a larger brigade that had recently joined with Forrest's. Cory was sure they were good fighters, but he wanted to be with Forrest, figuring that was where the action would be the thickest.

The horses pounded over a hill and down the far slope toward another creek. A couple of roads converged at a ford. Cory looked past the creek and saw the roofs of buildings and a church steeple in the distance, a couple of miles away. That was most likely the settlement of Lexington.

There were woods beyond the creek, too, and Cory suddenly realized that if he were the Yankee commander, he would use those trees for cover and try to stop the Southerners at the ford. He was about to call out a warning to Forrest when he saw that the general had slowed his headlong pace. The other cavalrymen followed Forrest's lead. They rode toward the ford at a brisk gait, but nothing like the gallop of a few moments earlier. Forrest was waiting for something . . .

Guns crackled along the creek to the north, and Forrest clenched a fist triumphantly. "That'll be Gurley's Alabamans," he said. "The Yankees were waiting right where I thought they'd be." Forrest thrust his fist into the air. "Charge!"

So the Yankee commander, in trying to set a trap, had instead been caught in the jaws of another. The main body of Confederate cavalry thundered down the hill while the men waiting for them were swung around to the left to deal with the threat coming from that direction.

Cory saw muzzle flashes flickering in the shadows under the trees on the far side of the creek. A cannon roared and belched smoke. A shell screamed through the air and burst among the cavalrymen, spilling a couple of horses off their feet. A man shrieked in pain, but the sound faded almost instantly, torn away by the passage of the wind that buffeted Cory in the face.

Instinct made Cory want to empty his pistol toward the Yankees, but he knew they were still too far away. He waited until the charge had swept closer to the creek, then lifted the gun and aimed at the trees. The Colt bucked in his hand as he squeezed the trigger. He thumbed back the hammer and fired again then again and again as he rode across the creek, water splashing high in the air from the hooves of his horse.

It was chaos in the woods as the Alabamans attacked from the left flank and Forrest's three Tennessee regiments carried out the frontal assault. Cory spotted one of the cannons and spurred his mount toward it. As he fired, though, the Colt's hammer fell on an empty chamber. One of the Yankee artillerymen yelled a curse and swung a long pole at him. Cory barely had time to recognize the makeshift weapon as one of the cotton-wrapped swabs that the gunners dipped in water and ran down the cannon's barrel after each shot to extinguish any sparks left behind. Then the cudgel slammed into his chest and swept him out of the saddle just as if he'd ridden into a low-hanging tree limb.

He crashed hard to the ground, the impact of his landing knocking all the air out of his lungs. Gasping for breath, he rolled over and saw another blue-clad trooper lunging toward him. This one brandished a rifle with a bayonet attached to the barrel, and he clearly intended to bury that length of sharp steel in Cory's body.

Cory remembered that he had emptied his right handgun. In fact, the empty revolver was still clutched in that hand. He had hung on to it somehow when he fell. His left hand streaked to the other holstered Colt, and the thought flickered through his brain that he hoped the gun hadn't fallen out of the holster when he tumbled off his horse.

The Colt was still there. Cory's fingers closed around the walnut grips. He palmed it smoothly out of the holster and tipped up the barrel as he drew back the hammer. The Yankee cried out in horror as he saw the muzzle of the Colt lining up on him, but it was too late for him to stop his charge. The pistol boomed, and the soldier jerked as a slug drove into his chest. He stumbled and tried to throw the rifle and bayonet at Cory as he died. Cory flung himself to the side, away from the bayonet.

Cory kept rolling and came up on his feet. His chest was numb from the blow that had felled him, but his arms and his legs worked. So did his trigger finger. He fired three times into the clump of artillerymen around the cannon. One man spun off his feet, while another staggered and clutched his side. The others broke and ran. The wounded man reached out for some support and laid his hand on the barrel of the gun. He screamed as the flesh of his palm began to bubble and smoke from the intense heat of the barrel.

Cory shot him again, knocking him to the ground.

In a matter of minutes, the Union forces abandoned any idea of resistance, and the rout was on. Forrest's men rounded up many of them, taking them prisoner, but as the Confederate cavalry began to pursue the ones who were getting away, Forrest called them back.

Cory heard the general shout the order. He was thumbing fresh rounds into one of his revolvers and fitting a cap onto the nipple of each cylinder. It would have been all right with him if the cavalry had ridden down and killed every one of the Yankees. He closed the Colt, holstered it, and broke open the other gun to reload it.

Forrest trotted up on his horse. "You're afoot, Mr. Brannon," he commented. "Are you all right?"

"I imagine I'll be sore as hell tomorrow," Cory replied, "but right now I'm fine, General." He slid the second Colt back in its holster. "I'm a little surprised you deliberately let some of those Yankees get away, though."

Forrest's eyes narrowed and glittered with anger. "You forget that you're a civilian, Mr. Brannon. The way our boys were suddenly all around 'em, howlin' and killin', they probably think our force is two or three times bigger than it really is. That's exactly what I want 'em to think."

Cory shrugged. He grasped the logic in Forrest's thinking. He just hated to see any of the Yankees get away unbloodied.

Reports began to come in from Forrest's subordinates. The Yankees had had two cannons set up, both of them rifled 3-inch guns. Now that they were in Confederate hands, Forrest asked one of the officers, "Would you care to take charge of these pieces, Lieutenant Morton?"

The lieutenant, a pale-faced young man who wasn't even as old as him, Cory thought, nodded eagerly. "Thank you, General," said Morton.

"Put 'em to good use, lad," said Forrest. Then he looked over at one of the prisoners who was being led up to see him. "Who's this?"

The Yankee, whose uniform bore the insignia of a colonel, stiffened and saluted Forrest. "Col. Robert G. Ingersoll, General, at your service, sir," the Union commander introduced himself. "Is this the army of your Southern Confederacy that I have so diligently sought?"

"It is, sir," Forrest replied solemnly.

Cory thought the Yankee colonel was a pompous stuffed shirt, but Forrest was civil to the man and promised him and his men fair treatment and an early parole and release. That didn't surprise Cory; Forrest might take as many prisoners as he could during this raid, but he wasn't interested in keeping them. Disarming them and obtaining their sworn oaths not to continue hostilities for a set amount of time was enough for the general. Bloodthirsty in battle he might be, but once the combat was over, Forrest reverted to being an officer and a gentleman.

And this fight was definitely over. Cory was already looking forward to the next one.

Chapter Fourteen

THE RAIN SEEMED TO be over for a while, and Cory didn't mind that. The sky remained overcast most of the time, however, matching the grayness of his mood.

If it had been up to him, he would have pushed on with the cavalry toward Jackson immediately, but Forrest seemed to be content with the day's work even though it was only early morning. The cavalry, rejoined now by Captain Gurley's Alabamans, moved toward Jackson, but at a leisurely pace. Again Forrest ordered plenty of drumming from his small corps of musicians. The drums brought out the people in the houses they passed, and these Tennesseans stared in wonder at the long column of cavalry—apparently without taking note of the fact that it was also a thin column.

Cory understood the bluff that Forrest was running and approved of it despite his impatience to close once more with the Yankees. The Federal forces gathered in Jackson probably outnumbered Forrest and his men by as much as four to one— but the Yankees didn't know that. The fact that Forrest was able to ride unimpeded to within a few miles of the town was proof enough of the Yankees' ignorance of their true strength.

Forrest called a halt late in the afternoon and ordered his men to make camp, adding that they could build as many fires as they wanted. That evening, Cory sat in on the meeting with the regimental commanders in which Forrest gave them their orders for the next day.

Once again, Forrest was splitting his army. Col. George G. Dibrell's Eighth Tennessee would circle to the north and strike the rail line at Webb's Station, some eight miles from Jackson. The Alabamans and a battalion from the Second Tennessee would head south, their objective being several bridges on the railroad leading to Corinth, Mississippi. If they could manage to burn or disable those bridges, they were to proceed westward to the other rail line, the one running southwest to Oxford, where Grant was headquartered.

In the meantime, Forrest and the rest of the cavalry would demonstrate toward Jackson itself, keeping the Yankees there worried and occupied.

Cory found himself nodding in agreement as Forrest explained the orders. The general had come up with a good plan, he thought. Cory mulled over his options and decided to remain with Forrest the next day. Even though Forrest and the men with him would serve more as a distraction than anything else, Cory was confident there would be some fighting before the day was over.

He didn't sleep well that night. His dreams were haunted by the sounds of battle and the flashes of gunshots. He tossed restlessly in his bedroll as the screams of dying men echoed through his head.

He pushed all those thoughts out of his mind the next morning as he rode with Forrest toward a long ridge not far east of Jackson. On the slopes beyond the ridge, Cory saw crosses and headstones under the arching, winter-bare limbs of trees. When he looked closer, he saw movement at the crest of the ridge.

Forrest laughed. "The Yankees are making their stand next to a cemetery," he said. "How appropriate."

Cory looked at the gravesites laid out across the hillside and swallowed hard. He had tried all morning to work up the same sort of killing rage that had gripped him the day before, but so far he hadn't been able to manage it. Now all he could think about was that this should have been a place where the dead could rest in peace, rather than having a battle fought next to them in which even more would die.

What was wrong with him? he asked himself angrily. Ham Ryder was dead, cut down in the prime of life by the Northern invaders. Cory had been Ryder's friend, so his only thoughts should be of vengeance.

He lifted a hand, wiped the back of it across his mouth. He wouldn't cut and run. He would fight if it came to that. He had answered every call, done everything he could for the cause of the Confederacy. That wasn't going to change.

But he knew, suddenly, that he couldn't live simply to kill. He felt vaguely ashamed of the savage emotions that had surged through him the day before as he watched the Yankees fall. He'd had his vengeance, and it had tasted oh so sweet at the time, but now there was only bitterness in his mouth.

The realization did nothing to change his resolve. He would fight to the best of his ability, and he would kill to save his own life and to help win the battle.

But no matter how many Yankees he killed, it wouldn't bring Ham Ryder back to life. It wouldn't do a damned thing for the Texan who had befriended him and then fallen at Fort Donelson. And Captain Farrell, the man who had lifted him out of the morass and helped him to make something of himself, would still be dead. What's done is done, Forrest had said, but Cory recalled a line from the Bible that summed it up even better.

Let the dead bury their dead.

"Halt!" Forrest shouted.

The long, thin line of cavalry stopped. Cory wondered if the Yankee officers on the ridge could study them through field glasses and tell how many of them there were. To the rear, the drummers continued playing, as if an entire division of infantry were coming up right behind them.

"We'll let 'em take a nice long look at us," Forrest said. After a few minutes, he slowly drew his saber and raised it over his head. "Ready?"

Shouts of readiness came from both directions along the line of mounted men. Cory drew his revolver and gripped it tightly.

Forrest's saber slashed forward, and he shouted, "To the attack . . . *Charge!*"

The Confederate horsemen swept forward. Rebel yells echoed through the morning air. The advancing men set up such a racket that they must have sounded like at least twice their number to the Federal forces on the ridge. Musketry began to rattle, and smoke drifted over the ridge, but most of the shots went wild, whistling over the heads of the cavalrymen. As they reached the bottom of the ridge, they opened up with their pistols.

Cory wished he could guide his horse with his knees, like his brother Mac, so that he could draw his left-hand gun and blaze away with both weapons. That was what Forrest was doing. The general had sheathed his saber and had a Colt in each hand. The Yankees referred to him as "that devil Forrest," Cory had heard, and at the moment Forrest did indeed look satanic. He was grinning hugely, his dark eyes darting here and there, his jaw set in a determined line. The pistols bucked up in his hands, came down, bucked again. Cory was close beside him, trying to follow Forrest's example.

The Union defenders broke and ran without putting up much of a fight. By the time the Confederate charge reached the top of the slope, the Yankees were in full flight through the cemetery, dodging headstones and leaping over graves. Again, Forrest let them go, not worrying much about prisoners or pursuit.

He reined in and pulled up next to Cory. "Well, we spanked them again."

"Are we pushing on to Jackson?" asked Cory.

Forrest shook his head. "Let's see where they stop running."

The retreating Federal forces finally stopped along a creek that ran between the cemetery and the town itself. Forrest brought up a spyglass and studied their positions, then nodded in satisfaction.

"They're digging in, and more troops are comin' out from town to reinforce them. That's just what we want."

Forrest ordered his men to dismount and care for themselves and their horses. Clearly, he was satisfied with taking the cemetery and for the time being didn't intend to proceed any closer to Jackson.

Cory slipped his watch from his pocket. By this time, Colonel Dibrell's men were probably at Webb's Station. The Alabamans and the Second Tennessee might be burning those railroad bridges south of town by now, too. The Yankee commander in Jackson, thinking that the main threat was poised on his doorstep, was going to be mighty surprised when he started getting reports of the real damage going on outside of town.

The day was a long one for Cory. Forrest kept his men busy, shifting them around first one way and then another so that they gave the appearance of a much larger group to the prisoners. When Forrest got around to paroling the captured Yankees, they would take stories of the massive Confederate force back to their commanding officers. That strategy, effective as it was, made for a lot of sitting around and doing nothing for Cory.

Inevitably, his thoughts turned to Lucille. This was the nineteenth of December. In less than a week, he was supposed to stand up with her in the Methodist church and be married. No doubt she was carrying on with the preparations as if he were going to be there as planned.

Would she be devastated when he didn't show up? Would she be so angry that she would never forgive him? Was it possible that she might even call off the engagement?

Cory rubbed a hand over his face. If he left Forrest right now, he might make it back to Vicksburg by Christmas Eve. It would be a mighty close thing, though, and looking at it objectively, he had to admit it was likely he wouldn't reach Vicksburg in time. Besides, he had told Forrest that he would stay, and that was the same as giving his word.

He had given his word to Lucille, too, he reminded himself, just as he had given it to her father before that. And once again he was breaking a vow he had fully intended to honor.

Maybe Lucille would be better off if she *didn't* marry him. She needed someone who was more dependable. Cory realized that no one had ever been able to count on him for anything. He had run out on everyone, had let everyone down.

And now he was sitting here in the middle of a highly dangerous cavalry raid into Yankee-held territory feeling sorry for himself, he realized. The thought made him smile faintly and shake his head.

Lucille would understand, he told himself. She might be angry at first. Hell, she definitely would be angry. But she would forgive him.

The only thing he really had to worry about was Palmer Kincaid and how the gambler might try to take advantage of his prolonged absence to get closer to Lucille. If the gambler laid a hand on her, then Cory would kill him. Cory made that promise to himself.

Then he realized that he was making yet another vow that he might not be able to keep . . .

THE NEXT day, Saturday, December 20, Forrest left a small number of men posted on the heights east of Jackson and withdrew the rest of his force. Now was the time for stealth. As quietly as possible, the Confederate cavalry rode around Jackson to the north and then started up the rail line toward the towns of Humboldt and Trenton. It was Forrest's opinion that the Union commander in Jackson would launch an attack today on the force he thought was threatening him. If that happened, the handful of men Forrest had left behind would put up a brisk defense for a few minutes, moving around and shooting as fast as they could to make it look like there were more of them than there really were, then running like hell before the Yankees could roll over them. While that was going on, Forrest and the rest of his men would be raising holy Cain elsewhere.

Humboldt was first on the agenda. This was another rail-junction town, where the tracks of the Memphis and Ohio Railroad crossed those of the Mobile and Ohio. Colonel Starnes's Fourth Tennessee led the assault, sweeping in on the depot where the Union defenders tried unsuccessfully to repulse the attack. The Yankee garrison had no artillery, only small arms, and they were outnumbered. By shortly after noon, Humboldt was in Confederate hands, and Starnes ordered the depot burned. Other members of the regiment were detailed to burn bridges and tear up the tracks. The rails were levered up far enough so that ropes could be passed around them, then horses were used to pull the rails off the crossties. The ties themselves were rolled into bunches and set afire. Soon, columns of smoke were rising all over the countryside around Humboldt.

The soldiers paused in their work to watch in admiration as the ammunition stored in the depot building began to explode. Flames shot high into the air, and sparks cascaded down. The spectacle would have been a pretty one had it not signified such destruction. To the Confederates defending their homeland against the Northern invaders, it was a pretty sight anyway.

Farther north, Forrest himself, along with his staff and Cory Brannon and a good-sized force of men including Colonel Biffle's Ninth Tennessee, advanced on the town of Trenton. As they rode within sight of the settlement, Forrest raised a gauntleted hand to halt the column. He used his spyglass to study the situation for a moment then turned to the others with a grin.

"The Yankees have forted themselves up in the depot," he said. "It appears they've stacked bales of cotton and hogsheads of tobacco around the building to give themselves even more protection." Forrest extended the glass to Cory. "Take a look."

Cory lifted the glass to his eye and squinted through it. The squat depot building leaped into sharp focus, and he saw that Forrest was right. The Yankees had erected a thick wall of cotton and tobacco around the station. Cory saw the muzzles of rifles bristling through gaps in the makeshift barricade. He shifted the spyglass and checked the roofs of nearby buildings, spotting rifle barrels there, too. The Yankees had stationed sharpshooters around the depot to give it even more protection.

"They'll be hard to root out of there," Cory said as he handed the spyglass back to Forrest.

"Did you notice any artillery around that depot, Mr. Brannon?" asked Forrest.

Cory had to admit that he hadn't.

"And that shall be their downfall," said Forrest. "We'll keep them busy until Captain Freeman can bring up our guns."

He sent some of his men charging toward the town, drawing the fire of the Union soldiers in the depot and on the surrounding buildings. Cory leaned forward in the saddle, watching anxiously as the vicious rain of lead from the town knocked several cavalrymen out of their saddles. The Southerners returned the fire, and even without the spyglass, Cory was able to see one of the sharpshooters atop a building rise to his feet, double over, then topple over the edge of the roof, falling in a loose-limbed sprawl to the street below.

The cavalry broke off the attack and raced back to the main body of troops with only a few losses. By that time, the caissons and limbers had rolled up, and the gunners were moving their cannons into position. Forrest called over to Freeman, "Pour the fire into them, Captain!"

The batteries opened up a few minutes later, including the two 3-inch guns that had been captured from the Yankees the day before. Shells began slamming into the depot. The bales of cotton that had been stacked in front of the building were blown high into the air. Cory thought it looked like it was snowing as tiny bits of cotton drifted back down to the ground.

The bombardment was a short one. It took only three volleys before a Union officer appeared during a lull, stumbling out of the depot and waving a white flag tied onto a pole. Forrest smiled. "The battle appears to be over, gentlemen." He led the way proudly as the cavalry rode into Trenton.

Forrest reined to a halt in front of the depot and swung down from the saddle. The other members of his staff, including Cory, did likewise. The general stepped forward to meet the Union officer, who had cast aside the white flag and now had his hand on his saber. The Yankee drew the blade from its scabbard.

"I'm Colonel Fry, in command of this garrison, sir," he said, "and this saber has been in my family for forty years. Now I give it to you as a token of our surrender, General." He held the weapon out to Forrest.

Forrest took the saber, studied it approvingly for a moment, then said, "You are a Tennessean, Colonel?"

Fry's chin lifted defiantly. "I am, sir," he declared. Obviously, he was not going to apologize for also being a Unionist.

Forrest handed him the saber. "Take back your sword, Colonel, as it is a family relic. But I hope, sir, the next time you wear it, it will not be against your own people."

The words were gracious yet scathing, and as Colonel Fry took the saber, he looked down toward the ground.

The Union soldiers who had been inside the building filed out and stacked their rifles. The officers surrendered their handguns but retained their sabers as their commander had done. There were a lot of prisoners, well over two hundred. Cory watched them being lined up, then glanced toward the depot itself. To his surprise, he saw smoke curling up from the back of the building.

"General," he called, "the depot's on fire!"

Cory didn't know if Forrest wanted the building burned or not, but he was sure the general had not yet given the order to do so. Judging from Forrest's reaction to Cory's warning, destroying the depot was not in the plans. Forrest and Major Strange raced to the door, drawing pistols as they did so, and just as they got there, two last Yankee soldiers tried to come out.

Forrest planted the barrel of his revolver in the chest of one of the Yankees and growled, "Get back in there! And if you don't get that fire put out, you'll burn with it!"

In a matter of minutes, the fire had been extinguished before it could destroy the building and the supplies stored within it. Cory watched in amazement as crate after crate of ammunition was hauled out of the depot. Trenton was proving to be quite a prize.

By evening, Colonel Starnes had rejoined Forrest's force, as had Colonel Russell, falling back from Jackson where he had kept the Yankees occupied earlier in the day. The various groups of prisoners were consolidated and formed into squads so that they could be counted. Cory estimated their numbers at well over a thousand. And while that was going on, Forrest set up a table within earshot of the Yankees and had several couriers report to him. To each man, Forrest issued orders to be carried to a general, commanding him to bring up his forces. Cory didn't recognize all the names, and it wasn't until he saw some of the so-called couriers appear before Forrest more than once that he caught on to what Forrest was doing. The bluff was still being run. Any of those prisoners eavesdropping on Forrest's performance would be convinced by now that there were ten times as many Confederates in western Tennessee as was actually the case.

Forrest had missed his calling, Cory thought with a grin. If he hadn't been such a damned good soldier, he could have been an actor.

⌇

CORY LEARNED later that Saturday had been a bad day all around for the Yankees. While Forrest and his men were wreaking havoc in western Tennessee, down in Mississippi at Holly Springs, a Confederate cavalry force led by Gen. Earl Van Dorn had launched an attack, taking the garrison of fifteen hundred Federal troops completely by surprise. Before the Yankees quite knew what was happening, Van Dorn's men had captured them and laid waste to the huge supply depot established there by Grant. The Northern commander had been stockpiling supplies at Holly Springs for weeks as he prepared to begin his overland campaign against Vicksburg from Oxford. Now, with the warehouses at Holly Springs in smoldering ruins and rail-road service through western Tennessee disrupted by Forrest's raid, it would be impossible for Grant to attack Vicksburg.

Unaware of this for the time being, Forrest, Cory, and the rest of the force that had penetrated deeply into Yankee-held terri-tory had other things on their minds. First and foremost was get-ting back to friendly ground and doing as much damage to the Union cause as they could on the way. Forrest saw that his men were outfitted from the stores captured at Trenton. By the time they released the prisoners and broke camp the next morning, the Southerners had a surplus of ammunition, percussion caps, food, and even counterfeit Confederate money, a trunkload of which had been discovered in the depot. Cory had no idea why the Yankees would have had the counterfeit bills unless it was part of their plan to use them to disrupt the Southern economy. If that was the case the scheme likely would have failed, because the phony bills were easily spotted. Forrest had the counterfeit money distributed among the men so they could use it in lieu of matches and other counters when they were playing cards.

The reunited cavalry set off north along the railroad. Twelve miles from Trenton, at Rutherford Station, they found two com-panies of Federal troops. The Yankees saw the size of the force bearing down on them and wisely surrendered. Cory didn't regret the fact that there was no battle to speak of. He was glad he had come along with Forrest; he had owed that much to the memory of Lt. Hamilton Ryder. But he was no longer hungry for bloodshed.

Five miles farther on, at the town of Kenton, more Yankees were captured. All along the northbound route, Forrest dropped off work details to tear up the tracks. These groups leapfrogged each other, hauling off and bending rails and burning ties, caus-ing such destruction that it might be months before the Yankees could use the railroad again.

Cory rode alongside Forrest as the expedition continued northward toward Kentucky. Sleet began to fall as the group reached a swampy stretch of land along the Obion River. Where the railroad crossed this wide area of river bottoms, there were numerous bridges and trestles, and Forrest set his men to work destroying them. The sleet made it more difficult to find dry wood for kindling, but the cavalrymen managed, and for two days, Monday the twenty-second and Tuesday the twenty-third, dozens of columns of smoke rose into the sky to mark the destruction of the bridges.

They camped the night of the twenty-third in Union City, not far from the Kentucky border. As Cory sat by a campfire and sipped coffee, he pondered the fact that tomorrow was Christmas Eve. Lucille must have figured out by now that he wasn't going to return in time for the wedding.

Lord, she might even think he was dead! That thought made a worried frown appear on Cory's face. If there was only some way to get word to her . . .

But there wasn't, not this far behind enemy lines. Telegraph wires had been pulled down or destroyed along with the railroads, so there was no way to send a message from anywhere in this part of Tennessee. All he could do was wait until he got back to Vicksburg and explained the situation—he hoped that Lucille would understood.

Forrest remained at Union City through Christmas Eve, sending a party even farther north, across the border into Kentucky, to destroy the railroad bridge at Moscow. On Christmas Day he finally turned to the southeast again, following the Northwestern Railroad that would take him toward the Tennessee River. The raid had been a smashing success at an amazingly low cost—fewer than twenty-five men killed—but there was still the matter of getting back home.

The drenching downpours of early December returned the day after Christmas, slowing Forrest's progress. Reports also came in from the scouts that General Sullivan in Jackson had figured out finally where he was and was coming after him with a sizable force. Forrest cut south from the town of McKenzie, but the wide, swampy bottomland along the Obion River was once again in his path, and now the river had overflowed because of the rain, flooding the trail Forrest had intended to take.

Night fell early on the evening of December 28. Cory was riding with the group of officers accompanying the general. The rest of the column was strung out behind them.

Forrest reined in as he came to a long, narrow, earthen causeway that stretched out across the flooded river bottoms. Just enough light remained for Cory to see that the causeway was about a quarter of a mile long, and where it ended, a dilapidated wooden bridge began. He couldn't tell how long the rickety structure was; the other end of it was invisible in the shadows and the icy mist that was falling.

"The Yankees think to pin us in," Forrest said as he looked out across the causeway and the bridge. "They're so confident that they didn't bother destroyin' this path. Well, they'll pay for that overconfidence."

One of the officers said incredulously, "General, you can't mean to go across there! It's too narrow, too slippery. That bridge looks like it's ready to collapse."

"Well, we just won't let it," said Forrest, heeling his horse onto the roadway.

The rest of the general's staff hesitated. Cory lifted his reins and clucked to his mount. The horse started ahead at a walk, following Forrest. One by one, the rest of the officers rode out onto the causeway.

Cory's stomach clenched tightly as he glanced from side to side. The causeway was barely four feet wide, and nothing could be seen around it except black, icy water. A misstep would send both man and horse sliding into that water, and it was entirely possible neither of them would come back out.

Forrest rode slowly, letting his horse pick its way. Cory followed suit, trusting to his mount. The quarter-mile across the causeway seemed longer, but at last Forrest reached the bridge. Close up, it looked even worse than it had from a distance, thought Cory. Many of the planks were rotten, and the supports leaned dangerously.

Forrest turned in the saddle and said, "Have some of the men find forked branches in the woods. Cut them and send them forward. We'll use them for supports and added bracing."

The order went back along the line, and soon, along with the hissing of sleet and mist, Cory could hear the sound of axes biting into frozen wood. Troopers carrying the branches came along the causeway on foot, carefully making their way past the horses. They slipped into the water, which was not as deep as it had looked to Cory, and began shoring up the bridge.

Deep or not, the water was cold, and the workers emerged from it with their faces blue and their teeth chattering. "Build fires so those men can warm up and dry their clothes," ordered Forrest. Unlike earlier in the raid, when Forrest had wanted a lot of campfires to fool the Yankees into believing he had more men than he really did, now building fires might be dangerous. They were trying to avoid being seen. But without the heat, those men might freeze to death in their wet clothing.

Finally, Forrest was satisfied that the bridge had been braced up sufficiently. Once again he led the way, followed closely by Cory. The span shuddered and swayed under their horses, but it didn't collapse. When they came to the end of it, Cory saw to his dismay that they had to cross another of the narrow earthen causeways, this one just as long as the one on the other side. With Forrest still in the lead, eventually they reached solid ground once again, and Cory breathed a sigh of relief.

Getting the rest of the men and wagons and cannons across the river bottoms was an arduous, all-night job, but it was accomplished at last. Forrest and his men were on their way to Lexington, and from there it was only a short distance to Clifton, where they could recross the Tennessee River in the flatboats they had left hidden there.

The only problem was that the Yankees were waiting for them.

Chapter Fifteen

CORY REINED IN AND leaned forward in the saddle to peer through a gap in the trees toward the road at the bottom of the hill. A few minutes earlier, he had heard the tramp-tramp-tramp of thousands of feet and had carefully worked his way forward until he could see the road. What he saw was exactly what he had feared: rank after rank of blue-clad infantrymen moving along sluggishly through the mud, followed by a good-sized force of Union cavalry.

This was one of several Yankee columns moving around western Tennessee looking for Forrest, Cory knew. Other scouts had brought word that the Yankees were casting a net over the countryside in hopes of trapping the raider who had wreaked such havoc in the past week and a half.

Cory turned his horse and walked it quietly away from the Yankees until he had put enough distance between him and them to risk a gallop. He yawned as he rode. He hadn't slept the previous night, as the Confederate force was making its perilous way over the causeways and the rotten bridge, and there had been no chance to rest this morning, either. He had been out at first light, surveying the route that Forrest planned to take, finally earning his pay as a scout.

He rode back to where Forrest and the others were waiting in the woods near the town of McLemoresville. "Bad news, General," he reported as he dismounted in front of Forrest's makeshift headquarters. "There's a Yankee column moving along the road up ahead."

"How long?" asked Forrest.

Cory shook his head. "I couldn't see the end of it."

Forrest nodded grimly and said, "We'll wait them out, then. You'd better have something to eat and get some rest, Mr. Brannon. Once we start moving again, there may not be another chance for a while."

234 • James Reasoner

"Yes sir," Cory agreed. Food and maybe a cup of coffee sounded good, but sleep sounded even better.

After he had eaten he found a relatively dry spot underneath a tree and sat down with his back against the trunk. He was asleep almost instantly, exhaustion claiming him.

When he awoke, it was late afternoon. He bit back a groan of pain as he stood up. His muscles were stiff and sore from sleeping so long in such an awkward position. A look around told him that nothing had changed, except that all the fires had been put out so that the smoke wouldn't lead the Yankees to the woods where the Confederates were hidden.

They spent a long, cold, dark night waiting for the road south to be clear of Union troops. After everything they had done, all the riding and fighting and destruction, having to sit and wait chafed at the men. Some of the staff officers argued that they could break through the Federal columns, but for once Forrest decided on a course of discretion rather than aggression. Scouts were sent out again on the morning of the thirtieth, including Cory, and this time they reported that the road to Lexington was open and clear.

Forrest responded quickly, getting his men moving to the south. He sent a small force to the east with orders to watch for any Yankees coming from that direction. The cavalry moved steadily all day and camped that night not far north of a tiny settlement known as both Red Mound and Parker's Crossroads.

As they started south toward Lexington again the next morning, the final day of 1862, Cory was riding once more in the forefront of the column with Forrest and several of the staff officers. He wasn't scouting ahead this morning because he was confident that the outriders under the command of Capt. William Forrest, another of the general's brothers, would bring back any warning of trouble up ahead.

That warning came not long after the day's ride began. Scouts raced back to the column with the news that a large Union force was waiting at Parker's Crossroads. Cory's hands tightened on his horse's reins as he heard the distant crackle of rifle fire. Some of the outriders must have engaged the enemy.

Forrest digested the information, then growled, "By God, I'm tired of running from those damned Yankees. We're going on through."

Cory felt a quickening of his pulse. He was torn between the desire to avoid further combat and get back safely to Vicksburg, and the anticipation of throwing one last punch into the belly of the Yankee beast. Forrest waved his men forward, and a sense of eagerness swept over the entire group.

They approached the crossroads from a hill that enabled Cory to see thick woods on three sides—the northwest, southwest, and southeast—and a large open field with a ridge to the northeast on the far side of it. The Yankees were in the woods to the southeast, and as Forrest and his men came into view, they opened up an artillery barrage. Forrest responded in kind, calling a halt and ordering that Captain Freeman's and Lieutenant Morton's guns be brought up immediately.

The Confederate cannons opened fire a few minutes later and proved to be much more effective than the Yankee gunners. Some of the Federals had taken shelter behind a wooden fence at the edge of the woods, but as the bombardment began, the fence became a death trap. As the Confederate shells burst along the fence, huge wooden splinters sprayed through the air, every bit as deadly as if they had been metal shrapnel. The Yankees fell back immediately—at least, the ones who still could.

Forrest tugged lightly on his beard as he studied the situation. After a few moments, he said, "We'll keep them busy with the artillery while we flank them." The orders were issued quickly, and the Confederate force was split three ways. Forrest retained the largest group in the center, while smaller groups circled to the northeast and southwest. The force sent to the northeast would use the ridge for cover, while the soldiers making their way to the southwest would have to slip through the trees.

The artillery duel continued for a couple of hours until Forrest received word that everyone was in position. He drew his saber—a new one, a U.S. Dragoon model that he had liberated from the stores captured at Trenton—and brandished it. "Let's hit 'em, boys, hard and straight on!" he cried as he signaled for the attack to begin.

The cavalry swept forward. Cory had taken part in enough of these charges to know what was going to happen. He leaned forward over the neck of his horse as it pounded along the road and past the little trading post for which the place was named. The gunners ceased their firing at precisely the right moment. The cavalry drove into the woods, yelling and shooting, and the Yankees, already softened up considerably by the bombardment, broke and ran before them.

Cory emptied first one pistol then the other, seeing through the smoke that wreathed his head that several Yankees had gone down before his guns. He rode down another blue-clad trooper trying to bring a rifle to bear on him. The sounds of even more firing came from the flanks, and Cory knew that the maneuver Forrest had put into action was succeeding. The Yankees, despite their superior numbers, were pinched in from three sides and were being soundly defeated.

Spotting Forrest reloading his pistols, Cory rode over to join him. The general grinned at him and observed, "We're whipping 'em badly."

"Yes sir, we are," agreed Cory.

Forrest ducked suddenly as something whined through the air above them.

"General, are you hit?" Cory asked anxiously.

Forrest straightened and took his hat off, grinning as he looked at the hole a bullet had just torn in the crown. "No, but it was a near thing. I shouldn't think that I'd like to come any closer to death."

Cory couldn't argue with that, but before he could say anything else, a fresh wave of gunfire sounded from the rear of the

battle. He and Forrest both turned sharply in their saddles, surprised to hear the noise of battle coming from that direction.

One of the staff officers rushed up to Forrest, almost as wild-
eyed as the horse he was riding. "General!" the officer shouted.
"We're being attacked from the rear! The Yankees are on both
sides of us! What shall we do?"

Forrest's mouth quirked in a grimace as he clapped the
bullet-torn hat back on his head. "Then we'll charge 'em both
ways, damn it!" he growled.

The officer's eyes widened even more in disbelief. "Sir?"

Forrest shook his head. "How big is the attacking force in
our rear?"

"At least as large as the one in front, sir."

"Have Starnes and Russell mount a charge to keep them
busy," Forrest ordered crisply. "Everyone else is to withdraw to
the south as quickly as possible."

The officer nodded. "Yes sir!" He wheeled his horse to carry
out the orders.

Forrest glanced over at Cory. "By God, I hate to run, but I
won't see my men slaughtered needlessly. Why the hell didn't I
receive word that the Yankees were in our rear?"

"I don't know, sir," Cory said with a shake of his head. He
knew that he wouldn't want to be the men Forrest had sent out
to watch for just such a development. If the general ever got his
hands on them, he might kill them himself.

Colonels Starnes and Russell led their men in one more
charge, as Forrest had ordered, while the rest of the cavalry
rapidly started toward the south, skirting the edge of the battlefield. Cory saw a good number of men who had left their horses
tethered behind Parker's store cut off from their mounts by the
Federal cavalrymen sweeping in from the rear. They were taken
prisoner as Cory watched from several hundred yards away, and
although he felt sorry for them, he could do nothing to help
them. He wheeled his horse around and dug his heels into its
flanks, sending it lunging forward in a gallop.

The retreat was somewhat undisciplined but effective. The Southerners had made it past the trap that the Yankees had set for them, but their losses were higher than at any other time during the raid into western Tennessee. Cory saw the scowl on Forrest's face and knew how upset the commander was. He had been on the verge of one last magnificent triumph, only to have it snatched away from him.

Still, overall, the raid itself had been an unqualified success. Enough damage had been done to the railroads to render them useless to the Yankees for a long time to come. It was entirely possible, Cory knew, that what they had accomplished was nothing less than the salvation of Vicksburg.

He hoped fervently that was the case, but either way, he was ready to go home.

THEY REACHED Lexington on the evening of December 31 and spent New Year's Eve there. Scouts sent back toward Parker's Crossroads reported that the Yankees had not yet launched a pursuit. They were still licking their wounds from the battle, thought Cory. If that slowed them down even for a day, that would be long enough for the Confederates to reach the Tennessee River.

There had been some discussion about swinging back to the west for one final strike at some supplies Grant had stockpiled at Bethel Station, but the fight at Parker's Crossroads had eliminated that possibility from consideration. Forrest's only concern now was getting his men back across the river and out of Yankee-held territory.

On the morning of New Year's Day, 1863, reports from the scouts indicated that the Yankees were on the move again, heading south from the crossroads in at least a semblance of pursuit. Forrest soon had his men riding briskly toward Clifton. Some three hundred Confederates had been captured by the Union forces during the battle, but a nearly equal number of Yankees had been taken prisoner by Forrest and his men. Not wanting to be slowed down, Forrest paroled those prisoners without hesitation and without the sham of making his forces look bigger than they were. The need for that deception was over.

Cory knew he was going the wrong direction, that he was heading away from Vicksburg, but he decided to stay with Forrest until the cavalry was back across the river. It would be easier and safer to swing down through northern Alabama than to take a more direct route to Vicksburg.

It seemed like they should have reached the Tennessee by now, Cory thought around midmorning, but still they rode on without coming in sight of the river. The rain had stopped, but the roads were still muddy. Because of that, there was no dust cloud to warn them before a group of riders suddenly appeared in the distance in front of the Confederate force.

Forrest reined in and took out his spyglass. "Damnation!" he exclaimed a moment later. "More Yankees! They're like a flock of boll weevils."

The general was in a bad mood to start with, because Major Strange, who had been with him for a long time, was one of the men taken prisoner at Parker's Crossroads. With that sore spot irritating the general, Cory wasn't at all surprised when Forrest, without hesitation, ordered his men to charge the Yankees who had dared to get in their way.

Once again the riders surged ahead. Pistols cracked and carbines boomed. Cory saw the muzzle flashes coming from the barrels of the Union weapons. He was down along the neck of his horse, urging the animal on to greater speed. He felt as much as heard the disturbance of the air around his head as bullets whipped past him.

Only a small group of Yankee cavalry blocked their way, no more than a regiment. Wisely, as nearly two thousand madly shouting Rebels thundered down on them, they broke apart and retreated. Forrest sent Starnes to the left and Biffle to the right

to complete the rout. Those Yankees who surrendered were dis-
armed and left where they stood, staring after the Confederates.
There was no time for prisoners now.

With the way open again, Forrest and his men pushed on
hurriedly, finally reaching the river around midday. The wide,
icy river looked beautiful to Cory.

"Get those boats raised!" ordered Forrest as they came to
the small creek where the flatboats had been sunk. Men slipped
into the water and tied ropes to the submerged ferry boats,
which were then hauled out and quickly patched.

There was always the danger that a Yankee gunboat might
come along, so the cannons were floated across the river first. As
soon as they were on the other side, Freeman and Morton set up
their guns to cover the rest of the crossing. Forrest sent men back
down the road with instructions to "come a-runnin'" immediately if they caught sight of any Yankees approaching.

"There's no time to take the horses over on the boats,"
Forrest said. "They'll have to swim for it. Everyone dismount!"

Cory wasn't sure the horses were going to cooperate with the
general's decision. He wished his brother Mac was there; Mac
could get almost any animal to do just about anything he
wanted. But Mac was in Virginia somewhere, serving with Jeb
Stuart's cavalry the last Cory had heard.

Cory swung down from the saddle and led his mount to the
edge of the river. Other men were doing the same. The animals
were balky, which came as no surprise. The water was cold and
the current was swift.

One of the flatboats was drawn up to the bank beside Cory.
He stepped out onto it and tugged on the reins. His horse gingerly put one hoof in the water, then another. Cory edged farther out on the boat.

"Good idea, Mr. Brannon!" Forrest called from the shore.
"Get one started and the others will follow."

A couple of soldiers were standing nearby. Cory said to them,
"Get on here and pole us out."

The two men hesitated for a second then did as he said. Cory realized he had just given an order, and the soldiers had obeyed it. That was definitely an odd feeling for him. He'd never been in command of anything in his life.

The men pushed the boat away from the bank. Cory held tightly to his horse's reins, and the animal came grudgingly into the water and began swimming. Behind them, more horses were being pushed and prodded into the river. The herd instinct sent them swimming after the leader. Soon there were dozens of horses in the Tennessee, kicking their way toward the far shore.

Meanwhile, the wagons were brought across on the other flatboat. Some of the men, unwilling to wait, began chopping down trees and lashing them together to form crude rafts.

Cory's flatboat reached the eastern bank. He hopped off, catching himself as he slipped a little in the mud. His horse climbed out of the river and shook itself off. Cory patted the animal encouragingly on the shoulder. The rest of the horses began splashing up out of the river, while more swam across from the other side.

Cory watched during the afternoon as the flatboats kept up a constant shuttle across the river. It had taken all night and most of the next day for the horse soldiers to cross the Tennessee the first time. This day was different. By eight o'clock that evening everyone was across, even General Forrest, who had waited almost until the final trip. That didn't surprise Cory. If the Yankees had shown up at the last minute, Forrest wanted to be on the same side of the river so he could take part in the fight.

Two weeks had passed since Forrest and his men had ventured into western Tennessee, outnumbered, badly equipped, bent on a task that most sane men would have considered impossible to accomplish. But accomplish it they had, and now they were returning in better shape than when they had left, with more arms and ammunition and other supplies than they had taken with them. It was quite an achievement, Cory thought as he rode away from the river with the others. He and Ham

242 • James Reasoner

Ryder had helped make it possible by slipping into Memphis and bringing the percussion caps to Forrest, but after that, everything had depended on the general's daring and audacity and the fighting ability of his men. Cory regretted any hard feelings he might have caused by missing his wedding, but he was proud to have been among Bedford Forrest's men on this raid into Yankee territory.

He just wished that Ham could have seen this day.

Forrest nudged his horse alongside Cory's. "I suppose you'll be taking your leave of us now," he said.

"Yes sir, I'm afraid so. I have to get back to Vicksburg and mend some fences."

"I'd be glad to have you remain a part of the brigade. You seem to bring luck with you, Cory."

Cory frowned in surprise. "I've never thought of myself as particularly lucky, sir."

"Then you haven't thought long enough," said Forrest. He drew the gauntlet off his right hand and reined in to extend it to Cory. "You may not be an officer, Mr. Brannon, but you are a gentleman and a fine fighting man, to boot. Good luck to you."

Cory clasped Forrest's hand and felt emotion swelling in his throat and tightening around his chest. "Thank you, sir," he managed to say. "And good luck to you, too."

Forrest released Cory's hand and saluted him. Cory returned it, then wheeled his horse. It was late, but he could at least get started toward Vicksburg. He would head south along the river, he decided, then cut west after he had crossed into Alabama.

"Give my best regards to Miss Farrell," the general called after him, "and be sure to tell her it's not my fault you missed the wedding!"

Tired though he was, Cory couldn't help but grin as he rode into the night.

Chapter Sixteen

WEARING THE BEAUTIFUL WHITE wedding gown she and her Aunt Mildred had made, Lucille stood in front of the mirror attached to the dressing table in her room. A crack ran through the upper right corner of the mirror. It had been fine until a few days earlier when a shell from one of the Yankee gunboats had exploded less than a hundred yards from the house. The blast had shaken the ground and made the mirror crack.

It was bad luck to break a mirror, thought Lucille.

Then she put her hands over her face and began to sob.

It was Christmas Eve morning. The day should have been a happy one simply because it was in the middle of the holiday season. Even more so, this should have been the most glorious day of her life, since it was her wedding day. At least it was supposed to be. The Yankees and their infernal shelling certainly had dampened any holiday cheer that might have made itself felt in Vicksburg. And it was impossible to have a wedding without a groom.

Cory, thought Lucille, *where are you?*

It had been over a month since he had left for Tennessee. The trip shouldn't have taken more than three weeks, he had said, and yet he hadn't returned. Had he and that young lieutenant run into the Yankees? Lucille had asked herself that question a thousand times since it had become obvious that Cory wasn't going to be back when he said he would. Could he have been hurt somehow?

Was he dead?

Three simple little words that she tried determinedly to keep from creeping into her head. It was impossible not to wonder, though. She believed that he was still alive, but she couldn't be sure of that. Not until she had seen him again with her own eyes and hugged him so tightly that he would think she was never going to let him go.

And after that he would have some mighty tall explaining to do about why he was late.

She would forgive him, of course. She might be angry, but all that really mattered was that he was alive. Already, in her prayers, she had started making a covenant with God: Let Cory Brannon return to her alive and well, and she would do anything, anything at all, that the Lord led her to do.

She had thought back, time and again, to the months when they had been separated earlier in the year. All during that time, she had believed that he was alive and that he would find her. She had been convinced that if anything had happened to him, she would know. She wanted to believe that was still true, which was why she had insisted on continuing with the preparations for the wedding as if there were no doubt that Cory would be there. She knew Aunt Mildred and Uncle Charles had tried to point out gently to her that Cory could have been delayed, that he might not return to Vicksburg by Christmas Eve. They didn't want her to be hurt too badly, she knew.

But they didn't understand. Admitting that something could have happened to Cory was the same thing as giving up on him, at least in Lucille's mind. She was going to remain as optimistic as possible.

At times like this, though, here at the eleventh hour, when she was dressed in the beautiful gown and waiting to go to the church . . . she just couldn't help it. The tears began to flow, and she couldn't stop them.

She was vaguely aware of the door of her room opening behind her, and then she heard her aunt. The older woman rushed across the room and placed a comforting arm around her shoulders. "Oh, my dear!" she said. "My poor, poor dear!"

Lucille turned toward her, and Mildred embraced her and started patting her back. "He's not coming!" Lucille said between sobs. "H-he's not coming!"

"There, there, girl," murmured Mildred. "I've never seen a young woman with as much faith in a young man as you have in Cory Brannon. Don't give up now, dear. He could still get here in time."

"B-but the carriage is waiting! It's time to go to the church!"

"Well . . . ," Mildred bit her lip for a moment, then said, "Perhaps he went straight to the church. Perhaps he's waiting for you there."

Lucille raised her head and looked at her aunt. "Do you think so? Do you really think he might be there?"

"It's certainly possible."

Lucille began wiping tears off her face. "Then we should go down there and see. If Cory's not there, we'll wait for him."

"Yes." Mildred nodded. "I think that's a good idea." She took a lace handkerchief from the pocket of her dress and dabbed at Lucille's eyes. "Let's just wait a few minutes more, until your face isn't so red, dear. Then we'll go."

Lucille summoned up a smile and nodded in agreement. Cory would be waiting at the church when they got there.

OF COURSE he wasn't.

Lucille told herself she was surprised when she didn't see him there, waiting for her with a big smile on his face, but she really wasn't. Not deep down. Deep down her faith was slipping away by the minute, running out like sand in an hourglass.

Plenty of other people were waiting at the church. She saw Lt. Jack O'Reilly and Palmer Kincaid sitting in separate pews close to the front of the sanctuary, as well as several other officers from the home guard and the army, and family friends from Vicksburg. As Lucille stood in the rear of the church with her aunt and uncle, several of the guests turned to glance at her. There was an air of impatience in the church. It was Christmas Eve, and people wanted to be home with their families.

"I'll wring that boy's neck, I swear I will," muttered Uncle Charles under his breath. His wife shushed him.

Lucille managed to smile weakly again. "I'm sure it's not Cory's fault," she said. "He'd be here if he could."

Kincaid got up from the pew and walked back toward them. He looked very handsome in an expensive dark gray suit, a frilled silk shirt, and a diamond stickpin in his red silk cravat. He shook hands with Charles Thompson, nodded pleasantly to Mildred, then took Lucille's right hand in both of his.

"I knew you'd make a beautiful bride, my dear, but even so your loveliness today is breathtaking," he said.

"Thank you, Uncle Palmer," she said. "I . . . I just wish Cory was here to see me . . ."

Kincaid frowned slightly. "Where is the boy? I never thought he'd miss his own wedding."

"He hasn't returned from his mission for General Pemberton," Uncle Charles said stiffly.

"Going to Tennessee, wasn't he?" asked Kincaid.

"That's right."

"That's a long way." Kincaid patted Lucille's hand and smiled at her. "I sure he would have been here if he could."

She nodded, feeling tears burning in her eyes again. She took a deep breath, determined not to cry. Not now. Not here.

Kincaid went back to his seat, and Charles Thompson drew his wife aside. "How long are we going to wait?" he asked Mildred. He whispered the question, but Lucille heard it anyway.

"As long as it takes," Mildred replied sharply.

Lucille turned to her aunt and uncle and said, "No."

Both of them looked surprised. "What was that?" asked Uncle Charles.

"I said no," she repeated, a little shocked at how strong and firm her voice sounded. She certainly didn't feel that way. But it was time to face facts: Cory wasn't coming. And as the one who had been left at the altar, it was up to her to break that news to the guests.

She lifted the veil from her face and threw it back over her head, then started walking down the aisle toward the front of the church. Aunt Mildred cried softly, "Lucille, no!" and Uncle Charles said, "Wait!" but she ignored them both. She had this task to do, and postponing it wouldn't make it any easier.

She heard the buzz of surprised conversation from the guests as she walked down the aisle alone. The minister stood at the altar watching her and looking confused. When Lucille reached the front of the church, she turned to face the puzzled guests.

"Hello, everyone," she said, raising her voice so that she could be heard. She could summon up plenty of volume when she wanted to; after all, she had grown up taking soundings on the bow of the *Missouri Zephyr* and shouting "Mark twain!" up to the pilot in the wheelhouse.

She went on, "Thank you for coming here today. It means a great deal to me that you wanted to share this . . . this special day. But . . . but I'm sorry to announce that there will not be a wedding today."

In the back of the sanctuary, Aunt Mildred and Uncle Charles looked stricken. They weren't embarrassed by what had happened, Lucille sensed. They were just sad for her.

"My fiancé, Mr. Cory Brannon, has been unavoidably detained and will not be able to attend the ceremony that was planned for today." She paused and took a deep breath, forcing herself to go on. "I'm sure the nuptials will proceed when he returns to Vicksburg."

Most of the women looked scandalized. Some of the men looked down and tried to hide the grins that had appeared on their faces—*The boy must've lost his nerve,* they had to be thinking—while other men frowned and shook their heads in stern disapproval. Everywhere Lucille looked, though, expressions of sympathy and concern appeared on the faces of the guests, male and female alike.

They felt sorry for her. For one of the few times in her life, people were pitying her. She didn't like that, didn't like it at all.

She wanted to scream at them, *Go home! It's over!* But she knew she couldn't do that. So she kept the brave smile on her face and said simply, "Thank you again for coming."

People began to stand up and shift around. The low hum of conversation quickly grew into a buzz. Some of the guests started to file out of the church into the overcast Christmas Eve afternoon. Lucille stayed rooted to the spot where she stood in front of the altar.

Lieutenant O'Reilly came over to her, looking as neat as ever in his uniform. He held his hat in his hands as he said, "I'm truly sorry things didn't go as planned, Miss Farrell."

"Thank you, Lieutenant."

O'Reilly gave her a weak smile and turned to leave. As he passed her uncle, he paused and said something quietly to Charles Thompson, who nodded grimly in agreement. Then Mildred took hold of his sleeve and tugged her husband along as she came down the aisle to Lucille.

"Oh, my dear, I'm so sorry," Mildred said as she hugged Lucille again. "I never saw such a brave thing in my life as the way you stood up in front of all those people."

"What did the lieutenant say to you, Uncle Charles?" Lucille wanted to know.

Still scowling, he ignored the warning glance his wife shot at him and said bluntly, "He said that young Brannon ought to be horsewhipped. I had to agree with him."

"Charles!" scolded Mildred.

"Well, it's true. I thought very highly of that lad. I depended on him while we were dealing with the railroad and the wagon train. Oh, I knew he had an impulsive streak . . . but to not show up for his own wedding! And to my niece!" He shook his head, clearly unable to comprehend how anyone could do such a thing.

"There won't be any horsewhipping or neck-wringing," Lucille said. "I'm sure Cory has a very good reason for not being here. He could even be—" Her voice broke as her control threatened to slip away from her. "He could be—"

A shudder went through her, and she still couldn't finish the thought. As her eyes blurred with tears, she saw that all the guests had left the church, and she was thankful for that much, anyway, as she started to cry.

Aunt Mildred hugged her and tried to comfort her, while Uncle Charles stood by harummphing and looking solemn. He finally said, "I'm sure the boy's fine. He can take care of himself, I tell you. I've seen it for myself. The lad's a survivor."

Lucille looked up, the light from the church's candles shining on her tear-streaked face, and said, "He had damned well better be."

⌇

COLONEL THOMPSON had left the running of the supply line from Texas in the capable hands of Allen Carter, who proved, day by day, that the Confederate army had lost a potentially fine officer when his leg was blown off at Manassas. On a solemn and sober Christmas Day, a courier appeared at the Thompson house, bearing the news to the colonel that the Yankees were steaming down the Yazoo River toward Chickasaw Bluffs, north of the city. Thompson was summoned to a meeting with General Pemberton and the other officers responsible for Vicksburg's defense.

As they clustered around a table in Pemberton's office, the general announced, "I've received word that General Van Dorn's attack on the Union supply depot at Holly Springs was a smashing success, gentlemen. All of Grant's stores were either captured or destroyed."

"Good news indeed," said Thompson. "What about General Forrest's raid into western Tennessee?"

Pemberton shook his head. "No reports have been received from Forrest; at least, none that have been passed on to me."

Thompson had begun to wonder if for some reason Cory had gone along with Forrest on the raid. Cory was acquainted with the general from Fort Donelson and Shiloh, so it wasn't impossible that he would have accompanied Forrest. It would have taken a powerful motivation for the young man to miss his own wedding, however.

Pemberton went on, "I intend to move troops north to Chickasaw Bluffs to repulse the Yankee advance. General Smith will be in command of the operation."

Maj. Gen. Martin Luther Smith, who at one time had been in charge of all of Vicksburg's defenses, nodded his head in acknowledgment of the task ahead.

"Colonel Thompson, can you spare some men from the home guard?" asked Pemberton.

"Of course, sir," Thompson replied. Pemberton was just being polite; the troops in the home guard were his to command, just like those in the regular army. "I shall take charge of them myself and in any capacity you deem appropriate."

Pemberton shook his head. "No, Colonel, I'd rather have you here in the city. Your men will be part of the Provisional Division, under General Lee."

Gen. Stephen D. Lee was sitting across the table from Thompson. A distant relation of the famous military family from Virginia, Lee was an artillery officer who had risen to command a division. He assured Thompson, "We'll take good care of your boys, Colonel."

Thompson tried not to scowl. The discussion continued, but he no longer felt that he was a part of it. He had volunteered for a combat command, only to have the idea summarily dismissed. True, other than the skirmish with the renegades who had attacked the wagon train, he had not actually been in combat since the Mexican War, more than a decade earlier. But he felt certain he would have acquitted himself well—if he had been given the chance.

When the meeting broke up, Thompson walked slowly back to his home. The city was still abuzz about the battle of Fredericksburg, which had taken place earlier in the month in

Virginia, north of Richmond. The Yankee army, under the command of Gen. Ambrose Burnside, had tried to cross the Rappahannock River and capture the city of Fredericksburg, but they
had been defeated soundly by the Confederate defenders.
Thompson had read all about the battle in the newspapers, as
had everyone else in Vicksburg, and the smashing Southern victory had done a lot to improve morale in the city. If the Yankees
came to Vicksburg, people told themselves, they would get the
same sort of hot lead welcome that had been waiting for them at
Fredericksburg, with the same result.

Well, the Yankees were coming, Thompson told himself,
and he would have liked to be able to do his part in thrashing
them. That was not to be, however. He was a soldier and would
obey orders, even if it meant sitting and waiting.

His time would come, he thought. Sooner or later, Vicksburg
would need him.

⁓

As EXPECTED, Confederate troops clashed with Union forces at
Chickasaw Bluffs on December 28, 1862. The Yankees under
Gen. William Tecumseh Sherman had steamed up the Yazoo
River, and when they disembarked from their transports, they
found themselves facing a broad stretch of swamp ground with
the steep bluffs behind it. Vicksburg was only three miles south,
following an overland route, but the bluffs stood squarely
between the Yankees and the town.

And the Confederates were dug in securely with artillery
and fourteen thousand riflemen. As the Federals tried to
advance across the swamp toward the bluffs, they encountered a
devastatingly effective bombardment and volleys of rifle fire
that cut them down like a scythe.

Sherman had not expected to encounter this much resistance. Grant was supposed to be pressing Vicksburg from the
northeast, drawing off enough of the defenders so that Sherman

254 • *James Reasoner*

could break through with his thirty thousand men and take the city from the north before the Rebels knew what was happening. Obviously, that was not how the situation had developed. The Confederates might be outnumbered by two to one, but they held the high ground and took full advantage of it.

Grant had tried to get word to Sherman of the destruction of the supplies at Holly Springs and the havoc being wrought along the railroads in western Tennessee by Bedford Forrest, but the message never reached Sherman. Left to operate on his own, Grant's subordinate had no choice but to order his men to fall back to the Yazoo and temporarily abandon the effort to take Chickasaw Bluffs.

The next day, the twenty-ninth, Sherman tried again, sending his men on a flank attack against the left side of the Confederate line. That proved almost equally futile. The Yankees were able to battle their way to the foot of the bluffs, but only with enormous losses. And once there, they found themselves pinned down by Rebel fire coming from directly above them. It was a bitter pill for Sherman to swallow, but he had no choice except to order another retreat. Otherwise all of his men would have died for nothing.

Still unwilling to admit defeat, Sherman began planning yet another attack, but before anything else could be done, nature intervened. A thick fog rolled over the swamps along the Yazoo, so dense that a man could hardly see his hand in front of his face. Seeing anything more than a few yards away was impossible. The fog itself might have been a blessing to the Union if Sherman's men had been able to use it as cover for a sneak attack on the Confederate defenses, but it was soon followed by a driving rain. The Yazoo began to rise, leading both General Sherman and Adm. David Porter, the commander of the boats that had brought the troops up the river, to worry that they would all be washed away by a flood. Grudgingly, Sherman withdrew completely from the Yazoo, having Porter ferry his men back down the river and across the Mississippi to the town of Milliken's Bend.

So far, the Yankees had made—or attempted to make—four assaults on Vicksburg, two by land and two by way of the great river. All had come to naught. A less stubborn foe might have given up.

But Vicksburg was still the key to the Confederacy, as Abraham Lincoln had put it, and the Union president wanted that key in his pocket.

~

LUCILLE CAREFULLY packed away the wedding dress in a cedar chest. She closed the lid and promised herself that she would not look at the dress again until Cory had come back to her.

It was January now. In Tennessee, as one year turned to the next, Braxton Bragg had attempted to recapture Nashville, only to be turned back by the Yankees at the battle of Stones River. In Vicksburg, two weeks had passed since the wedding that wasn't. Still there had been no word from Cory. Uncle Charles had told her he suspected Cory had gone along with Forrest on the raid into western Tennessee. Lucille had to admit that sounded like something Cory would do. He knew Forrest and looked up to the cavalry general. Lucille felt a pang of hurt deep inside whenever she thought about the possibility Cory had preferred going into battle to marrying her. That wasn't the way it was, she told herself. If Cory had gone with Forrest, he would have had a good reason. But it still hurt.

At least Forrest had gotten back safely, without many losses among his men. Uncle Charles had learned that much from General Pemberton a few days earlier. A wire had come from Bragg in Tennessee reporting Forrest's success in his mission, as well as the failure at Stones River, which would only make Bragg even less likely to come to the aid of Vicksburg.

There *had* been losses, though, and if Cory had been with Forrest, he could have been one of them. Lucille had no way of knowing, and she repressed the thought.

But she had decided that it was foolish to leave the wedding dress hanging in her wardrobe. After putting it away, she came downstairs and went into the kitchen, where she found her aunt making biscuits. As usual, Mildred was trying to stretch a meager amount of flour as far as it would go.

"What have you been doing, dear?" Mildred asked without looking up from her work.

"I put my wedding dress away," replied Lucille. "It's in the cedar chest."

That got Mildred's attention. She turned around with flour dusted on her hands and said, "Are you sure that was the right thing to do? Cory could be back—"

"Cory will be back whenever he's back," Lucille said. "If he ever comes back."

"Oh, I'm sure he will."

"The dress has nothing to do with it, either way."

"Still, I hate to see you lose hope . . ."

Lucille's hands closed, and the fingernails dug into her palms. Was that what she was doing? Losing hope? Had she given up on Cory? Did she believe now that he was never coming back?

A knock on the front door made her gasp and spin around. Could it really be him, come home to her at last? That thought sprang into her head, even though she didn't want it to. She didn't want to get her hopes up, not after she had been disappointed so many times in the past.

Still, she had to know. "I'll see who it is," she said, leaving the kitchen and heading along the hallway toward the foyer.

She almost broke into a run.

Checking herself, she walked to the front door, took a breath, and opened it. Palmer Kincaid smiled at her and lifted a hand to his hat. "Good afternoon, Lucille," he said. "How are you?"

"Oh," she said. "It's you, Uncle Palmer."

If he was offended by her tone, he didn't show it. In fact, he laughed lightly. "Sorry I'm not that fair-haired lad of yours. If I was Cory Brannon, I don't think wild horses could have dragged me away from marrying you, my dear."

"Cory has never needed wild horses to drag him anywhere," Lucille said dryly. "Come in, Uncle Palmer. It's cold out there on the porch."

Kincaid took off his hat and stepped inside. "Indeed it is. I thought the winters in the South would be warmer and fairer than this."

"We're not *that* far south," Lucille said as she started to close the door behind him. As she did, she glanced down the street.

A man was riding along the street, she saw, a man who had evidently come a long way. His shoulders slumped wearily, and his horse plodded slowly on its way. The man's hat was pulled forward, shielding his face, and the collar of his coat was turned up against the chilly wind. All Lucille could tell about him was that he had a short, sandy-brown beard. She decided she had never seen him before and closed the door.

Then she froze as she turned back into the foyer.

Kincaid stood there, his hat in his hands, looking at her with a puzzled expression on his face as her eyes widened in shock. She knew who that rider was. Somehow, *she knew*.

Wheeling around, she threw the door open, burst out onto the porch, and flung herself down the steps to the walk. She flew across the yard, out the gate and into the street.

"Cory!"

Chapter Seventeen

IT HAD BEEN A long ride through northern Alabama and then across Mississippi, following much the same route he had taken when he walked it six months earlier. Many of the obstacles were the same, too: Yankee patrols that had to be dodged, lack of provisions that led to a lot of hungry nights, sheer boredom, and loneliness. One difference was that the weather was miserably cold now instead of miserably hot. But Cory had pushed on stubbornly anyway, holding an image of Lucille in his mind that he followed like a beacon, its shining rays cutting brilliantly through the darkest night.

He finally came to the Southern Mississippi Railroad and followed it west through Jackson—remembering the *other* Jackson, the one up in Tennessee where the Yankees had congregated to wait for an attack by Bedford Forrest that had never come. The past few weeks had a decidedly bittersweet tinge to them. Cory was proud that he had been part of such a successful raid, but he wouldn't have gone along with Forrest in the first place if he hadn't wanted to avenge Hamilton Ryder. And he had missed his wedding, too, which was bound to have hurt Lucille.

As he rode along the railroad right of way, he thought about the little girl called Maggie. He and Pie had met her back in the summer when they were walking to Vicksburg for the first time. She and her mother, Sarah, lived on a farm somewhere around here. Cory thought about looking them up and saying hello. Maggie's father had been killed in the war, but the little girl didn't know that, or at least she hadn't when Cory and Pie met her. Cory was curious as to how they were doing, but he decided not to take the time. He was too anxious to get back to Vicksburg and be reunited with Lucille. The next time he came this way, he promised himself, he would definitely stop in and visit the family.

He felt his excitement growing when he finally came within sight of the city. The massively imposing courthouse stood atop the bluff, dominating the landscape as always. At least it hadn't been blown away by the shelling from the Yankee gunboats, Cory told himself. His impulse was to urge his mount into a trot, but he couldn't do that to the horse. It had carried him a long way already and deserved the slower pace. He would be there soon enough.

But when it came to seeing Lucille again, that could never be soon enough to suit him.

Vicksburg had sustained more damage from the Yankee gunboats during the time he was gone. He saw a couple of buildings with their walls caved in from exploding shells, and some houses had burned down in fires started by the bombardment. Fewer people were on the street, too, and many of those who were had a furtive air about them. Cory saw people looking over their shoulders, as if they expected mortar shells to come crashing down on them at any moment.

Finally, he was on the street where the Thompson house was situated. A cold wind blew at his back, and he hunched his shoulders against it. He wanted to lift himself in the stirrups and crane his neck so that he could look farther down the street, but he suppressed the urge and forced himself to ride normally.

He couldn't restrain himself, though, when he suddenly heard a familiar and much-loved voice shout this name. His head jerked up, and he saw Lucille running into the street. Cory's heart seemed to swell until it filled his chest and closed off his throat. He pulled back on the reins and brought the horse to a stop, then dropped quickly from the saddle. He let the reins fall loose in the street as he started running toward Lucille. He was acting purely on instinct now, giving no thought at all to what he was doing. All he was thinking about was Lucille.

She was hurrying to meet him, her shoes slipping a little in the muddy street. As they came together, Cory caught her up in his embrace and drew her tightly against him. Their mouths found each other as her arms wound around his neck. Cory literally staggered a step from the intensity of the kiss.

Her body was warm and round and full in his arms, her mouth hot and sweet and urgent. Blood roared in his head. Joy flooded through his entire being.

After an unknowable amount of time, Lucille finally took her lips away from his and pressed her face against his chest. "You're alive, you're alive, you're alive," she babbled. "Thank God, you're alive!" Abruptly, she lifted her head to stare up at him, wide-eyed. "You *are* alive, aren't you, Cory? I'm not just imagining this?"

"I'm alive," he told her. "I'm all right, Lucille."

She took her arms from around his neck and put them around his waist instead, hugging him so hard that he could barely breathe. "I thought you must be dead," she whispered. "Don't you *ever* scare me like that again!"

He buried his face in her thick, honey-blonde hair, breathing deeply of its fragrance. "I'm sorry," he murmured. "I'm sorry about the wedding, sorry I couldn't be here."

She looked up at him again. "Where were you?"

"Tennessee. I had to go with General Forrest to destroy the railroads so the Yankees couldn't use them."

"You *had* to go?"

Cory took a deep breath. "To settle the score for Ham."

Lucille put a hand to her mouth and said in horror, "That young lieutenant?"

Cory nodded grimly. "He was killed. We were doing a job together, and it . . . it was my fault . . ." Cory couldn't go on.

"I'm so sorry, Cory. You can tell me all about it later." She gently pulled on his arm. "Come on. We'll go inside. You can say hello to Aunt Mildred and Uncle Palmer."

"Kincaid?" asked Cory, more sharply than he had intended.

"That's right. He's paying us a visit today. In fact, when he just now knocked on the front door, I thought for a second he might be you."

Not hardly, thought Cory. His joy at seeing Lucille and holding her again was tempered slightly by the knowledge that Palmer Kincaid was still making his presence known.

Only slightly, though. Right now he was so happy that nothing could spoil his mood too much.

Something nudged his shoulder, and he saw that his horse had followed him down the street and come up behind him. He chuckled and took hold of the reins again. Placing his other arm around Lucille's shoulders, he turned and walked toward the Thompson house.

Mildred had come to the gate and was smiling broadly as she saw Cory and Lucille coming toward her. Up on the porch, Kincaid stood smoking a cigar. The gambler wore a friendly smile as well, but Cory didn't trust it. He wondered if Kincaid had hoped that he would never come back. That would have left the field wide open for him to make advances toward Lucille.

"Cory, I'm so glad to see you!" Mildred exclaimed as he and Lucille came up to the gate. She moved closer to him and hugged him, kissing him on the cheek. Then she stepped back and said, "My goodness, you look like you haven't had a decent meal in weeks!"

"That's true enough," Cory told her with a grin. "Nothing to compare with your cooking, Mrs. Thompson."

"Oh, go on with you! I'd make a welcome-home feast for you tonight if I could, but . . ."

Cory nodded. "I understand. Supplies are getting scarce. Are they still coming in from Texas on the railroad?"

"For now," said Lucille. "Uncle Charles is worried that the Yankees are going to move into Louisiana and cut off that route, though. He can tell you all about it when he gets home later."

"He's here in Vicksburg?"

"He never went back after the wed—"

Lucille stopped short, and pain appeared in her eyes. Cory felt a surge of guilt. Lucille had been so happy to see him that she hadn't thought all that much about the wedding and how he hadn't been there. But now she had been reminded of it, and all the hurt feelings came rushing back.

"I'm sorry, Lucille," he said. "I wish I could make it up to you, but—"

"We'll talk about it later," she said firmly. "Right now, I'm just glad to have you home, Cory."

Kincaid came down from the porch and along the walk. "Let me echo those sentiments, Cory," he said as he extended his hand. "Welcome back to Vicksburg."

"Thanks," Cory said simply as he shook the gambler's hand.

"You've certainly had this little lady worried," Kincaid said, pointing with his cigar to Lucille.

"I'm sorry about that. If I could have gotten word to anyone, I would have. We tore up the telegraph lines along with the railroads, though."

"So your mission was a success?" asked Kincaid.

"Very much so. Grant had to pull out of Mississippi. I heard that he's gone all the way back to Memphis."

"Memphis isn't that far," Mildred said with a frown. "And the Yankees are still shelling the town from the river from time to time."

"They won't give up," said Cory. "They want it too much."

"Well, they're not coming today, so why don't we all go inside and get out of this cold wind?" suggested Mildred. "I'll see if I can scare up some tea."

That sounded good to Cory. Of course, anything that involved being around Lucille sounded good, he thought. He said, "I'll take my horse around back to the shed and see to it, then I'll come on in."

"Let me give you a hand," Kincaid offered.

Cory would have rather not had the man's company any more than necessary, but he couldn't turn Kincaid down without being impolite. "Thanks," he said and started to lead the horse around the fenced yard toward the narrow alley that led to the rear of the property.

Kincaid strolled alongside him, puffing on the cigar. "I'd be very interested in hearing about your experiences in Tennessee, Cory. I don't get to participate in any military actions myself."

"You could enlist," said Cory.

Kincaid smiled thinly. "I don't really think I'm the type to function well in the army. And I have my own responsibilities here, too."

"Running a saloon and gambling hall?"

"Someone has to keep up the morale of the citizenry."

There was a cold edge in Kincaid's voice. They understood each other, thought Cory. And neither liked the other.

"And I've been keeping an eye on Lucille for you," Kincaid went on as they reached the back of the house and Cory began to unsaddle the horse. "She was very upset when you didn't show up for the wedding, you know."

Cory wasn't going to be chided by the likes of Kincaid. He grunted as he heaved the saddle off the horse and set it aside in the shed. "It couldn't be helped," he said curtly.

"You would have been proud of her. She got up in front of all the guests and announced that there wasn't going to be a wedding—"

"There's going to be a wedding," Cory cut in. "Now that I'm back, there'll be a wedding. You can count on that."

"Oh, I am," said Kincaid. "But not as much as Lucille. I'd suggest that you not disappoint her again. Otherwise she might . . ." The gambler puffed on the cigar and blew out a cloud of smoke. ". . . call off the whole thing."

Cory looked at Kincaid. The gambler's face was smoothly shaven, and he smelled of bay rum. He had an air of well-fed contentment about him. Cory's face, on the other hand, was covered with beard, and he knew that he smelled like horse and sweat and smoke. He hadn't looked in a mirror in a while, but he certainly felt gaunt and haggard. And at this moment he was filled with the impulse to put a fist right in the middle of Kincaid's smirk.

"Lucille won't be disappointed," he said matter-of-factly. "I'm going inside."

"Of course," Kincaid said around the cigar.

They went through the house's back door, and Cory found himself in a warm kitchen filled with the smells of spices and cooking food. He paused and breathed deeply, enjoying the wonderful sensation.

Lucille stood at the table with her hand on the back of a chair. "Sit down, Cory," she said. "I'll pour you some tea."

Cory took off his hat and hung it on a nail by the door. He was looking forward to a bath and to scraping the beard off his face, but that could wait. He sat down. Lucille got the teakettle from the stove and filled the cup in front of him. Carefully, he lifted the bone china cup and inhaled the steamy vapors rising from the tea. He sipped the tea and closed his eyes for a moment in sheer pleasure.

Lucille stood behind him, her hands on his shoulders. Mildred was back at the stove making biscuits. The only thing spoiling the moment was the presence of Kincaid, who leaned against the wall and smoked.

After a few minutes, he excused himself, "I suppose I'd better be going. I don't want to intrude on what is, after all, a family reunion—of sorts."

Quickly, Lucille said, "Oh, you're not intruding, Uncle Palmer. You can stay as long as you like."

Kincaid smiled and casually waved a hand. "No, that's all right. I have business to attend to anyway." He started out of the kitchen, then said, "Come see me when you get a chance, Cory. I really would like to hear about your trip."

Cory nodded, not really meaning it. He intended to stay as far away as possible from Kincaid's waterfront dive. There had been a period in his life when he had spent a lot of time in such places, but no more.

Lucille saw Kincaid to the front door, and Cory worried about her the whole time she was gone. When she came back, she sat down at the table across from him and reached out to clasp one of his hands in both of hers. He sipped the tea and looked at her, content just to let the joy of being in her presence wash over him.

A short time later, the front door opened, and Cory heard the familiar footsteps of Colonel Thompson in the hallway. The colonel came into the kitchen and stopped short at the sight of the bearded, hollow-eyed young man sitting at the table with his niece.

"Cory?" Thompson exclaimed. "Is that you?"

Cory squeezed Lucille's hands, then stood up and faced the colonel. "Yes sir, it is," he said. "I'm finally back."

Thompson had dressed in civilian clothes during the time when he and Cory and Pie had been setting up the supply line from Texas. Now he was in the uniform of the Mississippi Home Guard, resplendent in the crisply pressed gray tunic and trousers, with a red sash around his waist and even a plume tucked in the band of his hat. A saber in a brass scabbard was belted around his waist.

He extended his hand and said formally, "It's good to see you again, my boy. You're looking . . . well."

Cory laughed and took the colonel's hand. "I look like blazes, sir, and I know it," he said. "But I'm happy to be back, and that's the main thing."

"Yes, it is," said Thompson. "Yes, it is." Suddenly, still gripping Cory's hand, he gave into an impulse and threw his other arm around Cory, thumping him on the back. "Lord, but it's good to see you again, son."

Awkwardly, Cory returned the embrace. "Thank you, sir."

Thompson stepped back and frowned. "I seem to recall saying a few weeks ago that the next time I saw you, I was going to wring your neck."

"Charles . . . ," Mildred said in warning tones.

"Something was mentioned about horsewhipping, too," Lucille put in helpfully.

Cory took a deep breath, let it out in a sigh. "The wedding," he said, with a heartfelt sigh.

"Indeed," Thompson said sternly. "I assume that you have a suitable excuse for breaking this dear girl's heart?"

"My heart's not broken," said Lucille. "Just wounded a little."

"Yes sir," Cory said to the colonel. "I'll tell you all about it—"

"After supper," Mildred put in. "That'll be soon enough for a bunch of talk about the war. Right now, you men shoo out of here, so Lucille and I can finish preparing the meal."

Thompson took Cory's arm. "Never argue with a woman, lad. It's the biggest waste of time and the greatest danger on the face of the earth."

"Oh, go on with you," Mildred said affectionately. "Take the boy into the parlor. Smoke a pipe or something."

"Do you *have* a pipe?" Thompson asked Cory.

"Uh, no sir."

"I have an old briar you might like. Come along."

Cory glanced over his shoulder at Lucille, hesitant to leave her even for a little while. She smiled, though, and motioned for him to go on.

It was all right, he told himself. From now on, they had all the time in the world.

THAT EVENING, the four of them sat in the parlor, and Cory told the others about the raid into Tennessee. Colonel Thompson and Mildred were on the divan, while Cory sat in an armchair near the fireplace. Lucille sat on the rug next to his right leg, one hand resting on his knee.

"You really should be making this report to General Pemberton," Thompson said before Cory began. "But I suppose we can go to his headquarters tomorrow and meet with him."

"Yes sir," Cory said with a nod. "I'd be glad to tell the general all about it."

Tonight, he started with the encounter he and Ham Ryder had had with Bedford Forrest, and the subsequent meeting with Bragg. He continued with Forrest's orders that they remain in Tullahoma and then go to Columbia with him. Glossing over certain parts of the story, most notably concerned with Miss Arabella and the things they had seen in her house, he told of how he and Ryder had slipped into Memphis to retrieve the firing caps that Forrest so urgently needed.

"We were on our way back to meet up with General Forrest at the river when . . ." Cory's voice broke, and he had to struggle to go on as the painful memories flooded over him. "We rode into a Yankee patrol. When we tried to get away, of course, there was some shooting . . ." He drew a deep, shaky breath, and Lucille's hand tightened on his knee. Cory drew some strength from that and was able to go on. "Ham was struck in the back. He managed to stay on his horse and lead me to safety, away from the Yankees."

Thompson said softly, "Mortally wounded?"

Cory nodded. "Yes sir."

Mildred asked, "Were you able to give him a decent burial?"

Cory looked down at the floor. "I wasn't able to bury him at all. I had to leave him there so I could get back to General Forrest as quickly as possible. So many of his men . . . well, they would have been helpless if the Yankees had caught them without those percussion caps."

"How horrible it must have been for you," Mildred said quietly.

"You had no choice," said the colonel. "You had to complete your mission. I'm sure the lieutenant would have told you the same thing."

"He pretty much did . . . before he died." Cory laid his hand on Lucille's where it rested on his knee. "The worst of it is, the whole thing was my fault. I was riding in front, and I had dozed off because we'd been in the saddle for so long. I didn't see the Yankees in time. I could have saved us both if I had."

Colonel Thompson frowned, blew out his breath gustily, and said, "Nonsense!"

"Sir?"

"I said it was nonsense, this business of your blaming yourself for the lieutenant's death. You're a human being, and human beings are fallible. Deprive them of sleep long enough and they doze off. It's inevitable."

"But I should have—"

Thompson leaned forward and said, "There are such things as fortunes of war, Cory. No one can control them. No one can know why a bullet misses one man and strikes another. Those decisions are in the hands of a higher power."

Slowly, Cory shook his head. "I don't know. I still think—"

"It's out of our hands, I tell you. Fortunes of war." The colonel settled back against the divan. "Fortunes of war."

After a moment's silence, Cory said, "I'd like to believe you, sir. At any rate, I found the general's camp near the river crossing, and by then I felt like I had to go along with him on the raid. I felt like I owed it to Ham."

"That didn't bring him back, though, did it?"

Again, Cory shook his head. "No sir. It surely didn't."

With the pain of reporting Ham Ryder's death behind him, Cory was able to go on with the story, telling the Thompsons and Lucille about the way Forrest had bluffed the Yankees into thinking that western Tennessee had been invaded by a much larger force than was really the case. He explained how they had torn up the railroad lines, looted and burned warehouses full of supplies and ammunition, pulled down telegraph wires, burned bridges, and generally wreaked havoc with the plans concocted by Grant. Then came the tale of how the Confederate cavalry had made its way back to the river, including the battle at Parker's Crossroads.

"Once we got back across the river, I took my leave of the general," Cory concluded. "He would have been pleased to have me stay with him, but I knew I had to get back here."

"Quite a story," murmured the colonel. "I'm sure General Pemberton will be fascinated by the military aspects of it."

"That's all I intend to tell him, sir." The rest of it, Cory knew, was private.

"There was a battle near here, too, you know," Thompson went on. "Up at Chickasaw Bluffs. General Sherman thought to ferry his men up the Yazoo to that point, then have them come overland against the city. He was repulsed with heavy losses. But he might not have been had not General Pemberton been able to concentrate his defenses in that area. If Grant had still been advancing on us, I fear our forces would have had to be split, and the outcome could have been quite different."

"Then we helped to save Vicksburg," Cory said.

"Indeed you did."

Cory sighed. That made him feel a little better. Ham's sacrifice hadn't been for nothing.

"There was quite a battle in Virginia, too, last month."

Cory's head lifted. Virginia was his home and in a way always would be, no matter where he roamed.

"At a place called Fredericksburg," continued Thompson. "Are you familiar with it?"

"Yes sir. I've been there. It's on the Rappahannock River, north of Richmond."

"A Union general named Burnside tried to cross the river there and capture the city, but he failed. It was quite a triumph for the Confederacy, according to the newspapers."

"You have brothers in the army in Virginia, don't you, Cory?" asked Lucille.

He nodded. "My brother Will is in the Thirty-third Virginia under Stonewall Jackson, and my brother Mac is serving with General Stuart's cavalry."

"Then they were there," Thompson said.

"But I'm sure they're all right," Mildred said quickly. "Otherwise we would have heard. Your sister writes to you with news of the family, doesn't she?"

"Yes, ma'am. Cordelia's good about that. But with the war going on, letters get lost sometimes."

"Have faith, lad," said the colonel. "From what I've seen of the Brannons, they're a lucky bunch."

"So I've been told," murmured Cory. He looked down at Lucille, who was smiling up at him and holding his hand. "And I can't argue with that. No sir, I can't argue at all."

Chapter Eighteen

T HE DEFEAT AT CHICKASAW Bluffs was not the last bitter pill that Gen. William Tecumseh Sherman had to swallow that winter. After withdrawing from the Yazoo River, he and his men bivouacked at Milliken's Bend, a small settlement on the west bank of the Mississippi about ten miles upstream from Vicksburg. Shortly after that, several thousand reinforcements under Gen. John A. McClernand showed up. Since McClernand, who had achieved his rank through political connections rather than military expertise, technically was Sherman's superior officer, he assumed command of the Union forces at Milliken's Bend, much to Sherman's disgust.

Gen. Ulysses S. Grant shared Sherman's low opinion of McClernand. It was possible that McClernand might decide to launch an offensive of his own against Vicksburg, and if he did, the inevitable blunders he would make might put the Union army in danger of being destroyed completely. Grant moved quickly from Memphis to Milliken's Bend to snatch command out of McClernand's hands.

Although the Yankee gunboats under Adm. David G. Farragut still sporadically shelled Vicksburg, Grant knew that bombardment alone would never be enough to subdue the city. The swampy bottomlands that surrounded so much of Vicksburg's inland boundary made overland attacks difficult, as Sherman's misfortunes at Chickasaw Bluffs proved. Still, Grant was determined to carry out his mission, even if his methods had to be rather far-fetched.

The next attempt certainly fit that description. During the previous summer, Union forces had begun digging a canal across the base of the Swampy Toe peninsula, a long, narrow projection of land directly opposite Vicksburg formed by the horseshoe bend of the Mississippi River. That effort had soon been abandoned, but now Grant resumed it, reasoning that if the canal could be completed and the river could be diverted into it, Union ships could pass up and down beyond the range of Vicksburg's guns. While that would not put the city in Federal hands, it would accomplish one of the Union's main goals, which was to open the river to traffic once more.

The work was cold, muddy, and miserable. Despite the chill in the air, gnats seemed to thrive, and clouds of them hovered blindingly around the soldiers who were trying to dig their way through the muck. Still, they persevered and might have succeeded, if not for heavy rains in January that caused the river to rise and wash away everything they had done. The only thing the Yankee effort really accomplished was to cut the supply line from Texas. The tracks of the Shreveport, Vicksburg, and Texas Railroad ran all the way to the end of Swampy Toe, so now the railroad's terminus was in Union hands. The locomotives sat idle in Monroe, Louisiana, so the Yankees couldn't capture them and make use of them.

Grant abandoned the idea of the canal but didn't give up on taking Vicksburg. An attempt was made to divert the river at Lake Providence, forty miles north of Milliken's Bend, into the swamps west of the Mississippi. Plenty of fingerlike creeks and bayous existed in the area, and if they could be connected somehow, they would form a network that would lead back to the Mississippi far south of Vicksburg. Again, the effort involved a great deal of digging and slogging through mud and swamp, which meant that progress was extremely slow, and again it failed when it became obvious that it would take years to complete such an operation.

The Yazoo Pass expedition was Grant's next idea. Ferrying troops up the Yazoo hadn't worked, as Sherman's failure at Chickasaw Bluffs proved, so Grant decided to bring them down the Yazoo instead, through the Yazoo Pass that connected the smaller river to the Mississippi and across Moon Lake. That would allow the troops to go ashore farther to the northeast and bypass Chickasaw Bluffs on their way to Vicksburg. The first obstacle to Grant's plan was that a levee had been built across the mouth of the Yazoo several years earlier, closing the pass. Early in February 1863, Grant solved this dilemma with the prudent use of large quantities of explosives. The blast blew a huge hole in the levee and sent the waters of the Mississippi flowing rapidly into Moon Lake. The water took with it Union gunboats and troop transports.

The Yankees were on their way to Vicksburg—again.

CORY WAS aware, at least to a certain extent, of what the Union forces under Grant were doing. Colonel Thompson kept him informed, telling him what was discussed at each meeting with General Pemberton. It was a sad day when they learned that no more supplies would be coming in from Texas on the railroad.

"Well, our efforts were fruitful for quite a while," the colonel said after delivering the unwelcome news. "A great deal of supplies were brought into the city by way of the railroad. As bad as our situation is, think how much worse it would have been by now without what we accomplished."

Cory could only nod in agreement. It seemed to him, however, that all their efforts might have just postponed disaster. The Yankees were tightening the noose on Vicksburg. Food was growing more and more scarce, though no one was starving to death—yet. In the long run, having enough ammunition might be a problem, too.

But at least he was with Lucille again. He could withstand almost anything as long as they weren't separated, he told himself. They began planning another wedding for the middle of February. This one, however, would be a small ceremony, with only a few friends and family invited. The mood in Vicksburg had changed, and somehow, Lucille insisted, a big wedding just didn't seem appropriate anymore.

Cory didn't care. The important thing was that soon he and Lucille would be married.

The potential guest list for the ceremony grew by a couple on a day late in January when two unexpected visitors arrived at the Thompson house. Cory and Lucille were in the parlor, talking quietly, when a knock came on the front door.

"I'll get it," Lucille called to her aunt, who was in the kitchen. Cory followed Lucille into the foyer. As she swung the door open, they both were startled to see Fred Carter standing there, an arm around the waist of his father. Allen Carter was gray-faced and exhausted, and there were lines of pain around his eyes.

"Fred! Mr. Carter!" Lucille exclaimed. "Come in, come in. What in the world are you doing here?"

Cory wondered the same thing. He had assumed that when the Yankees swarmed onto Swampy Toe and idled the railroad, Carter and Fred would have stayed in Monroe.

"Pa's real tired," Fred said as he helped his father into the parlor. "Can he sit down?"

"Of course. Cory, help Fred get Mr. Carter onto the divan."

Cory took Carter's arm, and carefully, he and Fred lowered the man onto the divan. Carter was breathing hard. He sighed as he leaned back against the cushions, then reached down to massage what remained of his right leg.

"Damn thing started acting up on me," he said. "Beggin' your pardon for the language, Miss Farrell."

"That's all right," Lucille told him. "Where did you two come from?"

"Monroe," Fred answered. "We walked."

"The whole eighty miles?" Cory asked in surprise.

Carter nodded. "Yeah. Dawson at the wagon yard offered to let me have a couple of horses, but I don't take charity."

"How did you get across the river?"

"Found a fella with a skiff. He was willing to risk the gunboats and bring us across—for the rest of the money we had."

Lucille sat down at the other end of the divan. "But why did you come to Vicksburg?"

"We're goin' to fight Yankees, Pa and me," Fred announced proudly.

"Once the railroad stopped running, there was no point in taking the wagon train back to Texas," said Carter. "We kept hearing about how there was going to be a fight over here, so we decided to come see if we could get in on it."

Cory and Lucille exchanged glances, but before either could say anything, Mildred appeared in the doorway of the parlor and said, "My goodness, if it's not Mr. Carter and Fred!"

The young man grinned at her and greeted her in return.

Mildred came into the room and hugged him, then took Carter's hand. "It's so good to see you again," she said. "But why aren't you in Louisiana?"

Carter seemed to have recovered some of his strength. He didn't look quite so haggard now. "Like I was telling Cory and Miss Lucille, Fred and I came to get in on the fight once the Yankees get here."

Mildred frowned. "The good Lord willing, the Yankees will never reach Vicksburg."

"Yeah," said Carter, but he didn't sound convinced.

Neither was Cory. He knew the Yankees wouldn't give up and go away once Grant had set his mind to something. He remembered how doggedly Grant had come after Fort Henry and Fort Donelson, and how the Union commander had turned the tide on the second day at Shiloh when it looked like the Yankees were whipped. Grant might be defeated—anything was possible—but Vicksburg would not get off lightly in the process.

"Well, I'm sure Charles will be glad to see you again," Mildred said. "Do you have a place to stay?"

"Figured we'd find us a place in some army camp."

"Nonsense. You'll stay right here with us."

Fred grinned and nodded, saying, "I'd like that," but Carter shook his head.

"We don't take charity."

"It's not charity," Mildred said sternly. "If you're here to help defend the city, then we're all indebted to you. It's only right that you and Fred have a decent place to stay."

"Please, Pa," Fred put in. "I want to stay here with Cory and Miss Lucille. And Pie. Where's Pie?"

"He left," Lucille said gently. "Remember, Fred? He and Miss Rachel went to Texas."

"Oh, yeah. I remember now. Miss Rachel sure was pretty. Not as pretty as you, though, Miss Lucille."

Cory said to Carter, "I think you should stay, too, now that you're here. But I'm not sure it was a good idea for you to come in the first place. You'd have been safer in Monroe."

"I had to be doing something," declared Carter. He thumped his right thigh with his fist. "After I got home from Manassas with my leg shot off, I pretty much gave up for a long time. Didn't figure I'd ever be good for anything again. But the colonel gave me a chance, and I proved myself. I couldn't go back to being useless again. I just couldn't."

"Well, I'm glad the two of you are here, and I'm sure Charles will be, too," said Mildred. "And no more arguments. You're our guests, gentlemen."

Carter shrugged, admitting defeat. "Thank you, ma'am."

"Are we staying?" asked Fred eagerly.

"Looks like it, son."

"Good. I like it here."

❦

THE NEXT unexpected arrival was not nearly as pleasant. Colonel Thompson, who was as glad as the others to see Carter and Fred again, brought home a letter one day early in February. Cory recognized the writing on it as soon as Thompson gave it to him.

"It's from my sister, Cordelia," he said as he broke the seal and unfolded the paper.

He was standing in the middle of the parlor as he read it. Lucille and Mildred were on the divan, both of them mending clothes. Carter sat in the armchair near the fireplace, while Fred sat crosslegged on the floor in front of the flames. Colonel Thompson took out his pipe and tobacco pouch and began to pack the old briar as he watched Cory read.

Suddenly, Cory paled, and his fingers clenched on the paper, crumpling it. Lucille noticed his reaction immediately and put her mending aside. She stood up and quickly came to him.

"Cory," she said, putting a hand on his arm. "What is it? What's wrong?"

He lowered the crumpled letter and swallowed hard. "My . . . my brother Titus," he said hoarsely. "He was at Fredericksburg. I . . . I didn't even know he was in the army."

Lucille's eyes widened in shocked understanding. "Oh, no," she whispered.

"He was killed," Cory said flatly. "They weren't able to recover his body, but there was no way he could have survived, Cordelia says. Mac and Will were there. They didn't see it, but they talked to people who did."

The others in the room stood up and surrounded Cory, reaching out to him in sympathy. Colonel Thompson clasped a hand on his shoulder and asked, "Your other brothers, they came through the battle all right?"

Cory jerked his head in a nod. "Yeah. Will and Mac are all right, Cordelia says. But Titus . . ."

She put her arms around him. "I'm sorry, Cory. I'm so sorry."

"He . . . he didn't even get a proper burial . . ." Thoughts of Ham Ryder, his body left lying under that tree, came back to him, and the pain they brought with them dug deeply into him.

A few moments of silence went by, then Colonel Thompson said quietly, "I hesitate to bring this up at a time like this, but General Pemberton had news today."

Cory took a deep breath, smoothed out the letter from his sister, folded it, and tucked it inside his coat. He turned to the colonel and blinked back the tears in his eyes. "What is it, sir?" he asked.

"He's received word from agents in the Union camp that Grant is about to launch another offensive on the city. He intends to blast open the Yazoo Pass and ferry troops across Moon Lake and down the Yazoo."

Cory was only vaguely familiar with the geographical features Thompson mentioned, but he understood the general idea of Grant's plan. "He's still trying to get around Chickasaw Bluffs and come at the city from the northeast, isn't he?"

Thompson nodded. "That's right. But General Pemberton intends to stop him before he can get anywhere close to Vicksburg. The general has already put out the call for men."

"Count me in," Allen Carter said without hesitation. "I'm ready to see some action again."

Without daring to look at Lucille, Cory said, "Me, too, Colonel. I'll go." He had to go to avenge Titus.

"No!" exclaimed Lucille. "You can't, Cory. You haven't been back from Tennessee that long. We . . . we haven't even gotten married yet!"

Cory turned toward her and rested his hands on her shoulders. She stared up at him in disbelief, tears shining in her eyes.

"It won't take long," he told her. "It won't be like what happened in Tennessee."

"How do you know that?" she asked in a whisper.

Colonel Thompson put in, "I think the lad's right, Lucille. General Pemberton plans to block the waterways with fallen trees so that the Federal boats can't get through. It's entirely possible there won't even be a battle. But we need to have a force ready to meet the Yankees just in case."

Lucille didn't appear to have heard him. She was still looking into Cory's eyes. "You're going, aren't you?" she said.

"I have to," he said miserably.

"Why?"

The question took him by surprise. "What?"

"Why does it have to be you, Cory? When I first met you, you didn't give a damn about anything. Who appointed you the . . . the savior of the goddamned Confederacy?" She was shouting by the time she finished.

"Lucille!" Mildred gasped. The colonel and Allen Carter looked surprised, too, and Fred was staring at Lucille with his mouth hanging open.

Cory shook his head. "It's not like that. I'm just trying to do the right thing—"

"What about the right thing for us? I forgave you the last time, Cory, but if you leave me again, I . . . I just don't know if I can."

Cory felt something ripping inside him. This was one of the worst moments of his life, and though he wanted desperately to change things, to fix everything that was broken, he couldn't see how. All he could see was Lucille's tear-streaked face—and Titus's dead body lying in a heap of corpses on a frozen battlefield.

"I'll go, Colonel," he said. "Put me down as a volunteer."

And a damned fool, he thought bitterly.

LUCILLE'S ANGER was like a blanket of ice covering her. She tried to shrug it off, but she couldn't. During the few days that Cory remained in Vicksburg before leaving with General Pemberton, Colonel Thompson, and the other men who were going up the Yazoo to stop the Yankees, she barely spoke to him. Her heart went out to him every time she saw the pain and sorrow in his eyes. He had just found out that his brother was dead, after all. He had to be hurting from that. And yet he hadn't let it stop him from doing what he believed was the right thing. Lucille told herself she should be glad he was so devoted to protecting Vicksburg.

But she couldn't. She wanted him to be selfish for a change and care more about protecting himself. That way he would be all right, and she wouldn't have to endure any more sleepless nights while she wondered if she would ever see him again.

Would any of them be all right if the Yankees took Vicksburg? Or would the battle destroy the city and everyone in it?

War was complicated enough to start with, and love just made it worse, she decided.

The day Cory, Uncle Charles, and Allen Carter left wasn't hard on her alone, Lucille knew. Aunt Mildred was being separated from her husband, and Fred Carter, unexpectedly, was being separated from his father. Ever since they had left Monroe, Fred had thought that he was going to fight the Yankees, too, but Carter refused to take him along.

"You need to stay here with Mrs. Thompson and Miss Lucille," Carter told Fred as they all gathered in the parlor to say their good-byes.

Fred was wearing his hat and coat and had a pouch full of supplies slung over his shoulder. He stared at his father and said, "But you told me I could come with you!"

"To Vicksburg," Carter said firmly. "I told you that we'd come to Vicksburg together. I didn't say anything about you going on anywhere else."

"You're going! I want to be with you, Pa!" Fred started to cry.

Carter looked angry, embarrassed, and sad all at the same time. He put his arms around the young man and hugged him. "Listen, son, I don't want to be apart from you, either. But I can't be worrying about you all the time. That's why I need you to stay here. You'll be safer."

Mildred tried to help by patting Fred on the shoulder. "And we need you here, too, Fred," she said. "My, you've been so good about chopping wood and fetching water and helping out any way we ask you to, I just don't know how we'd get along without you now."

Fred let out a wail and clung more tightly to Carter.

Lucille's instincts made her try to help her aunt. Together, they pried Fred away from his father. Fred threw his arms around her, still sobbing. Lucille disentangled herself as gently as she could. She was crying now, too, partially out of sympathy for Fred and partially because she didn't want to say good-bye to Cory. When he put a hand lightly on her shoulder, she turned and practically flung herself at him, hugging him so hard she was surprised his ribs didn't crack.

"I . . . I'm sorry, Lucille . . . ," he began.

"I know," she said between sobs. "J-just hold me."

"But I want to tell you—"

"There's n-nothing you can tell me. I know you h-have to go. Oh, Cory . . ."

Mildred was crying now, too, and Cory, Uncle Charles, and Allen Carter all had tears in their eyes. Somehow, the whole thing suddenly struck Lucille as comical. There was so much crying going on that the sorrow lost its meaning. Incredibly, she began to laugh.

Cory looked down at her in amazement as he held her. "Lucille?"

"It's all right, Cory," she told him, stifling her laughter as she rested her face against his chest. "It's all right. You just come back safe to me, hear?"

"Then . . . you're not mad at me anymore?"

She lifted her eyes to meet his puzzled gaze. "I'm mad as blazes at you," she said honestly. "But you don't have to do everything in life just to make me happy, do you?"

"I wish I could."

"You can't. Not and be Cory Brannon." She came up on her toes and kissed him lightly. "Now go on, before I realize that I've momentarily lost my mind."

"All right," he said slowly. He kissed her again, harder than she had kissed him, then let her go and turned toward the door. Carter and the colonel were ready to go, too. The three of them left quickly. Lucille and Mildred and Fred stepped out onto the porch to watch them walk toward downtown Vicksburg and Pemberton's headquarters. The women stood on either side of

Fred and put their arms around him. He was still sobbing wretchedly. He shouted, "Pa! I want to go, Pa! Come back!"

Carter just turned and waved, as did Cory and Charles.

Fred shrieked, "Pa!"

Sharply, Mildred said, "You hush now, Fred. You're just making it harder on your poor father."

"But I want to go with him!"

"And I'm sure he'd take you if he could. This is what war is about, Fred—people being apart when they don't want to be. It's a hard lesson, but it's one we've all had to learn."

"He'd take me with him if he loved me!"

Mildred moved in front of him and looked up into his face. "You listen to me, young man. Your father loves you more than anything or anybody else in this world. That's why he's trying to do what's right for you. You may not understand it and you may not agree with it, but don't you ever think that your father doesn't love you!"

Fred blinked rapidly and sniffed a few times, then said, "Really?"

Mildred nodded. "Really." She took his arm. "Now come along inside." She led him to the door, then paused and looked back over her shoulder at Lucille, who was still standing at the railing along the edge of the porch, staring down the street where the three men finally had gone out of sight. "Lucille, are you coming in?"

"In a minute," she said.

"Don't stay out here too long, dear. The wind's cold today."

Not really, thought Lucille. For the first time in days she actually felt warm again.

Chapter Nineteen

CORY HATED SWAMPS. The stink of stagnant water and decaying vegetation, the gloom of the shadows cast by the moss that grew so thickly from the trees, the heavy oppressiveness of the air, even in winter . . . those things were so alien to the farmland where he had been raised in the Virginia Piedmont. A few days of marching through the swamps along the Yazoo River northeast of Vicksburg made him feel as if he would never be clean again.

He had been given a rifle when he volunteered with the Mississippi Home Guard. He took special pains to keep it and his pair of revolvers from rusting in the damp weather.

It took two weeks to reach the spot where the Yalobusha River merged with the Yazoo, and a miserable two weeks they were. Even if everything went well, it would be the end of February before they could return to Vicksburg, Cory suddenly realized, and that meant there would be no February wedding for him and Lucille.

Well, a March wedding . . . a spring wedding . . . was even better, he told himself. With any luck, the weather would be more pleasant by then.

Some of the Confederate forces had gone ahead to set the trap for the Yankees. Huge trees grew along the banks of the Yazoo, and men had set to work with axes and crosscut saws to fell as many of them as possible. The trees toppled into the river so that their huge trunks formed a barrier the Federal vessels could not pass until they had been hauled out of the way. That would take a great deal of time and slow the Yankees' progress even more than the narrow river channel already had.

That delay gave the troops from Vicksburg the time they needed to get ready. For several days after they arrived at the mouth of the Yalobusha, Cory and the others labored almost around the clock, piling up bales of cotton and sandbags until they had a high, thick wall that bullets wouldn't penetrate. This massive breastwork on the eastern bank of the Yazoo overlooked a bend in the river, so that the Yankees would be right in the sights of the Confederate guns.

Eight cannons were ferried upstream and hauled into position. When they were ready, their barrels pointed toward the Yazoo, one of the artillerymen laughed and said, "This here's a regular fortress now. I reckon we ought to call it Fort Pemberton, after the general."

The name caught on. Two thousand troops manned Fort Pemberton, and they were ready for the Yankees.

Several days passed with no sign of the Union steamboats. The delaying tactics upriver must have worked, thought Cory as he stood his watch, rifle propped on the pile of sandbags in front of him and his eyes fixed on the Yazoo. Scouts had been sent up the Yalobusha and the Tallahatchie to make sure the Yankees hadn't shifted their invasion route over to one of those streams, but it wouldn't really matter if they had. The Tallahatchie flowed into the Yalobusha and the Yalobusha flowed into the Yazoo a short distance above Fort Pemberton, so the Yankees had no hope of sneaking past the defenders unseen.

A hand fell on Cory's shoulder, and he looked over to see Colonel Thompson crouching next to him. "How goes it, lad?" he asked.

Cory slapped at an insect crawling on his face. "All right, Colonel. But I'd like to know why there are still so many bugs around in the middle of winter."

Thompson chuckled. "It seldom gets cold enough in these parts to kill out all the insects."

"It's below freezing a lot of nights."

"But not far enough below, I suppose. At any rate, the tiny creatures are almost always with us, making a constant annoyance of themselves."

"Like the Yankees," Cory muttered.

"Yes, but the Yankees have a more potent sting."

Cory sighed as he watched the river. "I wonder how Lucille is doing."

"I'm sure she's fine, and so are Mildred and young Fred."

"I wish Fred hadn't carried on so when we left. It was hard on Allen."

The colonel nodded. "Of course it was. But he had to do as he saw fit. I don't think it would have been a good idea for the boy to accompany us, either. Now, if Private Jones had still been around, that would have been a different matter entirely. We could have certainly used him."

"Yeah. I miss Pie." Cory looked over at Thompson. "You know what happened back there in Louisiana, don't you? With Grat and Rachel, I mean?"

"I have a pretty good idea. Somehow you got the young woman out of the boarding house, and then she and Private Jones absconded to Texas."

"That's about the size of it," admitted Cory. "Pie told me to tell you he was sorry about how everything turned out. He had to do what he did, though."

"I must admit I was somewhat disappointed. You two gave me your word you wouldn't go back to the boarding house."

"We never set foot in the place, sir," Cory said.

"Oh, come now. There's no point in maintaining the fiction after all this time—"

"But we really didn't. Lucille went into the house and got Rachel. It was her idea."

The colonel's eyebrows lifted in surprise. "Lucille?"

"Yes sir. So Pie and I kept our word."

For a moment, Thompson looked like he was about to explode with anger. Then, abruptly, he laughed. "My niece is an extraordinary young woman."

"Yes sir," agreed Cory. "I've thought that for a long time. It's been over a year now since I first met her."

"A busy year for us all."

"Yes sir."

Too busy, thought Cory. It had been a year filled with fighting and death, with tragedy and separation. A year filled with war. There was no other way to look at it.

And the future stretched out darkly in front of them, holding the promise of nothing but more of the same . . .

ᑐᓄᕽ

LUCILLE WAS alone in the house when she heard the knocking on the front door. Aunt Mildred and Fred had gone downtown in hopes of being able to buy some more supplies. Fred had carried the wicker basket Mildred used for her marketing. They would be lucky if they came back with the basket filled even a fourth of the way to the top. Spring was just around the corner, as the old saying went, but it was not going to be a season of plenty in Vicksburg.

Lucille went to the door and opened it to find Palmer Kincaid standing on the porch. He swept off the dark brown beaver hat he wore and smiled at her. "Good afternoon to you, Lucille," he said. "How are you?"

"Just fine, Uncle Palmer." She stepped back into the foyer. "Come in. It's been a while since you've come to visit us."

"My business keeps me busy. Of course, it's not how it was in Cairo, mind you. The Staghorn was quite an establishment. Always bustling."

"I remember." Lucille took his hat and ushered him into the parlor. "I think after I was old enough to understand some of the things that went on there, Father was a bit leery of allowing me to go in. I always wanted to see you, though."

"The feeling was mutual, my dear. I always looked forward to your visits. Your beauty brightened up the place like the sun never could."

Lucille laughed. "You're going to make me blush, what with all those compliments, Uncle Palmer."

"Don't you think you're old enough now you could just call me Palmer? After all, you'll soon be a married woman."

"Oh, I don't know. You've always been Uncle Palmer to me—"

"Things change," said Kincaid. "You've changed, Lucille."

Her finely drawn eyebrows arched in surprise. "I have?"

Kincaid clasped his hands together behind his back and stood in front of the fireplace. "You certainly have. In the short time I've known you, you've grown from a little girl into one of the most beautiful women I've ever seen. Quite possibly *the* most beautiful."

Lucille felt her face growing warm. "Uncle Palmer, now I really am blushing—"

"Palmer," he said, unclasping his hands and coming a step toward her. "Call me Palmer, Lucille."

Suddenly uneasy, she moved toward the divan and crossed behind it, putting it between them. For some reason, she said, "Aunt Mildred is out in the kitchen—"

"No, she's not," Kincaid interrupted. "I saw her and that boy leave a short time ago. They looked like they were going marketing." The gambler shook his head. "Sad to say, they probably won't have much luck. Provisions really are beginning to grow scarce in Vicksburg. I can hardly get enough whiskey to meet my needs."

"The city can get along without whiskey."

Kincaid smiled. "You wouldn't say that if you happened to own a tavern."

Lucille relaxed slightly. If she could keep him talking about his business instead of going on about how lovely she was, she would be more comfortable.

"I'll certainly do what I can to help," Kincaid went on. "I have my finger on what little river traffic there is. If you need extra supplies, let me know and I'll see what I can do."

Lucille shook her head. "That wouldn't be fair. Everyone is facing the same hardships—"

"I don't care about anyone else. You're the only one in Vicksburg who matters to me, Lucille." Kincaid paused, then added, "Because of my friendship with you and your father, of course."

Lucille wasn't so sure about that. For the first time in her life, she noticed the way Kincaid's eyes dropped to the thrust of her breasts against her dress and lingered there. The things that he had said to her earlier, all that about how beautiful she was, those were things a man might say to a woman he was trying to . . . to make love to, she thought. She swallowed, suddenly nervous again.

"Why did you come here today, Uncle Palmer?" she asked. Her hands were resting on the back of the divan. They tightened as he came closer to her.

"Because I decided that I've waited long enough," he said, his eyes intent on hers.

"I . . . I don't know what you're talking about."

He shook his head. "Don't tell me that," he said, his voice suddenly taking on an edge of anger. "Don't tell me you haven't known how I've felt about you for years now."

Still gripping the back of the divan, she drew herself up straighter and squared her shoulders. "I think you'd better leave now, Uncle Palmer."

"Damn it, don't call me that!" he burst out. "I'm not your uncle, and you know it. You know I want you, too. By God, I've wanted you ever since you were fourteen years old!"

She shook her head and cried, "Stop it! Don't talk like that! I don't want to hear it."

His hand shot over the back of the divan and grabbed her arm, and she cried out again. "You will hear it!" he said savagely. She tried to pull away, but he was too strong. "I've watched you with that boy you say you're going to marry—if he comes back alive. Before you spend the rest of your life with him, you need to know what it's like to be with a real man!"

He pulled hard on her arm and she fell forward, tumbling over the back of the divan. She sprawled on the cushions, and suddenly he was on top of her, holding her down, kissing her. His mouth pressed hard against hers, bruising her lips. His hands pulled at her clothes.

She fought back, twisting from side to side and trying to throw him off. Kincaid's weight made it hard for her to breathe, and she felt a wave of dizziness and revulsion wash over her. Blackness was closing in around her, and she was afraid she might pass out. She couldn't do that, her brain screamed at her. If she did, she would be helpless to stop him from doing whatever he wanted.

She tried to claw at his face with her fingernails. He caught both of her hands in one of his, but she was able to tear her right hand free. Her fingers found his left ear, gripped it hard, and twisted with all her strength.

Kincaid shouted in pain, and the crushing weight went away from Lucille. He rolled off her and fell to the floor next to the divan. He flung his left arm up and batted her hand away from his head, then clapped his hand over his ear and spewed curses.

Lucille pulled herself to her knees and tried to scramble off the divan past him. He threw an arm around her waist and knocked her down. She kicked at him and started to crawl away, but he caught hold of her ankle and jerked her back. She rolled over and slashed her nails toward his face again, making him flinch. Her ankle came loose from his grip. Sitting on her rump, she pushed away frantically, sliding across the parlor floor toward the fireplace.

She lunged and grabbed one of the pokers from its stand. Coming to her feet, she swung the poker at Kincaid, missing by at least a yard as he darted back. Lucille caught her balance and raised the makeshift weapon again. She didn't think about the fact that she had regarded this man as a friend for years, nor about how shocking his unexpected assault was. All she thought about was that if he came any closer to her, she would split his head open with the poker.

"Get out!" she screamed at him. "Get out, damn you!"

He extended a hand toward her. His ear was red where she had twisted it, but she hadn't torn the skin. "Lucille, you're making a mistake. I can do things for you—"

"Get out!"

"I can be of help to your family. I can be the best friend you've ever had."

"Stay away from me," she said, her voice shaking. "Get out of this house and don't ever come back!"

He laughed coldly. "I could take that poker away from you, you know."

"Go ahead," she dared him, too furious now for caution. "Try."

Kincaid hesitated, and for a second she thought he was going to come after her again. She wasn't afraid now. She *wanted* him to give her an excuse to flail away at him.

Finally, he said quietly, "You'll regret this day, Lucille." With that, he straightened his clothes, turned, and stalked out of the parlor. A moment later, she heard the front door slam.

She turned toward the window to make sure he had really left. When she saw him walking stiffly away from the house, reaction to everything that had happened suddenly hit her. She dropped the poker to the rug at her feet, then, gasping and sobbing, she began to rub her hands over her mouth where he had kissed her, as if she could wipe away the vile memory of what he had done.

She fell to her knees in front of the fireplace and cried for a long time. How long, she never knew. But finally, the tears stopped and her stunned brain began to function again. She knew that Cory had never liked Kincaid, and now she understood the reason why. He had been able to see the things she never had. He had seen the way Kincaid must have been looking at her for years.

And if Cory knew what had happened here today, he would try to kill the gambler. Lucille was sure of that.

That couldn't happen. Cory had dodged death plenty of times, but anyone's luck could run out. Kincaid was an evil, treacherous man. Lucille didn't want Cory anywhere near him in the future.

Which meant that Cory couldn't find out about this, and neither could anyone else.

Lucille got to her feet, wiped the tears away, and tugged her dress into place. Thank God it wasn't torn, she thought. In fact, once she put the poker back in its place and straightened the rugs, no one would be able to tell from the looks of the room that anything unusual had occurred.

She took a deep breath and told herself that she had to get busy. Aunt Mildred and Fred would be home soon.

And she prayed that Cory would be, too.

PALMER KINCAID was still livid and in pain when he stalked into his office in the rear of Cochran's, the waterfront tavern he had won in a poker game shortly after arriving in Vicksburg. His ear ached like blazes where that little hellcat had nearly twisted it off his head.

He took off his hat and slammed it down on the desk. A chuckle came from a shadowed corner of the room.

Kincaid spun around. Survival instincts well honed by years of living on intimate terms with danger sent his hand under his coat to grasp the butt of a pocket pistol.

"No need for that, Kincaid," said the man who sat there on a cane-bottomed chair. "Besides, if I wanted you dead, you would be already. You're much more valuable to me alive."

Kincaid grunted and took his hand away from the gun. "You'd do well to remember that."

"Oh, I never forget it," said his visitor. "How about one of those cigars that you smoke?"

Kincaid hesitated. "They're expensive," he said, "and they're not that easy to get anymore since the Yankees have control of New Orleans."

300 • James Reasoner

The visitor just waited in silence.

"Oh, all right," Kincaid said after a moment. He reached into his vest pocket, took out a cigar, and handed it to the man in the corner. The man took the cigar, carefully trimmed the end of it with a little knife he took from his pocket, and then scratched a lucifer into life on the sole of his boot. As he held the flame to the tip of the cigar, its glow illuminated a lean face with a lantern jaw and deep-set eyes. The man puffed on the cigar until it was burning properly, then shook out the match, sat back, and blew out a cloud of smoke.

Kincaid went behind his desk and sat down. As he did so, his visitor said, "You looked upset when you came in. Something wrong?"

Kincaid touched his sore ear, then forced himself to take his hand away. He shook his head. "Nothing important," he said. What had happened between him and Lucille Farrell was personal and no business of the man in the corner.

But that didn't mean he would forget about it any time soon. Kincaid's eyes narrowed as he remembered Lucille's reaction to his decision to finally tell her the truth of how he felt about her. She would be sorry about what she had done. He had made that promise to her, and now he renewed it to himself.

"What are you doing here?" he went on.

"I told you when we left Cairo that I'd come to see you when the time was right." The visitor puffed on the cigar again. "Now it is."

"It's about time. Don't forget, you promised me a handsome payoff."

"And what would you do if the damned Rebels offered you more than I have?"

Kincaid laughed. "Take it, of course."

"That's why I trust you, Kincaid. You have no morals at all. As long as the money is right, you're the most loyal man on the face of the earth."

Kincaid brushed that aside. "What are we going to do?"

"You know that Federal troops are on their way down the Yazoo River?"

Kincaid nodded. "Quite a few men have gone up there to stop them." *Including that bastard Brannon*, he thought. It would certainly help uncomplicate matters if Brannon somehow stopped a bullet during the fighting.

"Our gunboats are still being prevented from shelling the city properly by those batteries along the bluff. If something could be done about those, so that we could strike against the Rebels from the river as well, the overland attack would have a much better chance of succeeding."

"So we're going to sabotage the Confederate batteries?"

The visitor nodded. "I'm not sure how, just yet, but that's my plan, yes. Our plan, I should say, since we're in this together, Kincaid." He raised his eyebrows. "We *are* still in this together, aren't we?"

"You're a suspicious man."

"Suspicion serves me well."

"I'm with you," said Kincaid. He opened a drawer in his desk and took out a bottle and a couple of glasses. "In fact, I think we should have a drink to seal the bargain."

The visitor stood up and came closer to the desk. "That sounds like a good idea to me."

Kincaid pulled the cork in the neck of the bottle and poured the drinks. This was a fine bottle of brandy, and he had been surprised to find it among the stock behind the bar, since Cochran's generally served the rawest, least expensive whiskey possible. Kincaid had appropriated it for his own use immediately. Such luxuries were much too fine for the backwoodsmen and river trash who patronized the establishment.

He was still angry over what had happened with Lucille, but she would come around, he told himself. When the war was over, as it soon would be, he would be a rich, powerful man, able to take any woman he wanted. And Lucille would not be able to tell him no.

He handed the other glass to his cautious visitor and said, "To victory."

Jason Gill raised his glass, clinked it against Kincaid's, and repeated, "To victory."

CORY CROUCHED behind the barricade with Allen Carter to his right and Colonel Thompson to the left. All along the line of cotton bales, men waited with their rifles ready. A tense air of anticipation hung over Fort Pemberton. A short distance back from the breastworks, Gen. William Loring, who was in command of the Confederate defenders, paced back and forth.

"Be patient, boys," he called out. "The Yankees will be here soon enough."

The first time Cory had seen Loring, he had been struck by the general's resemblance to drawings he had seen of William Shakespeare. Loring was mostly bald on top of his head, had longish hair around his ears, and sported a mustache and sharp goatee. Cory had no idea if Loring knew that he looked like Shakespeare, and he hadn't broached the subject with the general for fear that Loring would think he was crazy.

The general was right about the Yankees—they were coming and they would be there soon. The scouts had brought the news that the fallen trees and the boats that had been sunk in the river channel had slowed considerably the progress of the Union vessels, but the obstacles hadn't stopped them. In fact, as Cory peered upstream now, he could see smoke drifting over the tops of the trees and knew it came from the stacks of the Yankee boats. When he listened hard, he could even hear the chugging of their engines.

Without taking his eyes off the river, Allen Carter said, "Damn, I hate the waitin'. I'd rather fight than wait, any day."

"I suspect most soldiers feel the same way," said the colonel, "especially when they know that a battle is inevitable."

"Get it over with," said Cory. There was a dull ache behind his eyes.

"Exactly."

The sound of the engines was louder now. There was more smoke pouring into the sky. With an abruptness that was startling, the nose of one of the Yankee gunboats poked itself around the bend in the river.

"Fire!" Loring shouted as the rest of the vessel came into view. "Give them blizzards, boys! Give them blizzards!"

Cory intended to do just that. He lined the sights of his rifle on one of the openings in the gunboat's cabin and squeezed the trigger. The rifle kicked hard against his shoulder as it belched smoke and flame and lead. He knew the likelihood of his bullet actually hitting that narrow slit was slim, but if enough of the defenders fired at those openings, some of the shots would penetrate the gunboat's cabin.

As the rattle of rifle fire came from the barricade, so did the heavier roar of the cannons as the artillerymen got to work. Water geysered into the air around the gunboat as the first shells splashed into the river. The cannons on the boat began to fire, but their shells either fell short or slammed harmlessly into the thick barrier that shielded the defenders. Several shells in the next volley from the Southern batteries hit their target, crashing into the gunboat's hull. Cory saw the vessel shudder heavily as he reloaded and got ready to fire again.

A second gunboat came around the bend and immediately encountered one of those "blizzards" of lead that Loring had ordered. Half of the Confederate artillerymen concentrated their fire on the second gunboat, and this time their first volley was accurate. Both boats sustained considerable damage in a matter of moments.

Cory had squeezed off half a dozen shots by the time the gunboats stalled in the water and then began to reverse. A triumphant shout went up from the defenders. "They're runnin'!" Allen Carter whooped. "Look at 'em go!"

Cory rested his reloaded rifle on the barricade but didn't fire again. The gunboats slid quickly back around the bend, out of sight. Cory turned to the colonel and asked, "What about the Union troops?"

"Back upstream, most likely," Thompson replied. "They sent the gunboats ahead to run the gauntlet, so to speak, and find out the strength of our position."

"Then they could come back?"

Thompson nodded. "Of course. One battle does not a campaign make."

Cory had been afraid of that. If the Yankees abandoned the idea of making their way down the Yazoo, then he and the other defenders would be free to return to Vicksburg. But he wasn't going to be that fortunate. Today's action was just the first thrust by the Yankees.

Despite the chill in the air, he was sweating, Cory realized. He wiped his forehead, then wiped his hand on his trousers.

"Are you all right, lad?" asked the colonel. "You look positively ill."

Cory rested his hand on his forehead again. It felt hot, even to his own touch. "I don't feel so good," he said. "Like I might have a fever."

"Why don't you go back to camp and lie down for a bit?" Thompson suggested. "I don't believe the enemy will come back today."

"Reckon that's what I'll do." Cory stood up, and as he did so, a wave of dizziness hit him. "Damn," he muttered, then he fell to his knees and pitched forward onto his face.

As he lost consciousness, his brain was crying out, *Lucille!*

Chapter Twenty

OVER THE NEXT FEW days, as the Yankees made several more unsuccessful attempts to break through the Confederate defenses at Fort Pemberton, Cory spent most of his time sleeping in the rough lean-to he shared with Allen Carter. The slumber was hardly restful, however. Fever dreams haunted him, strange and vivid and unsettling. Lucille was in some sort of danger, and he couldn't help her. He heard her calling his name, but he couldn't find her. As he tossed and turned in his bedroll, in his mind he was searching frantically for Lucille. He cried out to her, and her voice began to fade.

More than once, he woke up drenched in sweat.

Although the fever broke, each time it went back up again. There were several physicians among the defenders, but all they could do under these conditions was advise that Cory be kept as quiet and comfortable as possible. None of them could be certain what had caused his illness. Some swamp-borne pestilence, more than likely. Fevers were common in areas such as this, although they usually struck during the summer instead of the spring.

On March 20, 1863, after one more exchange of shots with the defenders of Fort Pemberton, the Yankees began steaming north up the Yazoo toward Moon Lake, reported the scouts. Finally, they had given up.

That was the same morning Cory awoke clear-headed and ravenous. He was weak, but as he ate the hardtack and drank the coffee that Allen Carter gave him, he felt strength seeping back into his body. He wasn't ready to believe he was really over the illness that had felled him, however. He had rallied before, only to suffer yet another setback.

Colonel Thompson glanced into the lean-to on his way past. "You're looking better, Mr. Brannon. I hope it lasts this time."

"So do I," said Cory. "Where are the Yankees?"

Carter answered. "Headin' north as fast as they can, their tails 'tween their legs. They've given up on the Yazoo."

Cory looked up at Thompson. "Is that true, Colonel?"

"It is," Thompson replied with a nod.

"Then that means we'll be going back to Vicksburg." Cory couldn't keep the excitement out of his voice.

"Some of the men will remain here in case the Yankees double back, which isn't considered likely. But the Home Guard is indeed returning to Vicksburg. I'm not certain that you're up to traveling, however. You're just now beginning to recover from your illness, if indeed you have shaken it off."

"What's the date?" During his delirium, Cory had completely lost track of time.

"March 20th," Carter told him. "Ain't that right, Colonel?"

Thompson nodded. "It is."

Cory put a hand to his head. He had been gone from Vicksburg—and Lucille—for well over a month. Another wedding date come and gone with no marriage. Well, he told himself, at least this time there hadn't been any elaborate preparations to go to waste. Lucille hadn't been left at the altar this time. That was small consolation, but he hoped it was enough to keep her from being too angry with him.

"I can make it back," he said. "I don't care how weak I am, I can make it back."

Thompson chuckled. "I suspect you're right. Very well, then. The two of you can prepare to move out with the rest of the Home Guard."

Cory swallowed the last of the coffee, washing down the final bite of hardtack. The unpalatable stuff had never tasted so good. He was going home.

THE YANKEES did double back, just as Colonel Thompson had mentioned they might, after meeting with reinforcements during their retreat up the Yazoo. Their return to Fort Pemberton, which was still strongly defended, was as unsuccessful as the first foray, and after only two artillery duels, the Union boats turned north for the final time.

While this was going on, Adm. David Porter of the Union navy hit on the idea of using yet another series of interconnected waterways to circumvent Chickasaw Bluffs and approach Vicksburg. Steele's Bayou, which intersected the Yazoo ten or twelve miles north of the city, led to Black Bayou, Deer Creek, and the Sunflower River. If they were indeed connected, the Yankees could make a two-hundred-mile circle that would eventually put them only a few miles northeast of Vicksburg. Having scouted out the landscape personally, Porter convinced Grant and Sherman of the feasibility of his idea and began transporting artillery and supplies along the twisting waterways while Sherman's troops followed behind.

Porter encountered many of the same troubles as the Yazoo Pass expedition: narrow, shallow streams; tree branches that hung down nearly to the water in places and caught on the boats' smokestacks; channels that were easily blocked by Confederates who felled trees across them and sunk obstacles in them; and deadly accurate sniper fire that raked the vessels from time to time. Finally, Porter abandoned the idea, reasoning that if he continued, he would wind up with his boats stuck in the swamps where they would be easy prey for the Confederates. He backed away and returned ignominiously to Milliken's Bend.

All of Grant's plans had come to nothing. He had spent several months trying to find a suitable way to attack Vicksburg from the north but was finally forced to admit that it simply could not be done. As he had realized from the start, the best overland approach to the city was from the east. But getting his troops in position to launch such an attack would be risky at best. He would have to transport them down the Mississippi until they were well south of Vicksburg, cross the great river, and swing back to the northwest. No doubt the Confederates would oppose them every step of the way. Still, that was the only option left open to him.

Spring had arrived, and the winter rains had stopped. The roads would soon be dry, and the Union army would be on the march again.

CORY DROPPED off the wagon in front of the Thompson house, followed by the colonel and Allen Carter. They had been able to hitch a ride from General Pemberton's headquarters. The short ride didn't help much, after the long march from Fort Pemberton, but as tired as they were, they were glad to save any steps they could. The colonel was in the best shape of the threesome. Cory was still thin and weak from his illness, and Carter's right leg above the wooden peg throbbed painfully with every step. "I don't mind the fightin'," he had said more than once, "it's the marchin' I hate."

Fred was sitting on the porch, and he sprang to his feet as he saw the threesome climb down from the wagon. "Pa!" he shouted as he rushed down the steps and out the walk. He slapped the gate open and threw himself into Carter's arms.

"Hello, son," Carter greeted him warmly as he patted him on the back. "How are you?"

"I'm fine," Fred replied, so happy he was almost crying. "How about you?"

"A lot better now that I'm back with you." Carter hugged him tightly.

Lucille and Mildred had heard the commotion, and their faces lit up as they came out onto the porch. They exchanged big smiles. Lucille began to shift back and forth on her feet, and after a moment, Mildred laughed and said, "Land's sake, girl, go on and run out there."

"It's not very dignified," said Lucille.

"Neither is being in love. Go on."

Lucille grinned and took her aunt's advice. She hurried down the steps and ran to meet Cory. He held out his arms toward her and drew her into his embrace. Their lips met.

After the kiss, Lucille stepped back a little and looked him up and down. "You're so thin!" she exclaimed. "What happened to you out there?"

"I was a little sick for a while," Cory explained, "but I'm a whole heap better now that I'm back with you, Lucille." He took her face in his hands and kissed her forehead, her nose, her mouth. His hands slid down to her shoulders and then his arms went around her again and held her to him. He was trembling slightly, whether from weakness or sheer joy at being reunited with her, he didn't know.

The colonel held out a hand to his wife as she approached, intending to solemnly shake hands with her. Instead, Mildred took his hand and then threw her other arm around his neck, pulling his head down for a kiss. Thompson looked startled. Mildred drew back. "I'm taking some of my own advice," she said and kissed him again.

Eventually, the six of them wound up in the parlor, and the colonel told Lucille, Mildred, and Fred what had happened at Fort Pemberton. "Other than the sterling efforts of our artillerists, it really wasn't much of a battle. We were never in any real danger."

That was stretching the truth a little, thought Cory. The Yankee gunboats had gotten off quite a few shots, and some of those shells could have reached the Confederate defenders. But luck had smiled on them, and nearly all of them had survived the ordeal unhurt.

"What's going to happen now?" asked Mildred.

"It's difficult to say. General Pemberton told me that while the Yankees were coming down the Yazoo, they also tried to navigate some of the streams to the northeast of the city but were turned back once again. Grant is an intelligent man. Surely he'll see that it's impossible to take the city from that direction."

Fred said, "Maybe they'll give up and go home and leave us alone from now on."

Cory wished he could believe that. "If Grant can't get at us one way, he'll try another."

Thompson nodded. "I'm afraid you're right. He appears to be quite stubborn about the matter."

"Well, I'm going to hope that Fred's right," said Lucille, and the young man beamed at her. "I'm going to hope for the best." She was sitting next to Cory on the divan, and she moved closer to him. "This time it's going to come true."

Cory knew what she was talking about—the wedding. He didn't want to disappoint her again. He ought to promise her that, come hell or high water, they would be married, and soon. And nothing the Yankees could do would interfere.

But he had seen the way fate worked, and too many hopes had been snatched away from him. As long as the war was going on, one day at a time was the best any of them could hope for.

THAT EVENING after supper, Cory stepped out onto the porch and leaned on the railing. Night had fallen, and the stars were out. Most of the nights were clear now, the winter overcast having been displaced by spring. In only a couple of weeks, the air had warmed considerably. Cory breathed deeply of it tonight. It wasn't as crisp and clean as it had been in Virginia, because quite a few unpleasant odors drifted up from the riverfront, but he still enjoyed filling his lungs and blowing out the breath in a long sigh. He knew that he should have been content.

But something was bothering him, and he couldn't quite pin down exactly what it was.

The front door opened behind him, and he heard soft footsteps. A moment later, Lucille came up behind him and placed her hands on his shoulders. She rested her head against his back, leaning into him so that he could feel the soft warmth of her body.

They stood like that for a while in silence, and then she said quietly, "It's so good to have you home, Cory."

"And here I thought you'd still be mad at me," he said, trying to make his voice light.

Lucille shook her head. "No, I'm just glad to have you back, safe and sound."

Cory turned around so that he was facing her. He slipped his arms around her waist. Her breasts rested boldly against his body. She kissed the line of his jaw, then moved her lips down into the hollow of his throat and along the side of his neck. Cory closed his eyes as he held her, and his heart began to pound harder. He wanted her so badly the need throbbed in him like an ache. And judging from the way she was nuzzling his neck, Lucille was excited, too. Ever since he had met her and fallen in love with her, Cory had tried to keep any improper thoughts at bay. She wasn't some scarlet woman, some tavern trollop. He wanted to treat her decently.

But what could be more decent, he suddenly realized, than holding and kissing and . . . well, doing other things . . . with the woman he loved?

She lifted her mouth to his and kissed him hungrily. Blood pounded in his head. He was breathless when she finally broke the kiss.

"You . . . you'd better be careful," he managed to say. "I'm still getting over being sick."

"I don't care," she murmured. "I just want to be close to you, Cory. I don't want you to ever let me go again."

She placed a hand behind his head and pulled his face down to hers.

Suddenly, without warning, Cory knew what was wrong. He knew what had been bothering him ever since he and the colonel and Carter had come back to the house that afternoon. With an effort, he took his lips away from Lucille's and placed his hands on her shoulders. He stepped back, putting a little distance between them. The back of his legs bumped the porch railing.

"Cory, what is it?" she asked worriedly. "What's wrong?"

He swallowed hard, thinking that he was insane to be pushing her away at a moment like this. But he had to know. "Lucille," he said, "why are you doing this?"

"Doing what?"

"*This*. All the hugging and kissing and . . . and touching me."

The starlight was bright enough so that he saw her lips curve in a smile. "Don't you like it?"

"Yes, but—"

"Oh, I know it's not very ladylike, but I don't care. I love you, Cory. You're going to be my husband." Her smile became mischievous. "You'd better get used to it."

"I'd like nothing better, but why all of a sudden? You've been, well, touching me and holding me ever since we got back this afternoon."

"I missed you!" She sounded a little offended now. "Goodness, can't you understand that? I'm just glad to see you."

Stubbornly, he shook his head. "I think it's more than that. You seem sort of . . . desperate, Lucille."

"Well! I think that fever must have affected your brain, Cory Brannon. If my kisses bother you that much, I'll just stop!"

"No, that's not what I—blast it, Lucille!" He wasn't having to hold her away from him now. In fact, she was trying to pull free of his grip on her shoulders. "I was just worried about you. I thought something might have happened while we were gone—"

She froze, then suddenly put her hands on his chest and shoved hard. He had to let go of her and grab one of the posts holding up the porch roof, or he would have fallen backward over the railing.

"You don't know what you're talking about, Cory. Nothing happened, not a thing. I'm just glad to see you, that's all—or at least, I was. Now I think you've lost your mind."

She started to turn toward the door, and Cory said quickly, "Lucille, no. Don't go."

"I think it would be better. I know you're tired, and you've been through a lot. We just . . . we won't speak of this again, and in the future I'll try to control myself."

Cory bit back a groan of despair. Lucille was right—the fever must have affected his brain. If he hadn't started questioning her, probably they would still be kissing.

But he couldn't get the feeling of uncertainty out of his head, he realized as she went back into the house and closed the door behind her. Something *had* happened, something she didn't want to talk about.

The door opened, and Cory's pulse quickened. He sighed as Fred Carter stepped out onto the porch. Fred didn't notice the reaction, however. He was too busy looking up at the stars.

"Aren't they pretty?" he said.

"Yes," Cory said hollowly. "They're beautiful."

⌇⌇

BY THE middle of April, Ulysses S. Grant had finalized his plans. He sent General McClernand and his men south along the west bank of the Mississippi to break a path for the troops that would follow. In order to ferry all the men, guns, and supplies across the river, plenty of boats would be needed, and it would be quicker to bring them from north of Vicksburg rather than up the Mississippi from New Orleans. Admiral Porter's fleet prepared to run the gauntlet of the artillery batteries along the bluff at Vicksburg, and on the night of April 16, they did so, building up plenty of steam first and then making the dash at top speed.

The Confederates, however, had gotten wind of what was about to happen and were ready for the attempt. Abandoned houses on both sides of the river were torched as the Federal vessels approached from the north, and the glare from the blazes spread across the river, making the scene almost as bright as day. The Confederate guns began to thunder as the boats steamed into view.

Standing on the porch of the Thompson house, Cory, Lucille, the colonel, Mildred, Carter, and Fred could see the garish red glow in the sky and hear the booming of the guns. Thompson gripped the porch railing tightly and said, "If we can stop Porter, that will place quite an obstacle in Grant's plans."

Cory agreed. Tonight they were placing the fate of the city in the hands of the gunners on the bluffs.

Lt. Jack O'Reilly was at the battery he commanded, watching intently through field glasses and calling out aiming instructions to his men as the shells splashed into the river around the boats and threw up great columns of water. The firing was almost constant, and O'Reilly and the other men would have been deafened if they had not placed small wads of cotton in their ears to muffle the sounds of the explosions. That made communication more difficult, however, and several times the delay in understanding orders caused the gunners to miss their shots.

The Yankees didn't try to fight back. This was a mad dash, pure and simple. Three of the boats were damaged so badly by the bombardment that they were forced to stop and turn back, limping off to the north around the horseshoe bend. One by one, though, the other vessels made it, and O'Reilly uttered a heartfelt curse as he saw them sliding safely out of range of the Confederate batteries.

Word spread quickly through the town that the Yankees had been successful in getting past Vicksburg. No one knew exactly what that portended, but they could guess that it wasn't going to be anything good.

With his boats now where he wanted them, Grant's next move was intended to confuse the Confederate defenders. He ordered a cavalry raid that originated in Tennessee and swept down through central Mississippi. Led by Col. Benjamin H. Grierson, the Yankee cavalry proved to be equally as effective as

Bedford Forrest's had been at tearing up railroads, destroying stockpiles of supplies, pulling down telegraph wires, and burning bridges. This raid distracted the Confederate commanders, Pemberton in Vicksburg and Joseph E. Johnston in Jackson, Mississippi, and kept them looking east rather than south, where the real threat lay.

With the Confederate cavalry after them, Grierson and his men continued on through Mississippi, eventually fleeing all the way into Louisiana instead of turning back and attempting to return to Tennessee, where they had started out. The raid had served its purpose.

And yet Pemberton was not fooled completely. He sent several regiments to the south of Vicksburg to guard against a possible river crossing by the enemy. Grant countered by ordering a feint by Sherman up the Yazoo, in what appeared to be another in the long series of efforts to get at the city from the northeast. In reality, all the movement was designed to do was to prod Pemberton into recalling the troops he had sent south, and that was exactly what happened. Again Grant had successfully parried an attempt to block his plans.

The town of Grand Gulf, on the eastern bank of the Mississippi, was the spot Grant had selected for the river crossing. As Porter's boats approached, however, Confederate batteries opened up on them with a heavy fire. The thing Grant feared most was that his men would be slaughtered as he tried to get them across the river, so he immediately abandoned the idea of landing them at Grand Gulf and sent them farther downriver to Bruinsberg. The Confederates weren't waiting there, so on the final day of April 1863, Grant was able to start ferrying his army of forty-four thousand men across the river.

As soon as the crossing was complete, Grant sent McClernand's command to take the town of Port Gibson. From there, the Yankees would be able to outflank the defenders at Grand Gulf and capture that settlement, too, eliminating the threat from its artillery batteries.

That job was not as easy as Grant had hoped it would be. Brig. Gen. John S. Bowen, in command of the Confederate force at Grand Gulf, hurried his men to Port Gibson to block the Yankees. By digging in along the wooded ridges between the two settlements, the defenders were able to slow down and then stop the Federal advance for several hours, before Union reinforcements pouring up behind McClernand finally forced the Southerners to retreat. Before the day was over, both Port Gibson and Grand Gulf were in the hands of the Yankees, although not without the invaders' paying a price.

Grant was ready to move now, but instead of doing what might have been expected and following the Mississippi north toward Vicksburg, he swung his army sharply to the east instead, aiming directly at the state capital, Jackson. Joseph E. Johnston was in Jackson with a sizable force, and Grant reasoned that if he attacked Vicksburg first, he might well wind up trapped between Pemberton's army and Johnston's. If Grant could deal a defeat to Johnston and take Jackson, any Confederate reinforcements coming from the east would be cut off. That would allow Grant to march on Vicksburg without having to worry about any threat at his back.

Grant had his men living off the land and moving quickly, and during the early part of May the Union army raced across western Mississippi. Other than a few small skirmishes, the first serious resistance it faced came at the village of Raymond, where a force of twenty-five hundred Confederate troops was waiting for Grant's men. Although badly outnumbered, the Southerners struck first, using thick woods along a stream called Fourteen Mile Creek to conceal them until they were ready to launch their assault. Taking the Yankees by surprise, the fiercely fighting Confederates actually threw back the much larger force of the enemy.

The superior numbers of the Union army finally prevailed, however, and the Confederates had to retreat, leaving the way open into Jackson. A blinding rain helped to slow the Yankees for a while, but eventually they rolled on into the city, forcing Johnston to pull back or see his entire army destroyed. By the end of the day on May 14, Jackson was in Grant's hands.

At last, the Union general was ready to turn to the west, toward Vicksburg.

Chapter Twenty-one

SIX WEEKS HAD PASSED since Cory's return to Vicksburg from Fort Pemberton, and still he felt the effects of the illness that had laid him low during the Northern assault. He had not fully regained his strength, and he was still prone to attacks of chills and fever. The Mississippi Home Guard was engaged in digging more rifle pits east of the city and reinforcing the earthworks that had been erected the previous summer, but Cory was too weak most of the time to join in the effort. It bothered him that he couldn't carry his share of the load, but Colonel Thompson ordered him to stay home and rest. To Cory's protest that he wasn't officially a member of the Home Guard and therefore not subject to the colonel's orders, Thompson had replied, "Perhaps not, but you're engaged to my niece and living under my roof, so I expect you to honor my wishes."

Cory couldn't argue with that. He was definitely living under the colonel's roof, and he supposed he was still engaged to Lucille. It was hard to tell sometimes.

She had been cool toward him ever since their argument that first night. Cory had thought that they would be married as soon as possible after his return, but every time he brought it up, Lucille changed the subject. Although no one had ever really spoken of it, the marriage seemed to have been postponed indefinitely.

The talk in the city was all about the Yankees and how they had raced across the state to capture Jackson. As Cory and the others sat down to a sparse supper of biscuits and sorghum on the night of May 16, Colonel Thompson said, "I fear that we'll be facing Grant alone, with no possibility of aid from General Johnston. The reports General Pemberton received this afternoon said that Johnston has abandoned the capital."

"Grant's still got to get here," Allen Carter said belligerently. "I don't think he can do it. I've seen our defenses. Shoot, Fred and I have dug some of the rifle pits. We'll stop those Yankees."

Fred said eagerly, "Do I get to fight this time?"

The question, and the innocent enthusiasm with which Fred asked it, cast a pall over the table and made the young man frown in confusion. After a moment, he asked, "Did I say something wrong?"

Carter patted him on the arm. "Not at all, son. I just hope none of us has to fight. But if we do, we may need you."

They would need every man they could get, thought Cory. Even the ones like him who weren't in the best shape in the world. He was well enough to aim a rifle and pull a trigger, that was certain, and he wasn't going to listen to anyone who said otherwise—even Lucille.

The colonel went back to headquarters after supper. Cory was sitting on the porch a couple of hours later, enjoying the night air, when Thompson rode up and dismounted in front of the house. The colonel had a brisk air about him that alerted Cory to the fact that something had happened.

"What is it, Colonel?" he asked as Thompson came up the steps onto the porch.

"We've been ordered out to meet the Yankee advance," replied the colonel. "General Pemberton wants to try to stop them before they get to Vicksburg."

Cory put his hands on his knees and pushed himself up from the cane chair where he had been sitting. "Sounds like a good idea," he said. "Do we march in the morning?"

"No!"

The cry came from the doorway, not from Colonel Thompson. Lucille stepped out onto the porch and came straight to Cory. She put a hand on his arm and said, "You're not well enough to fight."

"I'm fine," Cory said. "I haven't had one of those fever spells in almost a week. I feel stronger than I have in a long time."

Lucille shook her head. "You're not well, Cory. You have to stay here."

"Why?" he asked, an edge of bitterness creeping into his voice. "You've been angry with me for weeks now, and you won't even discuss getting married anymore. Why do you care if I go off and fight the Yankees, Lucille?"

Colonel Thompson cleared his throat and said, "Ah, I believe I'll go inside and alert Allen and Fred to this development." He went into the house and closed the door behind him, leaving Cory and Lucille alone on the porch in the darkness.

"I care because I love you, Cory," she said. "I . . . I couldn't bear it if anything happened to you."

"You haven't acted like you care that much," he said. "Ever since that night we got back, you've changed, Lucille." He shook his head. "No, that's not right. You changed before that. You changed while I was gone the last time."

"Don't start harping on that again," she snapped. "That's nothing but your imagination."

"Maybe . . . and maybe you're trying to hide something from me."

"I wouldn't hide anything from you. I love you. You . . . you're going to be my husband."

"Am I?"

She stiffened. "Are you withdrawing your proposal?"

Cory suppressed the urge to curse angrily and said, "Of course not. I love you, Lucille. I want to marry you. I've wanted that almost since the first time I saw you, when I was nothing but a wharf rat and you were the grandest, prettiest lady on the whole blasted Mississippi River."

He felt her hand trembling where it rested on his arm. "Oh, Cory . . ."

She moved toward him and his arms went around her, catching her up in an embrace that brought them close. He leaned down to kiss her, one of the few times he had done so in recent weeks. She responded eagerly, with honest passion. He brought his hand up and slid his fingers through the thick blonde masses of her hair to cup the back of her head. When he broke the kiss, he whispered, "God, Lucille, I've missed you!"

"I've been right here."

Cory shook his head. "No. You left me for a while."

She came up on her toes. "Don't talk. Just kiss me."

For long minutes that was all he did, relishing the heat and the sweetness of her lips. Finally, though, they moved apart, and he said huskily, "I still have to go with the colonel tomorrow. I have to do what I can to keep you safe."

"Cory . . ."

"Like you told me once, I wouldn't be me if I didn't do these things."

Lucille laughed hollowly. "That's right, use my own words against me."

"It's not against you, Lucille. It's just . . . something I have to do."

"To avenge your brother? To settle the score for Lieutenant Ryder?"

Cory shook his head. "No. To protect you and your aunt and everybody else in Vicksburg. If that makes me one of the saviors of the Confederacy—"

She stopped him by putting a finger on his lips. "I didn't mean that," she said. "I'm glad you want to do the right thing, Cory. I'm just afraid."

"I'll be all right," he assured her. "I really am over being sick, and General Forrest told me I'm lucky, that I'm a survivor."

"Everyone runs out of luck sooner or later."

"Not me," he said confidently.

"Don't talk like that. Don't tempt fate, Cory."

"Why not?" Now that it was settled, he felt happy, almost giddy. "It's what I'm good at, tempting fate."

Lucille put her arms around his neck and kissed him again, and he wondered fleetingly if she was just trying to make him be quiet.

After a moment, though, he didn't really care what her motivation was. He was just glad to have her in his arms again, to be able to seize a precious instant of time such as this.

⌇

THE CONFEDERATE forces moved out well before dawn the next morning. Lucille hadn't slept. Throughout the night she had tossed and turned in her bed, worrying about Cory, worrying about the fate of Vicksburg itself . . . worrying about the lecherous Palmer Kincaid.

The gambler hadn't returned to the house since the day she had fended off his attack. If anyone thought his absence was unusual, they hadn't mentioned it. Cory had never liked Kincaid, so if he gave the matter any thought, he was probably just glad that Kincaid hadn't been around.

As long as Cory and Uncle Charles and Allen Carter were in town, Lucille didn't expect any trouble from Kincaid. If he found out that the men were gone, however, he might show up again. And this time, even Fred Carter would be gone, since his father had agreed to take him along. Lucille and Mildred would be alone in the house.

Lucille wondered if she ought to tell her aunt what had happened. She didn't want to, since so far she apparently had succeeded in keeping it a secret. It would be best, she decided, not to tell Aunt Mildred—unless she had to.

Everyone got up early. Lucille didn't think anyone had slept much, if at all. Cory was wearing the pair of Colts and had one of the Enfield rifles they had brought from Texas tucked under his arm. All the weight he had lost over the winter made his clothes hang baggily on him. Lucille had tried to take them up so that they would fit better, but she had been only partially successful. Cory still looked gaunt.

He wasn't feverish, though. Perhaps he was right about being recovered from the illness. Lucille hoped so.

After the men had eaten a skimpy breakfast and downed a few cups of coffee, they put on their hats, gathered up their weapons, and got ready to leave. Mildred carried a lantern onto the porch as they filed out of the house. There were hugs and kisses all around. Lucille stood for a long moment in the circle of Cory's arms. She had always prided herself on her ability to take care of herself—an independence that had been instilled in her by her father—but at a moment such as this, she relished feeling loved and protected. It was such a shame that the moment couldn't last.

Not while there were still Yankees to fight.

"There they go," Mildred said a few moments later as the men marched away down the street. "I pray they'll return soon, and safely."

Lucille nodded but didn't say anything. Her throat was choked with emotion. She watched until the predawn darkness swallowed Cory, and that was all too soon.

THE QUICK pace of the march was exhausting, but Cory forced himself not to pay attention to how tired he was. General Pemberton was taking more than two-thirds of his men out to meet the Yankees, some twenty-three thousand. A force of around ten thousand had been left in Vicksburg to protect the city and and serve as a reserve. All day long, the soldiers marched to the east without encountering any Union troops. That night, they made camp and dug in on a wooded ridge overlooking the fields of a farm owned by a man named Champion, about twenty miles east of Vicksburg. This ridge, which rose to a peak of some seventy feet, was called Champion's Hill, Cory was told by Colonel Thompson that evening.

"The general plans to make his stand here," said Thompson as he and Cory and both of the Carters sat beside a small fire and sipped from cups of the bitter coffee that was mostly roasted grain. "This ridge is the most defensible spot in the area, and it's directly in the path of the Yankees."

Carter looked over at Fred, who was sitting with a rifle across his knees. "You reckon you can shoot that, son?"

Fred looked surprised as he said, "You know I can, Pa. You taught me how to shoot."

"I never taught you how to shoot at a man."

"I can shoot at a target."

Carter took a drink of his coffee. "It's different," he said.

"How? Because the Yankees'll be shootin' back at us?"

"There's that," Carter said with a nod. "And there's knowin' that you're likely going to put an end to a man's life."

"Well, they shouldn't be down here tryin' to boss us around."

Carter shrugged. "There's that to consider, too."

Fred looked down at the ground. "I shot a songbird once."

It was his father's turn to look surprised. "You did? You never told me about that."

"I thought you'd be mad at me, 'cause it made me so sad. The bird was real pretty, and then I shot it, and then it wasn't pretty no more. Is it like that when you shoot a man?"

Carter swallowed hard. Cory and Colonel Thompson looked away, and Cory wiped a little moisture from his eye, probably from the smoke, he told himself.

"Yeah," Carter said, "it's not pretty. But sometimes it has to be done."

"I don't know," Fred whispered. "I thought I wanted to fight Yankees, but now I ain't so sure. Not if it's like shootin' birds."

Carter reached over and gripped his son's shoulder. "It'll be fine if you stay back here in camp, boy. Probably be a good idea. That way I'll know where to find you if I need you."

"It'd be all right, really?"

"Yeah. Really."

Cory was glad they had reached that decision. Enough had happened already in Fred's life to take away his innocence.

Being in the middle of a battle would have destroyed whatever was left.

Cory slept restlessly that night, so he was tired the next morning as the men crouched behind trees and bushes on the ridge and waited for the Yankees. Despite his weariness, his head was clear and he could tell that he wasn't feverish. He felt confident that he was strong enough to acquit himself well, no matter what the day might bring.

Not long after sunrise, gunfire began to crackle from the right of the Confederate defensive line. A short time later, Cory spotted Federal skirmishers darting forward across the fields below the ridge. He and Allen Carter, who was leaning against the tree to Cory's right, tensed, and Carter called over to him, "Here they come."

"I see them," Cory replied.

Colonel Thompson was somewhere along the line, making sure that the rest of his men were positioned properly. After a moment, Carter said, "Cory?"

"What?"

"I already talked to the colonel about this, but I want to ask you, too. If anything happens to me, will you see that Fred's taken care of?"

"Damn it, Allen!" Cory exclaimed. "Don't talk like that. Nothing's going to happen to any of us."

"You know better'n to count on that. I'd appreciate an answer, Cory."

"All right!" Cory said angrily. Then his voice softened and he went on, "Sure. If it's up to me, I'll see that Fred's taken care of just fine."

Carter nodded. "I'm much obliged, Cory." He lifted his rifle to his shoulder. "Looks like them Yankees are just about in range now . . ."

They were, sure enough, Cory saw. He settled the butt of the Enfield against his shoulder and waited for a good target to present itself.

The image of a bird, beautiful in its colorful plumage, flickered across his brain. He forced it out of his thoughts and curled his finger around the rifle's trigger. There was a flash of blue in the field below, and as the Enfield's sights settled on it, Cory squeezed the trigger.

The battle was on.

A volley ripped out along the length of the ridge, flame spewing from the muzzles of thousands of guns. Cory reloaded the Enfield, blinking rapidly because a vagrant breeze blew some of the powder smoke back in his face and stung his eyes. More of the Yankees were pouring into the field below, so he didn't bother aiming this time. He just pointed the rifle in the general direction of the Northerners and fired.

The artillery positioned atop the ridge opened up, sending shell and canister screaming down into the front lines of the Union advance. Dirt flew in the air, and so did the mangled bodies of men caught too close to the explosions. Smoke drifted down from the hill and over the fields.

Cory kept firing as fast as he could reload. He glanced over at Allen Carter and saw that Carter was doing the same. With a rustling of branches, bullets began to whip through the tree limbs above their heads. Leaves fluttered down around them, clipped by the hot lead. Cory looked down the slope again and saw that some of the Yankees had made it to the base of the ridge despite the heavy fire as they crossed the field. The Northerners were starting to make a fight of it now.

Something thudded into the tree trunk not far from Cory's head. Instinctively, he crouched a little as he leveled the rifle and fired again. Ricochets began to whine through the air.

The sound brought back memories of the Hornet's Nest at Shiloh. Cory had been in the middle of that hellish fight, and the bullets buzzing around his head sounded like he was in the middle of a real hornet's nest. This battle wasn't that bad—yet.

He brought the reloaded Enfield to his shoulder and fired again. From the corner of his left eye, he saw that some of the

Yankees, incredibly, were almost at the top of the ridge, battling every step of the way with guns and sabers and knives. Suddenly, the Union troops topped the crest, only to find themselves facing several of the Confederate cannon at almost point-blank range. Cory expected to see them blown to shreds, but an alert Yankee officer shouted a command and the soldiers threw themselves forward, landing flat on the ground. The cannon roared, but most of the shells passed harmlessly over the heads of the men, who were up again instantly, charging toward the batteries.

Cory yelled, "Allen!" and swung toward the Yankees, firing into them from the side, trying to turn back their daring thrust. It was too late. The Yankees were already among the artillerymen, savagely bayoneting them and crushing their skulls with rifle butts. If they could manage to turn those cannons back on the Confederate defenders, the rest of the line along the ridge would crumble.

Cory dropped his empty rifle and whipped out the Colts. The range was short enough for the handguns, and he began to fire them both as fast as he could thumb back the hammers and pull the triggers. He realized he was shouting incoherently in rage as he blazed away at the enemy, but he couldn't stop himself. The bullets ripped into the Yankees and spun several men off their feet. Cory kept shooting until the hammers of both guns clicked on empty chambers.

By that time, reinforcements were surging toward the middle of the line where the Federal troops had breached it. As Cory lowered the revolvers, he saw that the Yankees were starting to retreat down the hill. With a grin on his face, he turned to Carter and called, "Allen! Do you see that?"

Carter was leaning against the tree, his right hand pressed hard against his left side. Cory's eyes widened as he saw the blood leaking through Carter's fingers.

"No!" he cried. He jammed the empty Colts back in their holsters and ran toward his friend. He saw visions of Hamilton

Ryder and his brother Titus, but he forced them away and concentrated instead on catching Carter as the wounded man started to slip to the ground. Cory got an arm around Carter's waist and held him up.

"Get back to . . . the fight," Carter said. "Don't worry . . . about me."

"The hell with that," snapped Cory. "Let's get you back to the camp."

Carter might have argued more, but at that moment, his eyes rolled up in their sockets and his head fell forward limply. Cory thought for a second that Carter was dead, but then he felt the man's heart beating.

Forgetting about how tired he was, and how debilitating his illness had been, he started dragging Carter toward the rear of the Confederate lines. He had gone a hundred yards or so when suddenly Colonel Thompson appeared on Carter's other side. "My God!" the colonel yelled. "How bad is he hit?"

"Bad enough," replied Cory.

"Let me give you a hand."

Together, they half-carried and half-dragged Carter to the camp. Fred came running up when he saw them. "Pa!" he screamed. "Pa!"

"He's alive, Fred," Cory told the young man. "Help us with him."

Sobbing, Fred helped Cory and Thompson lower Carter onto his blankets, which were still spread out on the ground. Cory looked around and yelled, "Where the hell's a doctor?"

"I'm afraid the physicians have their hands full right now," said Thompson. "You'll have to do what you can for him, lad. I have to get back to the battle."

"But I'm not—"

"You're the only hope Allen has now," the colonel cut in. "He'll bleed to death if you can't stop it."

Cory knew Thompson was right. He nodded and dropped to his knees beside his wounded friend. Fred was still running

334 • *James Reasoner*

around and crying, so Cory said sharply, "Fred, stop that! Find me some water. Fred!"

The words finally got through to Fred, and he started rummaging through their gear looking for a canteen. Meanwhile, Cory ripped Carter's shirt open and exposed the wound. A bullet had gone through the front of Carter's left side and then torn out the back. The wound looked fairly shallow, Cory thought. The bullet might have glanced off a rib. Carter probably had a broken bone and he had lost some blood, but he could survive the injury if he didn't bleed to death.

"Here!" Fred said as he thrust a canteen into Cory's hands. He got a good look at the wound and started wailing again.

Cory gritted his teeth and poured water on the bullet hole, washing away some of the blood. He capped the canteen and tossed it aside, then tore a couple of large pieces of cloth off Carter's shirt, wadding them up and pressing them over the wounds. "Help me roll him onto his side," he said to Fred.

The two of them turned Carter onto his right side. Cory had Fred hold the makeshift compresses in place while he used Carter's belt to cinch them tightly against the wounds. Later, as soon as he could find some whiskey, he would use it to clean the injury. Right now, though, the compresses seemed to be slowing the flow of blood, and that was the most immediate danger.

Well, that and the Yankees, thought Cory . . .

꩜

THE CONFEDERATE line on Champion's Hill finally cracked and broke that afternoon, and General Pemberton ordered his men to retreat to Vicksburg. By that time, Allen Carter's wounds had stopped bleeding, but he hadn't regained consciousness. Cory looked around, found an empty ammunition caisson with a horse still hitched to it, and he and Fred piled Carter onto the cart. Cory took the horse's reins and led it while he and Fred walked alongside. The road to Vicksburg was jammed with thousands of men, many of them wounded, and several of them who were hurt too badly to walk were loaded by their friends onto the impromptu ambulance.

Colonel Thompson rode by a short time later. A line of blood ran down his face from a gash on his forehead. "How's Allen?" he asked as he reined in.

"I hope he'll be all right," said Cory. "He's still unconscious, but Fred and I managed to stop the bleeding."

"Good lads," Thompson commended them.

Cory looked up at him. "We got whipped, didn't we, sir?"

The colonel's bloodstained face was bleak as he nodded. "I'm afraid so. The Yankees were able to hit us with a flank attack that drove us from the hill. General Pemberton plans to make another stand at the Big Black River, but I fear we won't be able to hold them there, either."

"Then we'll just have to stop them at Vicksburg," Cory said. "The strongest defenses are there."

But even as he spoke the words and tried to sound confident, he realized that, finally, Grant had their backs against the wall. No one could help them.

Vicksburg would stand or fall on its own.

Chapter Twenty-two

Chapter Twenty-two

COLONEL THOMPSON'S PREDICTION PROVED to be correct—the Confederate defense at the Big Black River was ineffective. Two furious charges by the Yankees drove the defenders out of the hastily dug earthworks and sent them fleeing back toward Vicksburg.

Cory hadn't stopped at the river to join in the battle. He and Fred pushed on toward the city with the caisson carrying Allen Carter and the other wounded men. They didn't stop even when darkness fell but continued walking into the night.

Along with thousands of other retreating soldiers, they reached Vicksburg the next day. As the defeated, disheartened men poured into the city, the citizens of Vicksburg watched them with horror. Everyone had been counting on Pemberton and his men to stop the Yankee advance, just as the Northerners had been turned back every time before.

The defenders had never faced such a large force previously, however, thought Cory as he led the horse hitched to the caisson toward the Thompson house. There were hospitals in Vicksburg, but he figured they were all full of wounded men by now. The battle at Champion's Hill had resulted in so many casualties that private dwellings would have to be pressed into service as makeshift medical facilities. All the doctors in town would be kept busy for the next few days, hurrying from place to place and doing what they could for the wounded.

Some of the men on the caisson had families in Vicksburg and wanted to be taken home to recover from their injuries. Cory obliged them. By the time they neared the Thompson house, there were only three men riding on the ammunition cart—Allen Carter, a young man from Arkansas named Richards who had taken a bullet through the ankle, breaking it, and a

339

Texan called Howard who'd been shot in the thigh and the side. Cory didn't know if Howard was the Texan's first or last name.

Fred had walked alongside the caisson the entire way, sometimes reaching out to touch his father, as if to reassure himself that Carter was still there. Carter had been in and out of consciousness. When he was awake, he seemed to barely be aware of where he was, but from time to time he had caught hold of Fred's hand and squeezed it.

Now Cory told Fred, "Run on ahead and let Mrs. Thompson and Lucille know we're coming."

"All right." Fred hesitated. "Is my pa going to die?"

"I don't think so. Not if we can do anything about it, anyway. He'll have a couple of pretty good nurses once we get him home. Now you go ahead like I told you."

Fred nodded and broke into a run, trotting down the street toward the colonel's house.

Cory hadn't seen the colonel since the day before, but he felt sure he was all right. Keeping the retreat moving in a fast, orderly fashion had been a big job, one that had taken all the officers. Thompson would come back to the house as soon as he could.

A heavy boom sounded in the distance, followed a few seconds later by a high-pitched whine and then an explosion several blocks away. Through gritted teeth, Cory muttered a curse. The Yankee gunboats on the river were starting their shelling again. A moment later, the Confederate batteries on the bluffs began to roar in response.

Cory paid little attention to the bombardment. There was nothing anybody could do about death falling from the sky, so there was no point in worrying about it. He tugged on the reins, urging the weary horse on down the street.

A figure came hurrying out of a gate up ahead and ran toward him. Cory stopped as he recognized Lucille. Her honey-blonde hair streamed out behind her as she ran. Thankfully, she seemed to be unharmed. He dropped the reins as she came up to him and threw her arms around him.

He returned the embrace as she said, "Fred told us you were coming. Oh, Cory . . ."

"It's all right," he told her. "I'm fine. Allen's hurt, but I patched him up as best I could. These other men . . . they don't have anywhere else to go . . ."

Lucille gave him a quick, hard kiss, then stepped back briskly. "Let's get them all inside and put them to bed, so they can get some decent rest. That'll probably help them as much as anything."

She took the reins and led the horse down the street to the house. Cory looked over the place and saw that it was undamaged from the shelling. A surge of relief went through him. It was amazing how quickly he had come to think of this house as his home. That was because of Lucille's presence and nothing else, he knew.

Mildred Thompson and Fred Carter were waiting for them. Cory and Fred helped Carter down from the cart and supported him on either side as they helped him into the house. Carefully, they laid him on the bed in one of the bedrooms, then went back outside to find that Richards had already gotten down from the caisson and had an arm around Lucille's shoulders, leaning on her as he made his way up the walk. He smiled tiredly as she helped him into the house.

Howard, like Allen, was only semiconscious, and it took both Cory and Fred to get him inside. Mildred led the horse around back and unhitched it. The animal was army property, but no one was going to worry about that under these circumstances.

With the Yankees closing in on Vicksburg, there was nowhere to go anyway.

Cory went into the kitchen and looked in the cabinets until he found a bottle of whiskey. Knowing the colonel, it was strictly for medicinal purposes, but that was what Cory wanted it for now. He went into the bedroom where both Carter and the Texan were lying on the bed. Richards was sitting on the divan in the parlor, his wounded leg stretched out in front of him.

"We need to get those wounds cleaned and some fresh bandages on them," Cory said to Lucille.

"I'll find some clean linen."

He nodded. "That'll do fine. Fred and I will see what we can do in here."

Dealing with bullet wounds was getting to be nothing unusual for him by now, but still, the sight of the ugly, ragged openings in the flesh was disturbing. Cory didn't let himself dwell on the thought that it just as easily could have been him lying there shot full of holes. Dried blood had stuck the bandages to the wounds, so he had to soak them with whiskey before he could get them off.

As each bullet hole was exposed in turn, Cory poured whiskey into it. He had seen men put gunpowder in a wound and touch a match to it, so that the resulting fire would keep the wound from festering, but he wasn't prepared to go that far yet. Sometimes such treatment backfired and just caused a worse injury. The whiskey must have burned bad enough, because as he used it on the wounds, first Carter and then Howard moved around and groaned in pain, even though neither man fully regained consciousness.

Lucille came back with pads of cotton and strips of linen, and Cory used them to bandage the wounds again. Then he stepped back from the bed and said, "I reckon that's all we can do for them."

An attack of dizziness hit him suddenly, and he swayed on his feet, putting out a hand to catch hold of a chair back and steady himself. "Cory?" Lucille said anxiously. "Are you getting sick again?"

He shook his head again. "Nope, I'm just worn out."

Lucille put a hand to her mouth. "Oh, no. This is your bed. Where are you going to sleep?"

"Right now a blanket on the front porch doesn't sound half-bad."

"I'm sure we can do better than that."

If they had ever gotten around to getting married, they could share her bed, thought Cory, but he didn't say anything. Now that he and Lucille were together again, and considering the ordeal they might be facing as the Yankees converged on Vicksburg, he didn't want to dredge up anything bad out of the past.

She took his arm, and they went out of the room, leaving Fred sitting on a chair beside the bed to keep an eye on the wounded men. Mildred was waiting for them in the hallway. "Cory," she said, "where's Charles?"

"I'm sorry, Mrs. Thompson, but I haven't seen him since yesterday. I'm sure he's all right, though. He was just busy with the retreat."

"Was he . . . was he wounded in the fighting?"

"He had a cut on his forehead, but it didn't amount to much. Really, he was fine the last time I saw him."

Mildred nodded. "Thank you, Cory. I'll still feel better when I actually see him for myself."

"Yes, ma'am." Cory could understand the way Mildred felt. He didn't mention the fact that the battle at the Big Black River had taken place after Cory had seen the colonel. Thompson could have been mixed up in that fighting.

No sense in borrowing trouble, though, Cory told himself. Until he knew otherwise, he was going to assume that Colonel Thompson was unhurt and would soon be home.

Mildred bustled off to the kitchen, saying that she would fix all of them something to eat. Cory and Lucille went into the parlor. Richards pushed himself awkwardly to his feet, balancing on his uninjured leg, and tugged off his dirty campaign cap. "I'm much obliged for the hospitality, ma'am," he said to Lucille. "I don't have no family in these parts, and I reckon stayin' here with y'all is a whole lot better than bein' stuck in some crowded hospital."

"We'll certainly try to make you comfortable," Lucille told him. "Mister . . . ?"

"Richards, ma'am. Frank Richards."

"Well, you just sit down and take it easy, Mr. Richards." Lucille led Cory over to the armchair and told him to sit down, too. "I'll bring both of you some tea."

That sounded good to Cory. He nodded tiredly.

Lucille hesitated. "You weren't able to stop the Yankees, were you?"

Cory shook his head. "No, they just kept pushing us back. Like I've said all along, there are too blasted many of them."

"Aunt Mildred and I knew, when we saw all the soldiers coming back into town, that it hadn't gone well. I suppose it's all over now, isn't it?"

"It's *not* over," Cory said stubbornly. "The trenches and redoubts just east of town will stop them." He sounded more confident than he really felt.

"I hope you're right." She turned toward the kitchen. "I'll get that tea."

When Lucille was gone, Richards asked quietly, "Is that lady your wife, Brannon?"

"No," Cory said, "but we're engaged."

"Then you're a lucky man, 'cept this ain't a good time to be gettin' married." Richards shifted a little and winced at the pain in his broken ankle. "Ain't a good time for much of anything if you're a Southerner."

Cory couldn't argue with that. For two long years now, the war had raged. Before it began, no one had ever dreamed that it would last this long, or that it would claim so many lives. Cory rubbed his eyes and rested his head against the back of the chair and tried not to think about all the blood that had been spilled.

He was sound asleep by the time Lucille came back with the tea a few minutes later, and she didn't wake him.

HE WOKE to the sound of crying, but as he yawned and sat up, stretching stiff muscles, something told him the tears being shed were those of happiness and relief. When he got his eyes open, he saw that he was right. Colonel Thompson was standing in the foyer, hugging Mildred and telling her that he was all right. Mildred was sobbing with her face against the front of his uniform tunic. The colonel looked just like he had the last time Cory had seen him, except that the blood on his face had dried and most of it had flaked off. The cut on his forehead was ugly but not serious.

Lucille was waiting to hug her uncle. When she had, Thompson turned toward the parlor. Cory got to his feet and put out his hand as the colonel strode into the room.

"I'm glad to see you, Cory," Thompson said as he gripped the offered hand. "Thank God you made it safely."

"Yes sir."

Richards struggled to his feet and brought his hand up to salute Thompson. "Beggin' your pardon, Colonel," he said. "I'm a mite slow these days—"

"Sit down, Private, and let that be your last salute while you're a guest in my house." Thompson shook hands with him as well. "Col. Charles Thompson."

"Frank Richards, sir, private, Ninth Arkansas."

"Welcome to our home, Private Richards." Thompson glanced at Cory. "How's Allen doing?"

"He's holding on, I reckon," replied Cory. He didn't know what Carter's condition was, since he'd been asleep. "There's another wounded man in with him, a Texan called Howard."

Thompson nodded. "All the hospitals and aid stations are full. I expect there are as many patients housed in private residences as there are otherwise."

Cory hesitated to ask his next question, but he had to know. "Where are the Yankees, sir?"

"Approximately three miles east of the city, the last report I heard. Never fear, though. Our troops are manning the defensive positions in great strength. Grant will not be able to penetrate our lines."

346 • *James Reasoner*

That statement wasn't just bravado, Cory sensed. The colonel really believed what he was saying. And he was probably correct. Cory had seen the redoubts and rifle pits for himself. It would be difficult for the Yankees to get past them.

"I ought to go out there and lend a hand," he muttered.

Lucille came to his side. "You're too tired," she said. "You've done your share, Cory."

He shook his head. "Everybody has to do more than his share, if we're going to have a chance to hold off the Yankees."

"Somebody give me a crutch and a gun," said Richards, "and I'll go out yonder and take a few potshots at them fellas."

Lucille shook her head. "Men," she said. "All of you sit down. *Now!*"

There was no arguing with the tone of command in her voice. Colonel Thompson chuckled and said, "You should have been an officer, my dear."

As the men settled into their seats, Lucille told them that supper would be ready in a few minutes and then went out to the kitchen. Colonel Thompson and Richards started filling their pipes and talking quietly about the battle at Champion's Hill. Cory didn't pay much attention. The nap had made him feel more alert, but he was still somewhat stunned by everything that had happened. It was easier just to sit and try not to think about anything.

Inevitably, though, his mind turned to their current dilemma. Since the previous summer, almost everything he had done had been aimed toward postponing this day. Setting up the supply line from Texas, going on the raid into western Tennessee with Bedford Forrest, manning the barricade at Fort Pemberton . . . all that had been to protect Vicksburg from the Yankees.

And yet, here they were, trapped in the city with the Union army right on the doorstep. It had all been for nothing, he thought bleakly.

But not if Vicksburg could hold out, he reminded himself. The sacrifices would have been worthwhile if the city could stand. Already, Cory had seen how unlikely it was that the Confederacy could achieve a military victory in the war. But if the Yankees could be made to pay a high enough price, that might lead to some sort of settlement that would fall short of utter defeat for the South. Cory knew that he shouldn't even be thinking such things, that patriotic fervor should have him convinced even now that the Confederacy would triumph, but he had seen too much of the war to fall into that trap.

He looked up as some of Thompson's words caught his attention. The colonel was talking about the battle of Chancellorsville, back in Virginia. A week or so earlier, the city had been abuzz with the news that Robert E. Lee and Stonewall Jackson had dealt a humbling defeat to the Yankees. Reports of the Confederate triumph had done a great deal to bolster sagging morale in Vicksburg.

Thompson didn't look or sound happy about the news now, however. He went on, "I heard at General Pemberton's headquarters that Jackson is dead."

"Aw, no," said Richards. "Not ol' Stonewall."

Thompson nodded. "I'm afraid so. He was wounded somehow by our own forces, or at least that's the rumor. It was thought that he would make a full recovery, but he developed pneumonia, and the disease claimed him."

Cory hated to hear that. Like most Southerners, he regarded the general as a hero. Will was serving in Jackson's command, which meant that almost certainly he had been at Chancellorsville. Mac, too, because Stuart's cavalry also was attached to Lee's army. Cory hoped now, as he had when he first heard about the battle, that his brothers had come through it all right.

"Sometimes tragedy can come out of triumph," mused the colonel. "General Jackson's death is proof of that. But the reverse is true, too, and triumph can come out of tragedy. That's what we have to prove here in Vicksburg."

It would certainly be an unlikely triumph if the Vicksburg defenders could turn back the Yankees, thought Cory, but he supposed stranger things had happened. This was war, after all, and anything was possible.

"Supper is ready," Lucille called from the doorway of the parlor, and Cory suddenly realized just how hungry he was. He couldn't remember when he had eaten last, other than gnawing on a small square of hardtack while he and Fred and the wounded men were on their way back from the debacle at Champion's Hill.

Cory and Thompson helped Richards to his feet and into the dining room. Lucille offered to bring him a tray, but the soldier wouldn't hear of it. "Y'all have extended your hospitality to me, ma'am, and the least I can do is sit at your table."

Mildred had already taken a plate in to Fred, and she reported that Allen Carter and Howard were resting quietly. "I think it's a natural sleep," she said. "And that's what they need more than anything else."

Not really, thought Cory, but he didn't say anything. It wouldn't do any good.

What they all needed more than anything else was a miracle.

THE MOONLIGHT coming through the open door threw grotesque shadows and pools of silver on the floor. Lt. Jack O'Reilly sat on a keg of powder and took off his hat, then used his other hand to rub his eyes and his forehead. He was exhausted, but he couldn't let the men under his command know that. Here in the thick-walled powder magazine, no one could see him. He heaved a long sigh.

He had brought a driver, a couple of enlisted men, and a wagon here to this isolated hut to replenish the supply of powder for his battery of guns. The sergeant who was in charge of the magazine had unlocked the heavy door, then stepped back to let O'Reilly go inside. The driver and the other two men were waiting outside for the lieutenant to decide what he wanted. Then they would haul it out, load it in the wagon, and take it back to the battery on the bluff, half a mile away.

O'Reilly had felt a moment of dismay when he first stepped into the magazine and saw how much less powder and canister there was now. He recalled how well supplied the batteries had been when he first arrived in Vicksburg the previous summer. Now the magazine was less than half-full. There had been a lull in the shelling from the river during the past couple of weeks, but the activity of the Federal gunboats was picking up again, in concert with the overland attack from the east.

For a moment, O'Reilly had given in to his weariness and despair, but he forced himself back to his feet, clapped his hat on his head, and stepped out to speak to the enlisted men.

Other than moonlight and starlight, there was no illumination around the powder magazine. Torches of any sort were strictly forbidden, of course, because of the danger they might set off an explosion. In the darkness, O'Reilly saw the men he had brought with him only as patches of darkness next to the wagon. The sergeant leaned against the thick rock wall beside the door.

"Each of you bring out one keg," O'Reilly ordered his men. "It's not much, but we'll have to make it last. All of our shots will have to count from here on out."

He expected the men to obey him without hesitation, but none of them moved. He frowned in confusion. Lt. Jack O'Reilly did not like to be confused.

"What's wrong with you men?" he snapped. "Didn't you hear me? Now get those kegs loaded, right away!"

A laugh came from one of the men. "Load 'em yourself."

O'Reilly's jaw clenched and his eyes widened, and he could feel his face turning hot with anger. No enlisted man could talk to him like that! He was an officer, by God, and didn't have to stand for such insolence.

Furious, he swung around toward the sergeant, intending to inform the man that he had been a witness to insubordination

350 • *James Reasoner*

and might have to appear at a hearing. Before O'Reilly could say anything, though, he noticed that the sergeant seemed to be *sliding* sideways along the wall of the magazine. The moonlight showed a dark smear on the wall where he had been. Suddenly, the figure toppled over completely to sprawl loosely on the ground, his limbs in awkward positions.

"Well, he stayed propped up longer than I thought he would," said one of the men by the wagon.

O'Reilly knew by now that something was very wrong. He knew all the men of his battery, and he realized now that he didn't recognize the voice of the one who had spoken. Somebody had taken the place of his soldiers. He twisted back toward the men, his hand fumbling with the flap of his holster as he tried to reach his revolver.

One of the figures leaped toward him, swinging an arm. A club of some sort crashed into O'Reilly's right shoulder, staggering him. His arm and hand went numb, his fingers refusing to obey his commands. He pawed futilely at his holster.

The man swung the club at him again. O'Reilly lunged desperately to the side to avoid the blow. He opened his mouth to yell a warning, but before any sound could come out, one of the other men tackled him, driving him onto the ground. The lieutenant landed hard, with the other man's weight on top of him so that all the breath was knocked out of his lungs. As the man rolled off him, O'Reilly gasped for air and flopped on the ground like a fish out of water.

A boot sank into his side in a vicious kick. He couldn't cry out because he couldn't breathe. Instinct made him roll onto his side and curl up, trying to protect himself from further kicks.

One of the men dropped on top of him, cruelly digging a knee into the middle of his back. O'Reilly whimpered in pain. His hat had been knocked off, so his attacker was able to grab his hair and jerk his head up, pulling taut the line of his throat.

"You damned Rebels will have a hard time firing those cannon of yours without any powder," a voice hissed in his ear.

The same voice that had spoken so insolently to him earlier. The voice of a Yankee spy.

They were going to destroy the powder magazine! O'Reilly knew he had to do something, anything, to stop them. But he was helpless, his body wracked by agony, his right arm still numb, useless.

"We'll put all the bodies inside the magazine," continued the whispering voice, "and then when it goes up, nobody will ever be able to tell that you Rebs had your throats slit. Everybody will think somebody just touched off a spark when they shouldn't have."

O'Reilly tried to utter a curse, but he couldn't get any sound to come out. The man's knee was still digging painfully into his back. Suddenly, O'Reilly felt something at his throat, something that was freezing cold. There was a jerking motion, and the cold turned burning hot. Heat flooded out of him, in fact, and splashed down his chest. His body bucked spasmodically in the grip of his attacker.

Somewhere far in the back of O'Reilly's mind, he knew that his throat had just been cut and that he was mere seconds away from death. It was bad enough that he was going to die at the hands of a Yankee, but he couldn't let them get away with what they were trying to do.

Summoning up the last vestiges of his strength, he pushed himself off the ground and threw himself to the side, toppling the man off his back. O'Reilly's right arm was still useless, but he reached across his body with his left hand and finally found the snap on the holster flap. Awkwardly, he pulled the gun from the holster.

The heat had gone away and the cold was coming back, sliding up over him, encasing him in ice. His thumb looped over the hammer of the gun, and for an instant he thought he was going to be too weak to cock it. But then the hammer ratcheted back and locked into place.

"Stop him!" someone cried quietly.

O'Reilly tried to point the muzzle of the gun toward the voice, but he didn't really care now where the shot went. He just wanted to find the trigger . . . there it was . . . one more twitch of the finger.

The sharp crack of the revolver going off was the last thing that Lt. Jack O'Reilly heard as he died.

Chapter Twenty-three

PALMER KINCAID HELPED Jason Gill through the rear door into his office at the tavern and gambling hall. Gill leaned heavily on Kincaid and groaned as he clutched his left shoulder. Kincaid wouldn't be surprised if the bullet fired by that young Rebel lieutenant had shattered Gill's shoulder. The wound had bled quite a bit. Gill's coat was soaked.

"Lean on the desk for a minute," he told the Union agent.

"Damn it, I've got to lie down!" Gill protested.

"Not until I get the rug off the floor and put it on the divan. I'm not going to have you bleeding all over the furniture."

Gill groaned again, but he put his blood-smeared right hand on the desk to support himself while Kincaid spread the rug on the divan. Then Kincaid got an arm around Gill and lowered him onto the rug.

Gill's head dropped back onto the cushions. He began to curse in a low, pained voice.

"I couldn't agree more," Kincaid said as he opened the desk drawer and took out the bottle of brandy. "We certainly made a fine night's work of it."

"Shut up," grated Gill. "It's your fault we failed, damn it."

Kincaid poured brandy into a glass and drank it quickly without offering any to Gill. He turned toward the Yankee. "You're the one who had to torment the poor boy before you killed him by explaining our plans to him. And then you botched the job by not cutting deeply enough. If *I* had slit his throat, he never would have lived long enough to get his hands on his gun."

Gill rolled his head to the side so that he wasn't looking at Kincaid. "You still could have touched off the explosion instead of running," he said bitterly.

"Those guards were less than two hundred yards away. Once the lieutenant warned them with that shot, there was no time to waste setting a fuse." Kincaid picked up the bottle and dispensed with the glass this time. He drank straight from the bottle and then wiped the back of his other hand across his mouth. "And I'll be damned if I was going to stand close enough to that magazine to throw a match into it. The blast would have killed us, too."

"I don't mind dying, if it means those damned Rebels will suffer more before we send them all to hell."

"My life is worth more than that to me," said Kincaid. "If you value yours so little, maybe I should have left you there for the guards to find with the bodies of five of their friends. I'm sure they would have treated you kindly."

Gill didn't say anything, and after a moment, Kincaid went on, "Besides, I thought there wasn't supposed to be anyone at the magazine tonight except for one man."

"I didn't know that young fool was going to come up in a wagon," said Gill.

"I recognized that young fool, as you call him. His name was O'Reilly. I met him at the Thompsons' house. I've even eaten dinner with him there."

That finally made Gill look at Kincaid again. Gill's lips pulled back from his teeth in a grimace as he said, "Well, now he's screaming in the pit of abomination like all the other Rebels we've sent to their just reward."

Kincaid took one more slug of brandy and replaced the cork in the bottle. There was no point in arguing with Gill, he told himself. The Yankee really believed all the venom he was spewing, and besides, Kincaid's only interest in tonight's affair was the payment he had been promised. Instead, he said, "I'll fetch a doctor for you. Well, not a real doctor, perhaps, but a man I know who's quite experienced in dealing with gunshot wounds. If he's sober, he'll do a fine job of treating you. Before I go, though, I'll have my money."

Gill laughed harshly. "We failed, remember? The Rebel powder magazine still stands."

"That it does, but my payment wasn't conditional on the outcome."

Gill looked away again. "Go to hell. You'll not get a cent from me."

Kincaid sucked at a tooth for a moment, thinking. Then he went to the divan, leaned over Gill, and rested a hand on Gill's wounded shoulder. Gill cried out sharply as broken bones grated on each other.

"My money," Kincaid said. "You can give it to me, or I'll keep this up until you pass out from the pain. Then I'll search you, take it for myself, and have you thrown out into the alley to bleed to death. No one is going to miss you, Gill. No one."

"You . . . bastard," Gill panted.

Kincaid put a little more pressure on the shoulder. "The money."

When Kincaid let up again, Gill gasped, "In my . . . vest pocket . . . !"

Kincaid reached inside the man's vest and found the small leather pouch. The coins clinked together nicely. Kincaid tossed the pouch up and down on his palm a couple of times, estimating its weight, then stowed it away in one of his pockets.

"I'll get the doctor now," he said. "And don't worry about Ted. I'll take care of him out of my end of the deal." *But not with money*, he thought to himself. The man he and Gill had hired to help them could be paid off with a few bottles of rotgut whiskey, and Kincaid would keep all the money himself.

Gill's voice stopped him at the door. "Kincaid."

The gambler looked around. "What is it?"

"We're . . . through. I thought you . . . believed in the cause."

"You said it yourself, Gill. The only cause that interests me is the money."

"I hoped I was . . . wrong about you."

Kincaid laughed. "You were as right as you could be."

When he got back a short time later with Doc Phelps—who was only half-sober, but that wasn't bad for him—Gill was gone. The bloodstained rug was still on the divan, but there was no sign of the Yankee agent.

Kincaid shrugged and clapped a hand on his companion's back. "Go have a drink on me, Doc," he said. Phelps nodded eagerly and went back out into the saloon's main room.

So Gill was gone. That was fine with Kincaid. The Yankee would probably bleed to death in some alley before the night was over. Just as well, Kincaid told himself as he sat down at the desk and took out the pouch he had gotten from Gill's pocket. He opened the drawstring and spilled the gold coins onto the desk, looking at them with a pleased smile. He wasn't cut out to be a spy anyway. The acts of sabotage that he and Gill had carried out over the past few weeks hadn't been enjoyable at all, and Gill didn't pay that well. Now that Gill was gone, he could turn his attention back to other matters.

Such as Lucille Farrell . . .

WITH HIS bed occupied by Allen Carter and the Texan called Howard, and with Richards stretched out on the divan in the parlor, Cory made himself a pallet on the floor of the parlor and slept surprisingly well, although he was quite stiff in the morning when he got up.

He went into his old room and saw that Fred was still sitting beside the bed, intently watching Carter, who seemed to be asleep. "How is he?" whispered Cory.

Fred nodded. "He was awake a little while ago, and he ate some food Mrs. Thompson brought to him. I think he's going to be all right, Cory. The other man, too."

"Did you get any sleep last night, Fred?"

"I took a nap here in the chair." Fred yawned. "That was all I needed."

Cory thought about telling the young man to go lie down somewhere and offering to sit with the two wounded men himself, but he knew he couldn't. He had something else he had to do today. Lucille wouldn't like it, but he couldn't help that. He was sure the colonel intended to return to the defensive line around Vicksburg today, and Cory was going to go with him.

He squeezed Fred's shoulder and then followed the smell of coffee and bacon to the kitchen. Colonel Thompson, Mildred, Lucille, and Richards were sitting at the table. Lucille got to her feet as Cory came in.

"Sit down here," she said. "I'll get you some coffee and some food."

Cory took the chair and gratefully ate the meal that she placed in front of him. A couple of narrow strips of bacon, a biscuit, and a dab of preserves. The coffee cup was only half full. Better get used to it, he told himself.

As he ate, Cory asked Thompson, "Are you going out to the lines today, Colonel?"

"I should be there now," Thompson replied. "I waited thinking that you might want to go with me. And Lucille wouldn't let me wake you." He smiled at his niece.

Cory looked over at Lucille. Her face was expressionless. She might not want him to leave, but she wasn't going to come out and say that, he sensed. She was leaving the full weight of the decision to him.

The sound of an explosion made Cory forget about anything he might have said. The house shook violently, rattling dishes in the cupboard. Lucille and Mildred cried out in surprise and fear. Cory found himself on his feet without really knowing how he got there. He threw his arms around Lucille to protect her.

Another blast slammed through the air. Cory realized that the house itself had not been hit—not yet—but the explosions were somewhere very close by. Yankee mortar shells were dropping on the city, coming closer to the Thompson house than they ever had before.

A third explosion rocked the house, and this time Cory heard glass shatter in the windows. White dust from the plastered ceiling drifted down like snow around the people huddled together in the kitchen. As the echoes of the explosion began to die away, Cory heard a whimpering sound coming from somewhere else in the house.

"Fred!" he exclaimed. He hesitated to let go of Lucille, but she nodded and pushed him away, indicating that he should go. She followed him, in fact, as he hurried down the hall into the front bedroom.

They found Fred kneeling beside the bed, apparently unhurt but sobbing in fear as he leaned forward and lay protectively across his father. Carter was conscious, but he was too weak to push Fred off of him. He looked at Cory, silently pleading.

"I won't let them hurt you, Pa!" Fred cried between sobs. "I won't let them hurt you!"

More mortar blasts sounded in the distance, but these weren't nearly as close to the Thompson house as the first three. Cory bent over and took hold of Fred's shoulders, gently prying him up and away from his father.

"It's all right now, Fred," Cory said to him. "It's all right. Nothing's going to hurt your father."

Cory turned the sobbing young man over to Lucille, who hugged him and tried to comfort him. Turning back to the bed, Cory looked down at Carter and asked, "Are you hurt?"

"No worse than I was," Carter replied. His voice was still weak, but it sounded clearer and more coherent than Cory had heard it lately. "I thought Fred was going to bust these wounds open again, but I don't reckon he did."

"We'll check the bandages anyway." Cory did so as Lucille led Fred out of the room. Fred protested, but weakly. His adoration for Lucille made him go along with almost anything she wanted. Cory was thankful for that.

Carter was all right, and so was Howard. The Texan was awake now, too. He said in a voice that rasped from disuse,

"Sounded like them . . . Yankee mosquitoes was tryin' to . . . bite us again."

Cory grinned and nodded. "I'm afraid we'd better get used to it."

He could hear the Confederate batteries firing now and knew the Yankee gunboats would be steaming out of range after doing their damage. He hoped the city hadn't been hit too badly.

Thompson appeared in the doorway and said, "I need to speak with you for a moment, Cory."

Cory stepped out into the hall, and the colonel went on in low tones, "A lot of people have dug caves beneath their houses for protection from the bombardments. I believe we should give some thought to doing the same."

"I agree," Cory said, "but that'll be a lot of work and take some time."

"Better that than being caught in the house when a shell strikes it directly. Luckily, there's already a small cellar. All we'll have to do is enlarge it, perhaps move a few things down there so it will be more comfortable in case of an extended stay."

Cory nodded. "I wish Pie was here. He was mighty good at digging."

"I'm afraid you and Fred will have to manage as best you can."

"Wait a minute," Cory said with a frown. "I was going out to the lines with you—"

Thompson shook his head. "It's more important you get started down in the cellar. There are shovels in the shed out back. Mildred and Lucille can watch over the wounded men while you and Fred dig."

Cory wanted to argue, but he knew the colonel was right. He could do some good by going out and fighting the Yankees—but he might do even more to help protect Lucille and the others by staying here and working on the makeshift shelter.

"All right," he said grudgingly. "Fred and I will get the shovels, and we'll get started right away."

Thompson squeezed Cory's arm. "Thank you. I won't worry nearly as much today, knowing that you're here to look after the ladies and the wounded."

Cory nodded. He supposed there were worse things than fighting the war with a shovel for a while.

‿⁀

IT WAS May 19, 1863. As everyone in Vicksburg expected, the Yankees attacked that day, although Grant did not give the orders to advance until after midday. As the afternoon began to grow warm, the Union troops swarmed forward, concentrating their heaviest efforts on the northeastern part of the Confederate defensive ring that encircled the city. The Southerners were dug in there behind a stout, V-shaped earthworks known as the Stockade Redan. As the Yankees charged across the open ground toward it, deadly accurate rifle fire raked through them. Men in the front ranks were driven backward by the impact of the lead striking them, or else they managed to stay on their feet and stumble forward for a few more steps before tumbling to the ground. Within minutes, the troopers who followed were splashing through pools of blood as they charged.

The Yankees gained a little ground in the attack, then stalled. They were pinned down by the rifles of the defenders, and all through the long afternoon they lay there under the hot sun while bullets whined over their heads or thudded into the ground near them. Wounded men cried for aid or shrieked in agony. The only thing that brought any respite to these tormented men was the coming of night. As darkness fell, they were finally able to retreat without risking their lives.

The first assault on Vicksburg had ended in failure.

But it was not to be the last. Two days went by, and then on the morning of the twenty-second, the Federal artillery began a murderous bombardment. Grant had more than two hundred cannon with his army, and all of them were being used to lob shells at the Confederate stronghold. At the same time, the gunboats on the Mississippi joined in the fray, throwing their deadly mortar rounds at the enemy. Enough of the batteries along the bluffs had been put out of action so that the defenders were unable to drive off the boats. The roar of the cannon to the east and the heavy thumps of the mortars on the river to the west filled the air for hours. The people of Vicksburg crouched in their caves and cellars, listening anxiously to the sound of the bombardment falling on their city. The noise was like the most gigantic thunderstorm imaginable.

When the pounding by the Union artillery ceased, Grant sent his army forward again, this time along the Southern Mississippi Railroad. Thinking that the Confederate defenses must have been softened considerably by the rain of destruction falling from the sky, the Yankees were unprepared for the sturdiness of the resistance they encountered. A fortification known as the Railroad Redoubt, just south of the tracks, was still bristling with Southern riflemen, and they sent a devastating volley into the charging Federal troops.

Indeed, for all its sound and fury, the bombardment had done little actual damage to the Confederate defenses. North of the tracks, soldiers from Texas held back the Yankee charge, firing so accurately that men in the rear ranks of the Union advance had to clamber over the piled-high bodies of the troops who had led the charge. Grant poured more and more men against the Confederate line, to no avail. Despite falsely encouraging reports from the front, the aggressive Union commander realized that even an all-out frontal assault, such as he had tried twice now, was not going to breach Vicksburg's defenses. He ordered his men to fall back and curtly told one of his aides, "We'll have to dig 'em out now."

But Vicksburg was digging in.

GRUNTING AND sweating, Cory hauled the bucket of earth up the stairs, through the kitchen, and out the rear door of the Thompson house, where he added the dirt to one of the large piles that had sprouted in the back yard over the past few days. While the fighting had been going on, he and Fred had enlarged the cellar under the house to nearly double its original size.

Lucille met him at the door with a dipper of water as he started back in. Cory took it and drank gratefully. He frowned as he looked at his hands holding the dipper. They were covered with a layer of grime so thick it seemed impossible that they would ever come clean. But he was dirty all over, he told himself, after grubbing in the earth for four days like an animal.

"I think we'll be done soon," he said as he handed the dipper back to Lucille. He wished he could take her in his arms and kiss her, but he didn't want to get her filthy, too. "Tonight, Fred and I will take some furniture down there and fix some bunks for the wounded men."

"I hate the idea of living in the cellar," Lucille said with a little shudder. "It's almost like . . . like living in a grave."

"It's a lot better than that."

"Oh, I know. I just don't like it. After being raised out on the open river, it's hard being shut up anywhere."

Cory supposed that was right. The river wasn't open now, though. It was clogged with Yankee gunboats. For a change today, the mortars weren't keeping up their infernal thumping, and he couldn't hear the rattle of rifle fire or the roar of cannons from the defensive lines to the east. A silence that was eerie, coming as it did after all the commotion of the past few days, hung over the city.

"They're settling in for a siege, aren't they?" asked Lucille.

"That's what your uncle says." Colonel Thompson was back on the front lines today, although he had come home for a short time the previous night, after the Yankees had broken off their second attack. So far, the colonel had come through the fighting unhurt. Cory continued, "He says that Grant's smart enough to know by now that he can't take the city by force. So he'll try to starve us out instead."

"Can he do that?"

Cory laughed hollowly. "I don't know. But there's no way we can stop him from trying."

He had talked to the colonel enough to know that the Union forces had thrown a solid cordon around Vicksburg. A few scouts had managed to make it out through enemy lines and then back in to report to General Pemberton and the other officers. According to what they had seen, the Yankees were building a road north to the Yazoo River, so that supplies and reinforcements could be floated around to them. They were digging trenches and erecting earthworks of their own, too, so that the Confederates would have no chance of breaking out past them.

Cory's hand tightened on the handle of the bucket. "Well, I'd better get back at it. Thanks for the water."

Lucille nodded. "I wish there was more I could do."

There was a limit to what any of them could do, thought Cory. He didn't want to be too much of a pessimist, but he didn't see any way out of this trap.

He and Fred labored the rest of the afternoon. Starting out, they had torn down one wall of the cellar and then dug out the earth in that direction, packing down the dirt floor with their shoes as they went along, using boards from one of the nearby houses that had been wrecked in the bombardment to shore up the ceiling, and finally, now that they judged the space had been expanded enough, rebuilding the wall. Late that day, as he looked around the cellar by the light of a lantern, Cory saw an area that was seven feet high, twelve feet wide, and more than twenty feet long. There would be room for a couple of beds, the divan from the parlor, and several chairs. They might even bring down one of the rugs to put on the floor, he thought.

Mildred appeared on the stairs that led up to the kitchen. She looked around and said, "My, you two have done a wonderful job! When we're all done we'll have all the comforts of home down here."

Cory wasn't sure about that, but he summoned up a tired smile. "It'll protect us, anyway, when the Yankees start their bombardment again."

That wasn't long in coming. As night fell, the big guns opened up again. By then, Cory and Fred had set up one of the beds in the cellar. They helped Allen Carter and Howard from the room where they had been staying and down the stairs. Both of the wounded men had regained some of their strength, but they were still weak enough so that they couldn't do anything except lie in bed. Richards was able to get around on a pair of makeshift crutches that he had made, but he had to be helped downstairs, too. The two women stayed with the injured men while Cory and Fred carried down chairs, the divan, and a small table. Cory finally shut the door as the sound of mortar blasts began to grow louder. The line of explosions was walking its way across the city. The Yankees would probably claim later that they were shooting only at military targets, but Cory knew better. The more terror they could rain down on the citizens of Vicksburg, the greater the pressure to surrender would be on the military commanders.

A couple of lanterns illuminated the cellar. Lucille looked pale in their wan light as she came over and sat down on the divan. She said, "Sit with me, Cory," but he shook his head.

"I'm too dirty. You'd never get yourself or the divan clean again."

The earthen floor trembled under his feet as a shell exploded somewhere nearby.

"Do you think I care about that right now?" quizzed Lucille, and her voice shook a little, just as the ground had a few moments earlier.

Cory looked around the cellar. Fred sat cross-legged on the floor beside the bed, reaching up to grip his father's hand. Richards was sitting in a ladderback chair on the other side of the bed, talking quietly to Howard. Mildred was in another chair, her knitting basket in her lap, occupying herself with needles and yarn, although her face was pale and drawn. Everyone was seeking some sort of comfort, and Lucille was no different. And she was right, Cory told himself—a little dirt didn't matter at a time like this.

He sat down beside her, put his arm around her, and held her close as the explosions continued on into the night.

Chapter Twenty-four

ALL GOOD THINGS COME to those who wait, Cory had heard. He wasn't sure if that was from the Bible or some other book or just an old saying. But he supposed there was some truth to it. If everything had gone as planned, he would have been married to Lucille six months ago, in a beautiful ceremony in the church in downtown Vicksburg. Instead, they were going to be joined forever in the eyes of God and man in a dank cellar underground as yet another in an endless series of artillery barrages pummeled the city above them. It was still good, though, because at last he and Lucille would be married.

Colonel Thompson finished tying the string tie around Cory's neck. "There," he said as he stepped back. "You make quite a handsome groom, my boy."

"Lucille's an even more beautiful bride."

"Yes, well, that goes without saying, doesn't it?" Thompson chuckled.

They were standing in a corner of the cellar getting ready for the ceremony. Cory wore a suit borrowed from the colonel. The legs of the trousers were too long and the coat was not quite big enough through the shoulders, but it was the best they could do. At the far end of the cellar, behind the blankets that had been hung so that the women could have some privacy during the long hours they were all stuck down here, Lucille was getting dressed with the help of her aunt. Cory had seen the wedding dress—not on Lucille, of course, since that was forbidden until the actual ceremony—and he hoped it wouldn't get too dirty down here. It was a beautiful gown.

Allen Carter and Howard were sitting up in the bed. In the more than two weeks since the group had retreated into the cellar, both men had gained strength. Carter was getting restless, in fact, and wanted to be up and doing something again.

371

Unfortunately, there wasn't much for anyone to do, other than sit and listen to the explosions rocking Vicksburg.

Fred was pacing around excitedly. This was the first wedding he had ever attended, and he was looking forward to seeing Cory and Lucille get married. Richards was talking to the young man, trying to calm him down without much success.

Colonel Thompson patted Cory on the shoulder, then said quietly, "I heard some disturbing news this morning."

"About the siege?"

"Not directly. Someone at Pemberton's headquarters mentioned that on the night before the first Union attack, several soldiers were murdered at one of the powder magazines that supply the batteries overlooking the river. One of the men was Lieutenant O'Reilly."

Cory's eyes widened in surprise. "Jack O'Reilly?"

Thompson nodded solemnly. "That's right. The thinking is that someone tried to sabotage the magazine, perhaps even blow it up, but Lieutenant O'Reilly managed to get a shot off and alert some guards nearby. He was fatally wounded, however."

"Damn," Cory muttered. He hadn't been friends with O'Reilly, hadn't even liked the lieutenant, in fact, but he wouldn't have wished for O'Reilly to come to such an end. Of course, men were dying every day, but somehow being murdered in the night by saboteurs was different than dying in battle. "Does Lucille know?"

"I haven't said anything to her," Thompson replied with a shake of his head. "Nor do I intend to, at least not today."

"That's probably a good idea. She was fond of O'Reilly."

Footsteps sounded on the stairs as a balding, thick-bodied man descended from the house above. He carried a Bible in his hand and was dressed in a sober black suit. Thompson met him at the bottom of the stairs and shook his hand. "Reverend Emerson, thank you for coming."

"I am delighted to be here," the clergyman said with a smile. "It'll be nice to preside over a joyous occasion for a change. Most of the services I've had to conduct in the past few weeks have been funerals."

Emerson went around the room and shook hands with all the men. Cory was embarrassed when his stomach rumbled while he was talking to the minister. He hadn't eaten any breakfast. In fact, he skipped meals whenever he could, in an attempt to make their food last longer. The only thing they still had plenty of was cowpeas, and the hard little pellets weren't very good.

The blankets at the end of the cellar were pushed back, and Mildred stepped out from behind them.

"Are we ready?" she asked.

Cory turned anxiously toward her. The colonel said, "Indeed we are, my dear." He took Emerson's arm and led the minister over to an open area that had been cleared of furniture. Cory joined them, his eyes still fixed on the makeshift curtain.

There was no way to make music down here, but he seemed to hear the wedding march in his head anyway as Lucille stepped out from behind the blankets. A white, gauzy veil covered her face, and she carried a small bouquet of flowers. Without telling anyone, Cory had risked the barrage and gone out earlier to gather them from a flower garden down the street behind a deserted house. He had to swallow hard as he looked at Lucille. She was so beautiful that he felt her loveliness deep inside him.

His mind flashed back over all the months he had known her, from the first time he had seen her on the docks at New Madrid, to the hours he had spent with her in the pilothouse of the *Zephyr*, the weeks on the trail to Texas with the wagon train, and the time together here in Vicksburg. All of it leading up to this one special moment.

An explosion rumbled in the distance, then another and another.

Cory barely heard them. All his attention was fixed on Lucille as she walked slowly toward him. Her uncle moved in from the side and took her arm, escorting her the rest of the way across the cellar. When they came to a stop, Lucille was facing Cory at a distance of only a couple of feet.

"Well, we'll get started, I suppose," Reverend Emerson said. "Who gives this woman to be married?"

"Her aunt and I do, in the memory of her mother and father," said the colonel. He leaned over, gave Lucille a kiss on the cheek through the veil, then stepped back to stand beside Mildred and take her hand.

Fred Carter made a little noise of happiness as he smiled from ear to ear. His father shushed him, and Howard and Richards exchanged grins.

Cory and Lucille each took a step and turned so that they were standing side by side, facing Emerson. The minister continued, "We come here today to join these two fine young people in the holy state of matrimony. We'll dispense with the usual question of whether anyone knows of any reason why they shouldn't be married, because everyone here knows they were meant to be together. So . . ." He opened the Bible. "We'll proceed. Do you, Cory, take Lucille—"

The floor jumped under their feet, and dirt sifted down through the cracks between the boards of the ceiling. The roar of the explosion was loud as a shell landed close by. Fred cried out in fear, but his father took hold of his arm and said, "It's all right, son. It's all right."

Lucille was pale, and the colonel had his arm around Mildred's shoulders. The smiles of a moment before had vanished and been replaced with looks of grim expectation. They were all waiting for the next shell to hit. Cory tipped his head back and looked up at the ceiling, frowning as if he could hold off the bombardment by sheer force of will.

Several moments went by without another blast. Apparently, the one that had hit nearby had been a round fired at random. Finally, Cory looked down and turned his head so that his eyes met Lucille's. "I do," he said.

"But . . . I haven't finished the vows," sputtered Emerson.

"Doesn't matter," said Cory. "I do."

"I do, too," Lucille said.

"Well, this is a mite irregular, but I reckon you two know what you're getting into, so by the power vested in me by Almighty God and the sovereign state of Mississippi, I now pronounce you man and wife. May God have mer—no, dadgum it, I mean, you may now kiss the bride." Emerson closed the Bible and wiped a few droplets of sweat from his forehead. "I told you I've been holding too many funerals lately."

Cory didn't care what had been said or not said. All that mattered to him was that Lucille was his wife, now and for all time. He lifted the veil. She was smiling and crying, and he took her in his arms and kissed her, softly and sweetly, and for a few seconds nothing dared to intrude on their happiness.

Then the jolt of another explosion went through the cellar. Lucille gasped, and Cory lifted his hand to her face, stroking her cheek. "It doesn't matter," he whispered. "They can do their worst. We're together, and we'll always be together."

"Cory . . . ," she breathed.

The others left them standing there, holding each other. Colonel Thompson shook Emerson's hand again and said, "From the sound of what's going on up there, you'd better wait it out down here for a while, Reverend."

"I believe you're right, Colonel." The minister looked up at the ceiling. "Though fire may fall from heaven, it shall not consume us."

"Amen, Reverend," said the colonel. "Amen."

BY THE middle of June 1863 food was even more scarce in Vicksburg. People experimented with grinding up the cowpeas into meal, mixing it with water, and baking it into a sort of bread, but it was too awful to eat, cooking as hard as rock on the outside and still raw on the inside. Real flour, sugar, salt . . . all were in short supply. Fresh fruit and vegetables were worth their weight in gold. Beef—gone. Bacon, ham, salt pork—gone. Horses and mules were all that were left, and the taste was so bad that many could not stomach it. Few people ventured onto the streets of the city, at least during the day, and those who did were growing gaunt, as well as pale and hollow-eyed from being underground most of the time and seldom seeing the sun. Disease and malnutrition took a greater toll among the inhabitants than the constant Yankee shelling.

Although only a few citizens had been killed by the bombardment, the damage to Vicksburg's buildings had been severe. Many of them were now just piles of rubble, blown down by the explosions, or heaps of ashes, burned in the blazes started by the artillery shells. The Warren County Courthouse still stood proudly on the ridge overlooking the river, untouched, but it was one of the few landmarks in Vicksburg of which that claim could be made.

The Yankees had launched no more full-fledged attacks by their troops on the fortifications surrounding the city, although the Union sappers and engineers had tried to blow up some of the earthworks by tunneling under them and packing the holes with explosives. These attempts had done little good. The mines caused some destruction but few deaths, and when the Yankees tried to rush into the breach after one of the blasts, blistering rifle fire from the Confederates forced them back again and again. General Grant's frustration grew worse, but now that he had laid siege to the city, all he could do was wait out the Rebels—or give up and withdraw. And Grant was not about to do that.

Despite the grim conditions in Vicksburg, the populace was not without hope. Rumors abounded that General Johnston had returned to Jackson and would soon be on his way to Vicksburg with a large enough army to drive out the Yankees. When Cory asked Colonel Thompson if he thought that was true, Thompson could only shrug and say, "I don't know, lad. I pray that it is, because that's probably our only chance. But I'm afraid I'll believe the truth of it only when I see with my own eyes the backsides of the Yankees as they flee."

Cory and Lucille had spent their wedding night behind the blankets in the cellar, but conscious that the rest of the group was only a few feet away, they simply held each other through the night as the artillery shells fell above them. Not until early the next morning, when everyone else was sound asleep, had they made love.

Of course, spending most of their time underground, day and night had come to have little meaning for the inhabitants of Vicksburg. The Yankee bombardment went on around the clock some days, while on others there were unexpected lulls in the shelling. No one knew when such a respite would come or how long it would last, and in some ways, the silence was more nerve-wracking than the pounding of bombs.

The short rations were hindering the recoveries of Allen Carter and the Texan known as Howard, although both men were able to be up and around some now. They had no reserves of strength, however, and tired quickly.

Cory awoke shivering early one morning. He was trembling so badly that he woke up Lucille, too, who was snuggled next to him in the bedroll they had spread in a corner so that the colonel and Mildred could have the bed behind the blankets. His teeth were chattering as she rolled over to face him.

"Cory, what's wrong?" she asked anxiously.

"I . . . I don't know," he said.

But he did know. The sickness he had contracted months earlier in the swamps around Fort Pemberton had come back again. He had believed he was over it completely, but obviously that was wrong.

Lucille realized that, too. She pushed herself up onto an elbow and said, "You're having another attack." She put her hand on his forehead and almost jerked it away. "You're burning up! Oh, God, Cory!" She scrambled to her feet and hurried over to the hanging blankets, her steps guided by the single candle that was left burning at night. "Aunt Mildred! Uncle Charles! Cory is sick!"

"Lucille . . . ," he said weakly. "Don't . . ." He didn't want everyone else in the cellar disturbed because of him.

A moment later, Mildred came over to the bedroll and knelt beside him. She felt his forehead, just as Lucille had done, and nodded in agreement. "The fever's back, and so are the chills."

Thompson loomed up behind her, a worried frown on his face. "I'll get dressed and fetch a doctor," he said.

"Don't . . . don't go to so much . . . trouble—" Cory could barely talk because his teeth were chattering so hard. "Don't go out . . . Colonel."

"Nonsense. You have to have medical attention."

This was the worst attack since the very first one that had felled him, Cory sensed. From the way Lucille and Mildred had reacted when they touched him, his forehead must be blisteringly hot. To him, though, everything felt bone-numbingly cold instead. His thoughts were muddled, and when he tried to force them into some sort of coherent order, he found that he couldn't.

He laughed, but he never knew if he actually made the sound or if it was only inside his feverish brain. After the Hornet's Nest and the raid into Tennessee and everything else he had gone through, was this disease going to kill him? Bedford Forrest had called him lucky and a survivor, but maybe his luck only extended to bullets. The fever could kill him just as dead as a Yankee minié ball.

His eyes closed, and he slipped into unconsciousness.

⎯⎯

UNCLE CHARLES'S rank as a colonel in the Mississippi Home Guard was probably the only reason he was able to get a doctor to come to the house, thought Lucille. With all the hospitals in town still full of wounded soldiers, the physicians were kept busy night and day. But only a short time after the colonel left, he returned with a middle-aged, heavyset man whom he introduced as Dr. Mitchell.

Mitchell knelt beside Cory, pulled back his eyelids to examine his eyes, felt of his forehead and his neck, and listened to his breathing. Finally, when Mitchell straightened, he said, "It's swamp fever, all right. Some quinine would fix him up."

"Quinine?" asked Lucille.

"It's a sort of medicine made from the bark of a tree in South America," Mitchell explained. "From what I hear, the Indians down there have been chewin' the bark for years to protect themselves from swamp fever. We've known about it since the time of the Revolution, but not many doctors have much faith in it. I've seen it work, though."

"Do you have any?" Lucille demanded.

Mitchell shook his head. "Afraid not, missus. It's not that common. I don't know of any in the city."

Fear gripped Lucille. She said, "What . . . what will happen to Cory without it?"

"Oh, he might get better. Swamp fever comes and goes, comes and goes. It don't always kill a fella."

Aunt Mildred moved up beside Lucille and put an arm around her shoulders. "I'm sure Cory will be all right, dear. He's a strong young man."

Lucille swallowed. Cory might have been strong once, but for months now he had been pushing himself, using up more and more of his strength, doing everything he could that might help save Vicksburg for the Confederacy. On top of all that, he'd had to battle this stubborn illness. Both of them had thought it was gone, but now it was back, and there was no point in denying that this time it might kill him.

She brushed a hand across her eyes and blinked back tears. "What can we do for him?"

"Keep him cool when the fever's on him, and don't let him catch a chill when it breaks and he goes to sweatin'. If he could keep some food and water down, it might help." Mitchell shook his head. "'Course, food's gettin' mighty scarce for all of us, not just them that's sick."

"All right, we'll just have to get more food. Better food. That will help him recover, won't it?"

"Can't hurt," said the doctor.

The colonel said, "I'll gladly cut back on my ration so that Cory can have more." Words of agreement came from Carter, Howard, and Richards, too.

Lucille shook her head. The wounded men were already suffering from lack of enough to eat, and Uncle Charles was eating barely enough to keep alive so that Aunt Mildred would have more. None of them could afford to give up any of their food. And she herself was eating hardly at all, only a small bowl each day of the gruel made from cow peas.

"Nothin' more I can do here," Mitchell said. The colonel saw him up the stairs from the cellar, thanking him for coming.

Aunt Mildred squeezed Lucille's shoulders again. "I'm sure Cory will be all right, dear," she said. "We'll all pray for him."

Lucille nodded. She definitely intended to pray for her husband.

But she had the glimmering of an idea about something else she could do for him.

〜

CORY'S FEVER broke late in the afternoon, and within minutes he was drenched with sweat. Lucille allowed herself to hope that the fever would not go back up again, but she wasn't surprised when it did just that in the early evening. Cory was delirious. He kicked off the blanket they had spread over him and thrashed around feebly, muttering incoherently and sometimes crying out, lost in the grip of the fever.

Lucille waited until he had fallen into a restless sleep, then she left her aunt sitting beside him and went upstairs. Uncle

Charles had left earlier in the evening to return to Pemberton's headquarters, and none of the others were paying any attention to her. The shelling had stopped for the moment, but she knew it could resume again at any time with no warning.

She was going along the hallway toward the front door when a footstep behind her made her stop and turn around quickly. Fred Carter flinched back. In the dimness of the unlit hallway, she barely recognized him.

"Fred!" Lucille exclaimed in a low voice. "What are you doing up here?"

"I came to see what you were doing. Are you going somewhere, Miss Lucille?"

She took a deep breath. "Maybe."

"Can I go with you?" Fred asked eagerly. "I get really tired of sitting in the cellar."

"I know. We all do. But you can't go with me, Fred. I'm sorry."

"Where are you going?" he insisted.

Lucille came closer to him. "I can't tell you," she said, "and you can't tell anyone that I've left, either. Do you understand?"

Fred's eyes widened. "Are you running away from home?"

"No, of course not! I'll be back in a little while. I just have to go see someone."

"You'd better not go. The Yankees could start shooting at us again. You could get hurt."

"I have to," she said, impatience gnawing at her nerves. She had to do this while she still had her courage up, or she might not be able to bring herself to carry out the mission she had set for herself. "It's something that might help Cory get well."

"Oh! I want Cory to get well."

Lucille smiled. "We all do. So—for Cory's sake—will you not say anything to anyone about my being gone?"

"Well . . . all right. I guess not."

She leaned forward and kissed him on the cheek. "Thank you, Fred. I knew I could count on you."

That declaration of faith made his chest swell with pride. "I'll go back downstairs now."

"That's good. I'll see you later."

"Good-bye, Miss Lucille."

She turned and went hurriedly to the door. It was quiet outside except for some dogs barking in the distance. No one was moving on the street, she saw as she stepped onto the porch. Several houses in the neighborhood had been destroyed in the bombardment, and the ones still standing were all dark. The inhabitants were hiding either in caves or cellars below their dwellings, or they had abandoned their homes to stay in one of the larger caves under the city, some of which could hold several hundred people.

Although the night was warm, Lucille felt cold as she left the house. This wasn't the same sort of chill that gripped Cory, she knew. This was fear, pure and simple. Fear for Cory, and fear for herself. She didn't know if this errand would help save him, or even if she could find the place she was looking for. For that matter, it could have been destroyed in the shelling, as so many other places in Vicksburg had been.

But she had to try. It was Cory's only chance.

Walking through Vicksburg at night was like walking through a gigantic graveyard. At least, it felt that way to Lucille as she made her way across the city. She reached a street that went down a long slope toward the river and followed it. Twice she darted into the recessed doorways of abandoned buildings to hide as guard patrols went past. The soldiers wouldn't hurt her, but they would probably make her return home. A curfew was in effect, not that the citizens really needed one to keep them off the streets. The Yankees had taken care of that with their artillery and mortar barrages.

Finally, Lucille found herself close enough to the river to smell the water. This was a dingy neighborhood that had somehow been spared most of the ravages of the siege. She knew where the establishment she sought was situated. Uncle Charles had pointed it out to her one day when they were down here visiting the shore batteries.

Not only was the place still there, but a lantern was burning over its door, one of the few lights Lucille had seen since leaving the house. She took a deep breath, strode up to the door, and opened it, stepping inside the saloon and gambling hall known as Cochran's.

As soon as she did, a new fear hit her. She hadn't seen Palmer Kincaid for weeks. She didn't know if he was still in Vicksburg. He could have sold out. He might have just up and left without worrying about what he was leaving behind. If he wasn't here, she might have set herself up for trouble.

Of course, if he was, she might be in even more trouble . . .

The saloon was surprisingly busy. The air was thick with smoke, and Lucille heard the slap of cards and the clink of chips. Several men stood at the bar, and they turned to look curiously at her as she came in. She glanced around the room and decided that Cochran's was several steps below the relatively opulent Staghorn Saloon that Kincaid had run in Cairo. Circumstances had certainly changed for the gambler.

But then, that was true of all of them, she thought.

A couple of men moved away from the bar and came toward her, leers on their unshaven faces. The bartender ignored them and what they were about to do. Lucille felt like turning and running, but she knew that wouldn't do any good. The men would catch her, and besides, she couldn't leave without what she had come for. In a loud, clear voice, she said, "I'm looking for Palmer Kincaid."

"Won't we do, missy?" asked one of the men approaching her. "We can do anything for you that fancy-pants Kincaid can."

"I doubt that," rapped a sharp voice from an open doorway at the end of the bar. "Step away from that lady!"

Lucille felt a surge of relief as she saw Kincaid come out into the main room of the saloon. The two men who had been bent on accosting her turned away and went back to the bar, muttering to themselves. Kincaid strode briskly across the room and took Lucille's arm.

"It's not that I'm unhappy to see you," he said quietly, "but what the hell are you doing here?"

"I need to talk to you, Palmer." There was no *Uncle Palmer* this time. They had gone far beyond that, and they both knew it. "It's important. I . . . I need help."

A faint smile touched Kincaid's mouth. "So you came to me. I must admit, I'm surprised. Why don't we go back to my office and discuss your problem?" With his hand still on her arm, he turned her toward the door at the back of the room. "I must tell you, though," he murmured, "that there will be a significant price for my assistance."

"I know that," Lucille said. "And I'm prepared to pay it."

Chapter Twenty-five

Chapter Twenty-five

W OULD YOU LIKE A drink?" asked Kincaid when they were in the office and the door was closed behind them. "I had some rather good brandy, but I'm afraid it's all gone. If you don't mind drinking the same sort of swill those river rats outside are drinking, though . . ." He gestured toward a bottle on his desk.

"I don't want anything, thank you," Lucille said.

Kincaid grinned slyly at her. "If you didn't want something, my dear, you wouldn't be here. Not a lady such as yourself who's too good for a humble tavern keeper like me."

He wasn't drunk, but she could tell that he had been drinking heavily. His face was flushed, and his voice was slightly slurred. His eyes slowly went over her, lingering on every curve of her body as she stood in front of his desk.

"When you ran the Staghorn," she began, "you could lay your hands on just about anything you wanted, by one means or another."

"Quite true," he said, and something about his voice gave the simple words a lecherous tone. He continued to stare at her.

"Is it true here in Vicksburg, too?"

He shook his head and said, "I don't understand what you mean."

Lucille took a deep breath. "I've heard my uncle say that there's a . . . a black market in food and other commodities. That if someone has enough money, they can buy things that aren't generally available . . . if they know the right people."

"And you think I would be involved in something like that?"

"I think if there was money to be made, you'd do almost anything," Lucille said bluntly.

Kincaid looked at her stonily for a moment, then abruptly laughed. "You know me very well, my dear." He shrugged. "I have a few valuable contacts. A man in my line of work usually does. If you need more food, I can probably help."

"It's not just food. I need medicine, too."

Kincaid frowned in concern. "You're sick?"

"No, but my husband is." Lucille's chin lifted defiantly.

"Husband!" he exclaimed. "You mean you actually married that Brannon whelp?"

"Cory has some sort of swamp fever," she went on, ignoring the insulting question. "The doctor said that something called quinine would help him, as well as some better food. Do you have any? Can you get some?"

Kincaid held up his hands, palms out. "Hold on. We haven't discussed my payment yet."

"Whatever you want," Lucille said. "Anything."

"Anything?" Kincaid asked, the maliciously sly grin returning to his face.

"Anything," she repeated soberly. "If it'll save Cory's life, it's worth it."

Kincaid chuckled. "Some men might be offended by the tone of that response." He uncorked the bottle on his desk and took a swig from it. "I'm willing to forgive you, though." He gazed at her consideringly. "So you're a married woman now. I had hoped to be the one to introduce you to the delights of the physical act of love, but one can't always have what one wants, can one?"

"Will you help me?"

"Will you sleep with me?" Kincaid shot back.

"Yes." Her voice didn't even tremble as she said it.

"Here. Now."

Lucille shook her head. "No. Not until I have what I came for."

Kincaid took another drink. "That may be a problem. I have a . . . stockpile, if you will, but it's not here."

"Take me to it," Lucille said. "When I have what I need, you can have what you . . . what you want."

Kincaid frowned for a moment, then snapped, "Tomorrow night. That's the soonest I can help you. I'll take you to the place, and then you'll do whatever I wish."

Lucille nodded. "Do you have the quinine?"

"I can get some. That's why we have to wait until tomorrow night."

"All right." Lucille held out her hand. "It's a bargain."

Kincaid looked at her hand. "I'm not going to seal it with a handshake, if that's what you think."

He took a long step away from the desk, and Lucille had to fight down the impulse to turn and run. She let him take her into his arms, and his mouth found hers. Just as on that awful day in the parlor, revulsion swept through her, but she controlled it. She even made herself lift her arms and put them around his neck. His lips worked insistently against hers until she parted them. His tongue went into her mouth. She tasted the cheap whiskey he had been drinking and wanted to gag, but she forced down that reaction, too.

When he finally let go of her and stepped back, he said, "There, that wasn't so bad, was it? You may even enjoy paying your debt to me."

"I'll meet you here tomorrow night," she said. "What time?"

"After dark. It doesn't really matter when. I'll be here."

"So will I," she promised.

"You'd better let me accompany you back to your uncle's house. It'll be safer for you that way."

"I'll take my chances with the Yankee gunners."

Kincaid made a curt gesture. "I'm not talking about Yankees. If you leave here alone, some of that lot out there will follow you, and you'll wish they hadn't. They're bad enough in peacetime. With the war, they don't care about anything anymore."

Lucille saw that he had a point. She nodded grudgingly. "You can go with me."

"Good. Now that you've come around to my way of thinking, I wouldn't want anything to happen to you." He put on his hat and linked arms with her, leading her out through the barroom. His hard eyes warned anyone who was watching that it would be dangerous to follow them.

It was still quiet outside. They had walked a few blocks when Kincaid said, "You know, my dear, you really are just like me now. You'll do anything to get what you want."

She couldn't help but shudder at the thought. Kincaid felt her tremble and laughed.

She had been afraid of what Kincaid might try to do, but he made no advances toward her as they walked across the city. Evidently he planned to honor their agreement. When they reached the Thompson house, the night was still silent and the house was dark. This was one of the longest lulls so far in the shelling. Lucille took that as a good omen. Perhaps fate was finally smiling on her again.

Or perhaps not fate, because, as she reminded herself, she had just made a deal with the devil . . .

Kincaid kissed her again, then said, "Until tomorrow night." Lucille nodded but didn't say anything. She opened the gate and went up the walk to the porch then into the house, moving as quietly as possible. She was sure they had missed her down in the cellar by now, and she wondered what she was going to tell them. That she had gone out for a breath of fresh air, perhaps, taking advantage of the fact that the big guns weren't firing at the moment. That sounded plausible enough, she decided.

She glanced back from the front door, but Kincaid was already gone, vanished into the shadows. She stepped into the foyer and eased the door closed behind her.

The rasp of a match made her jump and cry out. She swung around sharply toward the parlor and saw her uncle standing there, holding the match flame to the wick of a candle.

"Lucille," the colonel began. "Would you care to share where you've been and what you were doing with Palmer Kincaid?"

THE NEXT evening, Lucille pulled up in front of Cochran's in a large wagon with four horses hitched to it. She had never handled a team like that before, but she managed fairly well, she thought. She set the brake and climbed down from the seat. Over her dress she was wearing a leather jacket that belonged to Cory, and a broad-brimmed hat was on her head.

For a moment, she worried that the place was closed because the lantern over the door wasn't lit. But the door opened when she tried the latch, and as she stepped inside she saw that several candles were burning. The customers who had been there the night before were gone, however. In fact, the only person in the place seemed to be Palmer Kincaid, who stood at the bar with a glass of whiskey in his hand.

He turned toward her, threw back the drink, then placed the empty glass on the bar. "Good evening, my dear," he said. "You look lovely as always, even in that pioneer getup."

She wasn't interested in his compliments. "Are you ready?"

"Of course. I'm a man of my word."

"You were able to get the quinine?"

"Certainly. It was rather difficult, however. If you were paying me in a different currency, I'm afraid I'd have to increase the price. However, under the circumstances, that hardly seems fair. You'll already be paying me everything you have."

Lucille didn't say anything. She turned and went back outside. Behind her, she heard Kincaid laugh softly to himself.

He emerged from the saloon a second later, clapping his beaver hat on his head. He offered her a hand, but she ignored it and climbed onto the seat of the wagon without assistance. Kincaid looked the vehicle over and said, "I don't recall anything being said about a wagon."

"I want it loaded with supplies, as well as the medicine," she said. "That's the only way you're going to get what you want."

"Now *you're* the one trying to change the bargain." Kincaid shrugged. "But very well. I'm sure you'll make it worth my while." He stepped up onto the seat beside her.

She lifted the reins. "Where are we going?"

He reached over and took the reins from her. "I'll drive, if you don't mind. I can find the place easier than I can give directions to you."

Lucille didn't argue with him. As long as they ended up where they were going, she didn't care who handled the team.

As Kincaid sent the wagon rattling down the street, a trio of explosions sounded, one right after the other, on the far side of town. Lucille jerked as the loud reports echoed through the night. Those were mortar shells bursting, she knew. By now, she could recognize the sounds of the various guns. To the east, the Yankee artillery began to roar. The Confederate guns barked a volley in response.

"Looks like our little romance will be accompanied by some music tonight," Kincaid said, evidently not worried about the bombardment.

He swung the wagon into a northbound street that paralleled the bluffs along the river. He was humming merrily to himself as he drove, Lucille realized. She thought about all the good times she had spent with this man when she was a child. She had loved him then, but she hated him now. She had been blind all along to the real Palmer Kincaid.

Or perhaps he had changed, she thought. Perhaps he hadn't always been as evil and mercenary as he was now. People *did* change, and not always for the better. Not even usually for the better, she told herself. The bad things in a person's life seemed to take root and grow faster than the good, and it was a constant struggle to keep them weeded out. Some people, like Kincaid, gave up the fight.

But she would never surrender, she told herself. Not as long as Cory lived.

His fever had been up and down all day. He'd been unconscious most of the time, and when he was awake he didn't seem to know her. Except for a moment late in the afternoon when she had been sitting beside the bed and his eyes had fluttered open. He had looked up at her, and his cracked and bleeding lips had whispered her name.

That was all he'd said to her today, but it was enough. He loved her. He would always love her, and she would always love him, no matter what she might do tonight to save him.

Kincaid veered the wagon off the street and onto a narrow trail that led down and along the face of the bluff, north of the Confederate artillery batteries. They weren't far from the great horseshoe bend in the river. After a few minutes of traveling along the narrow path, he hauled back on the reins and brought the team to a stop in front of a clump of brush.

"We're here," he announced.

Lucille looked around in confusion. There was enough moonlight for her to see the trail and the face of the bluff rising to their right. "Where?" she asked.

"Come with me." Kincaid hopped down from the driver's box, and this time when he turned back to help her, she let him, although her skin crawled at the touch of his hands on her, even through her clothes.

He led her over to the brush and pulled some of it aside. Beyond it, like a dark mouth, gaped the entrance to a cave. Kincaid took her hand and said, "Stay with me. It's very dark. But there's a lantern I can light when we get inside. The brush will hide the light from the Yankee gunboats."

They had to bend over slightly as they made their way into the tunnel. The crown of Lucille's hat brushed the top of the passage. If she hadn't been holding Kincaid's hand, she probably would have walked headlong into the walls of the tunnel. He guided her through its twists and turns and then finally said, "You can straighten up now." From the way his voice echoed she could tell that they had entered a larger cavern.

Kincaid scratched a match to life. After being in darkness for several minutes, Lucille's eyes narrowed at the flare of light. The gambler held the flame to a lantern wick, then lowered the glass chimney as it caught. A yellow glow spread out in a circle, showing Lucille a large, dirt-floored room crowded with crates and barrels and kegs, sacks of flour and sugar, baskets full of hams, bags full of apples and peaches. Her eyes widened in shock as she realized the cavern extended farther than she could see into the bluff. There was a tremendous amount of food here.

"My God," she breathed.

"Impressive, isn't it?" Kincaid said proudly. "My fortune. Right now, I'd rather have it than gold and precious gems."

She tore her eyes away from the food and said heatedly, "You could feed half the city with this!"

"But only half. The other half would still starve. Better to dole it out to selected customers who can afford to pay my prices. That way they'll be sure to survive the siege, and they'll still be grateful to me once it's all over."

"You bastard!" Lucille couldn't stop the words from coming out of her mouth. "People are dying up there!"

"People are dying everywhere," he drawled. "It's a natural condition of humanity."

Lucille took a deep breath and forced herself to calm down. "What about the quinine?" she asked.

Kincaid made a clucking sound and shook his head. "Perhaps I did lie to you a little bit."

Fear clutched Lucille's heart. "You don't have it?"

"I didn't say that. I was able to get only a small amount, although probably enough to cure your husband. The price for it, however, will be higher."

"I . . . I don't understand. What more can I do?"

Kincaid swept a hand toward the supplies and said, "For a wagonload of food, the price is that you give yourself to me."

"I already agreed to that!" Lucille said desperately.

"But for the quinine . . . you *stay* with me."

Lucille stared at him, not sure if she understood.

"I'll take the supplies and the medicine to your uncle's house and leave them there," Kincaid went on. "You'll remain here. Then, when I return, we'll go back to Cochran's. That will be your new home until I've made arrangements to sell the rest of what you see here. With that much money, we can leave Vicksburg and go anywhere we want. San Francisco, perhaps. I'm sure I could make a fine living on the Barbary Coast. But wherever it is, you'll go with me, and you'll never see Mr. Brannon again."

Lucille looked down at the floor, trembling. What Kincaid asked was impossible. She couldn't do it. Not even for Cory. And yet . . . she loved him. She had told herself that she was willing to do anything for him, that she was going to save his life no matter what sacrifices she had to make. Suddenly, her nerves calmed, and though her heart was still pounding furiously, she knew what she had to do. More than that, she knew that she was capable of doing it.

"Well?" Kincaid snapped, moving closer to her. "How about it? What's your answer, Lucille?"

She raised her head and said, "This." Her hand dipped into the pocket of the leather jacket and came out holding a small pistol. She lifted it smoothly, cocking the hammer as the barrel came up, and pressed the trigger. The sharp crack of the weapon filled the cavern.

Kincaid took a step back, his eyes widening in shock and horror as he lifted a hand to his chest. He looked down at the trickle of blood that came out between his fingers, then raised his eyes to her and gasped, "Lucille . . . ?"

"It was this or hang as a black marketeer," she told him. "Don't look so surprised, Palmer. After all, this is war."

He fell to his knees, then, as the life went out of his eyes, toppled to the side to land facedown on the floor of the cavern. Lucille slowly lowered the gun and replaced it in her pocket. Her hand was starting to shake a little. She had been able to remain calm until she had done what was necessary, but now the reaction was beginning to set in.

She heard voices and turned toward the tunnel that led into the cavern from the face of the bluff. Light glared and flickered in the tunnel, and a moment later, Uncle Charles burst into the chamber, carrying a torch. Behind him came Fred Carter, Dr. Mitchell, and several other men.

Uncle Charles stopped short when he saw Kincaid's sprawled body. "Good Lord!" he exclaimed. "What happened? We were waiting for you to come back out, but then we heard a shot . . ."

"Kincaid attacked me," said Lucille. "I had no choice but to defend myself."

Fred stared at the body. "Is he dead?"

Charles Thompson prodded Kincaid's lifeless form with the toe of his boot. "I'm afraid so. He was a gambler to the end, and it appears that he cheated the gallows." Turning and lifting the torch, the colonel surveyed the supplies stored in the cavern. "My God," he said in a hushed voice. "I never dreamed there would be so much."

So much, but not enough, thought Lucille. Kincaid had been right. Even distributed equally and carefully, these supplies wouldn't feed an entire city. They were only postponing the inevitable.

But perhaps a few people who might have starved to death otherwise would survive. And the quinine could save Cory. There might be other medicines here, too, that would save lives. The victories they would win as a result of this night would be small ones . . .

But victories nonetheless.

Uncle Charles and the other men began carrying the provisions out of the cavern. They had followed Lucille and Kincaid with other wagons, so that by morning, these supplies would be making their way to those they could do the most good. Lucille started toward the tunnel, anxious to be out of here, but Fred Carter stopped her.

Worriedly, he asked, "You're not mad at me, are you, Miss Lucille?"

"Why would I be mad at you, Fred?"

The young man shuffled his feet. "Well, for following you last night after you told me not to. And for telling the colonel where you went. I was just worried about you."

Lucille smiled and rested a hand softly on Fred's cheek. "No, I'm not angry with you. Not at all."

A relieved smile spread across Fred's face. "That's good."

Lucille patted his cheek and then left him to help the others.

She stepped out of the tunnel into the night and took off her hat as she breathed deeply of the warm air. In the distance to the south, she saw flashes of light from the river as the Yankee gunboats fired their mortars. The glare from the explosions in the city flickered overhead like heat lightning on a summer night. If a person hadn't known what they were, the lights in the sky would have been almost beautiful . . .

She had to ask herself if she could live with what she had done tonight, and as she did, Lucille already knew the answer. She pushed a few stands of the honey-blonde hair away from her face and put her hat back on. She had to get home.

Cory was waiting for her.

ON JULY 4, 1863, Cory stood on the porch of the Thompson house with his arm around Lucille and watched as the blue-clad troops marched past in the street. He was still thin and weak, but otherwise completely recovered from the illness that had ravaged him.

All morning the Yankees had been streaming into the city. General Pemberton had officially surrendered late on the previous day, after a meeting with his officers had convinced him there was no possibility of the army's being able to break through the Union lines. The men were sick, exhausted, and more than half-starved. The relief from General Johnston had never come. So on July 3, Pemberton had sent General Bowen to meet with the Yankees and negotiate a surrender.

General Grant—old "Unconditional Surrender" Grant—at first had demanded just that, but he had seen the wisdom of not having to deal with thirty thousand prisoners. The Confederate troops in Vicksburg would surrender their weapons and be paroled with the pledge that they would not fight again until an equal number of Federal prisoners had been released from Southern prison camps. And the Yankees, at long last, would occupy the city.

It had taken the Northerners a year and thousands upon thousands of lives, but the key to the Confederacy was finally in Abraham Lincoln's pocket.

On that somber Fourth of July afternoon, Charles and Mildred Thompson, Allen and Fred Carter, Richards, and Howard all stood on the porch with Cory and Lucille. Their eyes were drawn to a small detail of Union soldiers that turned up the walkway to the house. The young officer in charge of the group saluted Colonel Thompson, who stood there in uniform, as did Richards and Howard in what tatters remained of theirs.

"Sorry, sir," the lieutenant said, "but all Confederate military personnel must come along to surrender their weapons and officially give their parole."

"Of course," Thompson replied. Stiff with dignity, he descended from the porch, followed slowly by the two soldiers still recuperating from their wounds. Mildred sobbed softly.

The Yankee lieutenant glanced up at Cory and the Carters. Seeing that, Thompson said, "These men are civilians. You have my word on that, Lieutenant."

"Yes sir." Nodding, he led the detail away.

Lucille leaned her head against Cory's shoulder. "I guess the war is over for us," she said.

"The siege is over," said Cory. "The battle is over. But the war goes on."

"Not today," whispered Lucille.

Cory tightened his arm around her shoulders and placed his head against hers. "No, not today."

AT THE Warren County Courthouse, the Stars and Bars of the Confederacy was lowered, and the Stars and Stripes rose in its place. As Lincoln wrote to a friend in Illinois, "The Father of Waters again goes unvexed to the sea."